4 Cr

NEW VALUES

MARK·OLDHAM

N E W

VALUES ◁

Hodder & Stoughton

LONDON SYDNEY AUCKLAND TORONTO

British Library Cataloguing in Publication Data
Oldham, Mark
  New values.
  I. Title
  823′.914 [F]

  ISBN 0 340 41573 8

Hodder and Stoughton Editorial Office: 47 Bedford Square, London WC1B 3DP.

For my parents Marian and Kenneth Oldham
And my brother John. With Love and Thanks.

Dans les yeux les plus sombres s'enferment les plus claires
Paul Eluard 1925

IN THE YEAR OF OUR LORD NINETEEN HUNDRED AND THIRTY-EIGHT

PART ONE

There's little in taking or giving,
There's little in water or wine;
This living, this living, this living
Was never a project of mine.
Oh, hard is the struggle, and sparse is
the gain of the one at the top,
For art is a form of catharsis,
And love is a permanent flop,
And work is the province of cattle,
And rest's for a clam in a shell,
So I'm thinking of throwing the battle
Would you kindly direct me to hell?

Dorothy Parker, 'Coda'

'Slackhall, that's where flies go to in the winter,' people said, and the locals thought it was true.

Wreathed in smoke, its cobbled streets glistened wet by sombre gaslight during the long winter months. Snatches of sound echoed around the blanketing fog, the whirring glide and clank of a tram and the muted clatter of iron-clad clogs, as workers, heads bent low, wound their way to the mill, a distant buzzing like the drone of a hundred dying insects in their ears. The sounds filtered through the alleys and streets, ebbing and flowing like the soft pulsations of water under ice, and life continued unhurried like the gentle unfolding of the seasons. When the warmer weather arrived, the town would slowly fade, like an old photograph, the dark satanic mills oxidising in the anaemic sun. Time and tradition had left their marks; history had not failed this place.

The fallen in the Great War of 1914–18 were remembered in the town memorial. And the bricks and mortar of Slackhall stood for their own testament; the shabby houses were the annals of the town, the births, marriages and deaths among the broken valuables and second-hand furniture.

Julius Agricola ruled this land in AD 78, but as with all things, the Romans fell. Human bones and implements of war were buried in the dark soil along with memories. So in turn came the Saxons and Danes, and then the scriveners of the Normans with the Domesday Book, when much of the land was laid waste by fire and desolation. The pages of history fluttered by, the crusades and struggle for the cross, the Plantagenets, the Wars of the Roses.

The years disappeared; and with them those individuals, absurd and ordinary, who are no longer kept in mind. The houses grew and collapsed; time burned down the remembered shapes; crops grew and people were butchered; flames flickered across the sky and went out in 1745 when war came to an end on British soil. The aromas of the past drifted away, destroyed by the new smell of the present. The cotton industry spread along the river where once the Romans had bathed, and even fought, but now it was the dye-works which coloured the water magenta, not the sharp sword.

As moods change with the weather, so Slackhall changed with the light which played on its walls and chimneys. As the shadows of clouds slowly passed over undulating hills, the industrial smoke drifted and settled on the town, gradually staining the stones and vegetation, reaching into the tiny cracks and joints, filling them with the dusty residue of fires and oiled machines. And from the dull and greasy windows of the town, drab eyes could look up towards their benefactor.

Perched like a crow's nest at the top of a branching tree was the house which had swollen and grown from the sweat and toil of successive generations in Slackhall. The architecture had altered with the changing fortunes, extensions had been made, parts collapsed, until the rambling structure of Gothic extravagance was a place of many corners, stairways and passages, and its back faced the town.

The large gates were rusted, and no carriages or cars drove down the sweeping drive. The warped roof and crumbling stones no longer held revellers. The house was not the destination for weekends, and on the tangled lawns, no croquet mallets were swung. If the sun shone at a certain angle, the dark windows would reflect a strange desolation, as though the house were gutted and empty, and a façade was all that was left. But heart-beats could be heard within, and at night lights shone out into the darkness.

This was the outer atmosphere which nourished William Booth. As the sun rose and the house in which he lived sent its shadow down to the town, he lay half-awake, listening to the morning routines and watching through partially-open curtains as the smoke from a chimney drifted by. Blowing down, it meant there could be rain. Above him, within arm's reach, a huge pike's head protruded from the wall, the broad and fearsome trophy of a twenty-eight-pounder caught in Ireland, and now mounted on a wooden plaque. It was a malevolent creature with dull grey eyes, that stared with tranquil malice.

William slid his hands along its smooth and varnished surface in passive contemplation. The heinous tooth-fringed jaws were slightly open, room enough for his fingers to test the needle sharpness of their bristling carpet. Massing indiscriminately and growing inexorably towards the front as replacements for the vicious outer rim, they all curved back to form an inextricable attachment to the victim held within. Removing his hand was an extremely delicate operation, for even the tongue seemed similarly barbed. The passage was intended to be one way only.

Like some camera, William's eyes could record the whole detail of his room, while his head, without moving, lay within the nest of his pillow. Mounted on the opposite wall was a glossy celluloid chart with coloured illustrations of cockroach, lice and silver-fish, bedbugs and fleas, all much enlarged, embellished with the simple printed motif – KEATINGS POWDER KILLS ALL THESE. In the dreamlike world of early morning, William would meditate upon the complex anatomical drawings with their intricate mouth parts and segmented bodies, and within his mind he traced their delicate outlines.

Without moving a muscle and holding his breath, William could feel his body and the subtle pressure exerted upon it by the bedding. Slowly he stretched his fingers as though tensing them for an exercise on a musical instrument, until the sinews felt as taut as glass. He yawned.

The room seemed to drain all his energy. Turning over abruptly and pulling the sheets above his ears, he faced a small chest of drawers, the varnish cracked and peeling. Resting on the striated surface was an intricate brass picture-frame which looked as though it should have held a family portrait. The light, which dribbled into the room, reflected upon part of the glass, obscuring much of the detail but causing his eyes momentarily to return to focus.

He stared at the only part of the picture which could be made out, and as he curled his toes under the blankets, he wondered vaguely how long the painting had been in his room. The surface had become a looking-glass, he could make out part of his own head, his eyes blinked as though compromised. He gazed lazily at the single figure which could

11

be made out. It was a man, the biblical garb hinted at the subject, and the shadowy form had a bowed head, as though from grief or self-loathing, and the one arm which could be seen held on to a small bag. Unnamed he stood, and William had long ago decided the bag contained thirty pieces of silver.

William turned his head into the pillow and drifted into sleep, and his thin eyelids could not obscure the roving orbs beneath.

The sun still pressed down upon his dry skin, his pale eyes squinted from the dazzle, and in the heat haze, shapes trembled like a mirage as if the land were on fire. A warm wind blew steadily across the low hill, causing little eddies of spiralling dust which swept around the dull olive-trees at the foot of Mount Golgotha. The wavering shapes became more distinct until he could identify the constituent parts; it was only a matter of time before the crowd of people, mules and camels were upon him and he was enveloped in the haze of dust. His nose twitched from the acrid odour of sweat and animals; it was like a circus. Three bedraggled captives stood white-faced and gasping; one wore a crown of thorns. Smoke drifted silently through the bodies, and something was being roasted. A dyed monkey danced back and forth on the shoulders of a bearded man, and the sun glinted on some new, bright shiny nails. The music still continued, now accompanying the heavy blows of a hammer, and the prisoners managed to be shivering despite the heat.

The heavy executioner treated the bodies as though they were already dead meat. One by one the nails were driven home and the cheers of the crowd could not hide the tearing screams. William looked with amazement at the impaled limbs, the red blood. The thorn crown was wrenched from the last prisoner and submissively, he, too, was pulled to his execution. The executioner raised his aching arm and sent the nail crookedly into the wrist. The prisoner cried out. Cursing, the executioner tried to straighten the nail, tapping it this way and that – he was a perfectionist. The flies which had buzzed over the sweetmeats and beggars, now began to land on the naked bodies, feasting on the sweat and salty blood.

12

Three crosses were raised by the soldiers who spat on the twisting bodies, the rib cages heaving in and out, while in the blue sky carrion-birds began to circle, round and round and round.

The uncrowned head stirred slightly, and eyes as calm as the stilled water on which he supposedly walked passed over those assembled for his death, and as William was touched by the pale eyes he felt a cold hand clutch within his entrails, and it was as if he were falling, tumbling within himself in a dark abyss.

The cracking of the bone snapped through the air and angry insects buzzed, the swarming mass disturbed by the shattering of the crucified limbs.

'I thirst,' croaked the last prisoner. The rancid sponge was lifted on a spearhead, and the executioner reached up and placed a hand on the leg, as though patting some restless dog. The heretic's lips were ready to suck, but there was no cool relief for the executioner's spear drove into his side. A hoarse voice croaked a curse as the blood ran down, and he died with a look of surprise.

The three naked bodies hung blackening slowly in the strong sun, and it was only the flies which remained with them. The rest of the crowd began to leave the cruel place; Jerusalem seemed as white as bleached bone. Beneath the hot sun William sweated, and alone he found sun-crazed solace in the sound of the creaking wood of the cross. His mouth was dry and silently he watched the shadows of the cross lengthen . . .

In no time at all Nanny Bradshaw had opened the door and, stepping purposefully over to the window, pulled back the curtains as though the flimsy material were holding back a torrent of light.

'That's better,' she said, and talcum powder whirled in the thin beams of sunshine. The veil of sleep slipped from his buried head, and her creaking steps walked for a moment beside the creaking cross. He was awake. Standing before the light window, Nanny Bradshaw's polished and blunt body was shadowed, but William knew the expression she would be wearing on her uncompromising head.

13

'I've a busy day ahead,' she sighed, moving away from the window and wrinkling her nose at the insect poster. It always made her feel uncomfortable, her skin prickled and felt itchy. Within her folded arms shone an antiseptically clean white shirt, as well as a pair of precisely creased grey trousers.

'It's all right for some,' she said as she regarded William in the warm bed, and tried not to look at the open maw of the pike.

William, now sitting up in bed, watched silently as Nanny Bradshaw carefully placed his clean clothes at the bottom of the bed. As she straightened them with her broad hands, he was presented with a picture of Nanny stooping at his feet. The secret image pleased him. Her stays groaned as she stood up and he glanced at the picture lying innocently within its frame, recalling his dream. He closed his eyes.

'No dropping off to sleep,' commanded Nanny Bradshaw. 'We can't all spend the day in bed.' She smoothed down her heavily starched skirt and looked round the room as though she suspected something had been moved.

William was about to speak, but the question died on his lips as the languorous ringing of a bell broke the heavy air. She gave a desultory pat to the clothes and nodded to William. He looked away, and as she left the room the air seemed to rush in to fill the space she had taken.

He watched as the talcum powder slowly settled on to the carpet, and the bell still rang on. He knew Nanny Bradshaw had reached her destination as the sound was abruptly cut off. As though that were the signal for action, he hurriedly got out of bed. His bare toes absently wiped the talcum into the carpet and he tentatively glanced at the bedside painting. A restful scene met his eye. There were the respectful figures with bowed heads, a clear sky, and the pale gleaming flesh of the crucified. The blood was hardly noticeable. It filled him with a strange emptiness, and he could think of nobody with whom to discuss his unsettling dream. It seemed more than that; he could almost feel the warm sand under his feet, and as he made his way to the bathroom, he wondered if he ever talked in his sleep. He never noticed the temperature change as he stepped on to the cold linoleum and closed the door of the bathroom. Nanny had been at work, for a huge white

14

towel had been placed over the side of the bath, and a brand new bar of carbolic soap was waiting. He turned on the taps. Steam began to fill the room and he removed his pyjamas. Turning slightly, William regarded himself in a mirror, and as he watched, his image slowly disappeared into a faint blur as the mirror began to cloud over. The heat was oppressive and the very tiles seemed to perspire. He somehow hoped he would be able to wash away the vivid dream. Reaching over to the steamy mirror, he started to draw something and then almost angrily wiped it away, leaving a partial reflection of his own body. Switching off the taps, he climbed into the bath, and sank until his body was immersed. Lying full on his back, he floated in strange contentment.

Nanny had given up the personal supervision of his cleanliness nearly two years before, and the formidable scrubbings had ceased. He looked down through the clear water at his changeling form that was neither man nor child. With his head sticking out, the refraction gave the odd impression that whatever lay beneath was a distorted, unrelated remnant, and as he shifted, the image broke into fragments. Sliding down abruptly until his head was totally submerged, he cut out all the sounds of air. He had the sense of being outside time. Surfacing noisily and gasping for breath, he shook his wet hair about. He didn't feel frightened when he sank beneath the water. Rather, it made him feel secure. He had not washed away the spell of the dream, and in the overpowering isolation of the water, wondered about life. He thought of his long-dead parents, their images locked away in the threadbare photographs he used to summon their presence. He thought they would be watching over him and that the two spiritual guardians would make sure no harm could befall their son. He sniffed, but it was only the water getting in his nose, not the presence of held-back tears, and in so much liquid the gesture would have been futile.

He scrabbled in the bottom of the bath for the slippery soap, and then watched as the water became clouded like daylight with thunder.

A sudden knock splintered his solitude; he twitched with surprise and the reflection wobbled in time to his beating

15

heart. 'William.' Nanny Bradshaw's voice resounded in the tiled room like a crack on the head.

She knocked again.

'Did you hear me?' she demanded. 'It's time you were out of there.'

He heaved himself from the water. With rivulets trickling over his lean body, he inclined himself towards the door, listening to see whether she was still there. He could hear his own heart thumping softly and the faint lapping of the bath-water, but there was no sound of her lumbering gait retreating down the corridor. Reaching out for the coarse towel, he began to rub himself with water-wrinkled fingers.

He opened the door, feeling the cool indraught of air before he saw Nanny Bradshaw.

'About time,' she said, and although they were on the second floor of the large house, her claustrophobic presence made it feel as though they were in an underground cavern.

'I suppose you've left a mess for your Nanny to clean up,' her eyes straying past him into the bathroom, probing for the evidence.

He watched her with the stillness of a wound-down clock.

'The day a boy like you leaves no mess is the day your Nanny will retire,' she continued with an odd note of petulance entering her voice.

She sighed, and thought that her horoscope had certainly let her down. There was no mention of a change. As Jupiter was moving into the mid-heaven of her personal chart, it was supposed to be a time for affairs of the heart, not uncalled-for intrusions. As if she hadn't enough work to be doing, without being told to prepare a bedroom for the newcomer.

'I wasn't put on earth just to run around after you all day,' she said, ignoring his blank look, as unrevealing as the crystal ball she kept in her small room. 'Don't just stand there,' she snapped in an exasperated voice. 'Haven't I just told you what a busy day I have? I don't want you getting under my feet all day.'

Without having uttered a word, William made his way back to his bedroom, unaware that Nanny Bradshaw was thinking that it would do him good to have someone light a fire between his toes. She shook her head. After all, hadn't she

16

done her best for him? In her last visit to Mrs Makin, she'd told her that she'd brought that boy up single-handed. Mrs Makin had nodded sympathetically and offered her another piece of cake. The sponge was as generously dotted with raisins as the sky with stars, and the fortune-teller began to tell her about the imminent effect of Uranus in the twelfth house and that secret enemies could pull her down. She'd meant to ask for the recipe of that cake.

It was Sunday. The day given over to the Lord was also claimed by William, although he had no divine dispensation to such title. His actions were not directed by the planets, but his own pleasure, and with haste, he left, not even thinking that he was turning his back on God's day. Dashing down the stairs as though the house were on fire, he then came to an abrupt halt. Allowing himself a brief, painful smile, the Reverend Roe looked down on William, smoothing out his black suit and fastening one of the jet buttons which had burst open under the impact of the collision. The overtly fleshy body seemed to emphasise the skeletal quality of the hands which now slowly clasped themselves over his corpulent belly. Some people in Slackhall had wondered how Mrs Roe could bear to be touched by hands such as those, and it was the opinion of the town's gossips that his wife's periods of invalidity were due to the bulk of her husband's protruding stomach pressing into her delicate body when he made love to her.

'So William, where were you off to in such a rush?' The almost breathless quality of Roe's voice made it appear as though it were he who had been rushing. 'No doubt you were on your way to visit your grandmother.' He gave a smile as befitted a pillar of the community. 'Shall I lead the way?' His bony hand snaked out and, gripping the boy firmly, led him back until they came to the stairs to his grandmother's room. All the way up the stairs, William was conscious of the probing fingers of the reverend, which seemed not only to be gripping him but also feeling the thin muscles of his arm, as insistently as a bright light shining into closed eyes.

'Not as young as I used to be,' gasped Roe, as they finally came to the top of the stairs. 'Sorry if I leant on you William.'

On entering the dressing-room which formed the

17

antechamber to the bedroom, Roe was always struck by the strange timeless quality with which it was endowed. The possessions which littered the place had not been moved since she had become virtually bedridden. It was known for her to get someone to lift her into a bathchair and push her into the still room where she would sit and look at her dressing-table, now devoid of a mirror, and then, as if in a dream, her hands would reach out, but never touch anything. Opening the doors of the wardrobe, she gazed at the ravishing dresses that would never again rest next to her skin. Devoid of personal values, the repertory of her belongings waited in the wings and, being so superfluous, they exhibited a strange profundity. She stared at the clothes she had once loved, as if they were already those of one deceased and possessed the power of conjuring up her past. The fabrics were woven with memories, and she sighed at her foolish heart for making her undertake the pilgrimage. If she discovered some precious memory had been moved in the petrified room a cold anger would seize her, and her nights would have no rest until the culprit was dismissed. William often sneaked into the room, its odour, colour and shape being restful to him, and he would sit against the door which led to his grandmother's sanctum, listening to her steady breathing, and feeling quite safe.

There was no such feeling of peace as he accompanied Reverend Roe across the carpet. The lugubrious step of the vicar mirrored Roe's thoughts; for him, the room had no charm, its obsessional quality with the belongings set out with careful and rigid precision seemed to confront him with the process of mortality. He felt it macabre. He glanced down at William and couldn't banish the perverse life the boy must have lived in this strange interior world. Like a canvas of a landscape with the sky unpainted there was something distinctly unfinished about him. Stopping outside the bedroom door, Roe lifted his fleshless hand to the hard wood and knocked. Roe had the uncomfortable feeling that not only might he have awoken the slumbering invalid, but the room itself. He was not looking forward to this interview. As though not sure of the best course of action, he paused for a moment. Like Alice, he too wished to know the way he ought

18

to go. Grinning, William opened the door and almost stumbled over the threshold.

'Will-iaam, my-y de-ear,' drawled out the waking voice. 'We're all mad here,' heard Roe. He frowned to himself, why should she say that? Confused, he followed. 'Ah Reverend,' purred the voice, 'punctual as usual.'

The sound emanated from a huge four-poster, needlessly raised on a small platform. He smiled nervously towards the gloomy region, and placed his hand in a fatherly fashion on William's shoulder. Feeling the contact, William wanted to squirm away and his neck prickled.

Perched in the dusty, heavy, draped bed, the dwarfed body of his grandmother stared out. Eyes as bright and large as those of some nocturnal animal glinted in her shrunken head. The wasting disease affecting her body made certain parts of her physique appear abnormally large. Not only did her eyes tend to dominate her face, but also her more than generous mouth. When young, her full, pouting lips added a sensuous quality. Now, her broad and heavy mouth hung open, the pendulous lips trembling with a life of their own.

The morning sunlight did not seem to reach the interior of this room, the only window being veiled by yellowing lace, and the curtains never fully parted. She always preferred the light to be behind her, or not there at all.

'You woke me,' she said simply, and Roe shuffled slightly in case her voice carried a note of criticism, and he smiled more ingratiatingly than ever. 'I was having a dream.' Her speech was heavy and languorous, as if she were not sure whether she was awake or not. She fell silent and Roe had the worrying impression that her breathing had come to a stop.

She surrendered herself to the invisible mystery of her dream. She had had this dream before, it was as if her sleeping body wished to refine it, to iron out any creases from the rippling subconscious. It no longer had the power to frighten her, she was far too old for that and the years had taught her to listen to her own voice. She knew why she had dreamt it again, it was almost a trusted friend.

She was much younger of course, sitting in front of a crackling fire, the pages of a newspaper spread before her. 'Horrid Murder', said the headline, and she would tremble, the sheaves of paper rustling in sympathy. She always wondered how many people had read that the death of her husband was instantaneous, for when found, the right hand was in his greatcoat pocket, a mannerism quite usual for him when walking. 'Found in a shallow ditch.' She pulled her eyes away. A log had fallen in the fire and red sparks whirled up the chimney into the sky beyond.

The muzzle of the weapon must have been placed close to his breast and the beating heart it contained, for wadding had perforated his garments and some coarse blue paper had entered his body and was concealed in the sternum. She had never seen his body again, she did not wish to see the expression he was wearing at the moment of death when the pistol-shot rang out.

The assassins were found after one of them turned king's evidence, telling the tale which would send his own brother to the gallows. The paper rustled again, bringing her eye back to the verdict. 'Guilty', and when the accused heard it, he screamed out as God was his witness, he was innocent, and then fainted. When he was arrested, he had been travelling the country as a wizard, attending fairs and markets, setting up stall as a fortune-teller, but his own fate on the scaffold had not been foreseen. As he read the calloused palms under the warm summer sun, he watched the pile of coins growing, and perhaps gave thanks for the day he was discharged from the mill for belonging to the union.

The sun had stopped shining when the day arrived, and so she sat in front of the warm fire, reading the report. He gave way to a temporary frenzy and attempted to end his own life, but the executioner had already asked him his weight and measured his height, holding the tape at the nape of the neck soon to be snapped. He had blond hair and blue eyes, the colour of the sky, and they soon slipped into darkness as the hood was pulled over his head. He felt the gentle hands of the executioner place the heavier rope round his neck. They rested a moment. In the darkness, they could have been the hands of a girl, any of the girls he had taken, they all touched him like that. Then he was alone, standing for the last time, and the priest murmured about salvation. He smiled, he was closer to heaven than the priest, and then he realised the voice

20

had stopped. And he knew. In that moment, the hate welled up. The floor opened beneath his feet, the strong rope jerking his body back from the empty drop. The crack rang out a testament to the efficiency of the hangman, but not so swiftly that the curse wasn't heard, and before the limp body was removed from sight, the reports were already filtering out of the prison.

And then she would drop the paper containing the curse of a dead man, watch it fall to the floor and stare into the fire, the flames licking upwards towards the petition she had received. Oh yes, he had protested his innocence, thought that she would intervene. His childlike scrawl burned very well, the edges curled brown and she like Meleager's mother, prayed for his death as the paper twisted like his very soul, twisted like his body on the end of the rope. Another log would drop. She jumped at the sound and an ember landed on her dress; it always landed on the white dress. The crinoline would crumple and melt, and she would watch the flames take hold, the wonder of fire captivating her steady eyes. Then she would run, blazing like a torch. Chairs, curtains, carpets smouldered in her path, flickering into life, while the flames grew to be higher than her own body. She would clasp them to her, screaming their names, the names of those she loved. Wherever her eye fell, flames ignited. Her dead husband burnt away, and William's parents rushed to embrace her, only to be consumed in the roaring fire, and with a silent scream, she would look round for who else could help put out the flames of the curse. She heard the sound of a baby crying and woke up.

Roe's face wavered into view. She saw him through the heat haze of her dream. She let her head rest back into a pile of cushions. She felt the wig she wore slide slightly on her scalp, reached up to it, the colour of old meringue, and with as much charm as she could muster, adjusted it.

As the four clocks she kept in the room ticked away, she wondered how many seconds had passed as she lay in the bed.

'Punctual as usual,' she murmured.

'Perhaps,' ventured Roe, clearing his throat slightly, 'perhaps I should call back later.'

'What are you saying?' she said. 'What's he saying?' she asked William.

21

'He said, perhaps we should come back later,' repeated William, still feeling the fluttering presence of the reverend's hand. The clocks suddenly struck half-past the hour, except it was the wrong hour. She straightened herself slightly in the bed and smiled at William.

'Dawn is long over,' she said, and her eyes twisted towards the window.

'Ah yes,' said Roe at a loss, 'quite a beautiful sight I'll be bound. You have the better of me there.' Her breath seemed to whistle in the shadowed bed.

'And William,' she smiled, her voice taking on a new warmth. 'Your heart is in the right place, William,' she laughed, the girlish tone almost shocking from her withered form. 'You haven't told me what you are doing here. Perhaps you wanted to listen to a sermon by the reverend?'

She winked at William, and suddenly wished she could take a few steps towards him, even embrace him.

'He has his whole life in front of him, doesn't he Roe?'

'Ah, assuredly, assuredly.' He patted William on the head, not liking at all the wink and the reference to his sermons. He scented criticism.

'Ah, to be young, Roe,' her voice succumbed to a note of pity, 'to be young.'

She pushed the sudden unpleasant thought from her mind; she had a lot to do before she would give way to that inevitable call. It seemed wrong to think of dying, but sometimes she couldn't help it.

'What's the weather like?' she asked wistfully.

'Oh, quite fine, the sort of day you can see for miles,' said Roe.

'All the more reason not to spend the morning with old people,' she said gently, and looked about her room. 'I'm sure there are lots of things you planned to do.'

William knew she wanted him to go, he glanced at the sycophantic smile covering Roe's face, the reverend's aqueous eyes closed, and the corners twitched involuntarily as though he had been plunged into a religious trance. He couldn't understand how his grandmother wished to hear Roe. The sermons made him feel as though he were being lowered into a sea of some warm, soft, sticky substance, for

22

however hard you tried not to listen, something would always seem to stick to you.

'No time like the present,' she said, 'perhaps you would like your tea up here?' She smiled. 'You haven't done that for a while, perhaps you are getting too old?'

'Oh no,' he cried, and she felt her love warm; his devotion was unmistakable, he could never disappoint her.

'That's all settled then.' She gazed a moment at her grandson. 'Perhaps I shall have a little surprise for you.' She paused. 'Don't forget to say goodbye to the reverend,' she admonished, and watched as he shook hands with Roe and, trapped in her bed, followed his legs out of the room.

William's step had purpose. She sighed. She could almost detect an eagerness in his stride. She drew in a long breath and looked clearly at Reverend Roe. The vicar had adopted a sympathetic look, the one he usually reserved for the relative of a bereavement, and yet all the while he was commiserating with himself, languishing in this industrial backwater. The door clicked shut.

'Innocence,' she sighed, 'it never seems to last very long.'

'Ah, indeed not.' He fumbled awkwardly for the correct thing to say. 'He is a delightful . . . delightful,' his voice died out.

'I sometimes worry I have shielded him too much, there is such a lot he should know. Perhaps I shall talk to him, warn him he'll find it all so strange . . . the school,' she explained, 'I don't want him to think I'm sending him away.'

'Oh, he seems a sensible chap.'

'Everything will be spoiled, he could be so easily led.' She looked away. 'People,' she said menacingly, and stared at the draped window.

'If you wish,' said Roe tactfully, 'I shall have a little chat with him, man to man.'

'You,' the word pinned him coldly to the floor and he became aware of his pallid cheeks burning. He knew they would be crimson. He felt anxious at such anger, and a sweat began to break out on his body.

An overwhelming silence had fallen on the room, he shivered slightly, and she noticed.

'Someone walk over your grave?' she asked, her voice sounding far away. 'How is your wife?' she demanded.

23

He had the uncomfortable feeling that there was some veiled knowledge in the question. His dry lips parted slightly, but no sound came, he suddenly fell mute as he watched her clawed hand rustle beneath the pillows and with the uncut, nicotine-coloured nails like the broken talons of some trapped bird of prey, she pulled forth a crumpled letter and, without a word, laid it on the cover of the bed.

'Your wife,' she persisted.

'Ah . . .' stumbled Roe, 'it is so kind of you to ask, I shall tell her.' He stared at the strange envelope and blinked, '. . . much better though,' he said absently, trying not to think of whether he would find Florence with slurred speech, rambling eyes and the fumes of the empty bottle.

'It cannot be easy for you,' she said with unexpected sympathy, and he had to check himself from agreeing and spilling the sorry tale.

He had often wondered what it would have been like to listen to the breathless, embarrassed confessions of the Catholics. He had imagined pressing his avid ear to the partition, his rapt eyes closed as he concentrated on the fumbling advances young virgins would admit to.

'We manage, we manage,' his voice was distant and clipped, he still had the feeling that she knew that when Florence was indisposed, the only remedy was to lock away the alcohol. 'We all have our little burdens.'

She leant forward, and Roe's nostrils quivered as they detected the remote taint of decay, and he felt the sweat drip down the inside of his jacket.

'And the town,' she said, gesturing vaguely once more towards the window, 'how is it faring?' Her voice was polite, but uninterested, a macabre fakery of nostalgia.

'Little has changed, perhaps it's just easier to see the soot in the summertime.' Only he laughed at his little joke. 'But I don't think you'd feel lost.' He thought it odd that she should ask after the town as though some vague, mutual acquaintance.

'I no longer read newspapers,' she confided. 'It is a great relief, you know, just to live day to day. Perhaps I should feel guilty for not taking an interest, but I've lived through too many seasons. It's my family who are the important ones, not the changes outside.'

24

She spoke slowly and proudly and her words cast an eerie gloom in the lonely retreat she had forged for herself. Like many people all over Europe she had turned her head away, unwilling to become a spectator to the contemporary changes. The worrying speculation still ticked away like her clocks while plans were being drawn up, maps studied, and the relative efficacy of exhaust fumes and Zyklon B being researched.

'I still get to know what's going on,' she said with conviction. 'I don't ask to be told about all these things, but despite my barricades, the world outwits me. Even in this quiet place, I still hear the whispers, the fragments of life, perhaps the deaf have an easier life.' She sighed, but Roe felt agitated as her restless hands scraped the envelope which still lay on the cover; it was too light to make a depression.

'How long have I known you?' she asked ominously.

'Ah, now . . .' he tried to smile, 'probably longer than either of us would wish to admit to,' he squirmed slightly. Her face contorted, and it took him a few moments to realise she had tried to raise her eyebrow.

'Do you dream, Roe?'

'Ah . . . I . . . of . . . course . . .'

'My dreams, they wage war on me, remind me of those things I wish to forget, and they haunt my waking.' Her voice seemed to become thin and light, and he could hear the scraping of nails on the paper. The sounds filled him with a weary pessimism.

'Perhaps you would feel more at peace if we prayed together.' He brought his palms together as though obeying some physical law and her large eyes reflected the empty gesture.

'I have not asked you here for your moral or spiritual guidance.' Her voice was deliberately cold. 'Is it possible to have a soul without a body?'

Roe frowned at the paradoxical statement. She had phrased it like a rhetorical question. Her hand made a violent movement on the still bedspread, and her swooping fingers clutched the mysterious envelope. Fascinated, he watched her flourish it briefly in the pale and ghostly light. Roe felt instinctively that the paper was something disagreeable, but he had no idea what form the menace would take.

25

'You know my husband was shot?'

'Ah, yes a terrible thing, a tragedy, but I'm sure that God will . . .'

'Shot twice.' Her hand twitched. 'At close range, too.'

'We must learn to forgive and forg . . .'

'I dream about him,' she declared abruptly. 'Dream about him being shot.'

'You must try and fight this melancholia,' he said.

'I am too old,' she said simply. 'It is living and not living. I like things to be precise and invariable. My life has turned into stone. I lie in this bed and observe everything from here. The world is outside and I am here. I listen to the wind and the rain, and the birds call. Sometimes I can hear the town. I remain fixed in this bed and below me in the house many things happen, and, of course, I have my window.' She laughed. 'But perhaps I am too old, for even a starlit sky is dull to me.'

Roe listened to her stifling voice, the quiet horror of her words had become fascinating.

'I dream about the murderer of my husband. He was executed, no doubt you've heard all about it. There's no need to look so discreet. Perhaps you think I'm rambling?'

'No, no, I believe I can feel the torment you must have faced. Let us not forget the Scriptures. We must learn to turn the other cheek.'

'How simple,' she said bleakly. 'How simple and how stupid! Waking and sleeping, this is what I do, I give my priority to my dreams. They are full of reminiscences, and perhaps foresight. I have had time to think about it all.' She nodded her head up and down. 'Oh yes, you can see our future in the present.' She smiled, and rubbed her thumb along the edge of the envelope. 'For example, Roe, I perhaps know more about your future than you do. Everybody struggles in ignorance, but at least I know the experiences of your daily life are nothing, you are as much a hostage as I am.'

'Perhaps you are letting your imagination get the better of you?'

'Perhaps, we are all superstitious, even you, Roe. After all, what is God, prayer and after-life?'

'Mrs Booth!' he cried. 'I cannot countenance such

26

thoughts, and at your age, too. I should have thought God was a comfort to you.'

'I must wait and see. Perhaps you should give the devil his due. What can be more potent than a dead man's curse? And now I spend my days in this bed, and William is without his parents, and who is to know what else?'

'Only God,' declared Reverend Roe, 'directs the lives of men. I am astonished you are thinking in this way. Perhaps you should allow Dr Baldwin to visit.'

'Hypocrite,' she spat out. 'Don't talk about immutable faith. Don't you know that only dead men can afford to have secrets.'

'I believe I should leave at once. It saddens me to see you like this. I had hoped that over the years we had reached an understanding, and that the Blessed Communion I brought for you had meaning. I see I am mistaken. I confess I find all you have said bewildering. Everyone must grow old. I see many of our elderly, but none is like you. They will meet death with God, and yet at this time you reject him.' He shook his head. 'I pray that you do not turn away from the Church.' He gave a forlorn look, like someone who had missed the last train.

'Here it is,' she said simply. 'Perhaps it was wrong to have all this shilly-shallying. You'll see that what I said will turn out to be accurate.' She held the letter out to him. He found his eyes were irresistibly drawn to it.

'Did I tell you,' she said mysteriously, 'that recently I've had to dismiss one of the maids?' Her words evoked an unaccountable anxiety, and he cleared his throat. 'She had bright hair, red as the fire of destruction.' She smiled. 'It looked as though it could scorch her head.' She spoke with veiled ebullience and Roe felt a bewildering disorientation as the sound of his blood quickening its pace filled his ears. His hands began to twitch.

'I did not expect her to enter into correspondence.' Her words suggested an old-fashioned formality. She suddenly laughed in a brutal way.

'Let me see,' murmured Roe, moving towards the bed. 'You too . . .'

She watched him close in with reluctance. She hated the

27

contact of human flesh, it seemed to emphasise her own lack of substance. Her fingers jerked involuntarily as the bony hands of Roe touched her. The letter went skidding over the surface of the bed, and as they watched, it slid over the edge and disappeared from view under the bed.

Roe stared, his mouth opening and closing like some aquatic animal starved of oxygen and, with a gasping cry, he slipped under her bed. Emerging, he slowly pulled himself to his feet, and although the white envelope lay in his clenched fist, her eyes rested with shock and surprise on his head. Dangling down from his hair hung the vestiges of some unfortunate spider's lair. It looked as if one had actually chosen to weave its web on Roe's features.

He stood before her, and silently pulled away the spider's web, and straightened his white clerical collar. She looked up at the reverend as he slowly turned the letter around to inspect both the front and back as though it would reveal some clue as to the contents and origin, then swiftly he inserted his finger in the slit and pulled out the letter.

He knew it was her handwriting as soon as he saw the childish scrawl, which gave no indication of the adult nature of her body. He gulped, as though once more her pliant legs were wrapped round his corrupt neck. He almost expected to find strands of her red hair in between the sheets of paper. He tried to follow the lilting writing, to separate the words from each other. They seemed to flow together, mirroring the joining of their bodies. Even her writing had a carnal rhythm, the syntax dipping up and down. It was difficult to concentrate and he kept clearing his throat. He gave a trembling sigh, and looked up. His eyes were pale and vague, moving from object to object in the room, as though unable to decide where to rest. She remained silent, watching the crisis shudder through the reverend's body as the implications penetrated his tense mind. She shuddered, and stared for a moment at the distant sky.

'So,' she said to the dazed vicar, 'you are not the first.' The clocks suddenly chimed out, the sound unwholesomely clear. She continued, 'Or the last.'

'Who . . .' he croaked, 'who else knows of this?'

'Don't take me for a fool.'

28

She remembered the long red hair like some lion's mane, the strong young body which lifted her out of bed, and the small tongue which so charmingly protruded from between the red, red lips. A habit which had used to make her smile; now the very thought of that neat tongue left her filled with a sense of disgust. She could not help imagining that small pink tongue roving over the face and body of not just her son, John William, but the wretched figure of Roe, leaving a slimy trail of saliva as though a snail had just passed by. She closed her eyes to the bedlam of images.

He couldn't get it out of his mind. She was pregnant with his child, or it could be John William's, for as Elizabeth Booth said, he was not the first.

'She is with child . . . with child,' he whispered, and looked away from the figure on the bed as he spoke. 'She's only seventeen . . . seventeen, how was I to know? She obsessed me, I couldn't help myself, I even began to believe it wasn't the money. She gave me a lock of her hair.' He covered his face with his bony hands and tried to think it was all his imagination, pressing his fingers into his ageing skin. What a fool to think she would love skin like this.

'It must happen in many homes,' she nodded.

'Can you forgive me?'

He raised his head towards the ceiling. She watched his agitated lips move in confusion, beseeching divine forgiveness. She had thought for a moment he was wishing her to pardon him, she couldn't hear his words, the silence was filled with bitterness as tangible as an acrid smell.

'Heaven preserve us!' she said with fervour, her lips pursed at the tears which trickled down his gaunt cheeks.

'I'm sorry. I'm sorry,' his voice faded . . . 'a baby,' he sobbed.

'I . . . I don't condone,' she stammered. 'This is past the rights and wrongs, it is the remedy . . . the remedy.' She tried to keep her voice even, like the scales of justice.

'If people . . .' he whispered, his worried eyes darting around the room.

'I don't think you need worry,' she said, wishing he would hold his head up. 'I have written her a letter.' He would never know the painstaking hours she had struggled to make it

29

legible, and the words could never be wiped from her mind, they were as scratched in her consciousness as on the paper.

'The remedy,' he said quietly.

'It will not be born,' she said firmly. 'She is sensible; all she wants is the money. You both had your pleasure, and now comes the payment.'

'Yes,' he murmured, not truly listening to her words, but just the voice, for it was reassuring. He took a deep breath.

'There are women,' she said, 'every town has them.' She paused, as though the word left an unpleasant taste in her mouth. 'I shall leave the arrangements up to you and her. I shall see to the moneys,' she halted again, 'before and . . . after.'

'I wish it wasn't so . . .' He shook his head, unable to go on for the deep shame.

'You must tell her,' she said, 'there will be no problem with the money. You must make her understand that . . . she must understand, and there is no question of returning. None!'

'It must be painful for you, these . . . these, burdens, your own son.' He looked up at her trapped form. 'Does he know?'

'He . . . will . . . never . . . know.' She forced the words out, and there was a cold ccnviction in her voice, and hidden within, he sensed a threat.

'I'm sorry.'

'Please go away now,' she said wearily, her hand trembling in the direction of the door he had so innocently come through.

'Of course, of course . . .' He felt the questions tumbling round his mind, but sensed her agitation and fell silent. He knew he would take the money from her and hand it over, just as the letter had requested, and that the love child would be got rid of. Love child, he felt like laughing. 'With the merciful thou shalt show mercy.' He had not kept the ways of the Lord. He would have thought he would have been long past having children.

'It will be all right,' he said, almost forgetting the hammer blow of the news. 'She is sensible. She will take the money.' He remembered how her eyes lit up as she took the notes. 'I will see to things, clear up this unfortunate mess, don't worry, nobody will be any the wiser.' He was almost speaking to

30

himself, for Elizabeth Booth had sunk into her cushions, her eyes were closed and she didn't seem to be listening. He recalled asking the girl to stay. She had shaken her bright hair and opened the music box he bought her, swaying to the little tune, free and easy.

He still held the letter in his hand and he had made a mental note of the address. 'The letter,' he said, 'I'll put it on the bed for you.'

He doubted whether she heard his words. As his grip slackened on the envelope he felt curiously loth to leave it. He watched gravity take hold, and the thing fell down on to the bed. He tried to put his heart at ease as he left the room which held the danger to his position in Slackhall. He thought of himself as a poor man, a victim of fortune. Was this not indeed the unkindest cut of all? Yet as he slowly wound his way down the stairs, his face once more assumed the bland mask he would wear to his parishioners. He was an accomplished Thespian.

In the quiet of the bedroom, she opened her eyes. Her hands sluggishly moved towards the letter. Taking it in her rusty talons, slowly and painfully she tore it up, and with a cry threw the pieces into the morning sunlight.

She closed her eyes, an ability which gave her no relief. William would be coming to have tea with her. Her hands trembled. Would he see that her fingers were sticky not from jam but blood? Would he see the wolf's eyes staring out of the grandmother's clothes?

[2]

The upheaval of the world might have had its counterpart in the emotions of individuals. Aspirations and hope, conflict and petty tyranny could be found on the domestic front, as well as the battlefield.

William's eyes reflected none of this. The instruments of war had not yet cast their long shadows into this smug world. The *Picture Post* carried photographs of heroism, destruction, treason, death and misery. The captured images stared up forlornly from wherever the magazine had been so carelessly dropped.

As thousands were beginning to run in fear, William's legs began to carry him faster and faster. He ran down the dull passages, never noticing the peeling wallpaper or grimy paintwork. He lived in a land where you could run for joy. He slowed down. Panting, he recalled the years he had stalked these corridors, pretending he was evading enemy hordes, imagining every door held a secret threat. One by one, he had lost his tin soldiers. Perhaps he had demanded too much of them, ranging his chipped battalions in red and blue uniforms, watching them topple as a croquet ball smashed through their ranks.

He was standing by an old tapestry and suddenly became aware of muffled voices coming from the nearest door; he recognised the dry tones of his uncle. Taking once more to his heels, he dashed away, but was not round the corner before a pair of pale eyes caught sight of his moving form.

'There was a boy,' she said, sounding puzzled, 'running.'

'Ah,' smiled his uncle, 'that will be William. You needn't worry about him, he's off to school before long.' He laughed, his eyes tracing the outline of her body.

The smells of the kitchen seemed to cling to the very corridor leading to it, as though, over the years, the aromas of

32

cooking had embedded themselves in the brick. He started to feel hungry. Stepping into the tiled complex he was met by a dull heat. A fire always blazed away in the kitchen, even on warm days. Standing over a cold-looking pot sink stood Cook, she was separating the leaves of a cabbage, dropping the dark green ones into a colander after a cursory examination.

'Morning,' he said.

She jumped at the sound of his voice.

'You gave me a fright,' she exclaimed, smoothing down her apron. 'What's your game, sneaking up like that?' Her face was red and heavily veined.

'What's for breakfast?' he asked, his eyes catching the movement of a bright green mottled caterpillar which undulated into view among the cabbage leaves.

'Breakfast.' Her fat jowls seemed to quiver with indignation. 'You'll just have to see to yourself. I've only one pair of hands and now there's one more mouth to feed and only me to cope.'

He only half followed what she'd been saying, more interested in the caterpillar, which he thought was a cabbage-white. It reminded him that he hadn't got his killing jar with him.

The ephemeral lives of insects fascinated him. They buzzed and hummed through his mind. Even as a young child, he had played the cruel but fascinating game of taking spiders and placing them on another's web. The trembling web and scurrying back and forth absorbed many an afternoon. The garden never seemed to exhaust its supply of victims, and every morning it was covered with dew-dropped webs.

A splattering sound erupted from the range as something boiled over. With a huge groan, Cook barged past him, leaving an imprint of her floury hand. The sizzling continued, even though she had removed the heavy iron pan. She looked into the saucepan, wrinkling her nose. Her ferrety eyes darted to William.

'Look at this mess,' she declared, 'that good rhubarb's been ruined, and now what am I supposed to do?'

She banged the pan down, making some baking-trays

bounce. William shrugged his shoulders, he didn't like rhubarb anyway.

'It will have to be rice-pudding,' she said, 'with plenty of nutmeg.'

She sucked in the middle of her bottom lip, like the fluted edge of a piecrust and hoped this newcomer didn't expect lots of exotic things. She didn't hold with the use of lots of spices and herbs, and you weren't going to find frogs' legs either.

'Good plain English fare,' she said, 'that's what you get from my kitchen.'

She opened the oven door, the flat heat making the dry tips of her hair waft about as the smell of roasting beef plumed into the kitchen. William felt hungrier than ever. With a bent ladle, she basted the cooking meat, licking her finger as some of the hot juice rolled on to her dumpling hands. She eased herself up, wiping her hands down her apron and closing the door, and turned her red face to William. Like an over-ripe cheese her brow was beaded with little droplets of sweat.

'Jam and bread do you?' she asked. 'There's no time for anything else.' She gave a short, sharp laugh.

He poked absently among the cabbage leaves as she took out a white loaf from the bread-bin. She wiped a large knife leisurely on her apron, and then cut three heavy slices. Arranging them neatly, she spread a thick layer of yellow butter over them. She looked up at William and gave him an oily-mackerel smile.

'Kettle's on the hob,' she said, thoughtfully licking her thumb which had been neatly smeared with butter. 'I wouldn't mind a brew either, and you can ask your friend.'

She jerked her buttery thumb in the direction of the fire. As he followed her gesture, William was startled to see the figure of his tutor. Sitting with his back to the rest of the kitchen in a shadowy recess by the fire, Pewter could not appear more out of place. He was hidden partially by some flour-filled sacks and various boxes of provisions. Instead of books, he was surrounded by root vegetables. For the natural indweller of a dusty realm, the tiled kitchen was a curious refuge.

'Hasn't much to say for himself,' observed Cook, now

34

licking the jam off her fingers. 'Eat, drink and be merry. That's my motto. What about that tea then?'

William's eyes kept glancing at the tutor and then swiftly back at what he was doing, afraid lest some of the boiling water should scald him.

'Three sugars, and there's a drop of tinned milk,' said Cook, between mouthfuls of bread and jam.

She dabbed coquettishly at the crumbs which adhered to the side of her mouth. As William placed the steaming tea in front of her, she looked at it critically as though judging a vintage wine.

'The proof of the pudding's in the eating,' she said, and reaching down, lifted the cup to her mouth and drank. 'It'll do,' she said, 'although I like a drop more milk. Don't leave that jam and bread,' she instructed, 'not when I've gone to all that trouble, and the meal to get on with as well.'

She sighed like a soft jelly being turned out of its mould. Taking another sip of her tea, she decided if they wanted her to do outlandish things, like curry, she would hand her notice in.

'Can't stand around here all day,' she exclaimed, 'there's that cabbage to see to and the rice-pudding, and only one pair of hands.' She gulped down the rest of her tea. 'I don't know what he's doing in my kitchen,' she said, 'just comes in and sits down without a by-your-leave. You can tell him from me that this kitchen is a private area. Next thing he'll be wanting sandwiches.'

William felt embarrassed to convey a message that must have been audible to Pewter's own ears, and holding the cooling cup of tea, approached the seated figure.

The pile of burning logs provided a rosy glow, giving the pallid skin of the tutor the semblance of colour, and yet the man was such a dry stick it seemed an ill-chosen spot; if a stray spark should have landed upon him, it would have consumed him in seconds. Yet even a pyrotechnic display from Pewter would be miserly, his meagre flesh giving the flames little to burn. He was a physical anachronism, and attached to his gaunt frame hung the clothes from another decade. He wore a Victorian frock-coat that seemed well capable of holding another body. Although ill-fitting, the clothes had a pernicious effect; over the years, it appeared as though they were parasitic, and fed upon their wearer, secretly and ominously wearing down Pewter to the husk that now inhabited them. His spare body remained motionless, letting the fire's shadow create the illusion of life on his dry skin. His eyes were closed, but there all resemblances to a sleeping person ceased. Pewter had stationed himself in the kitchen with the one specific motive of intercepting his pupil.

He heard the banal exchange, his calm exterior belying the strong dislike he felt for everyday language. He would have denied the cook human speech, stopped her blubbering mouth which bubbled away like one of her cauldrons of stew. Ignoring the irrelevant conversation between Cook and William, his mind turned to reciting Homer.

Their voices faded like the very spirits who flitted around Erebus as Odysseus waited for Teiresias, the Theban prophet, to drink the dark blood of the sacrificial lamb. The fated seer, blinded for seeing a nude goddess, and speaking with the pure tones of Androgyne, had special significance for Pewter. It was only the Theban prophet who retained his intelligence among the dead. Freed from the repulsive and base temptations of the human condition, that would be true life thought the tutor, who had provided a hermetic environment for himself. Apart from sustenance and sleep, he had liberated his body from all superfluous desires. He had tried to unshackle the chains binding his intellect. It grieved him that the contents of his bulging cranium should be a hostage to the sweating, defecating stump that was his and man's burden. Like a charcoal burner, his mind devoured a forest of ideas, probing deeply among the red embers, and yet his own thoughts were as ashes in the wind. Time spent ruminating the thoughts of others or formulating his own ideas would have been the height of neglect. With single-mindeness he voraciously consumed the meditations, speculations and deliberations of the philosophers. The fragile fabric of his meagre body was a self-contained library of the works of the centuries. Conflicting notions were stored, he was not concerned with the truth, he merely harvested the profundity of people long dead. His barren pursuit provided no possibility of germinating his own concepts.

The only other thing to engage his attention was his pupil. With minute detail he had studied William, and beneath his eyelids he momentarily thought of the final lesson, and, to any observer, the mournful countenance displayed none of the Mephistophelean glee the tutor felt.

'I've brought you a cup of tea,' said William, addressing himself to the mute figure.

Immobile, in the sense of his own knowledge, Pewter allowed Odysseus and his companions to be blown from the halls of Hades before opening his eyes. As clarity began to spread across the soft unfocused eyes, Pewter never turned to face the youth, he merely indicated with his chalk-stained hand where to place the cup. Pewter had a bizarre deformity. The index finger on his right hand consisted of pure bone past the knuckle. Having no movement, the digit constantly seemed to be pointing at something.

'Sit down, sit down,' whispered Pewter's voice.

He waited until William pulled up a chair, and then he leant forward, bringing his heavily veined forehead close to William's.

'All is written,' he breathed, as though making some startling revelation. Pewter endeavoured to wink in a conspiratorial manner. The pale folds of flesh flapped over his eyes like sallow petals.

It was profoundly shocking that the taciturn tutor should change the way he acted. Such conduct was a shameless and brazen affront to the old Pewter. He winked again. Opening his brittle lips, Pewter attempted to smile into the chaste eyes of his charge, although he only created a feeling of profound melancholy. And then, to the surprise of William, and motioning the boy to silence, he scrabbled in his dusty coat and brought forth a small piece of slate, and started to write. Pushing the solid go-between towards the waiting hands, Pewter watched the fickle face of his student, who hunched his shoulders slightly. He could hear Pewter's breath.

'You finished with that cup of tea then?'

Cook had grown tired of them sitting there like dough which refuses to rise. Startled, William looked round, and

Pewter with a strange swiftness, snatched back the slate tablet.

She tutted as she bent towards the heat of the fire and picked up the brimming cup.

'That's a crying waste,' she declared, her big hand trembling with indignation. 'There's plenty that would be glad of a refreshing brew,' she stated, thinking how she wouldn't have said no to an extra cuppa.

'And another thing,' she said, 'this here is my kitchen, not the waiting-room at a station. You don't catch me hanging about your library, do you?'

She fixed Pewter with her little black eyes. Clumsily, she nodded her head in a self-satisfied manner, thinking that she'd got the better of a man of learning.

'Plenty of domestic agencies have been after me, you know,' she said with a touch of arrogance. 'Oh yes,' her voice becoming as tender as a well-cooked parsnip, 'I've had plenty of tempting offers in my time. I could have been at the Midland Hotel. They could be eating my almond slices in the tea-room.' She imagined all the businessmen and the ladies out shopping, sinking their teeth into the soft frangipane.

'You are what you eat,' whispered Pewter, his voice nearly drowned by the flickering flames.

The cook was momentarily silenced, as though thinking over the words of the tutor. Her eyes went misty and white, like coddled eggs. Suddenly, as though she had reached enlightenment and the eggs were done, they hardened into focus.

'Well, I don't take no account of vitamins, protein, and all this talk of nutrition. You can depend on wholesome food. Since Eve ate apples, we've been chewing our way without any interference in the kitchen, but I can't argue that a body needs food.' She laughed. 'I'd be in a right pickle if we didn't.'

'Snails, frogs' legs, snakes, raw fish, seaweed, monkey's brain,' chanted Pewter, his voice sinking lower and lower, until it resembled breathing.

'What's that?' she demanded, her nose quivering as though she could scent either burning cakes or sarcasm.

38

'Squid, octopus, armadillos, sloths, worms and beetles.'

'What do you mean, worms and beetles?'

'Food,' gasped Pewter, 'everything is food, even you!'

Cook backed away slightly, as though she expected the wizened man to attempt to gratify his hunger on her ample provisions.

'Never pick a quarrel until it's ripe,' she warned.

Pewter closed his eyes to the unsavoury woman, his papyrus lips crackled into a small smile.

'Let's carve him as a dish fit for the gods, not hew him as a carcass fit for hounds.'

'Nothing dirtier,' cried the cook, 'than those who eat that kind of muck. I wouldn't have believed my ears – worms and beetles! Even if I was starving, I wouldn't eat that filth, and I'm surprised at a teacher speaking out like that.' The cup and saucer trembled slightly in her hand. 'I've heard words I'd rather not have heard.' She turned to William. 'I'm quite within my rights to make an official complaint. I don't know what he's up to, but I'll not have it said that Mrs Ash lets those kind of things get into her cooking.'

'I'm sure he meant no harm,' explained William.

'He can say something when he wants,' said Mrs Ash, 'and very unpleasant listening it is, too.'

'I think he's tired,' said William, glancing at the stationary figure.

'We could all be tired,' came the peeved voice of the cook. 'No offence, but I don't think he's quite right. Just look at him, sitting by that fire, and then in the next minute talking about carving and eating you up.' She wagged her head back and forth. 'I don't feel safe, and that's a fact. To tell the truth it's made me feel quite jiggered.'

'Shall I make you another cup of tea?' asked William.

'Now that's a thought,' declared Cook. 'It's good for settling the nerves.'

'And I wouldn't worry about Pewter,' said William smoothly, and then tapped the side of his head silently as though indicating some mental problem.

'I knew there was a reason for all his malarkey,' she said, in response to the private information. She fell silent, wondering whether or not she should feel sorry for the unbalanced

39

man. 'Sympathy without relief is like mustard without beef,' she declared. As she plied the same spoon between the rice-pudding and the cabbage, William made her another cup of tea.

'That's better,' she sighed. 'Just tell him from me that I'm up to his old tricks, and if he wants cocoa and biscuits, he'd better apologise first.' She looked once more towards the tutor, thinking that she was a soft-hearted thing extending the hand of pity like that. By rights, if he'd wanted biscuits, he should provide his own.

'I'll tell him,' said William, and like a messenger boy, made his way back to the fire. Instead of a blazing fire, he could have been resting in the cool marbled halls of a necropolis. As sudden as a dagger thrust, he spoke.

'I have a message.'

He reached once more beneath his sombre coat, his eyes never leaving the watching boy. They were as cold as ice, despite the reflected blaze. He pulled forth the slate and handed it to his charge. As if relieved of some terrible burden, Pewter immediately looked more tranquil, and gazed piously at William's confused face, concealing that the tedium of the wait had made him malign.

'Boy,' was the first word on the slate. Coming from the hand of Pewter, it almost seemed an endearment. There was something unnerving about the melodrama, and if at first William had wanted to smile, the thought no longer crossed his mind with Pewter crouched by his elbow like a vulture. He read on. 'Your early years are filled with uneventful happiness. I have taught you the rudiments of knowledge and your education at my hands is almost complete.'

William looked up from reading the strange homily, and gaining no further understanding from the dark eyes, returned to the words of bitter wisdom.

'Human nature takes its course. You are becoming a man. Life and its explorations will seem infinite, but you are already on the journey to the tomb. Man has but a short life on this earth, the soil is heavy with unnumbered humankind, lost generations have fed the worms. Human experience has been my jailer, I am shackled to the legacy and stored sensations of others, intensive reading has been my youth and lover. Words drawn by pen held my faithful eye, and exquisite syntax imprinted a caress as subtle as an adoring kiss. Oh astonishment! From this sombre corner I should look out and see the treasures of life. Man's destiny is strewn with folly, error, sin and avarice. With dreams and chimeras he fills the enigma of life.

'I have not dealt with anthropology. Clinical experience leads me to believe that you will strive for experience, originality and excitement. You will succumb to the distraction of pleasure. Your isolation has made you the perfect study, you will represent the human condition, a victim and manifestation of inherited traits. You may feel anger; it is as nothing to me, your feelings are as transitory as a flea-bite. You are the son of man and woman. The final initiation into your apprenticeship for life will take place tonight. Arrive at midnight precisely. Tell nobody, and do not speak to me again.'

Scarcely had William read the last word before Pewter snatched the slate and swiftly erased the secret tidings.

William glared at the tutor's face curving into a leer. Somehow, Pewter had managed to touch a raw nerve of vulnerability. He saw Pewter smile, as though aware of the despicable bond he had formed. It was a smile of superiority. Angrily he got up from his chair.

'What makes you so sure?' he growled.

Pewter once more closed his eyes. The humiliating gesture was not lost on William.

'I'll not be there. You can keep your useless lesson. You won't command me,' he said, and then knocked over his chair which noisily clattered to the floor. 'You're simple-minded,' he cried, and then stalked out without another look at his surroundings.

'Hey,' shouted Cook, who had turned at the sound of the falling chair to see William open the door to the garden. 'Mind that draught.' There was no response except for the slamming door.

'What's all that sour grapes about?' she asked.

But even before William had left, or Cook asked her question, the teacher had resumed the internal recitation of the Odyssey. All that remained as a testament of William's

41

frustration were a few motes of dust which whirled round in their own vortex and gently settled on the clothes of the still figure.

'From beast to man and back again,' he suddenly whispered, and then fell silent, leaning his body towards the consuming fire.

[3]

As Reverend Roe made his way from the large house, his eyes scarcely distinguished the streets upon which he walked. His distracted mind did not register the doffed hats of those who passed by, and they in turn, thought the vicar was becoming too important by half. As he approached his own residence, he had the crazy impulse to walk straight past, to carry on down the road away from all the weary memories. He sighed. He could not leave his prosperous stipend and they would be expecting him; he was due back for a meal. He pressed the bell of the vicarage. The wait was interminable and he raised his hand to his throat and adjusted the band of his collar, the same hand he often used in caressing the bright red hair. As though it were strangling him, he fiddled and messed with the choker of pure white.

The door was opened by Bethsheba. In the whole of Slackhall there was no other dark skin to match that of Bethsheba. The legacy of his father-in-law's missionary zeal turned her dark face to Reverend Roe.

'There's a caller,' she said. 'I showed her into the parlour.' Roe managed to stifle the impatient click of his tongue.

'Where's your mistress?' he asked, and as Bethsheba's eyes turned towards the stairwell, he nodded.

'Will you want refreshments?'

'Who is it?' he asked.

'The headmistress of the girls' school.'

'What can she want?' he muttered, while Bethsheba thought how tired he looked, and wished that she'd improvised some excuse and not let the woman stay. She treated Roe with the same reverence she used for the imported God which her ancestors accepted at the point of a knife.

'The refreshments,' she reminded him.

43

'Ah, no, I shall just offer her a small sherry. We have some left?'

Bethsheba nodded and fumbling about, handed him the small key for the cabinet which held the drinks. It lay cold in his palm like a recrimination from his wife. He watched as Bethsheba heaved her heavy body towards the stairs. As it was Sunday, she had crammed her large feet into a pair of shiny black shoes, which looked two sizes too small. A mound of flesh stuck up above the leather where the shoe dug into her foot. With a pious inclination of the head, Reverend Roe opened the parlour door, and casting a glance round the room, let his eyes rest on the prim and proper figure of Cecilia Royce.

'Ah, Miss Royce,' he said to the rising form, 'what an unexpected pleasure.' He extended his hand and as she shook it, he wondered briefly why she was wearing gloves.

'I'm so sorry to disturb you,' she said, 'I'd hoped to catch you at the church.'

'I was detained,' he explained.

'And how was Mrs Booth?' asked Miss Royce.

'As well as can be expected.'

'A remarkable woman,' said the headmistress with feeling. 'It will be the end of an era when she dies. Slackhall wouldn't be the same.'

'Ah, indeed,' he said, indicating that she should once more resume the chair.

'It must be a fascinating place,' she said, sitting down. 'Goodness knows what wealth of things they've got tucked away there.'

'Pardon?'

'The Booths,' she explained. 'They must have so much hidden away in that old house, I'd just like to have a good root through. They probably don't know what they've got themselves.'

She moved about impatiently on the seat, as though she could scarcely contain herself from rushing off to the building there and then. Roe managed to smile, curling his lip over gritted teeth. He remembered that he'd opposed her appointment as headmistress, but had been in a minority on the board.

'Could I offer you a little drink?' he said.

'Oh I couldn't possibly,' she gasped, recalling the reason for her visit.

It seemed to Roe that her remark sounded as though she were making an official complaint. He slipped the key back in his pocket and turned to look at the headmistress. There was something distinctly overstated about her face. The bulging eyes he found most disturbing; they had a strange probing quality as though they found every-thing in life of some interest. He doubted whether the suggested drink would have softened their unremitting intensity.

'And what may I do for you?' he asked, wishing she'd get to the point of her call.

She sighed, momentarily closing her eyes.

'I've had to expel a pupil.'

She said it quickly as though the very sound of the words left a nasty taste. Roe couldn't quite see what this had to do with him; it would be a matter for the governors. She opened her eyes. The painful staring continued and the vicar wondered vaguely whether she used eye-drops. He felt his own eyes smart in sympathy.

'I had no choice,' she said forlornly. 'She was consuming alcohol at school.'

'Alcohol,' exclaimed Roe, 'I am sure under the circum-stances you will receive the full backing of the governors. Speaking personally, I think there was no other option. How shocking.' He fell silent, wondering whether he'd just imagined hearing raised voices upstairs. 'Shocking,' he repeated, his ears quivering for any stray sounds. 'Of course,' he said, speaking slightly louder than necessary, 'there may be those who might question whether discipline at the school is as it should be.' He knew what effect his tactless remark would have.

'I can assure you that this is an isolated incident. This girl is not like the other pupils.'

'Clearly,' he said sharply. 'One presumes drunkenness is not widespread.'

'I'm afraid I blame the parents,' she said with conviction, choosing not to consider the thin, trembling shoulders of the mother who was sobbing over the disgrace. 'She is a problem child.'

'I am sure you do,' he demurred, thinking that the headmistress was the sort of woman to be a suffragette and that the standards of the school had fallen accordingly.

'Normally, I wouldn't have bothered you with this sort of thing,' she said. 'It's not just the fact the offence was so . . . so . . .'

'Scandalous,' he said, remembering the time she had politely informed him that someone else was going to present the school prizes; some woman or other.

'That,' she said, 'is what I'm hoping to avoid.'

'Well, we shall just have to hope your firm action is an end to the shabby little incident, and that no other children are contaminated.'

'I think you'll understand my concern if I tell you the name of the child is Ethel Coffin.'

'Ethel Coffin,' he repeated, spinning the incongruous name round in his mind. He remembered it, but couldn't recall why.

'You had to give permission for her to attend.'

'Aah . . . the Catholic child,' he said, now understanding her worry, 'how unfortunate.'

For a while, neither of them spoke and Cecilia Royce presumed the reverend to be contemplating the ramifications of her action. Fiercely, she reminded herself that there was no other course. The Reverend Roe meanwhile had suddenly been overwhelmed by his own problems. It was as if the room in which he stood melted away, and once more he was listening to the dry tones of Mrs Booth.

'The remedy,' he murmured, scarcely aware he'd said it out loud.

'Yes,' she said, thinking the utterance was directed at her.

'What?' he said, the vagueness and confusion of his mind becoming apparent.

'You mentioned a remedy.' She paused and frowned. 'Did you hear a strange sound?' she asked.

'Sound?' he repeated abstractedly, as though his speech had been reduced to a form of mimicry.

'There it is again,' she said. 'I think it's coming from

46

upstairs.' It was as though she were on some treasure hunt, unable to refrain from unravelling the clues.

'I think it came from outside,' Roe said, cursing the stupid woman for making such a fuss.

'No, no,' she said blithely, 'I'm sure it was upstairs. I have good hearing.'

'Do you?' he muttered.

This time the moan was unmistakable, even he could no longer deny it. She watched him from the chair, aware that she had unwittingly stumbled across some private grief. Her heart sank, and she opened her mouth to say something, and then thought better of it.

'Would you excuse me a moment,' he said, and before she found her voice, he had swiftly taken himself from the room.

She sat a moment, crossing her legs in a restless way as if she were in some waiting-room. She looked around, taking in the sombre furnishings and wished she'd accepted the sherry. Her gloved hands began to rub the faded material of the chair and as the heavy silence descended, she began to go over the distressing events leading to this ill-chosen visit.

It had started with having words with Mrs Withington. What was the point, she'd asked the secretary, of telling girls that they couldn't wear jewellery, when she came in wearing such a vulgar display? Of course, she'd known the woman was highly strung, but the ensuing floods of tears and threats of resignation hadn't helped her own peace of mind. The woman seemed to have got it down to a fine art; nobody could be that sensitive to criticism. It was a good job she was patient, for she had been sorely tempted to accept the proffered resignation.

Perhaps it was this unpleasant scene which had led her astray. She'd needed to get out of the office, and though it wasn't her practice to check on the girls' toilet at that time of day, that was where fate took her practical feet. She'd heard the commotion, raised voices; some of the girls were having an argument. The imprecations vibrated through her body, and she increased her pace. As she rounded the corner, her eyes took in the gross kneeling form and flushed cheeks of Ethel Coffin. She had sighed inwardly to

47

herself, wondering how any parent could let their child get into that state. She had made many attempts to encourage the child to lose weight, but the fat which rippled round the girl's body was impervious to her exhortations. It was almost impossible to catch Ethel with her mouth empty. She had been amazed at the gaunt forms of Mr and Mrs Coffin, who were as thin as Jack Sprat. Children could be very cruel, it was in their nature; she had told the Coffins that very thing. She had considered telling them some anecdotes about the nastiness of young girls, but had fallen silent before the two stiff faces. They had a doglike devotion to their daughter.

Ethel had not seen her standing at the bottom of the corridor, and she had watched as the girl slowly raised herself from the floor, reaching inside one of the many pockets of her voluminous dress. Carefully she pulled out a little package, and with as much delicacy as her broad fingers were able to muster, she began to unwrap the contents. Miss Royce watched as a secret look of pleasure suffused the fat face. But before she managed to open her mouth, the silence was broken with a deep moan. Ethel looked down at the unwrapped contents of her pocket and was confronted with twelve crushed biscuits.

Ethel threw out her hand, causing the broken biscuits to scatter and roll down the corridor. Miss Royce stared in disbelief as the pieces of biscuit came hurtling towards her. Ethel Coffin, still unaware of the presence of her teacher, continued the dull moan. It was as if her very essence mourned the destruction of the biscuits.

Accompanied by the sound of crunching biscuits, Miss Royce strode towards the bulk of Ethel. Turning her broad head in the direction of the noise, and seeing the uncompromising attitude of Miss Royce, Ethel cut off the sound and as quickly as she was able made off towards the entrance of the toilets.

In the tiled sanctuary, the rows of chipped pot washbasins provided no hiding-place and the mirrors tacked along the wall displayed various portions of Ethel's body, each emphasising the predicament she was in. The only course open to her seemed to be the further retreat into the darker cubicles which lay behind her. Miss Royce appeared in the washroom. She scanned the place for Ethel, and seeing the girl pressed into the toilet, looked directly into her frightened eyes, only to be met with the swift slamming of the door.

Rattling the door, it was clear to Miss Royce that Ethel had slid the bolt across, complicating the matter of her removal.

Hearing the voices of more children, Miss Royce decided that she would place the toilets out of bounds, and that the girls would have to use the staff washroom. Clapping her hands in an authoritative way, Miss Royce herded the girls along the corridor.

The boiled sweet was submitting the last traces of its being to Ethel's mouth. Soon she would be without sustenance and reality would have to be faced. Her body's awareness had been heightened by the influx of glucose, and as she shifted her weight within the dark confines, she felt capable of attuning her senses to hidden spheres. Just as Joan of Arc had her visions when she heard bells, so Ethel was more receptive to such an occurrence after eating boiled sweets, although up to now no voices had imparted messages to her, forcing her to take up arms for a worthy cause. However, Ethel's ears were not seeking to pick up the murmurings of St Catherine or St Margaret, she was straining to pick up the slightest noise outside. Ethel contemplated manoeuvring her body in order to look under the bottom of the door to see whether the patent leather shoes of Miss Royce were silently waiting.

Grasping hold of the side walls of her cubicle, Ethel attempted to ease her vast bulk slowly to the floor, but gravity was not on her side, and as her swollen fingers vainly clawed at the slippery gloss paint, Ethel's descent could not be stopped, and her body experienced the unique feeling of moving faster than it had ever managed in the past. Having the air knocked out of her well-padded lungs, Ethel gasped like some prize koi carp. As the trembling in her body subsided, she became aware that her head had reached the correct level to see under the door. Ethel squirmed to achieve a better view, and realised with mounting panic, that she was stuck. With her broad legs splayed out around the toilet bowl, her heavy arms were pinioned to her side and her shoulders dug into the door. Like some upturned tortoise, Ethel had no means of raising herself. Sensing the utter hopelessness of her situation, Ethel succumbed to her sizable gut reaction, and screamed.

Miss Royce reacted instantly to the piercing noise, knowing exactly the source. She wondered how she had managed to lose grip of the reins of her school. Yet as she reached the lavatory she felt her composure returning, and eased the pressure of her nails which had been biting into her hands. Ethel's screams seemed to have lessened in volume, the noise began to disintegrate into stifled sobs like some ebbing tide. Miss Royce smirked at herself in the row of mirrors, and knew the school was once more in her command.

'Ethel Coffin, you must report to my office at once.' Pausing to check her dress in the mirror, Miss Royce began her progress towards the exit, 'After you have swept the corridor,' she added.

'I can't,' came the muffled voice of Ethel Coffin. The words stopped Miss Royce in her tracks.

'There's no such word as can't in my school,' she hissed icily. 'You will do as you have been told.'

'But I'm trapped,' wailed Ethel.

In the various mirrors in the room the reflected images of Miss Royce raised their eyes in unison as though seeking divine inspiration. Measuring every breath she took, Miss Royce contemplated the new piece of information.

'How are you trapped?' she asked.

Ethel, who was finding the angle of her body more and more uncomfortable, began to wail again. Hoisting her lightly starched dress in her hands, Miss Royce, as graciously as she could manage, got down on her hands and knees, and crawled towards the toilet door, as though it were some sacred shrine and she were a wretched penitent. She peered under the opening. The shock of seeing Miss Royce made Ethel cease her crying. She gulped back her sticky tears, and in the cramped confines of her oesophagus, began to choke. The snuffling ululation made Miss Royce click her tongue in an aggressive manner, but as she watched the blubbery head sag and loll in front of her, she realised that the girl was not

50

functioning properly. Phlegm bubbled out of the corner of her sagging mouth, and a muffled gurgle wheezed out from the bluish lips. Seizing Ethel's damp head with both manicured hands Miss Royce pulled it from under the door. It emerged with a dead plop. Ethel's asthmatic drone rattled on while Miss Royce inserted her hands once more under the door, scraping her flesh as she squeezed them between the rough wood and the unyielding fat on Ethel's back.

Attempting to simulate the manoeuvres she had been taught in the airy spaces of a church hall, Miss Royce pressed down on Ethel's body, in a vain attempt to influence the movement of her ribcage. Miss Royce had never attempted the life-saving technique on a sentient being, the classes had used a dummy. The instructor had been extremely keen on the correct training in the instance of dealing with a person struck by lightning. Miss Royce knew the necessity of dragging the prone body to shelter, although a lone tree in an empty field would not suffice. The instructor had felt Miss Royce to be more competent than some other women.

'You, Miss Royce,' he said, 'have a head on your shoulders.'

He then gave her a white smile from the tanned mask of his face. The consternation the remark caused almost made Miss Royce forget that she had to ask the dummy whether it had eaten any breakfast that morning.

Unfortunately, the prone carcass of Ethel was not as straightforward as the demonstration dummy, nor was the girls' toilet the exact location Miss Royce had imagined she would put her life-saving techniques to good use. She had often seen her picture in the local newspaper, underneath the dramatic headline 'Headmistress saves life of Instructor'. The fantasy scoop went on to explain how the instructor had invited Miss Royce on a hike, and the tragedy occurred when a sudden storm hit them on the fell. The instructor was struck by a fateful bolt of lightning. The resourceful Miss Royce dragged his unconscious body to the shelter of a nearby wall, and while the cool rain beat down, pressed her warm mouth to his supine lips, and gave him the kiss of life, her manicured hand gently undoing the belt on his tight shorts, which as she

51

knew, could constrict the instructor's breathing. Having brought the instructor to consciousness, the heroic Miss Royce battled her way through the unyielding elements to get help. The article concluded with a comment from the recovering instructor, stating he always knew Miss Royce was his best student, and in his opinion she wasn't just a pretty face, she had a head on her shoulders.

Bowing the only head she had, to the task in hand, Miss Royce allowed herself a brief moment of panic as she imagined a different headline, 'Death of a local schoolgirl'. The realisation that the girl could be the instrument of her removal as headmistress made the uncaring hands exert more pressure. Her bitterness proved to be her saviour, as Ethel's pummelled body responded to the violent beating.

'Oooooowoah,' was the sound which greeted her return to reality, and Miss Royce relished the scream, which earlier had caused such annoyance. Now she wanted the keening to continue.

'How are you feeling, Ethel?'

'You saved my life,' came the devoted reply.

'Well, not exactly, Ethel, you see I've been trai . . .'

'Oh yes,' interrupted the girl's breathless whisper, 'I've been saved. I feel as though I've been born again, and you brought me back to life, breathed into me, and although I've been dead, I'm not now. I've been saved, and I don't know nobody.'

'Anybody,' interrupted the headmistress, 'anybody, not nobody.'

'Well I don't know anybody,' said the reborn Ethel, 'who've come back from the dead like I have. I must be unique.' The tone of self-satisfaction was obvious, as though Ethel were attempting to take some credit for the miracle.

'Well, remember it was I who saved you, Ethel.' Miss Royce almost felt compelled to raise her hands in the air and add, 'and my healing hands.'

'But,' continued Ethel, 'I don't suppose anyone can be brought back from the dead. It stands to reason doesn't it?'

Miss Royce was now beginning to feel that the girl's familiarity must be contained. Never had a girl spoken to her

52

without being spoken to first, and certainly never interrupted her. Miss Royce wondered if she didn't prefer the old Ethel rather than the reborn version. She must quell the child's morbid fascination with dying, a product no doubt, of Catholic mysticism.

'Ethel, I think we shouldn't forget why it was necessary for me to utilise my life-saving and first-aid knowledge. I'm sure your memory cannot have been affected by the ordeal, and of course any explanation of what has happened would necessitate a close scrutiny of your actions leading up to the accident. You know that I would have to fill out accident forms in triplicate.'

The headmistress's voice quietly flowed around Ethel's protruding head, the subtlety of the message dissipating between Miss Royce's mouth and Ethel Coffin's ears. As Miss Royce continued to weave a plausible explanation for Ethel to use to explain the bruises which were beginning to show on her round face, the wonder of her experience was solidifying in the girl's mind. She must have been to heaven, although she couldn't really remember very much, so nothing much must have happened, but just because she couldn't remember anything, that made it easier to think of the kind of things which would happen to you in heaven.

'So,' concluded Miss Royce, 'I think the less said about it the better. I'm sure that's for the best. I'm not going to have to fill out any forms in triplicate, and you won't get into any trouble.'

'I've been to heaven,' said Ethel.

'I'm sorry, dear,' said Miss Royce. 'What did you say?'

'I've been to heaven,' said Ethel, 'and,' she continued, 'it was wonderful.'

'Nonsense.'

'The angels had hands just like yours, Miss Royce,' said the reborn voice of Ethel.

The headmistress snatched her hand away as though it had been scalded by the words, although the thought couldn't help occurring to Miss Royce that perhaps her hands were like those of an angel.

'The angels also gave me lots to eat,' said Ethel hopefully.

'Well, they shouldn't have,' said Miss Royce, thinking it

53

was now best to humour the girl. 'You get quite enough to eat for your school dinner.'

'I also drank some wine,' said Ethel, wondering whether she was taking the idea of filling in the gaps a bit too far.

Miss Royce frowned at the concept of under-age drinking. Slackhall would not put up with it.

'How much did you drink?' demanded Miss Royce, forgetting in the vigour of her disapproval that the inquisition was being carried out on the suspect disclosures of a fat girl who was sticking out from underneath the door of a toilet.

'Lots.'

The word had slipped out of her podgy mouth before she could help it. The eyes of Miss Royce lit up with a zeal which any prohibitionist would have recognised, and any drunkard feared.

'You are drunk,' concluded Miss Royce. 'You have been drinking in my school, and in your drunken temper you threw gingerbread biscuits down the corridor aimed at me. You then rushed to hide, or probably poured your liquor down the toilet, collapsing in a drunken stupor.' She glared triumphantly at the bewildered girl. 'I can smell alcohol on your breath,' she said.

'It's only a boiled sweet,' squeaked Ethel.

'Don't interrupt me with your drunken protests,' continued Miss Royce. 'I'll not have drunks in my school. I shall write to your parents explaining the situation and how I saved your life when you were in a drunken stupor and could have died from inhaling your own vomit.'

'But, I wasn't sick,' wailed the reborn Ethel.

'I shall have to recommend that you are to be expelled. I'm not going to have the rest of my girls corrupted. I'll get the caretaker to release you from the position your vice has got you in, and then you can leave the school premises. You, Ethel Coffin, are expelled.'

Miss Royce had risen to her feet to utter the last few words. She didn't feel it dignified to expel a child while sitting on the floor.

'But I've just been to heaven,' wailed Ethel.

'Don't tell lies, you drunken child. I wouldn't be surprised if you were the ringleader behind the gang flicking ink at

54

teachers' white cardigans. Don't think I won't get to the bottom of all this. I'll wish to speak to you when you've sobered up.'

As Miss Royce walked from the girls' toilet, the trapped girl screamed: 'I've been to heaven, I've been dead and was raised up again. Not nobody can die and come back from heaven.'

'Not everyone,' came the curt voice of the headmistress.

Like some nocturnal intruder, Reverend Roe returned to the room. So silent was his entrance that he was afforded the opportunity of observing Miss Royce some minutes before she was alerted to his presence. She did not appear to have shifted at all. He could not resist creeping nearer, but the floorboard creaked and he was betrayed. Cecilia Royce confronted the startled Roe, frozen in a ridiculous attitude like a stylised expressionist character adopting the posture of stealth, one leg raised, the other touching the tell-tale floorboard. His arms were balanced like an Egyptian wall-painting, and thus caught, he tried to give a natural smile.

'Thought you'd dropped off,' he said, relaxing his arms until they hovered at his side. 'Ah . . . my apologies.' He moved himself further into the room, and she sank back into her chair. 'Well, I mustn't detain you,' he said, thinking that she looked as though she were getting too comfortable.

'Was everything all right?' she asked. 'You seemed to be gone for so long.'

'I believe you have had a little nap,' he declared, giving her a playful smile. 'It must be all the worry. The diocese business took only minutes.'

'Minutes?' she said in a puzzled voice. 'But the moaning.' Her eyes blinked rapidly.

'I'm sorry. I'm not precisely clear what you mean.'

'There was a dreadful moaning, I heard it,' she looked beseechingly at the vicar. 'The moaning came from upstairs.'

'I heard no moaning,' he said blithely, stroking his white clerical collar. 'Well, no rest for the wicked.'

She turned to look at him, thinking that his skin had a disconcerting pallor. 'I'm sorry if I disturbed you,' she said sullenly.

'Not at all, not at all. What are we here for, if not to help others?' He ushered her out of the room and glanced nervously up the dark stair-well. 'Did you have a coat?' he asked.

'I think it was hung up over there.' She watched as the reverend darted over to the hanging garments, and feverishly sorted through them, almost tearing hers from the peg. 'I brought a parcel with me,' she said.

It was difficult to tell whether it was his teeth that clicked with impatience, or his knees as he bent to search.

'Parcel, parcel, parcel,' he muttered under his breath. 'Ah! Here it is.' He flourished the package in the air and in his vigour the brown paper split, sending some gaudy material cascading to the floor.

'I'm so sorry,' he declared, picking up the slippery, liquid-looking fabric.

'Dressmaking?' he asked, thinking the colour was ghastly.

'For the school,' explained Miss Royce. 'We are putting on a historical religious pageant.'

'Ah, how commendable. And this?' he questioned, holding the violent purple towards her.

'For Salome and the dancing girls.'

'Dancing girls?' He dropped the material into her open palms. 'I think perhaps I should have been asked about the suitability of the play. It is a Church of England School.'

'All the governors will be invited,' she said.

'Purple is not a colour for young girls,' said Roe, 'and Salome is not a fit and proper subject. I hope this has nothing to do with the Wilde play?'

'Really,' declared Miss Royce, thinking the man was a philistine. 'This is 1938. I feel that today's children should be made to appreciate culture. This is a classical performance, and the girls will be learning ballet.'

'On your head be it,' said Roe, giving a twitching smile to the little pun. 'If I were you,' he said hurriedly, 'I would not get too carried away with modern ideas. Remember we are only in Slackhall, this is not a place that takes kindly to new things.'

'Thank you for your advice,' she said. 'Naturally, I did not think that you would be shocked.'

She gave a brief smile and walked out into the strong sunlight. He watched her striding shadow for a few seconds, and then thankfully closed the door on to the summer's day.

Roe climbed the staircase very slowly and the lively façade he displayed to Miss Royce crumbled into a haggard ruin. He was tortured by the fear that one day his wife's drunken bouts would be discovered. At least Dr Baldwin was discreet.

If it were possible for a colour to represent the inner soul of a person, to express their very essence, then the colour most appropriate to Florence Roe would have been grey. Not the sullen, brooding grey of a stormy day, or the pale, delicate grey of the smoke from factory chimneys. The grey which would represent Florence Roe would be mid-grey, an indiscriminate colour, neither too dark nor light. A colour which reeked of compromise. But the parlour game of analogies had never encompassed Florence Roe, and nobody was called upon to describe her grey aura.

From the gloom of the landing, Reverend Roe pushed open the bedroom door and almost reeled from the overwhelming fragrances, the mingling perfumes that clouded the air with their unyielding sweetness. He could feel the onset of a headache. Enclosed within the heady odours, he took in the smiling inertia of his wife, perched on the bed. Her complexion was pink and healthy looking. It was as though in the process of embalming a dead body, the undertaker had been a little too generous with the rouge. She created the impression that she was resting, just having returned from a bracing walk. The midday sun poured through the window, the Venetian blind had been rolled up, and the hot, ripe summer day shimmered through the haze of perfume.

Roe watched the animated movements of his wife's hands. Florence Roe was busy knitting.

'Have you had a nice time, dear?' Her whimpering voice pattered across the room as though not sure whether it should have raised itself at all.

He clenched his fists, and it seemed to him that she tried to make a sensuous movement on the bed.

'I have had to entertain a guest,' he snapped. 'Can you

understand me? I had to entertain a guest, while you made drunken scenes.'

He looked down sternly on Florence Roe, as though willing her to stand up to him. She put her knitting down, and wiped her red eyes with a small handkerchief. She rubbed them with an almost shocking amount of vigour.

'I'm sorry. I'm sorry. I just wasn't feeling very well this morning and I thought I'd have a pick-me-up. I had earache, and I thought it would soothe the pain.'

'Must you always apologise,' he barked. 'I had the headmistress downstairs, and you were groaning and moaning up here. If you don't care about your own reputation, think of mine. I warn you, I'll stop covering up for you one day. You'd have to go to some institution.' He watched the tears dribble down in flushed streaks as they scored lines in the red powder.

'I had an earache. It gave me terrible pain. I'm sure the headmistress would have understood that I had to moan a little.' She sniffed. 'I'm not as strong as you, I'm a weak woman.' She trembled as delicately as a jellyfish, oscillating in currents not of its own making.

'Earache, toothache, cramps. These are your excuses. You are a drunk. Do you know a child was expelled from the school for drinking? Perhaps it's just as well we had no children.'

'It's not my fault. It's not my fault,' she sobbed. 'I'm just not strong. The doctors said that, and they said I should have a little pick-me-up, and I don't even like the taste.' Her hands were pulling at the knitting, slowly unravelling the stitches. 'I'm sorry, I'm sorry. Please don't be angry with me. Tell me you still love me,' she pleaded, wiping her trembling hand across the stained face.

'Love!' sneered Roe. 'I am married to you, and that's all that binds me.'

'Then I don't love you,' she wailed, and flung the knitting towards the mirror.

'Bethsheba,' he shouted. 'Bethsheba. Come here at once.'

He watched his wife's reflection swaying in the bright mirror. He felt as though he were overseeing the beginnings of her madness. The soft ululations continued, and as he waited for the arrival of Bethsheba, he watched the strange

58

occurrence within the reflection. The bright tears trickled down from her eyes, shining as they fell into the sunlight. The splashing tears were the last thing of value she would give to her husband. Her moist eyes looked towards the mirror, and he shuddered. They seemed to burn into him, and the tears ceased, as though evaporating into the heat of the room, and she made the discovery that she could no longer cry.

[4]

The bright light caused him to squint slightly. The gentle gloom of the house had tricked him into thinking it might rain. He stepped through the lush vegetation, glad there was no water to splash on his bare legs. William forced his way through the tickling ferns, sending up little clouds of insects. The old pathways of the garden were now overrun with wild green, it was only his feet which told him there was stone beneath the undergrowth. A slight breeze rustled its way through the stalks, stroking him with its brief presence, and then once more he felt the steady warmth of the sun. He bent to pick a long stem of grass, and paused to listen to the surprising multitude of sounds. Behind him, some of the leaded windows had been flung open to let the summer in, and he could hear the faint strains of some music, which filtered from his uncle's radiogram.

Further away, he could make out the distant barking of dogs and as he slipped the frayed end of the grass into his mouth he tried to sort out the different cries of the birds. Their chattering crowded the air. He could hear a curlew reaching into the blue sky and the warning burst from a distant pheasant. He brushed some humming flies away from his head. He followed his shadow away from the house with its rows of staring windows. The land had once been terraced, but an architect's ruins were all that remained, and as William clambered down the ha-ha, it would have looked to any curious eyes as if he had fallen off the edge of the world.

Leaving the ha-ha behind, William pressed on, the long grass speckled with cuckoo spit. Each white blob contained a tiny larva and sometimes he dallied, trying to remove as many of the soft little bodies as he could from their protective environment, and leave them exposed in the hard sun to dry out. He wiped the trailing white from his leg, feeling the little

60

body of the insect squash; he breathed in the warm grass and sighed.

The lamentations of Orpheus were casually blown on a stray breeze. *A dio terra; a dio cielo, e sole, a dio.* William tossed the stalk to one side and threaded his way through what would once have been a neat lawn. From the centre of an ornamental pond towered the other occupant of the green realm. The old statue was faded and covered in pale patches of moss. The cloven feet rose to the muscled body and from the sweeping beard leered the face of a satyr, the stone eyes staring unceasingly at nature run riot. From its head grew the horns of the beast, wound about by the dry tendrils of a vine long dead.

The whole area held an atmosphere that was both languid and remote. He paused a moment in the stillness. The tall weeds and grasses swayed and the stalks meshed the ground with slender shadows imperceptibly binding the fabric of the abandoned place. The faint fumes of the tangled rose-beds hovered in the dazzling air. No longer confined, they had spread into large thickets, and the heavy heads bowed towards the petal-strewn grass. The large banks of roses had created their own arbour, the gloomy scent capturing any stray breeze and creating a haven of mysterious tranquillity. As though about to pick one of the luxuriant blooms, his hand strayed towards the tangled mass, and then paused. Beneath the hesitant hand lay the heavy white head, crawling with greenfly.

There was a dull splash from the marbled pond and he wandered over to its edge, the bent vegetation marking his path. The still surface hardly reflected the blue sky, and the dank green algae subdued all the brightness which played on the water. Nature had taken hold, and where once there might have been oriental carp there now were frogs, toads, newts and myriads of water insects. Like everything else, in the neglect it had come under the possession of forces which did not value the transient work of man.

A discarded jamjar nestled by some reeds, a testament to William's frequent visits. He would collect the larvae of the Great Water Beetle placing the largest specimens in the glass prison, which served to magnify the occupants slightly for the

61

boy's round eyes. Here he beheld the spectacle of the insects growing hungry and turning on themselves. Like some Roman emperor at the amphitheatre, he would sit in rapt concentration as his aquatic gladiators feasted on each other. Their fleshy, segmented bodies could move with a hunter's swiftness. They grasped the victim in scimitar-like jaws, and inserting the sharp mandibles into the enemy they pierced the opponent's hide. When the wounded larva once more lay passive, the other would begin to feed, sucking back the internal juices along the same route the poison had been injected. Sometimes, as William watched the fluid pumping up the insect's body, the legs and feelers of the empty shell would twitch feebly, as though some form of life remained.

He had also seen a feeding larva attacked itself while feeding off its victim, the insects forming an intricate geometric design in the jamjar. There was something pure about the unthinking brutality. They were killing machines, as efficient as anything constructed in factories of war. When only one larva remained, he would treacherously tip the victor on to the grass, and with revulsion watch it vainly struggle to reach some watery sanctuary. He dropped the jamjar into the water, as though he no longer wished to perpetrate such crimes, and left the pond.

He was heir to this benighted place. It was as if the warm air and matted vegetation had entered into some complicity. The scents of summer dulled the wits, and gave the unsettling feeling that behind the sweet smell there was something more unpleasant awaiting discovery, something under the surface. William was in love with the garden.

His restless form seemed out of place in these enervating latitudes. He strode through the languorous scent of the flowers towards the boundary where he could make out the shining leaves of the wood. He did not loiter, but the trees remained remote. They stood aloof as though they had all the time in the world to wait for his arrival. His rustling step sent up a startled pheasant and he watched it fly into the shadows. A random gust of wind sent a flurry of hawthorn blossom tumbling through the air like a scented drift of snow. He brushed the stray petals from his hair and, unadorned, he reached the border of the wood. The sound of the crickets which spread from the fields seemed to cease, as if the heavy branches which kept the light from reaching the ground wove a spell of silence. The gnarled trunks of the ancient trees cast their shadows like a frontier and, without a backward glance, he slipped between then and was soon lost to sight.

Within the confines of the trees his footfall was deadened in the rotting leaves and soft loam. Away from the dry heat, the gloomier region was as refreshing as if he'd been doused in a cool stream. Clustered about the oaks and sycamores were huge swathes of wild ferns, luxuriant growths as extravagant as ostrich-feather fans, their gentle movement cooling the air, and far above, the sky was shielded by the carapace of leaves. Some had the veins which ran through them etched on the surface by the bright sky. The smell of earth was heavy in the sunless air.

William made for an open glade, the definition growing clearer until he broke into the sunlight once more. A woodman's axe had once been at work; littering the clearing were dank stumps, their sides covered with gilled fungus. In the flat heat of the opening, William could smell the drying wood, and grass once more clustered around his feet.

The woodland had been opened up for a midsummer-night's party and the boughs of surrounding beech trees had been festooned with streamers. Here, Elizabeth Booth had danced like Titania beneath the coloured paper lanterns, the faerie wings of gauze shimmering in the light of fireworks. The party gown now lay mouldering in her dressing-room, shut away in the darkness. She had told him of the party, how they had ordered tables, chairs and small tents to be set up, with Japanese lanterns illuminating the way from the house. Not wishing to cause their guests any discomfort or inconvenience, a huge wardrobe was constructed, in which the masked revellers hung their cloaks and coats after walking across the neat lawns to the wood. William had found it, and now this place was his secret.

The two enormous doors were firmly closed, but it was possible to discern a tender pathway through the stiff grass which led up to them. Foxgloves reared up among more ferns, and the grass was filled with bluebell leaves, the flowers having long died down.

63

The still varnished surface of the wardrobe shone as though gilded by the sunshine. Briskly he strode up to the threshold, raised his arm as though about to swing open the doors of his secret refuge, and knocked politely. The branches of the surrounding beech trees rustled, and the sound of the knock faded into the bright sky. His wavering shadow seemed to mirror the uncertainty; it raised an insubstantial arm as though about to knock again, and then lowered it beneath the towering bulk of the door until the shadow was that of a waiting boy. He had turned his head away as though to leave, when a furious scrabbling erupted within.

'Go away!' declared a disembodied voice. 'I'm not receiving anyone today.'

'It's only me,' he said with a childlike laugh. There was a moment's silence.

'Makes no difference,' replied the voice. 'We're still not receiving anybody, unless,' it added, 'you've got a visitor's card.'

He searched about his pockets and brought forth a crumpled piece of paper. He wafted it nonchalantly before the tiny keyhole, as though performing a ritual that had become somewhat perfunctory with frequent repetition.

'Keep it still,' screeched the voice from within.

There was a rapid click, and a brown wrinkled hand shot out of the partially-opened door and snatched the card. The door shut even more suddenly.

'That's better,' murmured the voice, and he could hear a further banging about, and the rasp of a match being struck. 'I've got better things to do than receive visitors all day long, you'd think some folk didn't have jobs to go to.'

The voice nattered on like the shrill chattering of an agitated bird. He sat down patiently in the long grass and listened to the irritated exclamations which punctuated the serene warmth, and closing his eyes, he waited calmly.

The huge door reared open with a groan, a trickle of red rust fell from the great hinges, and the shadowed interior was flooded by the strong sunlight. William had nodded off, and awoke to the foot digging him in the side.

'Get up from there, you vandal, don't you dare lie there.'

Sitting up, he looked at where his back had just lain, and

among patches of bare earth, he realised he had sprawled through a ring of darker coloured grass, pressing some tiny mushrooms into delicate fragments.

'Honestly, it's only a few toadstools,' he said, brushing down his white shirt.

'You great hulk of a thing,' she said, and jabbed him in the side once more.

'Ouch,' he said. 'I didn't come here to be kicked.'

She looked down out of her wrinkled face at him, sitting within the verdant circle, and shook her head.

> 'He wha tills the fairies' green,
> Nae luck again shall hae;
> And he wha spills the fairies' ring
> Betide him want and wae;
> For weirdless days and weary nights
> Are his to his deein day!'

Her cracked voice whispered into the listening glade only to be met by the heavy flapping of wings as a crow flew overhead, casting a brief shadow over William's upturned head.

'Well I don't believe in fairies,' he said petulantly, 'and it was only an accident.'

'Oh yes,' murmured the little woman, looking at him with her uncanny eyes, 'accidents will happen.'

Standing before him, the dumpy figure of Mrs Grime gave him another shove.

'I heard you coming a mile off,' she said. 'You made enough racket to raise the dead.' She gave a barking laugh, like some fox.

'Well, it took you long enough to answer,' said William. 'How do you manage to see anything in there? I think you'd just dropped off to sleep.'

'I have my ways,' she said mysteriously, 'and I've been up half the day before you even raise yourself.'

She pulled one of her many scarves around her shoulders. The clothes she wore seemed very old, for their once bright colours had faded into pastel shades except for small patches which would occasionally flash into sight.

'Talking of sleep,' she said, 'you seemed to drop off pretty quick. Is there anything ailing you?' She peered closely at his face, her gnarled hand rough as it felt his skin. 'You look peaky,' she declared.

'I'm all right, Great Granny Grime, honestly.'

'I've got something that'll do you the power of good,' she said, and made off towards her strange abode. William followed her, taking care not to squash any more plants.

The strange secrecy that surrounded the glade encompassed the small woman. William had no idea where she came from, and instinctively told nobody at the house about her existence. Their relationship was founded on the silent complicity, and hidden from all eyes, she would show him the wonders of the wood. He watched as she scrambled around for one of her many potions. The interior of the wardrobe was cluttered with an odd assortment of items. Tacked to the side was a garish film poster, and stacked up in random heaps were small woven cages and baskets. She seemed to keep nothing in these cages, although sometimes he had noticed a few bloodied feathers stuck to the bars. Hanging from the roof were bunches of drying grass and herbs, the aromatic smell of which permeated the confined space.

'Here, get this down you,' her thin reedy voice piped up, and her luminous eyes watched as he took a swig from the bottle.

'Yeuch,' he cried, wiping his hand violently across his mouth, 'it's vile.'

'It'll do you more good than anything the doctor would give you. Scientists' stuff is made from rubber and oil; all that does is burn a hole in a person's gizzard.' Her bottom lip pursed into a wrinkled line, but her eyes seemed to flicker momentarily with a malign humour.

'Will it stop me having dreams?' he asked.

'Dreams?' she breathed. 'Everyone has dreams, why should you want to stop?'

'Oh it's nothing,' he said, looking away from her face which seemed suddenly to have been thrust very close to his own.

He could smell the very air she was breathing, and see the wrinkles which ran like canals across her skin. Even the hair on her warts and moles seemed to quiver with a strange anticipation as she looked into his innocent eyes. He could hear her breath rustling like dead leaves.

'You having nightmares?' she wheezed, her hand gently plucking at the bars of one of her many cages.

'No,' he said, 'just dreams.'

She put her head on one side, as though imitating an inquisitive bird. He found it disconcerting.

'Why do you have so many cages?' he asked.

Her fingers gave a brief, rattling crescendo against the bars of confinement and he watched as a single feather floated down to the floor. It settled gently among the blades of grass.

'Why, bless you,' she smirked, 'to put things in of course.'

William remembered that her favourite film was *The Man in the Iron Mask*.

'What's on at the pictures then?' she asked cunningly, making him jump as though she'd been reading his mind.

'I'm not sure,' he said, feeling once more the unease that had first surfaced in his strange dream. She ran her hand through a basket of ripe berries; William had no idea whether they were edible or not. 'The King Kong film I think,' he said.

'Shall we go and see it then?' she asked with a curious childlike eagerness filling her voice.

'It's supposed to be very frightening. Lots of women have fainted. The papers said it was a hazard to the health.'

'What's it about?' she cooed.

'A huge gorilla who goes around eating everybody, and falls in love with Fay Wray.'

'Well, I'll take my smelling salts along, just in case. That's as good a pick-me-up as any I know.'

With surprising swiftness, she jumped out of the wardrobe on to the soft grass and slammed the large door shut; the cages rattled miserably in the darkness. 'Shall we be off then?' The solitary cry of a wood pigeon came from nearby and William turned to look at the wardrobe; he could have sworn it came from there.

'This way.' She squinted obliquely at the bright sky, and despite the white sun, all he could see was the darkness of her round eyes.

Threading between the heavy trees, he struggled to keep

up with her and occasionally she would stop and paw at something, either on the bark of the tree or the ground, but she did it so swiftly, he could never make out what she deposited among her tattered robes.

As though suddenly tired out, she fell silent and stood, waiting for William. He could hear her wheezing breath scratching the heavy gloom.

'It's close in here,' she gasped. 'I reckon the weather's on the change.'

'You shouldn't have hurried like that,' said William.

'There's things to do,' she declared, and rubbed her side as though she had a stitch.

William could smell the sharp odour of her sweat, it reminded him of decomposing leaves. He frowned as though trying to remember something. It was too quiet.

'Listen,' he whispered.

'What's up?' wheezed Mrs Grime.

'There's something missing,' he declared.

'What can that be,' mused Great Granny Grime, 'I wonder?' She gave a slightly exaggerated frown, 'That's a real puzzler.'

'It's the sound of the stream,' cried William triumphantly.

'I don't hear it,' complained Mrs Grime.

'Exactly,' declared William. 'There's no sound from the water.'

'It's been very dry,' confirmed Mrs Grime, her eyes sparkling like the missing water. 'Strange how you noticed, like you were drawn to it.'

He never heard the little snicker.

'It must have run dry,' said William. 'Let's go and take a look.'

She followed his eager stare.

'We're right enough,' she muttered.

'I bet it doesn't run dry very often,' persisted William. 'It won't take a minute.'

'Curiosity killed the cat,' she said.

'What are you afraid of?' he asked. 'I'm sure the banks will be safe.'

'I'd leave well alone,' she said softly, and he suddenly found her holding on to his arm.

68

'I'm going,' he declared, and shrugged free. She thought three warnings were enough for anyone.

Transfixed, he looked down at the silent stones. He gave her a cheery wave, and sliding down the bank wobbled along the uneven surface of the bed. The green slime made it slippery and he soon gave up his precarious foray. Digging his hand into the soft moss, he pulled himself out, satisfied now that he had explored the phenomenon. He had been disappointed, but would never admit it as he picked up a pebble and slipped it in his pocket. Like a dog returning with a thrown stick, he panted his way over to Mrs Grime.

'Satisfied?' she cried in a sharp voice.

'Very interesting,' said William. 'I wouldn't have missed it for the world.'

'You disobeyed me,' she whispered oppressively.

He blinked uncomprehendingly at her and tried a faltering smile as though now unsure of the rules of their bewildering game. He couldn't help the stray thought that it was his land anyway.

'Shall we be finishing our walk?' she asked, and as though unaware she had said anything at all, she started to hum a little jig as they walked up the narrow little valley. 'It's probably stuff and nonsense,' she said with a little laugh, 'but we could do with some rain.'

'What's stuff and nonsense?' asked William, his feet absently crunching and scattering the beech-nuts.

'Red Beck. That's what this place is called.'

'I know,' said William, brushing away a spider that had just dropped on to his arm.

'But do you know how it got its name?' She stood before him and thrust forward her crinkled lower lip. Her eyes screwed up, and she laughed into his sullen face. It sounded as though she were mocking the sunlight. 'This whole place was once dyed red with . . . well, I'm sure you can guess. It was once a battlefield. That's why this stream is called Gore Brook. Soldiers of the olden days died here. They probably helped the trees to grow so tall. I don't think it was right to let those scientists come grubbing about, not very wise that. A graveyard, that's what this place is, and the bones should have been left to rest. Unnatural the way they want to root about,

69

digging and poking things that don't rightly concern them.' There was a ghastly animation about her face, and suddenly she flourished her hands in front of William. 'There must have been plenty of red hands round here, dripping they must have been. It's said they were all betrayed, sold down the river by one of their own.' She gave a little laugh. 'Cursed him they did, cursed him and this place with their dying voices.' She turned and started to walk further up, the incongruous sunlight playing on her wheezing form. 'Strange,' she said, 'how it was. Like this place called you.'

As if in a trance, he followed her over the sweet-smelling grass, which must once have reeked and steamed like an abattoir. He shivered with strange apprehension as he walked through the spindly patches of shadow; they pierced him like invisible spears.

'We need a summer storm,' she panted, and wiped away at the sweat which beaded her brow.

'What do you mean?' he suddenly demanded, and grabbed at her shoulder.

'You've a terrible curiosity, that's for sure. You might regret satisfying it.'

'What's wrong with the river?'

'Bless you,' she chortled. 'It's not the river-bed, that's just the start. It's bad luck to see it run dry. They cursed it, you see, just as their bodies ran dry, everything draining away into the bloody stream.'

'Well, what are you doing hanging about if this place is cursed?'

'So many questions, my little friend,' she grimaced. 'You're willing to listen now though. It's a rum old world. Here we are chatting away where once you couldn't have heard yourself speak for the groaning and moaning. Mind you, there's been groans a-plenty through the years, and no doubt there'll be more to come.' She sighed and rubbed her gnarled hands together. 'Old beliefs die hard, and to my way of thinking, the old ways are the best ways. Oh, they all think they know better; like them scientists snooping and sneaking. Learning's no use when the end comes, they should have asked all those who were burnt and stabbed what use is learning when the flames take hold. There'll be scapegoats a-plenty when the time comes.' She gave him a knowing wink. 'Fear and hatred and curses, a very potent mixture that, quite unsettling.' She gave a little burp. 'And now the river's run dry, if you get my meaning.'

'So I'm cursed,' he said, and thinking how absurd the words sounded, laughed.

She scowled and darted further away towards a larger clearing. Dust and spores twirled in the beams of sunlight and he never noticed her lack of shadow. As though still unable to resist his curiosity he trailed after her and soon wrinkled his nose as he inhaled an unwholesome fragrance which seemed possessed of the very sweetness of corruption.

She stood beneath a flowering tree, reached up and took a branch; the petals fell like dying butterflies, garlanding her straggly hair with their soft touch.

'Some think the elder smells like corpses,' she said, obviously not minding the unpleasant smell of the leaves and flowers, and then started a little rhyme:

> 'Judas he japed
> With Jewen silver
> And sithen on an eller
> Hanged hymselve.'

She shook the leaves once more. They rustled like a death rattle.

'Oh, yes, old Judas hanged himself on an elder. It's a tree for treachery, strange that you don't like the smell.' She sniffed deeply. 'Now there's another thing, hanged men's curses are very potent things as well.' She rustled about in her faded clothes. 'Take a look at this,' she cried, and stepping forward, she flourished a strange card under William's nose.

'He's hanging by his foot though,' said William.

'Why, bless you, so he is.' She looked at it thoughtfully for a moment and then hid it once more among her clothes. 'Not a very nice way to go that,' she declared, 'to be hanged by the neck until dead.'

'I don't suppose there's many nice ways of dying,' said William in a surly voice.

'That's true enough,' cried Mrs Grime, 'but perhaps some

71

is worse than others. Quicker for instance; it'd be worse to have it all dragged out.'

William felt uncomfortable, he found the smell of the elder stifling, and the talk mystifying.

'I had a friend who was hanged,' she said conversationally. 'He used to read the cards, but he never saw the hanged man, not that it means you're going to end up with a rope round your neck.' She laughed. 'That's another funny coincidence for you.'

'What is?' asked William. The good-natured face he generally wore with the old woman had slipped away.

'That friend I told you about, well he made a curse as he was hanged.' She pursed her lips and nodded her head up and down. 'Probably just managed it before the rope broke his neck.' She gave a quivering little chortle. 'Just in time, you might say.'

'So?' said William, deciding not to look at Mrs Grime but at the limpid sky.

'Well, here was me thinking it was as plain as the warts on my face,' she pulled absently at one of the dark hairs which emerged from her cheek. 'Like I said, I had this pal, met up with him on the fairs, and taught him a few tricks. Like a son, he was, to me.' She gave William a big, gap-toothed grin. 'I thought you'd have got the drift of things,' she said, sounding disappointed. 'What with the curse of the river attracting you like that. Why lad! It's in your blood.'

'What is?' cried William, growing exasperated.

'The curses,' she shrieked, and shook the branch with relish. She laughed to see him jump back.

'You ask your gran, she knows all about the curses of hanged men, and now you know about the curse of Red Beck as well. It's in your blood; like attracts like.'

He looked about him as though he expected to see neat piles of paper lying around, each one containing the curse of a dying man. Mrs Grime laughed at him.

'It's no good looking, you should have heeded my warning.'

'I'm going,' he said, and winced as her laughter danced around him.

'I'll not stop you.' She rocked backwards and forwards.

72

'You should watch yourself,' shouted William. 'It's trespassing what you're up to, and trespassers can be prosecuted.'

She held her sides, and wheezed in her laughter, as she straightened herself. She stuck out her livid tongue and wagged it back and forth.

'Just remember this,' she gibbered. 'You'll be back, and then we'll see what trespassers will be prosecuted.' She bobbed her head up and down. 'Judas,' she screeched.

She slapped her thighs, laughing hard, and then clutching her throat with both hands, she gave a bizarre imitation of hanging. Her eyes bulged out at him, and her purple tongue hung out limply. Then she rolled her eyes and arched her eyebrows coquettishly.

'I cursed you,' she groaned with the voice of a dying man.

Horrified, he backed away, his eyes on the bloated dark face and the squeezing hands; the veins on her neck bulged out. She burst out laughing. 'Boo! Boo! Boo!' she roared. He gave out a small yelp and took to his feet.

She sank to the floor, full of laughter. As she watched his lithe body race between the trees, she gave the odd half-hearted shriek and squawk, and then fell silent. She mopped her head again, and tried to steady her breathing.

'I'm getting too old for this lark,' she moaned, and wiped again at the sticky sweat. Fingering absently the key to the wardrobe, she threw it into the pile of elder blossom, and was consumed with a malicious laughter.

Snapping dead twigs beneath his feet, the boy sped through the massed trees. He could feel the pebble bouncing in his pocket, reminding him of the dead men's curse. He heard the cacophony of the dying soldiers, the screaming of the dead men, and the howling of the wood. He never made out the laughter which ran like a bubbling stream.

He saw the prize of the sunlit fields, and he could make out the ominous rhythms of the grasshoppers, sounding his retreat from the wood as surely as any bugle.

The hands grasped him so suddenly he didn't have time to cry out. Vainly struggling, his overworked mind thought this was the end and he closed his eyes to await his immolation. Instead he heard an alien voice, blurred and indistinct. It persisted around his bowed head.

'What is the matter? Why do you struggle so? What is the matter?'

William felt like fainting to the floor, but his body would not oblige with the dramatic gesture. Instead, he stood dazed and stupid, his lips not uttering a word.

'You're crying. What is the matter? Why does a strong boy like you cry? What has happened?'

The voice carried on, and still William didn't respond. He felt cool hands run themselves across his damp face.

'Here, let me get my handkerchief. Come on, blow your nose.' With great efficiency, the white hands busied themselves around William's head.

'I'm not crying,' he said. 'It's sweat, that's all, just sweat.'

'Well, I must say then, that this is the first time I have witnessed eyes which sweat. Perhaps this is what you do in England. Come on, hold your head up. Let me have a proper look at you.'

The firm fingers tilted the pliant head backwards until he was confronted with the face which owned the ministering hands. Two hard blue eyes stared down. It was difficult to say whether he found the firm pressure reassuring or oppressive. The face that accompanied the relentless eyes could not match their ice-cold strength. It was as if the majesty of the eyes would not let the rest of the features try and detract from their brilliance. Her face was as smooth looking as her hands, and probably just as cool to touch. She appeared like the Snow Queen, and he wondered whether his heart would grow colder and colder, the longer the eyes held him in their grip. He had no sister, like Gerda in the fairy tale, to come and rescue him from the icy enchantment. Her hair hung down limply, the colour of hay which had been left in the fields too long.

She searched William's face for any clue. She could see the resemblance to his uncle; they were very alike, except for the hair. It was a pity, she thought, that his hair was dark, so much nicer if he'd been blond. A sudden smile cracked her face.

'Well,' she laughed, 'at least I can see now that I haven't caught some wild creature from the wood. I think you almost look human.' She released the steady grip of her hands, but his face still tilted towards her. 'It is so hot,' she said, but it was hard to imagine her icy exterior succumbing to the sun.

'So, perhaps I should introduce myself, no? You English are so polite, I'm always afraid I shall be thought rude.'

'You're foreign,' said William, wondering what she was doing wandering through the garden.

'Aah, my accent gives me away.'

'I think your English is excellent,' said William. 'I'm a bit of a duffer at languages.'

'Duffer?'

'Not very good,' explained William.

'I shall remember it. "Duffer", it is so English, small and stuffy.' She gave a laugh. 'Would you like to sit a moment in the shade?' she asked.

He was suddenly shocked. How could he have forgotten so quickly. He turned to look at the waiting wood. He'd decided Mrs Grime was mentally deranged.

Her cool eyes saw him look at the trees with alarm. Something had happened in there, that was clear.

'I've got to get back to the house,' he said, and then wondered once more how she happened to be on their property. 'Did you climb over the wall?' he asked.

'Do I look as though I climbed over a wall?'

'I just wondered how you got into the garden.'

'I came the same way as you, from the house, William Booth. You see, I also know your name,' she said playfully. 'I am not being very fair. I shall tell you who I am.' She gave a curt little bow. 'May I present myself? Dagmar Ehrenhardt at your service.'

He stood entranced by her courtly introduction. Her blue eyes noted his smile.

'I hope we shall be the best of friends. You always need allies when you start out on something new.'

The trailing shadows of the overhanging branches wafted over them, and an embarrassed silence fell.

William fought to overcome his shyness, his hand froze as he extended it to introduce himself. A piercing cry vibrated through the air.

'What a curious sound,' said Dagmar. 'The warning cry of some bird. Either that, or something caught in a trap.'

William thought of the blood-spattered cages.

'Why are you staring so oddly?' asked Dagmar. 'It was just a bird.' He was aware of her cool breath as she moved nearer. 'Why, in the forests at home, you can sometimes hear the wolf howling at night.'

She ruffled his damp hair. Such cold hands, he thought.

'Should we go?' she asked, and turned her slender neck away. She stepped out on to the dry grass, hesitating a moment until William joined her. They were both conscious of the weight of the light that seemed to stretch its warmth over their bodies. Dagmar tossed her hair back in the sunlit world and breathed deeply.

'It would make a marvellous picture,' she said, shielding her eyes and scanning the distant fields. 'How far does your land spread?' she asked.

'All the farmers rent off us.' His voice was barely audible.

'I can smell the cut grass,' she declared, her foot brushed the long stems through which they were walking. 'Perhaps someone should cut this?' She gave a small laugh. It was evident that the garden was seldom used, but she didn't admire the untamed beauty, she thought it a mess.

'Nobody told me that you were staying at the house,' he said.

'Ah, that is probably because I am early. I did not know myself until earlier in the week.'

'How did you know me?'

'I saw you in the house.'

'Were you watching me?' he asked.

'You were running.' She smiled. 'I always seem to see you running.'

'Oh.' He absently pulled at the stalks of grass, letting his hand trail between the thin blades. 'Where do you come from?'

She was silent as though consumed by old memories.

'Can't you tell. Where do you think, with a name like Dagmar Ehrenhardt?' Her foreign voice seemed amused.

'Russia?'

'I should say not,' she cried, giving him a playful cuff on the back of the head. 'Do I look like a Bolshevik?' She smiled, revealing her teeth like pale gleaming ice. 'Germany, that is my fatherland, Germany.' Her voice trailed off.

'How long have you been away?' He didn't think he'd leave somewhere like Germany just to end up in Slackhall.

'Nearly a year.' She paused. 'Does that seem like a long time?'

He thought she sounded sad. Perhaps she had left behind someone she loved.

'It's hard to believe,' she said in a lonely voice, 'yet, despite the miles, I always carry a part of Germany with me, in my blood. And Germany has a part of me.' She gazed in a sentimental manner at the blue sky. 'We have many folk-tales in Germany,' she said, 'and in one of them, a young man was shooting at a witch, but the bullets went right through. Shoot as much as you like, she said, for it does me no harm. For know that my life resides not in me, but far, far away. In a mountain is a pond, and on that pond swims a swan. In the swan is an egg and in the egg burns a light. That light is my life.' She turned towards him. 'So you see, part of me is always in Germany, that is where my soul resides, far, far away.'

They walked on in thoughtful silence, and soon the haphazard outline could be discerned. The grey roof and tower which cut into the sky seemed twisted and warped; she'd noticed that William had been looking at it for some time. The air was rich again with the heavy fragrance of roses.

'It's so still,' she whispered, and then the statue caught her attention. However she turned, some part of the stone figure seemed to linger in her eyes. 'This thing,' she said, 'why do the English have such morbid things? It's a monstrosity.'

The face seemed to leer at her. If she had her way, it would be pulled down. There was nothing noble about it.

'Ouch,' she cried. William looked round, his eyes relaxing slightly when he saw she'd only stung herself on a nettle.

'Are you all right?' he asked. 'Just hold on while I find a dock leaf.'

'He did it,' she declared, glaring at the satyr. 'He heard me. Ah, this irritation.' She rubbed her leg vigorously, and watched William disappear into the vegetation. 'I shall go to the pond,' she called.

Warily she moved forward. She'd intended to bathe her inflamed leg, but gazing at the dank water, her mouth curled with distaste and she sat down on the warm marble rim. She tried to sit still, but it was as if the sun were focusing its heat on the sting; she squirmed, it was unbearable. She looked back at the oily surface. It was disgusting, but she craved some relief. Violently she hitched up her skirt and almost tore off her stocking. She hesitated a moment, and then plunged the leg into the stale smelling water. She shuddered as the slimy water plants twined round her leg. The water wasn't that cool. Her foot reached the bottom, sinking into the silt and she could feel it squelching up between her toes.

'William,' she cried out, 'please hurry.'

She waggled her foot about half-heartedly, clouding the water, and thought she felt something bump into her calf. Dagmar pulled the dripping limb from the water. It was probably crawling with disgusting creatures. She cursed herself for even thinking of putting her leg into it. She fanned herself in the stifling heat, and loosened the collar of her blouse while the bees droned in the banks of near-by roses. It was almost hypnotic. There was a lazy splash in the water, she had been right, there were things in it. She heard a rustling in the grass, and turned thinking it was William. Her eyes fell on two snakes, their tongues flickering as they slid over the grass in their mobile courtship and knotted together. They twisted and coiled, their undulations horrifying her. She remained static, fearing them to be poisonous and, unconcerned, the twining grass-snakes hissed through the stalks. A cool perspiration had broken out on her flawless skin. The roses stirred sluggishly. She closed her eyes to the fecundity, but it shuddered on around her in the swollen sunlight.

With the solemnity of an acolyte, William searched the matted vegetation, ripping aside the straying suckers and endless swathes of ivy, disturbing the huge flies from the shade of the leaves. A large shadow appeared on the tangled foliage.

'Well, this is a turn-up for the books. What gives you such an interest in gardening?' The dry voice startled William. He looked up from the undergrowth and was confronted by a pair of legs surmounted by the body of his uncle. 'I'm sure it's very fascinating crawling about the floor, but not quite the place to carry on a conversation.'

He kicked a clump of writhing weeds, and watched William rise from his hands and knees. He pulled out his cigarette-case, and proceeded leisurely to take one out and light it.

'William . . . Will . . . i . . . am . . . Now!' called Dagmar, her voice exposed her irritation.

'What's happened?' His usually tired voice seemed more animated, and his eyes focused intently on the boy.

'She's stung herself on a nettle. I was looking for a dock leaf.'

'Dock leaf!' exclaimed John William. 'We can do better than that. Go to the house and get some ointment from Nanny.'

'But . . .'

'No buts, just get a move on.'

He gave William a tap on the back of the head and watched him become half lost as he dashed off towards the house. Satisfied, he looked down at his neat trousers, and carefully wiped the bottoms with the long grass, staining them green. He hoped it would create the illusion that he'd been searching for the plant. He dropped the cigarette and, smiling, ground it into the soil.

'Oh William . . . do hurry up,' cried Dagmar.

As he neared the pond, John William could see Dagmar sitting on the broad edge of the marble slabs, her head turned away. He thought she looked like Garbo. His eyes took in the long white leg that was stripped of its covering of silk. Her stocking lay provocatively on the floor.

Dagmar suddenly turned and caught John William staring at her. Instinctively she smoothed down the skirt which had been rucked up. As though her movement gave him the order to advance, he strode towards her, swiping absently at the summer insects.

'Don't worry,' he called, 'help is at hand.'

He wondered if she'd realised he had just been standing there. Dagmar felt the tingling from the nettle sting spread along the curves of her body; she was aware of the emotions she had aroused in this man.

'You should have told me you were venturing into the

wild,' he said. 'I'd have made sure you kept out of danger.' He smiled.

She squinted slightly from the reflection on his light suit. He had a certain hard elegance, but she thought his eyes looked weak.

'Where is William?' she asked. 'He was supposed to be finding me something.'

'Ah yes, I tried to give him a hand,' he gestured to his stained trousers, 'but as we were having no luck, I thought it better he went back to the house for something.' He smoothed down his blond hair.

'What brings you into the garden?' she asked.

'The call of nature.' His voice was almost lost in her sudden exclamation of irritation as she rubbed the back of her leg.

'Here,' he murmured, 'let me have a look at the damage.'

Before she could protest, he took hold of the damp leg and, running his strong fingers down it, made the pretence of looking for the nettle rash. She made a small effort to extricate herself from the fervent hands. She felt his warm breath as he moved his head near the red rash.

'Please!' she exclaimed. 'I'm perfectly capable of looking after myself. It's not necessary for you to help. You'll just get your hands wet from my leg.'

'Let me dry it,' he said, and struggled to remove his jacket.

'No, no,' she protested. 'I can dry myself. You will spoil your expensive jacket.' She lifted herself from his hold. 'Your nephew will be here in a minute.'

'Is it still hurting?' he cajoled.

'It's fine. I was making a fuss over nothing.' She stood up, and looked down on his kneeling form, smoothing down her skirt.

'Perhaps I should kiss it better,' he smiled.

'How can you say such a thing,' exclaimed Dagmar.

'It's to suck the poison out.' He moved closer.

'There is no poison.' Her voice faltered.

He leaned forward, and looked as though he were about to collapse. The disconcerting image of a shot man crumpling to his knees flew into her mind. He was too close, his lips were almost touching her leg. She made no attempt to avoid him.

'Don't do that,' she said weakly.

He kissed her on the leg. She closed her eyes, and slapped his head.

'God damn it!' he cried, raising his hand to the source of pain. 'You shouldn't have.'

A German man, she thought, would have struck her back. His pale skin was already reddening.

'We are equal,' she said. He kept his hand on his head.

'You're a firebrand.' He gazed up at her.

'It is rude to stare,' she said, turning away.

'Isn't it rude to hit your employer?'

'Of course,' she said. 'You are within your rights to dismiss me.'

'Don't worry,' he said, trying to smile, 'you don't get rid of me so easily.'

Dagmar stared at him, and as he struggled to get to his feet, she struck him once more about the head. He cried out as one of her nails raked his skin.

'For God's sake,' he cried, 'there's no need to be so violent.' He looked up into her dilated pupils, her skin seemed to be glistening with sweat, like powdered glass. He thought how lovely she looked.

She turned away. 'This heat, it's oppressive.' Her abstract remark seemed as though she were uttering some apology.

Taking a fine silk handkerchief he dabbed at the bloody mark on his face.

'First blood,' he murmured, and gazed with a kind of adoration at the stain.

She averted her eyes, and giving a grimace of disgust walked roughly to the pond. Without a word he got to his feet.

She looked towards the stone satyr. 'I don't know why I'm here,' she said, and when she turned round he had disappeared, leaving the bloody handkerchief on the floor.

'Damn him, damn him,' she whispered fervently as she knelt to pick up the disturbing ensign. She thrust it angrily into her pocket, momentarily shocked that she even thought of him in English, his native tongue.

She was absorbed in staring at her reflection in the fetid water. It was as if she were looking at her drowned counterpart. Then she heard William's panting approach, she had almost forgotten his mission, all she could feel on her leg

81

were the lingering traces of the kiss. Her hands trembled as though from great fatigue as she tried to compose herself.

'I'm back,' he cried, almost tripping in his haste. He held out the ointment, and she noticed he'd cut his hand.

'What have you done?' she asked.

'Oh, it's nothing, just some brambles.'

He shrugged his shoulders and watched her put the cream on the bare leg. He blushed. She looked up and saw his adolescent infatuation.

'At least you are a proper English gentleman,' she said. He blushed some more. 'As noble as Siegfried.' She laughed at his puzzled face. 'I shall have to reward my little hero.'

Taking hold of William's shoulders, Dagmar drew the boy forward and planted a kiss on his brow. For a brief instant, he could feel her body pressed to him. It was as gentle as sinking into a drift of snow. Although her dry lips barely brushed his skin, he felt their cool presence and thought of the kisses of the Snow Queen, how they made people forget. In his eyes, Dagmar was perfect.

'Do you feel better?' he stammered.

'It is working already.' She smiled. 'It is just this heat.' She looked up into the sky, it seemed in the hazy distance was the vague beginnings of a black cloud.

'Look,' she said, 'I think it will rain.'

'It looks like millions of little flies,' said William. Dagmar shuddered at the idea.

She picked up her stocking and as she placed it in her pocket, her hand inadvertently touched the handkerchief.

'We should be getting back,' she said, 'before it rains, or the plague of flies arrives.' She laughed. 'I shall only feel better after a bath.'

They walked at first in silence, and then as if for something to say, Dagmar related the tale of Siegfried the hero, telling of his betrayal by Hagen. How the traitor Hagen learnt that Siegfried was not proof to all wounds, and persuaded the hero's wife to sew a cross on the vulnerable point; and instead of protecting the spot, he thrust the spear home.

She finished the tale as they reached the ha-ha. William climbed up the steep side, and Dagmar followed, but lost her footing. She grabbed out for the sharp blades of grass, but they slid viciously through her palm.

'Give me your hand,' said William, and taking it, he helped Dagmar up the slope. She looked down, her palm was bleeding slightly.

'Look, William,' she cried. 'We have become blood brothers,' and pulling her hand away from his injured palm, smiled.

The smile on William's face froze as he suddenly thought of his cursed blood, and now Dagmar had it.

'It will be our secret,' she said, wiping the propitious blood on to the silk handkerchief.

[5]

The darkness vibrated around William's bed as he waited for the dull chimes of the clock to herald quarter to midnight. The sultry air was not allowing anyone to rest easily.

When the familiar theme arrived it forced William to decide whether he should keep the strange rendezvous with Pewter. The events of the day had been burning gently and steadily into his tired mind, and it was the tutor who first kindled the fire with his mysterious message. William had been haunted by recollections of Great Granny Grime. He felt restless. He flung back the unbearable burden of the sheets, and lay sweating gently. His confused thoughts conjured chivalric dreams in which he rescued Dagmar.

As the minutes ticked away, the need arose in William and a hunger seemed to consume him, a hunger for knowledge.

William stole from his room. He would be early. He gave himself a proud smile. As he entered the silent corridor, the darkness was suddenly split by a blinding band of white light which poured from the edges of Pewter's door. Transfixed, William was illuminated in a pose of innocent surprise. His eyes reflected the sinister phenomenon. Then just as suddenly as it appeared, the light flickered and went out. Whatever plans William had formulated to surprise Pewter dissolved in the afterglow of the fierce light. He shivered in the oppressive heat, and couldn't help thinking of the kiss Dagmar had bestowed on his brow. He reached out and took the doorknob, and then paused a moment as though resting.

The terrible solitude was neatly shattered by the striking clock. With no chance to recoil, and with the glazed eyes of a somnambulist, he found himself in Pewter's room, the door closing quietly behind him. His first sensation was of an even more humid heat. William's eyes blinked, and before there was time to take in the room, the light blazed forth, hurling

84

him into a mere outline. While flickering shadows raced around, a stooping form coalesced into a darkened mass which slid along the bare floorboards, over William, and spread itself along the wall. It was the shadow of Pewter. Like some mad alchemist, the tutor stood motionless as the wild activity of light hummed round him. But the pyrotechnic display was nothing more than a lantern projector.

The huge metal contraption filled the centre of the room, shooting forth the torrent of light and causing the uncomfortable heat and a burning smell as though the dust of the room had been ignited. Pewter continued fiddling with the device, taking care that his flesh was not singed by the carbon rods.

'Very punctual,' whispered Pewter. 'It is just past the witching hour, but we shall not become slaves to phantoms.'

He turned back to the glowing instrument, leaving William floodlit. Moving out of the white light, William looked upon the barren interior. Yet just as Pewter would tremble at the sheer audacity of a blank piece of paper, so he must have groaned and slavered at the pristine expanse, and gradually he had broken down the subtle stratagem of the white. His characteristic scrawl started at the bottom of the massive wall, and black charcoal lettering covered the expanse; virtually the whole wall was a wasteland of fragmentary quotes from the writings of others. There was a bold sweep to the black marks, as if he had deliberated before making the first stroke. Under the gaudy light, William read some of the cluttered intellectual graffiti.

'Learning's golden gift,' said Pewter in a low but intense voice, and he gave the flicker of a smile.

William turned away from the wall. The phrases seemed to besiege him, and an unsettling déjà vu descended. His own gushing statements had been inserted incongruously among the musing of philosophers and scholars.

'What a piece of work is a man! How noble in reason! How infinite in faculties . . . the beauty of the world, the paragon of animals! And yet to me, what is this quintessence of dust?'

Pewter's voice echoed as if in a cathedral. William's fingers twirled a large globe of the world. That, and a sleeping pallet, were the only other items in the austere place.

A solid square of white light had been achieved.

'William,' the voice shimmered in the beam, 'your old master is talking to you.' Revolving as slowly as the globe, William turned to look at Pewter. The old man's eyelids seemed swollen, his body rustled like dusty tomes. 'My young apprentice, after tonight you shall no longer be my charge.' He raised one hand to prevent interruption. 'I shall be gone tomorrow. I shall melt into thin air. And, like the baseless fabric of this vision, the cloud capp'd towers, the gorgeous palaces, the solemn temples, the great globe itself, yea, all which it inherits shall dissolve, and like this insubstantial pageant faded, leave not a rack behind.'

William felt he was watching a strange tableau of a dream. Pewter held a palsied hand towards William. It contained a small vial.

'Drink it,' ordered Pewter.

The withered hand clutched spasmodically as William threw his head back and drank the cordial. It could have been poison, but he realised the shadowy figure had another purpose. He heard the noise of Pewter's breathing, he had closed his eyes as if overcome with the fatigue of sleeplessness.

'What time is it?' he said, but could no longer hear anything except the steady beat of his heart. His blood felt ablaze.

Like a passing wraith, Pewter stood in front of William.

'The sleeping and the dead are but as pictures,' he said slyly. 'I prove it thus.'

The magic lantern show began. The wall erupted into a blurred image, slowly sharpening into a black and white view of the house. There came a series of slides of William, who grew up as quickly as the slides were changed.

'Had I as many souls as there be stars,' the voice of Pewter whispered out into the beam of light like strands of smoke.

'Mother,' sighed William, as a picture flickered and was gone, replaced by the tangled wreckage of a crashed car, the stone mausoleum, the mute faces of mourners.

Pewter was weaving a hypnotic rhythm with the click of the changing slides, and the shifting patterns of black and white frames caused the light to ripple over the cross-legged boy. The heat from the projector was slowly building up, and soon the sweat was sliding down William's head. Pewter offered the boy pictures of sunlight, starlight, black upon white, white upon black.

The landscapes and seasons passed, sweet rain and parched fields. William was presented with the travesty of a grand tour.

Among the procession of alien places and things, the likenesses of those he knew; Elizabeth Booth, John William and Nanny Bradshaw slid into view, to be consumed in the clamour of other slides. The familiar was warped by the strange in the complex tapestry. Politicians, kings and popes vied with the burlesque. Human carnage, a skull and his grandmother, William felt himself falling into the tide of images.

A woman gave birth. There were all kinds of things he could have asked. He was dumb. The pressure of the flickering slides was like a physical weight. There was no time to think. He had become another screen upon which the tutor projected images. The couplings of animals, the flight of a bird, broken soldiers, pornographic studies. The revelation made no impression on the gently sweating figure. William felt possessed as the secret of life slid into his vision without a ripple. The kingdom of man was within him.

William's own head biting into a round shiny apple.

Like two tiny mirrors, his eyes reflected the same head biting into the same apple. He was lost in a symbolic world, the pictures superimposed one on the other. The last slide was left in the stream of light until the edges started to curl up and the head and the apple were consumed in a twisting, melting image. After a long time, William turned and looked at Pewter. The tutor was watching the slide of his apprentice dissolve, a pungent smell drifting in the smoky room. He smiled at William, his snaky tongue flickering out of his mouth like a small flame.

William closed his eyes, but the pictures were all within him now. He opened his eyes on the spinning globe. The world seemed much smaller now; he felt it slowly revolving within him.

Night slid into the room as Pewter switched off the projector. He reached down in the afterglow and pulled the drugged boy to his feet.

87

'Nothing of me that doth fade but doth suffer a sea change into something rich and less strange,' flickered his voice, his hot breath tickling William's ear. 'The higher you fly, the faster you fall.' He laughed, his tongue making a funny little noise as it danced over his withered lips.

He led the dreaming boy along the corridors. The bedroom door was open. William was as drained of colour as the slides. Pewter passed the dry husk of his hand over the boy's damp forehead.

'I'm only doing my duty. You must think about that, it is something you will know yourself.'

The real voice of the tutor spoke, it was quiet and emotionless. William moved his lips, but as Pewter lifted him into the bed, there was no sound. He patted William's hand, and looked at the head nestled into the white pillow.

'Goodbye,' he whispered, the word slithering into William's mind, the last word he heard Pewter utter.

The old man looked around the room, the outer rim of his nostril twitching slightly. He walked slowly to the door, his limbs moving with terse and austere precision. Patting the hand had been his gesture to humanity.

'*Consummatum est*,' he murmured, the sound dying into the night.

On the bed, William moved slightly. His face was white, and his breathing fast, and tears trickled from the corners of his closed eyes.

[6]

The sun rose in its usual place. Throughout the land, the flat wash of light fell on the heads of rich and poor, old and young. No storm had broken.

Some things could still be taken for granted. The chorus of crowing cockerels gradually spread across Europe along with the warm summer sun. It was early, but Bob Tunnycliff was already up and about, going through the bedewed fields. From his belt hung a dead rabbit, and over his shoulder a gun. It had been a good morning's hunt, and now he was off to check his new traps. He whistled as he walked. It was the 'Internationale', and the rabbit swung in time to his jaunty step.

In a warm olive grove, the same tune was being sung, but not with as much gusto. Four members of the International Brigade sang with dry mouths, two were lovers and held hands briefly. Enthusiasm and romantic ideals seemed obsolete when the firing squad waited. Two accepted blindfolds, the lovers decided to look at each other. Without warning the guns fired, offering darkness not the sun. Three died straightaway, one took longer, she only had a stomach wound and was bleeding to death until the second bullet arrived.

Dagmar had risen early, and found the note that John William had pushed under her door. She tapped it thoughtfully against her mouth, which wore no smile. She picked up the silk handkerchief, frowning momentarily at the dried blood, and along with the secret note plunged them into the darkness of her pocket.

In the short time in which she slept, it appeared providence had guided the feverish protestations of John William's pen.

89

She had captivated him as surely as she wished to captivate the house's occupants and the town outside.

The few words he'd penned hinted at the sensual encounter by the pond. In the surrendering to pleasure, and the fire of passion, Dagmar would blind her first ally to the new order she intended to forge.

Quietly she started to survey the sleeping house. As more light found its way into the corridors, it revealed the patches of damp and mould; the house seemed to be in the grip of spineless decay. She walked carefully, lest her clothes should touch the rotting walls. She swept along, like a broom, planning the changes she would bring. Clean white tiles bristled in her mind. They were so easy to wipe down with disinfectant, no mould would grow on them. She was interrupted in her survey by Nanny Bradshaw. The elderly woman's lips pursed as she saw the newcomer.

Dagmar's request to help with the early morning chores didn't suit, but she decided that at least with the foreigner in the same room there was no opportunity for her to snoop around. She would have the chance to tell the newcomer how things were done in the house.

'This can be your cup,' she said tersely to Dagmar, and indicated a tannin-stained mug. The German was wondering whether Mrs Bradshaw had scrubbed her hands that morning. Just because they were white was no indication; they could be crawling with germs. The cup looked positively filthy.

'I'm afraid I only drink my herbal infusion, Mrs Bradshaw.' She smiled sweetly as the older woman was piling sugar into the cups.

'And with no sugar either.'

'Well, I shall have to ask Cook when she arrives. We've not had much call for herbals before now. I'm sure it can all be arranged to your satisfaction.'

She watched with irritation as Dagmar took the chipped mug allotted to her, and before her eyes poured the fine sugar down the sink. Before Nanny Bradshaw could tut at the waste, Dagmar proceeded to wash the inside vigorously. Nanny Bradshaw just didn't know what Cook was going to say about such a carry-on. She wondered to herself, just who won the war anyway.

'It's a shame,' said Dagmar, 'how the house has been allowed to get into such a state.'

The milk was already pouring over the side of the cup before Nanny could do anything about it. The hairs at the back of her broad head quivered at the impertinence. It was Dagmar's helpful hand that had a cloth at the ready and efficiently wiped up the spillage. Nanny Bradshaw let the younger woman clear the mess, while all she did was clutch the side of the table with even whiter knuckles than usual.

'Can I get you a tray, Mrs Bradshaw?'

'The tray is under the sink.'

'Ah, yes,' said Dagmar, wondering whether that was a very hygienic place to put a tray used for humans. She had seen the cat; that could get into places like that. 'Here you are, Mrs Bradshaw.' Dagmar resisted the urge to give it a quick wipe over.

'By the way, everybody calls me Nanny Bradshaw, that's what I'm called in this house.' She brushed down her starched apron, and checking the tray, left the kitchen to the German.

The monarch had left orders not to be disturbed and so slumbered on. His prime minister was already up. His hand faltered as he shaved himself; the blood welled, seeming all the brighter in contrast to the white foam. If it wasn't bad enough having to go over to Parliament, now he would be sporting an unseemly little plaster. Someone like Winston was bound to notice. He wouldn't talk about warships. He dabbed the cut with a gentleman's precision, his eyes seeing a straight road that never alters. William slept on.

Fanny and Wilfred Coffin were beside themselves with worry. They had both sat down together on discovering their daughter had been expelled.

'I don't know what we're coming to,' murmured Wilfred.

The portentous remark was usually reserved for reading about the world in the paper. As though the summer air had given itself over to winter's chill, Fanny Coffin began to rub her thin arms, the wrinkled skin bunching up at the elbow like crepe paper.

'Alcohol,' their hearts missed a beat.

91

She had done her Catholic duty and had a child, and as she saw no reason to go through all that again, Ethel had become the voracious centre of their lives. As Ethel snored away in bed, Fanny Coffin brought down the photograph album, and with silent reverence put it on the table before her husband. The photographs had all been taken at the same place, serene floating clouds the invariable background. Their skinny lips trembled as the pages turned, and the portions of Ethel's form which the photographer could encompass seemed to become concentrated on her bulbous face. The head floated among the clouds. That's what Ethel had said her unexpected visit to heaven was like, full of clouds. Fanny Coffin's eyes nearly dropped out of her head when she saw Ethel drop a biscuit from lethargic fingers.

'I think my little girl is going to starve herself to death,' she sobbed to Wilfred, and she tried not to let the tears drop on the photographs.

'I shall write to Ursula,' declared Wilfred, just as Fanny's eye noticed the envelope stuck in front of the album. Inside was a card wishing mother and child health and luck for the future; the signature was that of Elizabeth Booth. 'I shall write to her at the convent,' intoned Wilfred, 'and we shall appeal for her help.'

'Yes,' said Fanny, thinking of the letter she too would write, nothing was too good for their Ethel.

It was Nanny Bradshaw who first discovered the disappearance of Pewter. As she slowly read the note pinned to his door, 'No more tea in future', she wondered whether the tutor was going to insist on a herbal infusion. She knocked to clear up the ambiguity, eventually opening the door.

The cupboard was bare. She gasped at all the scribbling on the wall. She thought she smelt a rat. Pewter had vanished just as the German arrived early, and then she'd seen the skinny chicken snooping about; she knew there was a connection. She squinted at the straggly writing.

'The thought whereof, doth like a poisonous metal gnaw my innards.'

The tray trembled as she read. It was her first clue. It would appear poison was used. She regretted calling him a queer fish when he wanted all the furniture removed. Nanny Bradshaw slowly moved around, looking for more clues. She couldn't wait to tell Mrs Makin about the incident. After all, the fortune-teller was the one who first recommended the detective novels to which she was addicted.

She thought she ought to sit down a minute, to get over the shock. She'd come round better if she had a bit of brandy to put in the tea. 'No more tea,' she thought, and sniffed. The poor man wouldn't be having tea where he was heading. William slept on.

Nanny Bradshaw balanced the tray like the scales of justice, and recalled the effect of Uranus in the twelfth house, secret enemies, that's what Mrs Makin had said, and how right, how right. She suddenly felt all alone.

As she paused to catch her breath, after climbing the stairs, she suddenly became aware of another impropriety. Gasping at the thought of someone sneaking into this room, she stared at the note pinned to the door. Snatching it down, she rushed straight into Mrs Booth's sanctum.

'Look, look,' rattled Nanny, 'the impertinence of it,' and flourished the envelope.

'Now, now,' admonished Elizabeth Booth, thinking she would nip in the bud the habit of just walking in, 'we mustn't forget our manners, must we.' That would be an end to the matter, she decided, and gave a forgiving smile.

'I've had a nasty shock,' declared Nanny, blushing faintly. Mrs Booth took a sip of the tepid tea. 'It's Pewter,' declared Nanny. 'He's vanished into thin air, and this was on your door . . . your bedroom door at that!' She pushed the letter forward. 'There were scribbled messages all over the wall,' she warbled. 'I've never seen the like of it. There's more to this than meets the eye.' She leant forward to try and see the contents of the note.

'Shall I summon the police?' she asked. 'They can strike while the iron's hot.'

'Police,' exclaimed Mrs Booth, perplexed.

'I knew the body wouldn't be there. They're too clever by half, and mentioning no names, I shall have to inform the police about those caught snooping around. I knew it would all end up in a bad way. I could feel it in my bones.'

'Nanny,' declared Mrs Booth. 'I haven't understood a word you're talking about. Why on earth should we call the police?'

'To find the culprit.'

'You're talking nonsense again,' said Mrs Booth, wondering why Nanny seemed to be taking the departure of the tutor to heart. 'Pewter knew that I had decided to send William to school, I must say I think he must have taken umbrage, but that's an end to the matter.' She handed the cup to the startled Nanny. 'By the way, Nanny, can you just take a little peek under the bed. I'm sure it's not being cleaned properly.' Elizabeth Booth decided the best course was to take poor Nanny's mind off the loss. Nobody had mentioned any romance.

'Disgraceful,' came the muffled voice. 'Why, it's full of dust and torn paper. I shall clean it myself.'

'Yes, you do that. Perhaps you should have words with the maid. Just do as you think best,' she smiled.

'You just can't trust anybody these days,' said Nanny. Mrs Booth thought the words were a poignant little confession about her affair with Pewter.

'Will you make sure those bits of paper are burnt? And if you happen to see Miss Ehrenhardt, could you ask her to come and see me?' She decided it would be too cruel to mention that the tea wasn't as warm as it might have been.

Nanny Bradshaw heard the voices before she reached the kitchen.

'Well, I'm sure that's all very fashionable,' said Mrs Ash, 'but it's usual for the staff to eat the same as the family.' She stopped as she saw Nanny.

'Ah, Mrs Bradshaw, just the person we need,' exclaimed Dagmar.

'Nanny,' came the sullen response.

'Aaah, many apologies. It's just that with a nanny you expect babies, and I see no babies.' Nanny Bradshaw wondered whether this was a piece of German sarcasm.

'Pewter's done a bunk,' she said.

'Never,' exclaimed Cook, wondering whether it was all because she'd said no more Garibaldis.

'A bunk?' questioned Dagmar.

94

'Upped and gone,' said Nanny. Her eyes were like gimlets as she watched for the response from the German. She decided Dagmar looked very guilty. 'Yes,' she continued, 'he's run out. That's left you in the lurch, hasn't it? I suppose you'll have to contact headquarters.'

'I assure you, I had nothing to do with the dog's disappearance.'

'Dog,' gasped Nanny. 'You need your mouth washing out. He was a brave man, how dare you call him a dog. Just who won the war, anyway?'

'I don't care for words like that in my kitchen,' commented Mrs Ash.

'I thought he was an animal,' explained Dagmar. 'I fear my English isn't as good as it should be.'

'You don't fool me,' declared Nanny, banging the tray down. 'I mentioned the police to Mrs Booth.' She thought Dagmar looked worried. 'And she wants to see you . . . now.' She smiled at Mrs Ash. 'It hardly seems worth the trouble of unpacking.'

'I see,' said Dagmar. 'Thank you for telling me.'

Her cool eyes took in the two women. She strode forward, and fumbling in her pocket, took something out and threw it in the fire.

'Well!' declared Mrs Ash, watching with wide eyes as Dagmar walked out.

'Quick,' called Nanny Bradshaw, 'we must save the evidence.' She deftly hooked out the package on to the floor.

Mrs Ash doused it with water, tutting slightly at the mess. Nanny prodded the smoking remains. She clicked her tongue with annoyance, as the blackened paper crumbled, but she had seen it contained writing.

'Instructions,' she declared with authority. Reverently she lifted the material. 'Blood,' she cried out, making Mrs Ash gasp and clutch her chest.

'You gave me a right turn then, Nanny,' she declared. 'How about a cup of tea with a little something added, just to settle the nerves.' She bustled over to the range. 'You wouldn't believe what that foreigner was asking. Said she didn't like any meat. I said there's nothing wrong with English meat, but all she wants is to eat vegetables. Talk about sauciness!' She poured the cooking sherry into the tea, licking her fingers when some spilt.

'No wonder she's such a skinny chicken,' declared Nanny. They laughed.

'It's a queer how do you do,' stated Mrs Ash, letting her eyes fall on to the smoking evidence. 'I'd put that in a teapot,' she declared. 'She doesn't take to tea either, so she'd have no business going in it.'

'That's a good idea,' agreed Nanny.

'Oh, she's taken on more than she can chew this time,' said Mrs Ash. Nanny gave a deep growling laugh. She couldn't see that skinny chicken tucking into her flesh.

Smoothing down the starched apron which contained the plentiful meat and gravies of her swelling form, she nodded at Mrs Ash and left the kitchen, clutching the teapot.

She would seek the advice of Mrs Makin as soon as possible. The fortune-teller would be able to get messages from the astral plane. They would have a séance. The murderer would be brought to justice, and she'd keep an eye on the German just as she would a rabid dog. William slept on.

Ethel Coffin woke from her slumber.

Downstairs her parents were composing the letters which they hoped would alter the unhappy future of their daughter.

'I've been to heaven,' whispered the fat girl in a drowsy voice. She recalled how in her flight from the school she'd been waylaid by a little wizened woman.

'What's a big, fine girl like you doing crying?' the old crone asked. 'I've got something to cheer you up,' and before Ethel could blink, she had placed a small cake in her palm.

She closed her eyes in bed as she once more tasted the mysterious flavours on the day her life had been saved.

'Remember,' said the little woman as Ethel consumed the gift, 'so mote it be,' and her dark eyes watched a passing car travel up the hill to the big house, noting the blond head of the passenger.

Although Nanny Bradshaw had known Dagmar had never been shown Mrs Booth's room, that would not impede her

96

pace. Dagmar would find the rooms on her own. It seemed to her, the further in she went, the drabber the atmosphere became. The narrow staircase leading up into the dressing-room had a horrible quietness. The curdled light caused her to blink, and she looked around at the flotsam which silted up the room, the final legacy of the presence of Elizabeth Booth before she had receded into the confines of her bedroom, the ebbtide of her departure leaving the remains of her life washed up and deserted. She wondered whether Mrs Booth had heard her approach. Wiping her gently perspiring forehead, Dagmar knocked. The clarity of the voice made her jump.

Inside, Dagmar had expected a cosy invalid propped up in bed and surrounded by fruit and flowers and family photographs. In contrast, the gloomy atmosphere of the room had an adhesive quality, and the sediment of the sick-bed clung to everything. Exposing herself gradually from the bedspread like some wizened pupa emerging from a cocoon, the arms and head of Mrs Booth lay uncovered unnervingly before the gaze of the German. Dagmar felt that if she had prodded the meagre flesh on this body the imprint would remain as on some overripe fruit.

For Elizabeth Booth, the sight of another firm body sickened her with the overpowering smell of health. The erect figure seemed almost to be challenging her own decrepitude.

She looked proud thought Elizabeth Booth, the sort of woman who would have been a suffragette. She remembered William's excited account of meeting this German in the garden. She'd had an effect on her grandson, that was clear. Her profile was imposing. She had ensured that all light was extinguished so she could see her new employee yet remain largely unseen. Dagmar felt slightly awkward as she stood at the foot of the bed, exposed to the scrutiny of the older woman.

'Ah, Miss Ehrenhardt I presume.' She laughed lightly, the girlish tinkling more appalling than any consumptive raspings. 'I hope you have been able to settle into our little . . . community. I thought I'd give you time to breathe before you start work, not that I shall prove to be a hard

97

taskmaster. You shall have time to pursue your own interests.'

Once more she laughed. Dagmar felt more unsure of herself than at any time since her decision to leave Germany. She had attempted to anticipate this interview, rehearsed answers to questions that had not been asked, and consequently felt at a loss for words.

She knew that she would have wished to know more herself. 'Desires to live with an English family, and learn their way of life' was all Dagmar had written for the agency who secured her the post. And here it was that she intended to become the torch-bearer for the Reich.

Mrs Booth continued in her strangely modulated voice. 'I suppose it will take some time to get used to living here, but I hope none of our little ways upset you. I remember when I first came to live here, it was all very odd at first. Still, you don't need me to advise you on that score. I hope that soon you will be able to meet some of the leading lights of Slackhall. I'm afraid I'm not up to entertaining any more, but of course, I'll provide you with letters of introduction, written by you. Ha, ha!' Dagmar was not sure she relished such a prospect. She would be in control of a vital commodity, but the role of emissary to Mrs Booth would be her passport into the very heart of the community. The ease by which she knew all the doors would be open to her made the simple conquest less sweet in her pale blue eyes.

'I must warn you, it's very quiet. Life passes slowly here, very slowly,' she sighed, the sound having a peculiar sustaining quality, as though her very sighs fanned the embers of her tired existence.

'I'm afraid the last few years have seen me retreat to this one room, and, of course, this house has many rooms.'

She watched Dagmar from the canopied bed, as the German allowed her eyes to take in the place, noticing for the first time the gaps on the dull brocaded wall, where pictures must once have hung.

'When you grow older, you are content with a simple life. I became quite obstinate about not wishing to know what's going on out there.' She motioned vaguely to the room. 'Quite content . . .'

'You are not the only one,' said Dagmar.

'Ah yes, that must be so,' she smiled, 'and, of course, as a nurse you must have seen the melancholia of the old.'

'I didn't mean . . .' started Dagmar.

'Please,' she interrupted. 'I have neglected many things of late, reflecting on nothing, deceiving myself with memories. I intend that to change.' She paused. 'And there's no time like the present. I've decided that you should first meet our good vicar and his poor wife. Shall we write the letter to the Roes? You'll find some writing things over there in the desk.'

It was clear Mrs Booth had prepared for her arrival, and somehow intended to use Dagmar to venture out into society, while she, like some grand puppeteer, directed the action.

'We'd better provide a bit more light for you.'

Turning to Mrs Booth, Dagmar saw the old woman gesture to a dark alcove. As Dagmar approached she realised the alcove was made up of several recessed shelves of polished granite, which bristled with weird configurations of tallow. As she struck a match, the shadows of stalactites and stalagmites of wax flickered over the room, and when she slowly began to light the wicks, the surrounding gloom did not seem to recede, but rather it sucked up the candle-light.

'Ah, that's better. Now I can see you more clearly, my dear. It's such a romantic light, isn't it?' Dagmar didn't feel that the tiny flames produced an intimate atmosphere. She felt exposed. 'Have you managed to find all you need?' Dagmar felt sure that the large eyes of Mrs Booth had watched intently as she removed the items from the drawer, and wondered why the woman was feigning such ignorance.

'Yes, I have all I need. The pen is very fine.'

'I'm glad you like it. It was a present from my son. Have you met him yet? I think he's a bit shy so he's probably been hiding ever since you arrived.'

'Oh no, I have met Mr Booth. He has been most kind in helping me settle in, sorting out someone to pick up my luggage, and he's offered to show me round the town.'

'Well, you must not let him monopolise you so much. I'm afraid I shall just have to keep you busy, won't I?'

Dagmar felt the eyes of Mrs Booth follow her as she moved back to the desk. It was as though the older woman were

99

waiting for her to make some mistake, almost willing it, like the audience at the circus who watch only for the trapeze artist to tumble to the sawdust.

'Shall I open the curtains properly?' asked Dagmar.

'Whatever for?' laughed Mrs Booth, 'I can see perfectly well.'

She gave a trembling cough, and watched the steady rise and fall of the German's strong rib cage.

'Do you wish some linctus for your throat?'

Elizabeth Booth listened quietly to the question and parted her lips slightly, only to make a weak little noise like the mewling of a drowned kitten. She saw the German's breathing increase slightly in pace. She gave another little sound.

'Shall I get a glass of water?' asked Dagmar.

Elizabeth Booth let the worried voice drift towards her. She watched Dagmar stiffen and lean towards the bed.

'Are you all right, Mrs Booth?'

The concern in her voice made the figure on the bed quiver with pleasure and, frightened lest this should give her away, she sought to quell the movement. She hadn't planned to do this, and almost regretted her subterfuge, but remained motionless. She did not speak. She could hear Dagmar's breathing; short and rapid.

'Is everything all right?'

She would let Dagmar come over and touch her. The tension was almost unbearable. She heard the heavy ticking of the clocks.

Dagmar had moved over to the bed trying to become accustomed to the gloom; the candles flickered as she reached out for one.

'Are you awake?' she asked, wondering whether she should summon someone, and as she edged forward with the candle, the hot wax dripped on to her hand.

Mrs Booth could sense the light behind her closed eyelids, and suddenly felt afraid. It now seemed wrong to pretend to be ill, as though perhaps she were rehearsing a role she might one day have to play. 'I am old,' she thought. Now she was playing dead and dreamed about dead people. She was much given over to dreams, it was becoming easier to think of other

100

times. She tried not to think about the abortion. If it was born, it would be her grandchild.

The wax dribbled down like a petrified tear.

'Mrs Booth,' whispered Dagmar, looking at the still face. It looked like an empty mask.

She could feel the warmth of the flame and remembered her dream about fire.

'What if she's dead, what if she's dead?' murmured Dagmar.

Elizabeth Booth was thankful for the return of darkness as she listened to Dagmar.

'They will blame me, they will think me to blame.' She had not imagined that the nurse would take on so.

'Damn, damn, damn.' Her voice sounded angry. 'What shall I say to John William?' she muttered to herself, 'what shall I say?'

Elizabeth Booth still heard the whispering voice. 'What shall I say to John William?' It panted into her like the very act of shame she saw them committing. She saw her son placing himself between the hands of the German. She had been deceived again. So soon, so soon, was she being free and easy with her son? One day she had been here, and already she was scheming.

She rolled open her eyes just as Dagmar was about to touch her and noticed that the German's face held no expression until it moved.

'Oh, Mrs Booth, you are awake.'

The candle-flames made the two eyes dance. She blinked, but remained silent.

Her mind seethed as though she had been plunged into a cauldron of passion. She saw the naked bodies rolling together, such debauchery in her home.

'You gave me quite a shock,' exclaimed Dagmar. 'I thought you were ill.' She peered at Mrs Booth once more.

'Why!' she exclaimed, 'you look quite pale. I hope I didn't give you cause for concern. How sweet of you to be so worried. It's such a caring thing to be a nurse. Why did you stop, my dear? Was it too upsetting for you? It must be difficult for a sensitive person to get used to all the things you have to do. I know I couldn't have done it for all the tea in

101

China. Talking of tea, perhaps I should ring for Nanny, a good strong cup of tea will do you the power of good.'

'No, no, really, I'm quite all right. I'm just relieved you had not . . .'

'Oh,' she laughed, 'you thought I'd pegged out. Goodness, I thought they trained nurses about things like that. What a shock all this must have been for you when I woke up.' Mrs Booth reached out one of her taloned hands and pressed the bell for Nanny Bradshaw.

Just as Dagmar began to feel the silence weighing down upon her, there was a knock on the door and Nanny Bradshaw entered. 'Ah Nanny, precise as usual,' said Mrs Booth. 'Would you mind bringing Miss Ehrenhardt and me some tea? I'm afraid I dozed off and she thought I had breathed my last.'

'I'll have two cups of tea here in a jiffy,' came her cunning voice. 'I don't know, what a morning it's been, what with Pewter, and then all this talk of death, it's like someone is trying to send a message through from the other side, to warn us. I wouldn't take it so lightly.'

Dagmar stared straight at Nanny Bradshaw, and studied the waxy face. She thought it likely that the skull could be of a deviant form. Dagmar felt a little surge of excitement at the discovery. The kindest thing to do, would be to put a bullet in the brain of such people. Shifting slightly in her seat, Dagmar's nostrils flared with pathological revulsion at the prospect of the circulating oxygen being consumed and exhaled by herself and Nanny Bradshaw. She breathed in as Nanny left the room.

'What did Mrs Bradshaw mean about messages from the other side? Does she dabble in some form of occultism?'

'Oh, I shouldn't think so. I can't quite see Nanny staring into a crystal ball.'

'I'm sorry,' frowned Dagmar, 'I did not mean these gypsy tricks. No, perhaps she performs some cabalistic rites, the sort Hebrews practise; some are taken in by such hocus pocus. Maybe Mrs Bradshaw can't help herself. It could be in her blood to practise such fetishism, you could not blame her, but such conduct must not be condoned.'

'Nanny is just a superstitious person, like many of her

102

generation. Those of us with more education may laugh at such views. No hoodoo, or voodoo or whatever it is goes on in Slackhall and I hope that's the last we ever hear of such talk. I'm sorry I have to speak to you in such a way, but if Nanny heard you, she would be most upset. She is a very devoted person, and worships at the church very regularly, so we'll say no more about it.' Just as if her word was made flesh, Nanny Bradshaw chose that moment to knock and enter the room.

'Ah, thank you, Nanny.'

With ruthless vigour she pushed a cup of steaming tea towards the flinching younger woman. Dagmar stared at the proffered cup as if it were a poisoned chalice. The quaint English custom of taking tea had suddenly been transformed into a subtle Chinese torture, and her body prickled.

The remorseless malevolence gnawed at the two women; it seemed only some form of violence could be the outcome. Yet Dagmar clutched the saucer, and raising the cup almost instantly to her lips, she consumed the strong tea prepared by the profane hand of Nanny Bradshaw.

'Well, that seems to have brought the colour back to your cheeks,' said Mrs Booth. 'Perhaps we can now get down to writing the letter.'

Looking Dagmar right between the eyes, Nanny Bradshaw relieved her of the cup, and picking up Mrs Booth's, left the room.

She remembered entering the service of the family; her long hair had been cut so as to fit under the cap she had to wear as the nurserymaid. Her silent acceptance of her life had slowly built up around her as true feelings were locked in and she had voluntarily thrown the key away. The house filled the horizon until she didn't wish to leave it. The family thrived on such loyalty, and in their lazy reliance, Nanny Bradshaw basked. The honorific title bestowed upon the virgin Dorothy Bradshaw lowered a coquettish bridal veil over her frustrations. There had always been times when she had felt that she had been overlooked, that her ministrations had been taken for granted, yet even when she was in such a mood, she was sustained by a favourite pastime of imagining the effect of her

103

death upon those she lived with. How they all wished they had told her how much she meant to them, and now it was too late, they would make amends by the size and ostentation of the funeral. She would be given an imposing monument; the grave would be covered with flowers, the waxed lilies mirroring the once living skin of Nanny Bradshaw. The inscription had been chiselled deep into the granite monolith, 'Mrs Dorothy Bradshaw', spread across the centre, and in high Gothic script above, 'In Loving Memory', twined round with flowers. Sometimes she filled in the front of the gravestone until there would be no room for more words.

There would be no such resting-place for Pewter. She rubbed her side in contemplation, perhaps Mrs Makin would do his horoscope.

While Nanny Bradshaw mused on the distant machinations of the stars, William awoke with a start. In his eyes there were no more the shadows of childish instincts, but instead a ripening look of erotic intensity glowed within, as he lay recalling the sexual revelations of the slides. He felt the cool lips of Dagmar once more on his trembling cheek, and as he discovered the secret relief for which he yearned, his fingers slipped in the wasted passion. Gasping and flushed he smiled a clever smile, and failed to notice the shackles had already been clamped firmly in place.

Leaving Mrs Booth in the half light provided by the steadily-burning candles, Dagmar made her way into the realms of daylight. As she reached the first window she flung it open and stuck her head out to take a deep breath of fresh air. Leaning out, she could see part of the garden's terrace, and the blurred heads of several roses in the distance. She made her way back to her room, and systematically opened all the other windows on the way.

Alone once more, Elizabeth Booth was overtaken by further introspection, it was as if in her subterfuge she had already made some acquaintance with death. Her exchange with Dagmar had caused imperceptible phrases from her confrontation with Roe to haunt her meditations. She would appease the German, those strong legs must march through the town on seemingly innocent errands, but once that was over, well, then there would be a further reckoning. She seemed to be staring at the flickering candle and the slow and steady flow of the wax, but in truth she was elsewhere.

Back in her room, Dagmar rifled through her still unpacked trunk until she extracted a small box with a victorious tug. In her haste to open it, she nearly spilled the contents on the floor, but having finally undone the catch, she removed a bottle of antiseptic. Throwing back her head, she gargled, as though the acrid liquid could excise the even viler taste of the tea produced by that deviant Bradshaw. To the mind of Dagmar such a cleansing was invigorating and when her blue eyes had screwed up in pain, they still managed a triumphant gleam. Wishing to take her mind off the quietly burning embers of discomfort she still felt but would not have admitted to, she went on with the business of unpacking. Carefully removing the paper from her cherished belongings she slowly exhumed her past which had been painstakingly stored away.

Dagmar was luxuriating in the touch and feel of her things, and soon they began to pile up around the kneeling figure. She had a collection of glass vases, their surfaces still shiny from such long storage. Seeing her finger on the cool glass, it was difficult to imagine the glee the same hands would have felt in hurling to the ground any such possessions of Nanny Bradshaw. She unpacked her gramophone records of Wagner. She hoped John William would enjoy listening to the Ring Cycle. The few books she possessed were also standard Germanic texts, Goethe lay alongside Schiller, and for contemporary works she relied upon the philosophic musings of the new chancellor. This she placed with great reverence upon her bedside table. She took out her clothes and placed them in the large wardrobe, concealing among the cotton and silk, a dark-coloured uniform of spotless material.

At the very bottom of the trunk lay a picture-frame face downwards concealing its contents, and alongside a bag containing Dagmar's embroidery. Removing the picture from the trunk, she looked around to see where to hang it. There were a couple of nondescript paintings already on the walls, and over the bed was a similar embroidery picture to the one she held. It said, 'Home sweet Home', and had a border of summer flowers. Taking care, she removed it from the hook and substituted her own work. Standing back, she straightened the frame slightly and smiled at a job well done; the room now looked more like home, the picture adding the finishing touch. In bold print she had carefully stitched the three words: 'Work is Liberty', and a graceful border of hooked crosses ran round the outside.

'Have you just lost a loved one, dearie?' asked Mrs Makin, her wrinkled hands pawing those of Mrs Bradshaw sympathetically. 'In tragic circumstances?'

'Life's an open book to you,' declared Nanny Bradshaw.

'His vibrations are strong,' said Mrs Makin. Nanny blushed at the idea.

'The ring of Saturn was present on his hand,' sighed Nanny Bradshaw. 'I don't know his date of birth, or else I'd have asked you to do a natal chart.'

'Well, I told you about Uranus in the twelfth house. Have the enemies revealed themselves?'

'Oh yes, and thanks to your warning I had my wits about me.' Nanny Bradshaw smiled.

'Another piece of Battenberg?'

'I shall have to get the recipe off you some time,' declared Nanny, watching as Mrs Makin poured another cup of tea.

'There'll be thunder and lightning later on,' said the fortune-teller, looking out of the window. Nanny thought for a minute about the sparks that had flown in the kitchen.

'This person,' said Mrs Makin. 'I don't want to upset you my dear, but I have the impression that the missing one was somehow linked with their appearance.'

Nanny Bradshaw gasped.

'Just turn over a tarot,' instructed Mrs Makin, taking another sip of her tea.

'Queen of wands reversed,' declared Nanny Bradshaw.

'She's blonde-haired, blue eyed; I see opposition, jealousy and deceit.' She pulled a piece of marzipan off the cake and swallowed it. 'Turn over another.'

'Three of wands reversed,' said Nanny forlornly.

'It's not good, dearie, I needn't tell you that.' She gave an understanding little smile. 'There may be treachery. I wouldn't like to go any further at the moment.' She popped the remaining Battenberg in her mouth.

'Will there be a cusp?' asked Nanny.

'Now, now, don't get carried away,' instructed Mrs Makin. 'A little knowledge is often worse than a lot.' She gathered the tarot cards together. 'I hope that you've not been dabbling again.'

'Nothing I shouldn't,' said Nanny petulantly.

'Old Ptolemy had a lot to answer for,' she laughed.

'She's a foreigner,' declared Nanny. 'German.'

'The cosmic principles told me that,' said Mrs Makin, slurping slightly as she drained her tea. She watched Nanny Bradshaw look into the bottom of her cup. 'No point to that, dearie, you need the eye.' She straightened out some twigs of blossom that had been placed in a large vase. They were from an elder tree. 'She didn't mention no Christian Rosycross to you, did she?'

'Well, we don't have that much to say really, the only one she goes on about is that Hitler.'

'Just wondered,' sighed Mrs Makin. 'That Christian Rosycross, he's another German for you. Spent some time in Damcar. Ever heard of that, dearie?'

'Can't say I have. Is it in Germany?'

'Bless you, it's in Arabia, dearie, all sand and parched throats.' She laughed. 'You wouldn't catch me traipsing around, even if I was expected by the three wise men. I wouldn't go if you paid me.' Her eyes glinted like the pennies on dead men.

'She won't eat the flesh of animals,' declared Nanny, 'Mrs Ash told me; and she only drinks this herbal brew.' Mrs Makin raised her eyebrows.

'How's that boy of yours?'

'He seems to be taken a bit moody. He's always been highly strung, but it's like talking to a brick wall. Of course, I try my best. Why, I've brought that child up single-handed. He's almost flesh and blood. On the day of the disappearance I let him stay in bed, I thought he was running to a fever. And then when I told him about the school, there wasn't a whisper.'

'It's his age,' confirmed Mrs Makin. 'I always preferred

108

them as babies. Why, the number I've looked after, you couldn't count them on the fingers and toes I have.'

'And I bet there's no thanks either.'

'Oh no, and I only took a pittance from their poor parents, just to take the little lambs off their hands.'

'You are too soft-hearted,' declared Mrs Bradshaw.

'There are worse crimes,' confirmed Mrs Makin, 'and listen to who's talking.'

They smiled at each other.

'She's turned that boy's head, that's for sure.' Nanny Bradshaw shook her own. 'You wouldn't know I existed sometimes.'

'How ungrateful,' cried Mrs Makin. 'Mark my words, it'll end in tears.'

'They all think they know best,' sighed Nanny, 'but it will all come out in the wash.'

Mrs Makin pulled thoughtfully at a long dark hair which extended from one of the two large moles she had on her cheek.

'Well,' she said, 'I don't want to rush you, dearie, but I've got some company this afternoon, and I've got to get some baking done.'

Nanny Bradshaw lifted the heavy handbag off the floor and as she started to root through it, lilac talcum wafted into the room. Finding her purse she laboriously counted out the correct amount, and then as an afterthought, added a little extra.

'Much obliged,' said Mrs Makin, taking surprisingly little interest.

'Do you think it'll rain before I get back?' asked Nanny, not sure whether she should get her scarf out. 'I knew I should have brought that dratted umbrella.'

'A spot of rain never harmed anybody,' said Mrs Makin. 'You'll be all right, missus, the storm's not here yet.'

Mollified, Nanny Bradshaw made her way to the front door, stopping to adjust her hat in the hall mirror.

'Very smart,' said Mrs Makin.

'Same time next week?' asked Nanny.

'I'm afraid not, dearie, I forgot to mention, I'm off to visit my sister. I'll let you know when I'm back.' She noted the long face, and detected a twinge of regret for the little extra that had been left on the table.

Nanny gave a strained little smile, and smoothed down her coat. 'Well have a nice time,' she said, 'and hurry back.'

'It'll fly by, you mark my words.'

She stayed a few moments on the doorstep, and then with a quick sniff of the heavy air, she darted into her house. The diminutive figure moved with foxlike slyness back into the kitchen. Soon, it was filled with the sounds of ingredients being weighed, baking tins greased, and finally the mixing. Mrs Makin rolled up the sleeves of her cardigan and, doused in flour, she started to knead the bread dough.

'Fe fi fo fum, I smell the blood of . . .' She gave a little chortle, and raising her white, dusted arm, wiped it energetically across her nose. 'Be he alive or be he dead, I'll grind his bones to make my bread.' She sneezed.

She left the dough in a large bowl to rise, giving it one more friendly little tap before brushing down her arms. She glanced out of the window at the gathering gloom, and with a nod of satisfaction, went into the front room. As though she had something on her mind, she absently turned over a tarot card. 'The Hierophant,' she murmured, and gave a little smile. She scooped up the money, not bothering to pick up a shilling which rolled on to the floor, and deposited the whole lot in a drawer, already brimming with dusty coins.

The smell of warm bread began to permeate the pores of the tiny house. She had kept half of the mixture back, intending to finish her baking later.

Walking down the quiet street, the red-headed young woman kept looking at a crumpled piece of paper in her hand, as if trying to memorise the contents. Her lips moved silently as she counted down the house numbers. She heard a train leaving the near-by station and its whistle sounded forlorn. She sagged as if her strength was ebbing.

'Eleven, nine, seven,' she whispered, and then raised her trembling hand.

Mrs Makin was upstairs when the knocking began. She continued dabbing a little perfume behind her ears; it carried the pungent odour of crushed hemlock leaves. Patting down her greasy hair, she slowly made her way down the stairs. Short of breath, she wheezed gently as she opened the heavy door.

Reverend Roe stood quietly in the shadow of a lone tree. From the dull place he saw Georgette knock at number seven. When he opened his eyes, she had already gone inside. He could hear some boys and girls playing in a back alley.

'Just you sit yourself down, luvvy,' said Mrs Makin, 'and just give me that coat.'

'That's a nice smell of baking bread,' said the girl, her voice trembling slightly.

'It's a homely smell,' agreed Mrs Makin. 'It's my baking day. I always make my own bread. I usually do two batches, but I've run out of ingredients.' She gave a smile. 'Now slip that pretty dress off, while I get some little things and check that bread.'

Mrs Makin came back with a bowl of steaming water. She smiled up at Georgette, who was shivering slightly in her white slip. Her young breasts, already swelling with milk, rose and fell rapidly, as the girl took in the peculiar metal implements which lay in the water.

'Now dearie, just you drink this down, it's a little physic to make you feel better.' She watched intently as the girl downed the proffered glass.

'I'll be glad when it's over,' she sobbed. 'I wish I never did it.'

'Too late for that, luvvy,' said the little woman, easing herself down on to her knees. 'Now, Mrs Makin used to be a midwife so there's no need to fret. Why, it's as easy as pulling a rabbit out of a hat.' Her warty face gazed up at the drained face. 'Just you sit on the edge of the bed. That's right.' Her rough hand pushed up the slip. 'All the better to see you with,' she said.

Georgette's dulled eyes followed the little woman's movements in the dressing-table mirror. Her own pale hand fluttered down to rest on her slightly swelling belly. She wondered briefly whether it would have had red hair, and then winced with pain as all thoughts flew to her own anguish. She didn't even notice it was beginning to rain, the heavy drops rolled down the window.

111

'I didn't know whether you'd come,' said John William.

'Perhaps I'll regret it,' said Dagmar. Her hand trailed through the full roses. Their heavy heads were helpless under her fingertips.

A sudden silence seemed to devour them, with just the deep drone of the hidden insects in the congested air.

'The lull before the storm,' he murmured, and made as if to move closer to her. She noticed his long and slender fingertips.

'Are you very attached to the house?' she asked, avoiding letting him touch her.

'Of course. A strange question.' He snapped off the withered head of a dead rose. 'Do you miss your home?'

'Sometimes.' She turned as she heard distant thunder. 'It is different though. I feel for Germany something no English person could feel for England.'

'Oh, I don't know, we're pretty patriotic.'

'No, it's not the same. It is something we have in our blood. England is sleepy.' She shook some leaves and watched the flies move lethargically. 'See, just like the flies. They needed someone to shake them up. It is the same for you.' He shifted uneasily, and looked at the heavy sky.

'Just look around you,' she said. Her gaze lingered a moment on some black rooks which flew about the rim of the wood. 'You have let it get into this state.' She shook her head. 'Such neglect, and yet I see this as all of England.'

'Why have you deserted Germany, then?' He ran his fingertips over the pale hairs on her arm. She twitched herself away.

'I have deserted nothing; it is you who are throwing your life away.'

'I don't understand you,' he said, and smiled. 'You shall make me feel wretched.'

'Don't you see, I could never care for someone who had no . . . fire. Nothing moves you.'

'You do,' he said fiercely and moved forward, taking hold of her roughly.

'Don't,' she said faintly.

'Ssshh,' he said, his finger pressing gently on her lips, and moving swiftly he replaced his firm finger with his open mouth.

112

A sense of fatality hung in the air, under which the geometry of bodies cast changing shadows. Only the stillborn child was silent. It had blonde hair like its father.

The warm rain pattered on her upturned face as she gently intoned the one word, 'Vaterland, Vaterland, Vaterland'. Trapped within the pentacle of their spent embraces there seemed no room for subterfuge. They were bound together, Dagmar had occupied him as surely as the feet of any army, and there had been no resistance.

As their heart-beats slowed, he looked into her distant eyes. Her eyelashes darkened the rims like the shadows of forthcoming events. The rain came down, softening the outline of perception.

'Kiss me,' she said.

[8]

Walking with a marching beat, Dagmar made her way throughout the town of Slackhall, the grimy streets causing her to worry about getting her shoes dusty. The people seen within her blue, blue eyes lacked pigment, they faded into the grey background, even as summer was upon them, as though a light coating of ash from the many chimneys fell silently on everything.

A few noticed her strange gait; the loping stride she adopted made it seem as though a military band played silently for her. With a strategist's precision, she had already studied a map of the town, and now she progressed towards her target.

Her firm stride carried her past the town's cinema that William had shyly asked her to go to. It was advertising *King Kong*, which she'd informed him was the favourite film of her Führer. She was disappointed that the boy didn't appear to ask her more. Still it was early days; she was sure the noble and simple sentiments she carried would find root and germinate in Slackhall, just as they had in the villages and towns of Germany.

She paused as she reached the intricate railings of the graveyard. She could see the mausoleum of the Booths, the gloomy splendour of the cupola and pillars casting a baleful shadow. They had pre-eminence even in death.

Turning, she progressed to the vicarage, thinking vaguely how different this was to her homeland. For appearance's sake, she carried with her an incongruous bunch of flowers, the dusty roses shed a few petals as she knocked on the door. Standing, she considered the conversation with Mrs Booth, when she had been asked to relay a message to the vicar of Slackhall.

Dagmar was sure she could detect a certain falsity in the

114

words; the old woman had been preoccupied and the phrases of high morality seemed to conceal a baser message. The insistence had also puzzled her, as did her employer's enquiry as to whether her son or grandson had kept her from sleep with the radios they both had in their bedrooms. The veiled reference to the nocturnal proximity of the two males reinforced Dagmar's instinct that the old woman was somehow involved in some manipulation.

Her thoughts were cut short as the door swung open. Bethsheba asked if she could help, and as the figure on the doorstep stood mutely, the black woman was puzzled, seeing the loose arms hanging down at the side of the straight dress and the hand clutching tightly at a crumpled bouquet.

The town was truly degenerate thought Dagmar. She decided to ignore the negress, who had probably only learned a few stock phrases like a mynah bird.

'Thank you, I'll take those, shall I?' She extended her dark hand towards the flowers. Dagmar flinched away as though scalded.

'Don't you talk to me as though you know me.'

The words were spat out at Bethsheba who had now stepped back, the yoke of servility tugging her large body. It always seemed to shock her when she was confronted by such naked hatred for her, even though the treatment was common, if not usually so blatant. The mask of submission slipped into place.

Dagmar held out the letter of introduction. 'Take this to Mrs Roe.' The simple command set Bethsheba into motion, although her sense of oppression now weighed her down like a ball and chain.

Quickly reading the note, Florence Roe gave a little gasp of delight.

'Oh, how nice, we've got a visitor, Bethsheba, and she's from Germany. Just think, coming all that way, and now ending up in Slackhall. Isn't life strange.'

Bethsheba remained silent; she was slightly hurt that Mrs Roe hadn't noticed something was the matter.

'Oh, do bring her up at once. Don't leave her in the hallway. Quick, quick, is everything all right in the room? I must apologise for the mess, but we aren't prepared for

115

visitors, are we? Bethsheba, do you think there's time to dust round? Oh dear I suppose not. I hope she doesn't notice the dust.'

As she waited for the guest to arrive, her nervous fingers straightened and smoothed down her hair. She felt all shaky inside. Her palpitations increased as the door slid open and Dagmar entered. Florence Roe, consumed with stage fright, didn't move, and it was Dagmar who walked over, gazing at the frozen smile, her blue eyes noting a nervous twitch flickering away. As she held out the flowers, it was as though she had accidentally pressed some switch which sent the still figure into a frenzy. The words came tumbling out of her mouth taking Dagmar by surprise.

'Oh how kind, how kind. Why nobody has brought me flowers for so long. Did you pick them yourself? It must have taken you a long while, look at them all. I suppose you arranged them as well. I'm afraid I've no talent for such things. Would you arrange them in a vase for me? I know I'd spoil them if I did it. It really is very kind of Mrs Booth to send you over here,' she continued, thanking Dagmar as the German jammed the flowers into an empty vase.

Dagmar found it difficult to stare into this woman's eyes. They never seemed to rest in one place very long. They didn't even shift from the interrogating glare of Dagmar; they flowed round it. She realised Mrs Roe had stopped apologising and now seemed stuck. The confusion on her face made it look as though she might start to cry. Dagmar thought tears would come easily to this woman.

'Have you known Mrs Booth long?' She thought she might as well get as much information as possible.

'Goodness me, no, I don't know Mrs Booth at all, not in the personal sense. I'm sure that you already know more about her than I do. Why it's my husband who visits her. Of course, she sometimes asks after me, but we've never met. It's so kind of her to think of others with all her problems. She's a very selfless woman. My husband has the highest regard for her; you are very lucky to be working for her. I would love to meet her though.'

'What problems?' she asked probingly.

'It's just too terrible,' came her indiscreet voice, and

116

Dagmar settled back to listen to exactly what was too terrible.

As Florence Roe, with the garrulous ease of a traitor, told her tale, a stealthy smile wrapped itself around Dagmar's face, as, in her desperate need to please, the reverend's wife laid bare to the bone the scandal that was never mentioned in the house.

Florence Roe recounted the tale of the death of Elizabeth Booth's husband, lowering her voice to an insinuating whisper as though speaking in some church rather than in the privacy of her own bedroom. As she came to the end of the tale, Dagmar felt she possessed a route map of the family, the itinerary stopping at all the momentous events and, of course, no one would be any the wiser in the house.

'Oh dear,' she sighed, 'I hope you don't mind all the tittle-tattle. I'm just not used to having visitors . . .' She suddenly blushed, realising that in all the excitement of having someone call, she had forgotten her visitor's name. 'Oh goodness,' she thought, 'now she will think I am very rude.' She tried to sneak a look at the name in the letter, but it was just too obvious.

'Would you like a drink of tea?' she asked. 'I'll get Bethsheba to make one. I should have asked you earlier. You will think I've got no manners.'

'Please don't worry about it. I'm afraid I am not very keen on tea.' The thought of Bethsheba preparing a drink did not appeal to Dagmar, especially after the ordeal with Bradshaw.

'Perhaps you would prefer something else? Shall we be devils? What about some sherry? I know it's a little early, but it can be our little secret.'

She looked so eager that Dagmar almost felt like refusing, just to see her crestfallen, but instead she smiled her acceptance. Florence Roe rang for Bethsheba, who went over to a little cupboard and removed two glasses, and proceeded to pour the sherry.

'Most unusual to have a black for a servant. Is she any relation to Owens?' asked Dagmar with a curious detachment.

'Oh dear, I think you've confused me. Who are you talking

117

about now? I just spilled my drink a little. I hope it won't stain. Do you think it will?'

Dagmar got up and went over to Florence Roe, who seemed to go as limp as a rag doll as Dagmar took the material between her fingers and rubbed away at the spot.

'The black, is she related to Jesse Owens, the runner? They all look alike to me,' she continued, still rubbing. 'I saw him in Berlin, at the Olympics.' She looked down into the slightly glazed eyes of Florence Roe. 'Your nigger is fatter of course. I don't think she could outrun a pack of dogs.' She ceased her rubbing and a clammy look of contentment suffused Florence Roe's flushed face. 'There, I don't think it will stain.'

'Oh thank you, thank you.' Florence Roe clutched hold of Dagmar's hand as though drowning. ' I'm so clumsy, like a baby, perhaps I'm a little tipsy. What do you think? Aren't I naughty?' She tightened her grip. 'You've strong hands. I think your hands have authority, like a man's,' she simpered.

Dagmar tugged her hand from the embrace. Sitting down once more, Dagmar crossed her legs, the sound of stockings rubbing together made Florence Roe shudder, and fidgeting about with her own dress, her hands couldn't keep still, like a dying butterfly in a killing-jar, they flitted up and down as though conducting their own requiem.

'Oh, how wonderful, being able to go to the Olympic Games. I didn't even see the news at the cinema, see all those strong young bodies. What a fine sight that must have been. I read all about it, of course. Did you take part? Oh I think you must have. Let me guess, don't tell me.'

She hugged her knees as though taking part in a crash landing, and failed to notice her husband arrive. He stared in disbelief at the galvanised form of his wife, who, rocking herself excitedly in the chair, prattled on.

'No, don't tell me, don't tell me, I shall have it in a minute. Your hand is so strong, that must be something to do with it. Yes, I know, it must be a sport involving hands. But don't tell me, I shall guess it, just give me a minute.'

'Florence,' the word whipped through the air, and caused both women to jump. On hearing her husband's sepulchral tone, Florence Roe seemed to collapse, withdrawing whatever

118

animation had seized her, and reverted to a grey, nerveless creature. Dagmar noticed that Mrs Roe's usually wavering eyes seemed to be fixed on something, and following her betraying gaze, came to the empty sherry glass. The reverend had done the same, and without even acknowledging the seated German, he strode over to the tell-tale glass, lifting the evidence delicately. He raised it to his nose and sniffed. It was then that Reverend Roe noticed Dagmar, who had become an interested spectator. She now saw that the reverend did not twitch.

'Really, ladies,' he smiled, holding the glass aloft, 'I can't condone all this drinking, especially,' he added, 'as nobody offered any to me.' He chortled at his risqué remark, wondering who on earth this woman was, probably another representative of some charity or other. Damn Florence. What a performance he had interrupted. Goodness knows what the woman was thinking about it all. No doubt she was just as embarrassed as he was. He thought it would have been polite if she would announce that she had to leave now, but instead she just sat there.

'Florence, aren't you going to introduce me to your guest?'

Florence Roe bobbed her head and clutched the letter of introduction.

'You'll never guess,' she said, thrusting the envelope towards him with more vigour. 'Our guest was in the Olympics. I'm trying to solve what event. What do you think, dear?' She was now waving the letter in a most distracting fashion, as though emulating a starting flag for the sport in question.

'I'm sure I've no idea,' he said, 'what our . . . guest,' he spaced the words out with almost theatrical ease, 'competed in, although,' he added, 'I must apologise for my ignorance.'

Feeling almost excluded from the exchange between the husband and wife, Dagmar watched them both with the eyes of someone used to dissecting dead bodies. Here were tensions she could exploit.

'I am very pleased to meet you, Reverend. I have not been in Slackhall long, but I've heard your name mentioned quite a number of times.'

She extended her hand which Roe took to his own, and squeezed with a peculiar stroking quality, like a butcher testing the firmness of the meat. Roe himself was puzzled, he recognised a foreign accent, and wondered just who this young woman was. Her hand seemed to have been gripping his with equal vigour, she wasn't a timid virgin, not with a grip like that.

'I hope that all the reports you have heard have been favourable. I must sadly admit, I had not heard that we were to be graced by the presence of a distinguished foreigner, and I am at an even greater loss as I haven't been introduced.'

'Well, I shall remedy that at once,' she said. 'My name is Dagmar Ehrenhardt. I am from Germany,' she intoned.

'What an enchanting name, and where are you staying Dagmar? I hope you have somewhere comfortable. Our little town does not boast a very good hotel. We have none of your charming inns. Perhaps you would like to transfer your things here? I'm sure we can manage that.' His eyes glittered with the prospect of voyeurism.

'That is most kind, but you see I have a room of my own.'

'Yes,' butted in Florence Roe, 'she's living with the Booths; Mrs Booth sent her to see me.' Her voice sounded almost petulant, and before the other two could resume the conversation which excluded her, Florence Roe, in a breathless rush, attempted to monopolise things. 'I've been racking my brains, Dagmar. I know I haven't much sense, that's what Charles is always telling me, but I just know that it was either the discus or the javelin. Oh, do say I'm right.'

While his brain reverberated with the name of his tormentor, the voice of his wife penetrated his very marrow, and he shivered with guilt. As he looked at the lank-haired German, a sense of irony caused the corners of his mouth to twitch. 'Very well,' he thought, 'let her know what kind of house I reside in . . . a madhouse. She would recognise it.' He wished himself in the depths of the cool church.

Dagmar immediately felt that the motivations of Mrs Booth in sending her to this house had somehow been a form of admonition to Roe. His eyes were like a dark abyss.

120

She decided there would be no message, she would not allow herself to be a passive, extraneous pawn. To that extent she was no longer in the dark.

She smiled at the vicar and his anxious wife and spoke calmly.

'I'm afraid you must be disappointed. I didn't take part in any event, I merely opened some cages to let fly the white doves, a symbol of peace. It was very moving, though somebody had piled too many in the cages; there was not enough room, some didn't fly, just lay still.'

'Oh, how horrid for you,' came the trembling voice of Florence Roe. 'It's just too cruel, too cruel,' cried Mrs Roe. The tears had welled up in her watery eyes, and now she started to sob, her little shoulders shaking.

Roe could no longer shield the distaste he felt for his wife and for scenes of this sort. He had no doubt that the German would tell Elizabeth Booth about his wife's strange behaviour, and just to know that old crone could be feasting like a vulture on the dead marriage, made him clench his fist. With more than a vague sense of revulsion, he reached out for Florence's shoulders, and pinioned them against the chair back in an attempt to quell their sickening movement. At her husband's touch, which might have looked to some like a concerned embrace, she gave a shrill cry and pressed her head into his chest while her shoulders continued trembling like the dying birds.

Roe's gaunt head seemed marooned above the heaving body of his wife. It felt suffocating, and screwing up his eyes, he lifted her out of the chair, and in what seemed an ugly parody of the ardent groom, carried her to the bed. As he stooped to place his prostrate wife on the quilt, her arms snaked round him, and it became obvious he could not extricate himself from her embrace without Dagmar witnessing the whole thing.

Roe pressed down hard. A small vein pulsed in his neck like a coiled blue snake, an indication of the pressure he was using. At last her grip slackened and Roe pulled himself away leaving his wife sprawled like a discarded doll.

Roe wiped away at the sweat which now suddenly poured from his brow. He realised that he could have

121

strangled her. He turned to find Dagmar almost peering over his shoulder.

'I'm a nurse,' she said briskly, as if she meant to intrude further.

'A woman of many accomplishments,' he muttered grimly.

Roe felt he was almost too close to Dagmar.

'Shall I have a look at her?'

'No, no, she just needs to rest. I shall tell her how worried you were. She seems to have taken a liking to you Miss Ehrenhardt.'

'Perhaps I should just take a peek and see that she's breathing all right, that sort of thing.'

'She's quite all right,' said Roe more abruptly than he meant to, but he disliked such intensity, and wanted to remove this masculine woman from his house. 'I was just about to ring for Baldwin. He will check on Florence later. I know all this might seem a little heartless, but really we've found that to keep her very quiet is the best thing, you see. Had I been in, I'm afraid I would not have let you see my wife. This will be the second attack she has had this week. My wife is very delicate.'

'Yes, of course,' replied Dagmar. 'I did not realise. I should have noticed the signs.'

Roe's eyes had a hard glint in them, he now felt unbearable loathing for this woman who had acted like a spy from Mrs Booth, and talked of 'signs'.

'Well,' he said, taking hold of her arm like a parishioner's, 'don't worry yourself, I shall let you know how Florence is, although I assure you, she will be her normal self tomorrow.' He smiled grimly as he steered Dagmar down the stairs and heard himself referring to Florence as normal. 'Now then, did you have a coat?'

As Dagmar shook her head, Roe opened the door, and with consummate skill shook her hand with a subtle pressure which directed her towards the opening.

'Now,' he said, 'you must call again some time, and don't worry about Florence, although I think she'll be too embarrassed to see you for a while.' He emphasised the last words and couldn't restrain himself from a frivolous wink. 'Hope to see you in church.' Dagmar's mouth hung open. 'Give my regards to Mrs Booth, such a fine, fine woman, and,' he added, 'a devoted grandmother. How lucky you are working there.'

By this time Dagmar found herself on the doorstep and watched in disbelief as the door closed, Reverend Roe waving almost to the last instant when he retracted his arm before it could be severed and drop to Dagmar's feet.

9

Elizabeth Booth had scarcely known when she had felt so restless. She levered herself into sitting up, as though about to swing her useless legs out of the vast bed, but instead slumped back into the soft pillows. She noticed the sweat stains on the sheets; she loathed the idea of perspiring. With her scratchy fingers she tried to arrange the silk cushions over the marks. Exhausted from the task, she lay back and stared round her room. The candles were not lit, and the heavily swathed window filtered the sunlight.

She twisted the wedding ring on her finger as her mind's eye rested on the lingering image of Dagmar and John William. Like a water diviner, she saw the signs of lustful desires, her long abandoned body detecting hidden intimacy. The movement of limbs seemed to hint at the intertwining bodies.

When William had visited her, the movement of his body stalked through her mind. She had not wanted to see this. His every gesture suggested the amorous inclinations of an adult. His familiar face seemed shaded with a different hue. Even as she spoke to him, his eyes wandered away from her and she found it difficult to bear his presence, as though in some way she had been responsible for the loss of his innocence. She was puzzled when he blushed at the mention of Pewter. It made her uneasy. A silent suggestion formed of the stooping tutor somehow initiating William, and a cold shiver ran down her back, as if she were touched by a naked blade. She saw William being led like an animal to the slaughter. When she mentioned Dagmar, he was strangely silent, any comment had to be drawn out of him. Although she wore a smile which crinkled across her face like crumpled paper, she felt a creeping horror.

Already she saw the secrets in his eyes. A jealousy began to kindle in her breast. As she now lay awaiting Dagmar, her

124

eyes were like those of a pyromaniac. Yet, as the seconds passed into minutes, a weariness began to cloud them, as though the effort to sustain anger was now too laborious for her.

She tried to listen for the comforting sounds of the house, but she seemed suspended in a cruel silence. She remembered her conversation with Roe, saying she no longer cared whether it was daylight.

She momentarily closed her eyes, hoping to sustain her will. All the hopes and dreams were thwarted in the sterile, blue eyes of Dagmar. She would not be strong enough for a confrontation.

The blankets seemed heavy. Despair had started to spread like a virus through her hardened arteries. She was becoming lost in her dreams, but her thoughts did not float gently through her mind, they tore into her. She welcomed nightfall. The dark tunnel of her life stretched behind her, there seemed no light at the source and the dark corridor continued with no end to the gloom. She had spent her life for her family. Beneath her, she had imagined the lights being switched on, people bustling about, cooking food, smiling and laughing as they ate together, the way families do. That word 'family', the warm glow which she once felt filtering up to her from the house, like incense, was gone.

All that was left were ashes, like her memories. An empty futility, the progeny of wasted years. She took a deep breath, her yellowing skin trembled as if the effort of filling her lungs was too much. But as her weak body gently laboured she began to notice a febrile perfume exuded from the flowers Dagmar had picked. It clashed with the fetid atmosphere of decaying flesh. Her senses sharpened slowly, she could hear the ticking of the clock, and the rhythm of her own heart. The sheets restrained her, held her to the death-bed. She was no novice to life, but to die; her cold hands clutched the sheets and she concentrated on breathing. As the fate of all mankind loomed over her, it was still remote, impersonal, as though she had nothing to do with it. So many feelings seemed to consume her, buffeting her, as her resilience was severed, her fears walked freely in the sun under a cloudless sky. She realised she had lived alone, there was no hand to hold. Her hand twitched as though being pierced, and the tears mingled with the sweat. She had no strength to move the burden of her guilt and the thought lodged itself in her mind that she had paid for the abortion of her grandchild. She wanted to confess to someone. She didn't want to take that to eternity. It would be Roe's Judas hand which would throw the black earth over her coffin, the same hand which had delivered over her silver for the act.

Slowly she moved her right hand so that it clasped its lifeless partner. In this dreamless state, she let the gloom take over and stared with vacant eyes. She scarcely felt the strong hands which lifted her, felt down her limbs, or the blue eyes which stared into her helpless ones. The hands seemed to be pressing down on her. She made a feeble effort to brush them away, instead they settled on her like flies. A voice said something, but was too far away for her to hear. She wanted to tell, but her lips remained silent. They wouldn't move, not even to mumble out the prayers her mother had taught her. It felt as if she were being held, frozen under ice. She had forgotten winter kills.

10

Eight o'clock. The dull thudding of the church bell hovered in the calm evening, and still William lay in the grass, staring up at the sky, the longer stalks casting growing shadows over his face and body. He didn't even stir to brush away the tiny insects which made occasional forays over his hand. Alone, he had time to think, his thoughts trailing the passive clouds. At first, they were aimless like the dandelion seeds which floated hither and thither, wafted even by his gentle breathing. But as the solitude and shadows deepened, so his thoughts began to focus, and he squeezed his eyes tightly shut, as though prey to some inexplicable sadness. As he opened them, they seemed devoid of expression, unless there was a glint of hard determination shadowed by his eyelashes. There was no trace of tears.

Since Dagmar's arrival in the household, his landscape seemed to have changed. Familiar objects seemed strange to his touch, as though he couldn't remember whether they truly belonged there. Pewter had left, but the legacy remained.

William had been wrenched out of the childlike world. His discovery of the nature of men had not been so remarkable, yet the discovery made through his own body plunged him, like Alice, through the looking-glass into a new land. The rules would be different. He yearned to know more of the world Pewter had shown him. The brief glimpses had already blurred in his memory. Something was missing. Nothing and everything seemed true.

He no longer wished to run away to sea. In his solitude, he had formed a shell around himself. Just as he had thought his dead parents were his guardian angels, so he now thought the votive offering of his childhood would keep the darkness at bay, as though his state of grace were some precious marble, or favourite tin soldier that a frightened child would leave to pacify his nightmare, a bargain that could not be broken. He remembered Roe saying something about when you become a man you put away childish things. He had started the process with the rejection of Great Granny Grime. He shifted slightly as some stalks of grass pricked through his shirt into his back. Like pointing fingers, they reminded him of his perfidy. He had no intention of going back to see if she were still there. Unbidden, the images came of the little bent figure packing her bags and like a refugee taking to the road. The wardrobe would become the home of more hunted animals.

In the calm of the field he had no need of her now. It seemed he had imagined it all in his mind's eye like some fantastical game of dressing up, pretending with cloak and hat, crown and buckled shoes to be something other.

The smell of the earth clung to him. He had fallen into a climate in which the boundless skies had lost their distant innocence. The clouds hinted at the sombre storms to come. He was stripped of history and destiny and just lay there, staring up. It seemed to his fragile body that the sky could fall down, just as Chicken Licken foretold, preaching this strange foreboding to the other animals, right into the lair of Foxy Loxy, who licked his sharp teeth.

With the solid earth beneath him, William dreamed on, running his hand down his stomach, as if the touch of flesh made him powerless. Pewter had ensured that he was no longer empty inside, but the fragments of learning, his life so far, were all as insubstantial as the sunlight which disappeared behind the grey clouds. And should the sky fall, he would be no more remembered than countless other men whose shadows were cast on different fields, where now the light played.

Forswearing the simple delight of caressing himself, William knew that he now had choice. The thought momentarily dazzled him, and with a feeling of well-being, he stretched slowly. He closed his eyes as if overcome with erotic fatigue, and the cold smile of Dagmar reigned within his yearning mind.

He was wide awake when he heard the rustling approach of

someone. His face was vaguely flushed, and his eyes tried to hide the confusion of discovery.

He hastily sat up, running his hand through his heavy hair to rid it of tiny seeds and any straying insects. His white shirt was crumpled and marked by the grass upon which he lay, and he looked slightly raffish.

'You look like a noble savage,' said Dagmar.

He seemed to fall under the spell of her fanatic eyes. Like the Snow Queen, she reigned in his heart, which turned colder. He failed to notice the agitation that danced round her face.

Perhaps he will realise something himself, she thought, and uneasily fingered the imitation pearls which hung heavily round her neck. She had noticed that those Elizabeth Booth had were real.

'Did you think I was hiding?' asked William

'No, no, but we were worried at the house. We wondered where you could be.'

'So you are the search-party. I suppose I'll get into bother for missing dinner. How did you know where to look, anyway?'

'I didn't, it was just chance. What are you doing out here anyway, there's nothing?' She wondered why she didn't blurt it out, perhaps he would blame her for just standing there while his grandmother's life ebbed away, when he could be rushing to her side.

Dagmar tried to conceal her anxiety behind a thin smile. A few flies buzzed around her head and she wafted them away. It seemed as though they were attracted; she felt an invisible odour clung from the death-bed.

'It's your grandmother, William.' Her Teutonic voice was harsh.

'What?'

He strained his face up to her, and Dagmar clenched her heavy hands. She groped for the words, but clambering to his feet, William raced off over the field, and she stood there, looking after the receding figure like a hurt animal. He had not turned to her and she bitterly regretted finding him. It should have been someone else.

She had seen the same look of pain on the face of John

William, whose expression had crumbled before her cool gaze. His pleading eyes were weak, and she had no pity to give him, only barren strength. They had both gravitated to the matriarch, her rule had not been broken, the old ties were stronger than the brilliant new bonds the German had tried to forge. She sighed, and looked round the dreary field. From a promising start, things seemed to be slipping through her fingers. The crumpled grass where William had lain for so long was beginning slowly to unfold. Dagmar watched the slow serious movement. It seemed as though nature was covering the tracks, obscuring the presence of flesh, and given free rein it would slowly cover all the works of man. She didn't like it out in the wild.

She started walking in the direction of the house. She didn't wish to catch sight of William again and would go quietly to her own room. She felt a momentary inclination to linger in the decrepit garden, to see how things became when there was no order, but just as the hunter in a dark forest craves the sight of a log fire, so Dagmar longed for stone walls. She thought the sight of the tangled garden would only make her sadder.

A smile seemed out of place, but she had just caught sight of the figure of Reverend Roe, his jacket spread out like two bat wings as he rushed towards his benefactress. His fingers were struggling to fasten the buttons. It seemed in this moment of importance his belly had swelled out, and the agitated hands could not get the jacket to meet. He looked up and saw the German. She was the last person he wished to see. As he closed in upon her, he knew she was waiting for him and wondered whether the old woman had told her of his recent mission. He was still irritatingly struggling with the jet buttons on his long jacket. Reaching forward she pushed his hands out of the way, and pressing on his pliant stomach, closed the gap.

'You are too well fed, Mr Roe.' She didn't know why she had helped him.

'Well, we all have our little weaknesses.' He was not going to thank her for interfering, it was like being pawed by the hands of a man.

'How is your wife now?' She hoped to remind him of the

130

agonised embrace of Florence Roe, perhaps it was her scent she could smell.

'Ah, as well as can be expected, as well as can be expected.' It was almost, thought Dagmar, as though he repeated himself to add some reassurance to the sound of his pitiful voice.

'News travels quickly,' said Dagmar, staring momentarily at the house.

'I was summoned,' said Roe, licking his lips swiftly. 'And to think,', he rushed, 'I had only written to her yesterday, only yesterday.' He paused to look at her. 'I don't suppose you've seen the letter?' He fiddled nervously with the button.

'Letter?'

'Of course not, of course not,' he gasped. His eyes shifted under her puzzled gaze.

'It is important?' she probed.

'I should like to think she has seen it,' he said piously. 'A little thank you for all her good works.' He looked at her blank face and sighed.

'Difficult times,' he whispered.

'All things must change,' she exclaimed.

'Indeed,' he almost sneered, 'and I must away to the . . . family.'

He excused himself with a quick nod, and left her alone. As she walked to her room, her fingers idly played with two letters which lay in her pocket. Both addressed to Mrs Booth.

The darkness had set in and the naked bulb in her bedroom seemed to cast a harsh light.

Moving to the bed she lifted a discarded shirt, smoothing down the creases with a thoughtful, faraway look in her eyes. Suddenly, she buried her head in the black cloth, breathing deeply, as if trying to capture the scent of the wearer. She had fastened the buttons which ran up the front, lingering slowly, and looked over his shoulder as he stared in the mirror.

'It's like a uniform,' he said.

'You look masterful,' she said coquettishly.

He turned to look at his taut profile, smoothing down his blond hair.

'Take it off,' he commanded.

'Shall I start at the top,' she laughed, and slid her hand to his throat, 'or . . .' she paused deliciously, 'the bottom?' and they both watched as the mirror followed the motion of her seeking fingers.

She stared bitterly into the silent mirror; now it seemed to reflect her broken dreams. She wondered if Roe would be speaking of heaven. She bared her teeth, and threw the shirt on the bed.

'Without you then,' she snarled, and pulled out the letters. With uncanny instinct, she opened the missive from Roe.

Dear Mrs Booth,

How good it is to be able to report that the good works of which we spoke have now gone ahead. I hope that these glad tidings go some way to dispel those sad thoughts to which we are all so prone. Slackhall has much to thank you for, and what a comfort to know that your son is taking such an interest in the well-being of those who have fallen low.

One of these days, he will surprise us all, of that I am sure. You must forgive my digression, but as we get older, this world of ours seems more like an open book.

I must also commend you on your new companion, Mrs Roe and I felt that once more you walked among us. I am sure that you will find Dagmar very dependable. It is a trait I think among the Germans.

I regret to say it was not possible to get a receipt for the moneys you dispatched. I know how selflessly you have given, and I hesitate in making further demands, but I know you would prefer that I came to you once more, rather than troubled John William. My little stipend would not suffice for the works I have in mind, and I know how you spoke of the parable of the prodigal son.

I am sure that this is the last time I will trouble you, piece by piece we are restoring the fabric of this place. I know you will help. It shames me to ask such a generous soul.

Perhaps Miss Dagmar can act as the go-between, she would be the ideal carrier for such tidings.

I shall close now, but not before I forget to pass on the good wishes of an old retainer of yours. She wished to be remembered to you. I promised not to forget, and the silly child thought that you might have forgotten her.

Yours,
Charles Roe

Dagmar took her time to read it once more, the tone seemed to carry a distant, clipped hatred. Like some cypher, she puzzled over the words of the reverend. There was a connection with John William. She glanced at the black shirt.

If she was correct, she would be able to undermine the religion in this place. She would provide a more substantial diet for the people of Slackhall.

Dagmar began reading the second letter. The truncated phrases and writing caused her to pause and reread to make some sense of the rambling style. It seemed as though it were the work of a distracted mind, and towards the bottom of the page it was difficult to prise the words apart. It touched a nerve deep inside. Was this the contact she had been waiting for? It was as though a subtle whisper started up; this worried mother, a daughter who was starving herself to death, what better way of proving to the people of this place that there was a better way to live? This would be no mere illusion she would offer them, she would give this hopeless girl purpose. It would be no trick, the people would be able to see the transformation. She clutched the letter to her chest, and gave a little swaying dance round the bed, her ungainly movements looking grotesque under the harsh light.

'Ethel Coffin,' she whispered, 'Providence has chosen you.'

She burnt the letters, dropping the curling paper into the waste-bin. She switched the light out and watched the little red sparks pucker out, and after flinging off her clothes, slid between the cold sheets, wriggling her toes into the dark corners as though to make sure nothing was there.

She was soon lost in the memory of marching days, flags being raised on noble standards, arms stretching out in happy excitement, and torches, so many torches the fire warmed your face. It was like a bonfire.

133

The night rally, how that cool wind whipped through the aisles. It was a welcome freshness from the warm press of bodies to turn your sweating head into the gentle breeze. The torches wavered in graceful arches, the flickering shadows running red and black across the upturned faces, and then they flapped out, stretching themselves in a parody of a salute, so close to the heads.

Flames floated in the air, and high above, a dark cloud of smoke. The stench of it blocked up her nostrils, filled them with its curling sweetness of burning flesh.

She didn't hear the door gently open, or see John William look down on her sleeping head. He never detected the charred smell which hung over the bed, as he stooped to kiss her twitching head.

[11]

It had been raining steadily for three days. It seemed to betoken the end of summer. The community of the house was ruled by the needs of the sick-bed, the only visitors being the doctor, and less frequently the Reverend Roe.

Elizabeth Booth had had a stroke, and as Dr Baldwin shone a torch into her dim eyes and felt her moist pulse, he knew she was dying, but it seemed she would not go without making her family witness the death agonies. Nanny Bradshaw and Dagmar took it in turns to sit by the bed.

It would have been difficult to say whether Elizabeth Booth could detect the difference in the hands which dealt with her; the unfeeling efficiency of Dagmar and the trembling intensity of Nanny Bradshaw, who treated Mrs Booth as though her yellowing skin were fine white porcelain. The silver bell which had rung throughout the house now lay discarded and silent. Dagmar had noticed the discrepancy in the clocks' hands, and with Teutonic thoroughness pulled the room into line with the ordered ticking in the rest of the house. Night now fell with uniformity. The two attendants scarcely acknowledged each other, and a lingering silence fell over the whole house, broken by the occasional log which fell in the fire with a crackling hiss, and the persistent drumming of the rain on the windows. The candles remained unlit, an electric bulb illuminated the room which seemed to have shrunk to the figure on the bed. The silk cushions were removed to make it easier to change the linen, and somehow Dagmar had contrived to make the lair of Elizabeth Booth resemble a hospital room, pulling drapes, letting in the hazy light.

She had a dream; it danced behind her closed eyes. She bobbed about like a bottle on an ocean, sometimes

135

sinking, but always surfacing. Her heart was breaking. It broke.

When she opened her eyes, she was looking down from a height, and saw a figure lying on a bed. Floating, she watched the wrinkled skin below her shudder on the rattling indrawn breath. It was possible to define the shape of the skull beneath the thinning hair. It was no one she knew. Suspended in the air, she had no compulsion, it was a nerveless existence.

Days and nights passed without disturbing her floating form. Familiar features flitted beneath, unaware of her invisible vigil. The visitors plucked at the strings of her memory like a breeze through an aeolian harp.

With the wooden stare of a lotus eater, she looked out of the window, the landscape dripping down the grey pane.

She saw William reach out and take the shrivelled, unfeeling hand.

She saw John William stand in silence.

She saw Dagmar walk over and loop her arms around John William's taut neck, and draw the head down upon her shoulder.

She saw Nanny Bradshaw brooding, her waxy forehead creased with three symmetrical lines as she frowned at the sight of Dagmar.

She saw Reverend Roe crouching over the bed, and in the empty room watched his stealthy fingers frantically search through drawers.

She saw Dr Baldwin look down upon the still figure and sigh.

The floating body had an absolute emptiness, not even the desolate places of the world could mirror the abstraction of the ghostly condition.

She hovered, rising and falling like the wheezing chest beneath. Her floating form sagged voluptuously towards the bed, a heavy lethargy seemed to prod her in the back. The room was receding like a landscape seen through the wrong end of a telescope. The noises of the house clattered into the back of her mind, and once more she became burdened with feelings. She slowly closed her eyes. She felt a tug, as if like some fish she were caught on a line. A dull rumbling started in her ears, and she opened her eyes to stare at the cracked ceiling.

Her memory came back, as her chest laboured against the constricting blankets. Immobile in the cocoon of the bed, her mind thrashed about.

Elizabeth Booth was trapped once more in her body.

By the time Dr Baldwin arrived, Elizabeth Booth was pinioned in the precise folds of clean sheets and the phenomenon of her staring eyes was known to the house. Nanny Bradshaw took it as some portent that they had opened in the presence of the German. They looked accusingly at Dagmar, that's what she thought. There was no telling what things those eyes had seen as they protruded from her livid face; they looked like the empty hollow eyes of death itself. They'd given that skinny chicken a turn though, thought Nanny, pleased at the prospect of Dagmar getting her come-uppance. Those were the sort of eyes you would see on Judgment Day. No wonder the German was sweating, she'd got plenty to hide.

When she was alone with Mrs Booth, she resolved that she would try and get some sign from her, something which would point to what the foreigner was up to. The old lady wouldn't like the idea of being moved to another room so there wouldn't be any stairs to go up, and there would be a smaller bed, less of a nuisance, that's what the German had said. After what Mrs Booth would be able to tell her from her talks with those on the other side, she would be able to present a dossier on the secretary. In the huge stomach, a grin as broad as that of the Cheshire Cat spread itself. Oh yes, she'd pay back that trollop for her nastiness. She pursed her lips as Dagmar said something to the doctor. She thought nobody saw through her servile toadying, but she hadn't reckoned on someone like her. Before she had time to draw any more conclusions from Dagmar's behaviour, Nanny Bradshaw realised Dr Baldwin was telling them about the latest development.

'To be perfectly honest, I'm surprised she's managed to hold on this length of time. I think we'll just have to wait and see, but I'll have to give you some drops for her eyes. Conjunctivitis is already setting in. Whatever happens, I'm afraid she may lose her sight, although I can't really say that she's seeing us now, not in the sense that we see each other. It

137

just seems as though she's not ready to die. She's got hidden depths of strength, something is forcing her on and she's not going to let go easily. But we shall see. She's a very determined lady. I suppose she always was, and you don't need me to tell you that.'

She listened to them talk of her anticipated death, and the desperation she felt was being consumed by a slow anger.

While Dr Baldwin had been talking, Dagmar noticed that one of Mrs Booth's eyes seemed to move, either that, or the shadows gave the impression of movement. There it was again. She was sure, the watery bloodshot protuberance moved. She watched intently now, even ignoring the compliment the doctor had just paid her. Reaching out, Dagmar clutched Dr Baldwin.

'Look, look, she's moving.'

Struggling to free himself, Dr Baldwin moved towards the bed. Not only was the eyelid flickering back and forth, the eye itself seemed to roll sluggishly in the direction of the doctor until it stared directly at him. The others strained their necks to see what was happening, but apart from Dagmar and the doctor, nobody could discern the wild activity of Elizabeth Booth's right eye. Dagmar's hand secretly clenched itself into a peasant sign to ward away evil.

The hereditary folklore of witches clung to her like the smoke from the chimneys in a Bavarian village. From glaring at the doctor, the eye momentarily swam about in unfocused confusion, until, like a leech, it attached its gaze to the German. As Dagmar tried to move out of its determined vision, the eye followed her with tranquil malice.

Standing back, Dr Baldwin's movements were unnervingly followed by the right eye. He decided he didn't want to say anything in front of its unrelenting gaze, as though it would be able to lip-read anything he said. The others could now see Elizabeth Booth's head, and felt the presence once more of the old woman.

A warm surge of devotion flickered in the breast of Nanny Bradshaw. She alone knew Elizabeth Booth had truly returned. She had no need to listen for a heart-beat, or mess about probing and prodding, shining lights into this and that. It was a crime to carry on like that.

138

'She heard you carrying on like she was already dead and buried, didn't she?'

The accusing voice of the family retainer made the others jump. Nobody noticed that the eye on the bed flashed a quick look in Nanny Bradshaw's direction before returning to the tableau in front of the bed.

'Nonsense, nonsense,' said Dr Baldwin. 'I can assure you, Mrs Booth is involved in a struggle for life, and not eavesdropping on us.' He glanced once more at the bed and caught the wicked gleam of the living eye.

'Perhaps we'd better leave Mrs Booth for a while. She really must have perfect peace. Rest is the only medicine, complete rest.'

He ushered them all out of the sick-room, and in his own haste to leave, he nearly stood on the heels of Dagmar. She clutched the doctor again. He felt surprised that the nurse should have such a grip.

'She can't see us, can she? It's just an illusion that she's looking at you. She can't understand us. She's not listening to us, is she?'

'I can assure you, she isn't aware of what's going on around her. She might register movement, nothing more than that, just a reflex, like a chicken running after its head has been lopped off.' He hadn't meant to use such an ugly image, he must be tired. 'Yes, I'm afraid Mrs Booth isn't seeing what's going on here. It would be like an empty room for her, all your secrets will be safe.' He smiled at his little joke, but Dagmar had already looked away.

12

When Nanny Bradshaw made her way to Mrs Booth's room, she had something wrapped in brown paper under her arm. It looked the same size as a game box, as though she were going to play ludo with her employer. Elizabeth Booth was asleep, the blind eye staring sightlessly into the darkened room. Nanny leaned over and nodded to the vacant orb as though it could register her presence. Pulling up the chair, she eased her bulky body down. With eager fingers she pulled away at the brown paper and the scrabbling sounds penetrated the sleeping mind of Elizabeth Booth. Her right eye flickered open. She noticed the seated form of Nanny Bradshaw. How she wished she could smile at her. Her eye blinked gracefully in Nanny's direction, and although she had already become tired of the limited view from her immobile head, she looked out into the room with a visible dignity. She wondered if it would be possible to enter into some rapport with Nanny. If she would only look up from the package, she would wink at her. She hoped the old retainer would not be shocked by such familiarity and she would make the blink as formal as possible.

As Nanny's head was still looking down, Mrs Booth gave it a trial run. Nanny now proceeded to lay out a board on the quilt. Mrs Booth began to wonder what Nanny was up to. The strange preparations completed, Nanny turned towards the recumbent head, and as Mrs Booth winked at her, Nanny seemed to address herself to the blind eye, ignoring totally the gesture in the other. She leant forward, and began to talk in a voice which quivered with a strange intensity. It caused a prickling sensation over Mrs Booth's right eyeball, as though several flies had landed on the sensitive surface and fanned it with their veined wings.

'I've come as you knew I would. There won't be any prying

140

eyes tonight. We'll get to the bottom of this mystery.' She smiled at the dead eye. 'I've brought all the stuff so we might as well make a start, that's if you're ready?'

She brought her pallid face even closer to that of Mrs Booth, who had no idea what was going on.

'There's no telling what revelations might come,' said Nanny.

She lifted her employer as easily as a rag-doll until she was sitting up, and arranged the cushions to prevent her sliding down. Elizabeth Booth could see the board for the first time; it consisted of letters of the alphabet. Had she been capable of frowning, she would have done so; her eyes looked puzzled. She felt like some child's toy which was being positioned for an imaginary tea-party. As Nanny placed her hands on the board she would have liked to yank them away.

'If Mrs Makin could see me now,' wheezed Nanny, placing a wooden arrow under her employer's hands.

Mrs Booth couldn't help being intrigued by what Nanny was planning. She tried to concentrate on keeping her hand in place, but no connection was made. She might just as well have tried to spin straw into gold, the task was beyond her capabilities. However, like Rumpelstiltskin, Nanny Bradshaw seemed to have a solution, and with a piece of string fastened the arrow under her limp palm.

She looked into Nanny's face, it seemed to be filled with some dull longing. She tried winking at her. Nanny waited, and as the minutes passed, Elizabeth Booth began to grow cold. She really felt that she had indulged Nanny sufficiently now, and she wanted to be put back between the sheets of her bed. Nanny reached forward, and with a broad digit prodded the still hand as though encouraging it to do something. Nanny sighed as she saw it was the pressure from her own hands which made the arrow slide slightly. Clearly she had done something wrong. Looking down into the box, she pulled out a small instruction manual. Remembering Elizabeth Booth, she smiled into the silent eye.

'I thought I'd best be sure we set everything up good and proper. These ouija boards are supposed to be temperamental. No wonder no spirit is speaking to us, if we've done something to upset them. Perhaps you can get a bit of shut-eye while I read through this here manual, and then we can have everything hunky-dory, and find out what the flibbertigibbet has done to Pewter.'

Like the Cyclops she had now become, Elizabeth Booth closed her right eye, not in order to drift into sleep, but so that she could collect her thoughts. It seemed that Nanny thought she could commune with the spirits through her. Perhaps all this had been too much for devoted Nanny. If she could have spoken, she would have advised that she take a week off by the sea. Maybe she had a fond spot for Pewter – she had seemed most put out at his sudden departure – still nobody had told her that they were walking out, so it was no good crying over spilt milk.

As Mrs Booth was striving to understand what Nanny was doing, Dorothy Bradshaw had decided that they had gone wrong. She would have to try to contact the spirits more forcefully. She wondered whether they should call it a night, she didn't want to upset the spirits. Perhaps they had already arrived, curious about the ouija board, and here she was being inhospitable. That would never do.

'Mrs Booth, Mrs Booth.' She raised her voice slightly. 'It seems we've been going about this the wrong way. Oh yes, the spirits will be here all right, like bees to honey, the ouija board attracts them. But of course they don't know what we want, so either I'll spell it out for them, or I could write it down on a bit of paper.' She smiled at Mrs Booth. 'I think we should spell it out, otherwise we'd have lots of questions lying about for snoopers to find.'

Turning her gaze in the general direction of the ceiling, she swayed slightly. Mrs Booth still hadn't grasped that she was supposed to be the medium for the messages from the other side, but she could see Nanny wanted a séance.

The word spirit slithered into her mind, recalling the strange nightmare when she had been looking down into her own face, when she didn't know the names and shapes of living things.

Nanny Bradshaw took hold of Mrs Booth's hand. With great deliberation, she started directing the tied arrow to various letters, spelling out the message she wanted to reach those on the other side. It was difficult for Mrs Booth to follow the arrow all the time. She had to squint down to make out the letter and didn't have much faith in Nanny's spelling either. The concentration of the servant was almost painful.

'Where has the German hussy put Pewter's body?'

That was the question. Elizabeth Booth stared in disbelief at the figure. Even she, who despised the German, did not think she had done away with Pewter. As far as she knew, they had never met. Poor Nanny must be beside herself with grief to think such things. She wondered how the two of them must have fallen in love; it had the dimensions of a great tragedy. Nanny Bradshaw had lost her first love to the Germans in the war, so she must suspect them of ridding her of her second. Nanny had removed her warm hand from Mrs Booth's.

Nanny stopped staring at the roof, she was beginning to think the spirits had rejected them and wondered what would satisfy them. Would she have to undergo some form of penance? She looked beseechingly into the blind eye as though she would see reflected the answer she sought. Just as she was deciding that she would fast until the next attempt, the wooden arrow scraped itself along the letters, dragging the withered hand with it, like some unwilling captive.

Elizabeth Booth felt the tugging sensation which spread like a stain towards her elbow. It was not a pleasant feeling, and from such a sluggish start, her fettered palm darted between the letters in a tumultuous dance. Dorothy Bradshaw's eyes glowed as her stubby pencil took down the letters until they formed the message. The stark scribblings of Nanny Bradshaw filled the little sheet of white paper, and Elizabeth Booth's hand slumped back uselessly to the pointing arrow. She hadn't been able to follow the swift progress, and strained to see what Nanny had written, too surprised to be shocked by the phantom movement of her paralysed limb. Nanny placed the simple sheet of paper on the ouija board. Reading it upside down, Elizabeth Booth slowly translated the portentous remark, 'Hagen's Bane'. The two words lay there, innocent of the effect they were causing. Mrs Booth felt cold at the thought of the bald-headed teacher reaching out with his bony hand and directing the arrow for his strange confession.

143

'Hagen's Bane,' repeated Nanny. 'It could be a code word.' Her eyes gleamed at the thought of a spirit accomplice.

'Sounds foreign, there's definitely a foreign element.' She nodded into the abyss of the dead eye. 'German at that.' She tried to remember the German that Mrs Makin had been going on about, when the arrow started up.

'My poor heart,' she gasped, grabbing a pencil.

'H . . . I . . . S . . . T . . . E . . . R . . .' she spelled out, her lips forming the letters.

'Her Boss,' she breathed, and clutched at her bosom. 'I've heard her going on about that Hister. He's a pal of hers. I wouldn't be surprised if this here Hagen and Hister are brothers. What with this and the other evidence, the culprits will be uncovered.' She gave a contented smile, and rubbed her side to relieve the wind.

'Pardon.'

Nanny Bradshaw looked round the room and smiled.

She carefully undid the string tying the arrow to Mrs Booth's right hand and envisaged the possibility of material-isation, or at the very least, ectoplasm. Oh yes, she'd have a lot to report, both to the police and the *Psychic Monthly*. She was sure she'd make the front page. As she slid the body of her employer between the sheets, she smiled at the blind eye, the tunnel through which she felt the spirits reached. She patted down her hair as though looking into a mirror, just in case Pewter was still looking on.

'Well,' she said in a fey voice, 'that was a very good start. Communication has been established.' She patted Elizabeth Booth's exposed hand. 'Don't worry. When I write it all up, everyone will know you're the medium, and Pewter your spirit guide. Mind you, it was me that knew you'd remember the way back. Once you've crossed the river and the ferryman knows your face, he'll let you go free from now on. There's no telling what revelations will come. I'll leave this pencil and paper here just in case any spirit wants to have a quick word. It's not unusual to have the urge to do a bit of automatic writing after a spell on the ouija board. Not that I know from personal experience, I'm just not receptive, the power's not in me,' she sighed, and then beamed once more at the blank eye and tightened the grip on the unresisting hand.

'Still, you've been judged worthy.' She lowered her voice, 'Oh yes, many would give more than their right hand to do what's been allowed to you, and in the old days, there's many as burned for less than we've been up to.' She laughed, her podgy fingers pawing at her employer's pliable fingers. 'It's our little secret. We'll find out what that trollop's been doing. She said you were a nuisance! I knew that would bring you back as quick as a flash. I didn't tell you earlier, but I knew she was a bad fish as soon as I saw the skinny chicken. She doesn't drink tea either! There's no trusting a foreigner, and just who won the war anyway?'

She heaved herself out of the chair and leaving the pencil and paper on the quilt, left the room, her starched apron crackling.

As she walked along she thought it was only those who had a suffering vocation like Mrs Booth who would be receptive to the spirits. Her mind was lapped by small waves of pleasure, until, like a smooth pebble, there was no doubt that Pewter had sent her the message through the receptacle of Mrs Booth. She clutched at the note like a love letter.

Alone once more, Elizabeth Booth stared into the mottled ceiling, wondering just how many spirits were flocking round her bed. She felt as long as she kept her eye open, they wouldn't make a move. She had ceased trying to explain what had happened, perhaps it all had something to do with the curse on her family. She thought of Garside being responsible for all of this; his spirit could be swinging right in front of her now, swaying with the rhythm of the scaffold. She hoped morning would come soon.

As Nanny tucked away her ouija board, she wondered whether Pewter's spirit had followed her into her bedroom. She wasn't sure whether that was very gentlemanly to accompany a lady to her boudoir. She removed the message from her pocket. She had never believed she would receive a love-letter. A guilty warmth stole round her body. She decided that she would take no risks, and demurely slipped her voluminous cotton nightdress over her clothes. She let the starched apron fall to the floor, then struggled to remove her dress and stockings taking a certain risqué pleasure in the sly

145

patches of skin which flashed into view. She was proud of her white flesh. She flushed when she unlaced her corset and felt the familiar falling of her pendulous breasts. She had let her clothes fall with the provocative ease of a stripper; she was attempting to arouse the phantom tutor. As she unpinned her hair and let the greying locks cascade over her shoulders, her pale lips pouted. With trembling fingers she took the decision to remove her camiknickers. As the undergarment fell, Nanny felt wicked. She was like the whore of Babylon and giggled as she stepped out of the tangle at her corn-laden feet.

The bed was cold, but as she wriggled herself into the ready depression in the mattress she thought Pewter would be colder still. Her nightdress had ridden up to her thighs, exposing her bulbous knees. She quelled the urge to straighten it out. Her breathing was ragged and her eyes raked the darkened room for some subtle movement which might betoken the arrival of Pewter. Although she hoped he was already there, she was determined to lose her virginity to the incubus of the tutor. She parted her legs slightly with a shudder, letting the heat of her body escape. She imagined it would waft out into the room like steam from a kettle, bringing the thirsty Pewter to a brew more savoury than tea.

She remembered how Pewter loved his food, sucking marrow from the bone, crunching the fat, she would let him feast on her, wipe his greasy chin on the tablecloth of her freshly laundered flesh. She could almost feel the trembling progress of Pewter's skeletal finger. She waited, it was like death, her heated body began to cool between the barren sheets. Even ghostly fornication was denied to her, a bitter bile replaced the love juices, her bare-skinned body had been thwarted. She turned her head towards the faded wallpaper.

13

Looking out of the train window, Sister Ursula felt a vague regret. She disliked the rocking motion and ignored her fellow-travellers, especially when she noticed one had still retained his hat; she expected it to tumble from his head with the swiftness of the walls of Jericho. She knew he'd seen her habit and there was no excuse. Travel was heathen. She took some comfort from the fact that none of them was smoking, although with an hour still left, she wouldn't put it past any of them to light up, especially the one with the hat. He yawned without covering his mouth, and Sister Ursula stared into the wet interior. She would find it difficult to pray for him; she was sure he would smoke, for his teeth seemed stained with nicotine. She didn't belong to any of the places they slipped through, and she certainly didn't belong in this carriage. She could hear the rustling of papers as the other passengers read the world's news. Sister Ursula was not interested in the problems of the world; the large headlines about Sudetenland didn't register, her concern was for the immortal soul and for the other world.

The wooden sleepers clicked with the regular rhythm of rosary beads. The only landmarks which caught Sister Ursula's eye were church steeples; they were the milestones of her journey. Her thoughts wandered to the reason for her travel; the vast expanse of Ethel Coffin filled her mind, although the picture she had of her niece was a faded photograph image. She had the bulk, that was unmistakable, but the features were blank.

The train pulled into a station. The man left the carriage, giving a darting glance to the seated nun which pierced her like the fatal arrow which martyred her namesake, St Ursula. When she was a girl and knew the cloisters were for her, her burning vocation was to be worthy of St Ursula and her eleven

147

thousand virgins, slaughtered by the Huns outside Cologne. As a novice she had walked around the stone floors expecting any minute to be called upon to die for her faith. Like St Perpetua, she would have dreams of fighting the heathens in an arena, wielding a fiery sword with the oiled muscles of a man.

The train jerked her from her thoughts on beatification. She was nearly alone in the carriage now, no need to worry that somebody would start talking about what a mess the world was in. Sometimes she wished she could grow a beard like St Uncumber, not to revolt a pagan husband, but to discourage conversation. The train began to slow down. She had failed to notice that the railway had left the undulating hills and had entered the grimy enclosure which went by the name of Slackhall. She just hoped Wilfred was there. She certainly wasn't going to lift her suitcase from the rack, that was a man's job.

The train disgorged its passengers with the same ease the dragon did with St Margaret. Sister Ursula saw her brother hurrying along to meet her.

'Did you have a nice journey Ursula?' he gasped a little like a landed fish. 'You've arrived just in time.' He coughed violently, running a drab hankerchief up to his mouth. 'It looks like rain, you must have brought it with you.' He smiled at his sister, his purple lips almost apologising for the gesture. Sister Ursula did not smile at her brother.

'Wilfred.'

Mr Coffin regarded his sister with the same awe as a burning bush. 'Please collect my suit-case from the carriage, I don't want it to be whisked away to some other place.'

Wilfred Coffin emerged from her carriage, the heavy suit-case nearly scraping the floor as his thin arms strained to lift it.

'Where is Fanny?' she asked.

'Oh, she's back at the house. She'd have liked to come to the station of course, but what with it looking like rain, and arranging for someone to sit in with Ethel, well, we thought it better if she stayed put; but I know she would have liked to be here. She said she'd be thinking about us, and she'll have a nice warm cup of tea waiting for us when we get home.' He looked anxiously into her face to see whether she looked

148

more annoyed, but it was difficult to tell. 'We're very grateful that you could come and help us. We're just about at the end of our tether. I should warn you that Fanny looks a different woman. What with all the worry, she's really lost weight, and her nose has gone all thin; she's got a thin nose, it's all sharp,' he sighed, and Sister Ursula tried to allow her severe face to assume a sympathetic look. In her heart of hearts, she believed she had already started with God's help to lift the troubles from the shoulders of her brother, the sympathetic look was the first step.

As Wilfred's shoulders trembled under the strain of the suit-case, his sister made off down the platform, leaving him to walk in her slipstream. She was trying to imagine how Fanny Coffin could possibly have lost more weight. Without being too personal, her nose was always thin and sharp, not like her own, which she saw as being aquiline, not thin and sharp.

She walked with a terrible vengeance, grinding her shoes into the pavements. She suddenly realised she did not know the way to her brother's home. Wilfred was still trailing in her wake; she couldn't understand why he was so frail – she always made sure that he ate his greens when he was young – and wondered whether Fanny fed him properly.

In the distance she could see the huge edifice of the Booths' house; it already seemed obscured behind a grey drizzle and she could also see the single spire of the church, a Protestant church at that. She felt it was a disgrace that the Booths' mansion should tower over God's own house. Even if Protestant. Such vanity would not be overlooked. If it was obvious to her eyes, it would be plainer to more exalted orbs than her own.

Still the Lord moved in mysterious ways, perhaps she had been sent to help more than her overweight niece; she no longer regretted her decision to come to Slackhall. In the grimy streets she might be permitted to perform a miracle; people would notice, and eventually there might be a new St Ursula. Her thoughts of adoration were cut short by the panting of her brother. She silently crossed herself for allowing such vain imaginings into her mind. It must be all the strain she thought; oh yes, travel did not suit her at all, she

149

would have to pray long and hard for such thoughts to cease. She just hoped she would not have to repent in public like Theophilus the monk. She would make no pact with the devil; she would drive his wicked temptations from her mind and prostrate herself before the Blessed Virgin.

She felt the first drops of rain on her face, and looked to see that Wilfred had failed to bring an umbrella.

'It's raining,' said Wilfred Coffin, and then held his hand out to test his theory. 'I said it would rain, and here it is. We'd better get a move on or else we'll get wet through.' He looked expectantly at his sister. Ursula was still standing looking at him, her black habit speckled with the dropping rain.

'I'm not going to walk anywhere in this pouring rain.' She started towards the nearest house. 'I shall explain to these people that we have been caught in this storm, and would they kindly offer us the shelter of their roof.'

Like a thin shadow, Wilfred Coffin followed his sister, and as he reached her, she had already knocked on the door. She waited, and then knocked again. This time she could hear the sound of somebody approaching.

The door swung open and a small unkempt woman stood on the doorstep. She wore a checked apron which had obviously seen better days, and her greasy hair hung in dark strands which seemed to wriggle with a life of their own. Sister Ursula thought she could do with a haircut, and began to feel perhaps it hadn't been the best choice of door. Even as she knocked she had noticed that the paint was peeling and the place was not in good repair. She tried to smile at the little woman, who appeared to have several strands of hair actually sprouting from her face, they were clustered around a mole.

'All right. All right. There's no need to bang the door down.'

She squinted up at Sister Ursula who was just about to begin her request when Mrs Wagtail jumped back into the darkened hall and began to push the door to. Sister Ursula's foot was in the way.

'What's your game, missus?' asked Mrs Wagtail. 'Do you belong to one of them religious organisations? You'll find no takers at number seven here. We don't want any of your pamphlets neither. It's a good job my Jack's not home. He'd send you off with a flea in your ear all right.'

'I think you are mistaken,' said Sister Ursula sweetly. 'We merely seek shelter.'

'Shelter is it,' said Mrs Wagtail. 'You on the run then? Get that foot out of my road, missus, it'll be the worse for you if you don't. We've no valuables you know, you'd best try some other house to rob.'

'There's been a misunderstanding,' said Sister Ursula, deciding that she couldn't leave this unsavoury woman to spread stories around like this. After all, she was here to perform good works. 'We want to come in out of the rain.' She held her hand out into the downpour.

'Oh, you do, do you?' replied the sceptical Mrs Wagtail. 'That's a good one that is. What do you think this is? I'll not have your sermonising in my hall, dripping water on the lino. I'll not deny Jack and I have the occasional glass of stout, but that's our own business, so there's no need to bother wasting your time trying to make us take the pledge. We're not temperance folk.'

'We're getting very wet out here,' persisted Sister Ursula, 'just remember the good Samaritan.' She gave a firm smile.

'As far as I'm concerned you can stay in the rain till kingdom come. Now get off with you. Just get that bloody foot out from under my door. I won't tell you again, we don't want no Jehovahs round here. Just push off.'

'Jehovahs,' cried Sister Ursula. 'I am Sister Ursula, of the Convent of the Precious Blood. There's no Jehovahs here.'

'It's all the same to me,' said Mrs Wagtail. 'We don't want any of that claptrap at number seven. There's nothing up with the occasional tipple. I'll bet you have the occasional drop of cooking sherry anyway.' Mrs Wagtail winked at the nun. 'Is he your hubby then, dear? Not much to say for himself, has he?' She had relaxed the door a little. 'They're all the same, men. My Jack now, he's an animal sometimes. Pardon me, I hope I'm not speaking out of turn, but he doesn't look as though he's got it in him. That's a blessing dear.'

'I'm not married,' protested Sister Ursula, crossing herself fervently.

'Well,' said Mrs Wagtail, 'if that doesn't beat it all, not

151

married you say. What's the world coming to, not married and then coming to the doors of decent respectable folks. Let me tell you, everyone is married at number seven. We don't want any shenanigans going on around here, coming up all brazen to the doors of strangers and announcing you're not married. It's shameless. Just what's your game? I shall call the police, there's children here at number seven. Mr Wagtail, he's very particular about them kids. Just wait till I tell him what you've been trying to fill their heads with. You're a shameless strumpet.'

'You are mad,' said Sister Ursula with conviction. 'You are not fit to look after children.'

'Who do you think you're calling mad? I'll have none of your bloody lip. My Jack will be back in a minute, you'd best be off before then or there's no telling what he'd do. Once his back is up, he could kill in anger, that's for sure.' Mrs Wagtail folded her arms over her ample bosom. 'There's no call for your trade around here, dear, you'd be best off in Manchester where I hear there's call for your sort.' She then gave the door a hefty shove and Sister Ursula nimbly removed her foot. Mrs Wagtail had strayed from the path, but she would still have someone to pray for her. Sister Ursula would add her name to the list.

Inside number seven, Mrs Wagtail held up the hem of her dress and did a strange little dance, walking and swaying down the hall back to her nostrums. Her knowing eyes were as dark as a deep sepulchre, and she licked her lips like a wolf scenting a dying man.

Wilfred Coffin had stood mutely during the exchange with Mrs Wagtail.

'I shall pray for her,' said Sister Ursula, and to Wilfred's dismay got down on to her knees on the wet doorstep. He wanted to tug at her wimple. He remembered all too clearly the words about Jack Wagtail and his temper. Sister Ursula rose from Mrs Wagtail's doorstep.

'Well I certainly feel that's been a good start to my visit. The poor woman was in need of someone to pray for her. She's worse than a heathen. There is a lot wrong with

Slackhall and your letter was timely, the Lord's work must be carried out. That house is idolatry.' She pointed at the Booths' home. 'Idolatry stares down at this town from every window. No wonder your Ethel has taken on so. There's a malaise in this place, I can feel it.'

She suddenly realised that she could also feel the rain soaking through her habit. She sighed at the sweet suffering.

[14]

Fanny Coffin had been peering anxiously out of the window, occasionally rubbing her thin arms as though they were covered in something she wished to remove. She had been relieved when she received no reply from Mrs Booth, and now knew that the old lady was at death's door. She was afraid of her sister-in-law, and she knew she could never live up to those hard standards Ursula set for herself. She also envied her the lack of responsibility, for she never had the burden of bringing a child into the world. She jumped when the doorbell rang, gave one last despairing look round the room, patting down her hair, scurried to the door.

'Did you have a good jour . . .' she stopped mid-sentence as she realised the person standing on her doorstep was not her sister-in-law.

'Mrs Coffin,' the person said.

'Yes, yes, I'm Mrs Coffin. There hasn't been an accident has there?' Suddenly she feared the worst and wondered whether she would be strong enough to hear the news. Poor Ethel, how could she tell her?

'I'm here on behalf of Mrs Booth,' and Dagmar Ehrenhardt held out her hand. As though in a dream, the trembling fingers of Fanny Coffin held themselves out, and she winced as they were squeezed. 'You sent a letter?'

Fanny Coffin felt slightly hysterical.

'Well, now,' said Dagmar, in a soothing voice, 'there's no need to be worried that what you said in the letter will go any further. I am a trained nurse, used to all sorts of illness.' She reached out and took the meagre arm of Fanny Coffin. 'Why don't you just tell me what's been going on. Is your daughter still starving herself?'

At the mention of Ethel, Fanny Coffin wilted in the strong

154

grip of the German who neatly stepped into the hall and shut the door.

'I think you have been very brave,' said Dagmar to the sniffling Mrs Coffin. 'It is not easy to be a mother.' She smiled agreeably.

The tip of Fanny Coffin's thin, sharp nose turned slightly red. She tried not to sob too loudly as Ethel might hear and be disturbed. She sniffed a few times, and pulling out a crumpled hanky, wiped her nose with shocking gusto, as though trying to rearrange her face behind the material and massage more life into her meagre features. Although she felt slightly awkward, Fanny Coffin also sensed a certain security. If anybody could help Ethel, it was this nurse.

'She's a very good girl, really. A little saint I used to call her.' She sniffed again. 'My little saint.'

'Where is the patient?' asked Dagmar.

'Oh, don't use that word. She's just under the weather, really. Mr Coffin and I have tried our best, we'd do anything for our little saint.' She nodded her head up and down energetically. 'Do you know, when Ethel was born, I heard a cock crow? What do you think about that?'

Dagmar smiled politely at Mrs Coffin. It seemed that this distracted woman had given birth on a farm. She didn't think it sounded very hygienic.

'Has she contracted Weil's disease?'

She decided to be blunt, otherwise she would never get to the root of the problem, it was the best way. She had always known those patients who had venereal disease by their reticent manner. There was something similar in the demeanour of Fanny Coffin, as though there was a guilty secret she would have to prise out of her.

'Pardon,' said Fanny Coffin, starting to feel worried about the imminent arrival of Ursula. Her gaunt cheeks began to burn with the complicated explanations she would be required to give. She knew Ursula would not be pleased, for she did not care for science. She looked at Dagmar and thought her eyes were like an X-ray.

'Come, come, there is no need for blushes. You cannot blame yourself.' She patted Fanny Coffin on the back. 'And

155

now we'd better see . . . little Ethel.' She was about to say 'the patient'.

Getting to her feet, Fanny Coffin started to shake her head. It was then she noticed Ethel standing in the doorway.

'Shut up,' was all Ethel Coffin said before stumping back into the lounge.

Dagmar stared in disbelief. She looked at Fanny Coffin, who had sunk on to the stairs once more, her face crumpled as the handkerchief she still vainly flapped in her useless hand. Deserting the mother, Dagmar entered the same room as Ethel. Chairs were swathed in elaborate embroidery, and hanging from a wall was a large wooden crucifix. Underneath sat Ethel Coffin. Although Ethel did not have the yellowing skin of jaundice, Dagmar noted that it seemed very greasy, and around the girl's mouth were lots of little spots. She decided she could not be on a healthy diet and next time she came she would bring some fruit. Ethel still failed to acknowledge her. It was as if the girl was in a trance. She stepped a little closer and noticed that her hair looked greasy as well, and the spots extended over her forehead. Some had little scabs; the girl had been picking at them. She looked at Ethel's fat fingers and saw that the nails were dirty; the girl was spreading infection on her own body.

Dagmar did not flinch with disgust or repugnance, rather she considered the solid shape of Ethel from all sides, admiring the singular determination that had created the edifice of flesh. She would remake this girl, teach her that the greatest virtue was to be found in order, and the joy of obeying orders.

She reached out a hand and took one of the biscuits which had been laid out on a plate adorned with a paper doily. The effect could not have been more instantaneous.

'You've no right to take those,' Ethel said. 'You should ask first. And why aren't you in black, where's your habit?'

'I have no bad habits, not like some girls I know. Eating so many biscuits is not good for you, you should eat fruit. Fresh fruit will clear up your complexion. I shall write a new diet for you.'

'Aren't you going to pray for me?' asked Ethel. 'Mother

156

said you would pray night and day for me. When will you start?'

'No, this is not the right way to carry on. What you need is exercise, and good balanced food. That will sort out all your problems. I shall come to visit you and we can have walks together. I can tell you about Germany, and you can tell me about England. You are unique, Ethel, and I'm sure great things are planned for you.'

'Oh yes,' agreed Ethel, 'I've been told that before. I've had my fortune told.'

'I can offer you something that is real,' exclaimed Dagmar, her blue eyes staring with cold clarity at the wooden cross. 'You are getting too old for fairy tales.'

'I've been to heaven,' murmured Ethel.

'You must speak up,' commanded Dagmar.

'They gave me a message for you, aunty', said Ethel quietly, her voice dissolving into a whisper. Dagmar turned. Ethel had called her aunty. She frowned. Was the child so unbalanced, or was she taking her for someone else?

'I'm not your aunty,' said Dagmar.

'Oh,' came the flat voice of Ethel, 'then the message isn't for you.' She took another biscuit and slotting it into her mouth began to chew it.

'What's Germany like?' asked Ethel. 'I'll bet it's not like heaven,' she added petulantly. 'Nowhere is like heaven.' Her voice seemed indistinct as she spoke with her mouth full of soggy ginger nut. Her face was absolutely expressionless.

Dagmar's heart beat quickly. She thought of how the blank eyes would soon begin to glow and later burn with a fierce ideological fire, and as a new Ethel arose in her thoughts, so did a large, cheering crowd to whom she presented her new follower. She smiled at her imaginings, rousing the slumbering spirit of the fat English girl just as the whole country needed to be awakened. She would replace the hunger of this child with something of more sustenance.

Tucking her hair behind her ears, Dagmar went over to Ethel and captured the fat girl's hand within her own.

'Oh Ethel, I shall tell you all about Germany, the dark woods, the high mountains, the brave heroes, the long rivers.

157

It's like heaven to me. Germany has a golden future, a golden future, and you and I shall share it, Ethel. That's what I meant when I said you were unique. Germany has chosen you, you will forget all about heaven. Germany will not dissolve like the clouds.'

'Do you have wine in Germany?' Ethel asked.

'Of course,' replied Dagmar. 'There is wine on every table, but there are more important things than that. I will give you thoughts that will intoxicate you more than crushed grapes.'

'I've had the wine though,' persisted Ethel. 'In heaven it was the colour of the sky. They said it was the blood of the lamb and it would cleanse everything.'

'Stop, stop,' cried a voice. 'Stop this blasphemy. I have arrived in time. I tell you to stop.' It made Dagmar and Ethel jump.

Sister Ursula stood in the doorway, her sodden habit dripping silently on to the floor.

'I shall pray for absolution. How I wish I could have blocked my ears from hearing. God sent me in time. Get down on your knees child, we shall pray together. Even though I shall catch my death, we shall pray first.'

'I don't need any prayers,' repeated Ethel, this time for the benefit of her real aunt. Sister Ursula threw her hands to her ears as though like St Anthony she were keeping temptation and the devil from entering her body.

She lowered herself to the ground, and clutching her rosary beads and the glinting silver cross, started to pray, her lips flapping together as she mouthed silently the intercession she sought.

'Only the Blessed Virgin was taken into heaven to be reunited with her soul. She was sinless,' exclaimed Sister Ursula suddenly, making Fanny Coffin's heart wobble. 'You are aiding the devil and all his works in your vain imaginings. Remember, every venial sin gives the utmost pain to God.' She raised her eyes heavenwards. 'If you should die without the blessing of the last sacrament, or absolution, the smallest venial sin will condemn you to one thousand years of purgatory.'

Outside, the elements added their support, the lightning

flashed, and after a few seconds the thunder rolled vigorously.

As soon as the Coffins had begun to pray, Dagmar sought
the anonymity of the heavy furniture, squeezing herself into
the bulky shadows. From the gloom, she looked out at the
bizarre tableau.

'There is no God,' whispered the German.

A crude flash of lightning revealed her presence to the nun.
Sister Ursula gave the German a look as sharp as the thorns of
Calvary.

Dagmar felt a sharp pang of recognition and it took her
completely by surprise. She thought the eyes of the nun
looked mad. Her grand designs suddenly collapsed like the
citadel of the gods in the finale of *Götterdämmerung*. It had
not occurred to her that there would be any competition over
the fate of Ethel.

Sister Ursula in turn had taken in the dead-pan face of the
German, and was wondering whether she knew it. Fanny
Coffin's head trembled as Sister Ursula slowly raised herself
from the floor.

As she moved, the damp material caressed her with an
unwelcome embrace. She looked at Mr and Mrs Coffin
as they followed her initiative. Wilfred coughed and seemed
to be shivering in the dank coat and they both leaned
towards her at the same angle, as though, like exposed trees,
their shape had been determined by a strong unrelenting
wind.

'Now, now,' she said with stern cheerfulness. 'It's not good
for the child to have too much excitement. She is over-
imaginative as it is.' She noticed the crucifix was slightly
crooked; she would mention it later.

'Are you Ethel's friend?' she said, in a stage whisper.

Dagmar swerved her way between the shadowed furniture
until her actual face could be seen.

'It's the nurse,' squeaked Fanny.

'A very noble profession,' said Sister Ursula, noticing
Fanny dig Wilfred in the side. She thought her brother looked
as though he were about to say something.

'I have to eat more fresh fruit,' announced Ethel, feeling
slightly left out. 'I want skin like the angels, and it's only right

159

that I should.' She was pleased at the gasp which emanated from the throat of Sister Ursula.

'I feel I am intruding,' said Dagmar, without any hint of artifice.

'I'm sure the good nurse knows best,' said Sister Ursula. 'I will certainly introduce a new diet for Ethel.' Her eyes lingered over the biscuits. 'Excess in eating is not good for the body or soul.'

'What about Germany?' cried Ethel.

Dagmar paused and began to open her mouth.

'We cannot detain the good nurse,' interjected Sister Ursula.

'I'll show you the way,' gasped Fanny.

'I'm so sorry,' murmured Fanny Coffin at the door, 'I don't know what possessed me to write like that, but as you saw, Ethel's a good girl, and I'm sure that Ursula will help.' She sniffed. 'I did try my best, I just can't think where we went wrong.' She held out her hand, but Dagmar failed to take it, instead she walked out into the falling rain.

Fanny scurried back into the lounge, only to be met by the plate of biscuits which had been sent spinning across the room.

'Pick those up at once,' ordered Ursula, her face burning as red as a cardinal. Fanny gasped at the command, and then fell to her knees collecting the broken pottery.

'Not you!' cried Sister Ursula. 'The child must learn obedience.'

She strode forward with the same steadfast expression that must have been on the face of St Boniface as he took an axe to the pagan oak-tree.

'I've a message for you,' said Ethel hurriedly. 'I have to deliver it.'

'Message?' queried Sister Ursula, pausing in her penitential advance.

'What's all this, Ethel?' asked her father.

'Let the child speak, Wilfred,' snapped Ursula, a strange sweat breaking out on her forehead. 'I must hear this . . . message.'

'You have served me well, you will serve me better.

160

Whoever puts the light out shall have life eternal.' Ethel gave a cunning little smile.

'That's very nice,' said Fanny, looking up from the floor, her eyes filmed with a glaze of pride, 'very poetic.'

'Who gave you these words?' asked Sister Ursula, backing away slightly.

'It was an angel,' cried Ethel. 'He was surrounded by a shining light and his eyes were as black as coal.'

'Aaaaaiii,' screamed Ursula, 'heresy, heresy, your face is as a burning wind and your voice the hissing of serpents.' She scratched her cheeks, plucking at the flesh.

'It was an angel,' cried Ethel, 'and it'll be worse for you if you don't believe me.'

'Ethel,' cried her mother, 'your aunty is only trying to help. We only want what's best.'

'Steady on, steady on,' muttered Wilfred.

'I shall pray for a clear manifestation of the will of God,' said Ursula. 'We shall see whether these are vain imaginings. I shall set you hard and humbling tasks. Remember Saint Euphrasia. She had to remove a pile of stones from one place to another, stone by stone, over and over, thirty times. It is my business to get to the truth, that is my task.' She sneezed.

'I don't think we've got any stones,' said Fanny, not thinking much of the idea. 'And you'll both catch your death if you don't go and change out of those wet things.' She eased herself from the floor, clutching on to the debris of Ethel's tantrum.

'Yes,' said Sister Ursula with surprising meekness.

She had felt momentarily disorientated. She frowned into the silent room. Something was missing. She couldn't hear the angelus bell. Ethel sank back into her chair, her bulk hidden by the brooding shadows. She watched as the nun walked out of the room and smiled to herself, thinking that soon the whole world would sit up and take notice of her. Even as she rushed home from school, there had been that little old woman who chased after her, to give her that little cake. She'd said she knew there was something special about such a fine girl. She saw her fat hand reaching out and the little cake drop into the open palm.

161

'Let him who has, have. Let him who holds, hold.' That's what she'd said, and Ethel had grinned back as she popped the little gift into her mouth.

And now she had her messages; she turned to the flickering fire and watched the flames dance.

'Had enough excitement for one day?' said her father, and he patted her greasy head.

15

Dagmar left the house, her back molars clamping down on the tender skin of her cheek. The rain had not succeeded in washing away any grime, nor had it brought any sense of freshness with it.

Gradually more people began to emerge from wherever the weather had sent them scurrying. They seemed to look round as though awakening from some long slumber and, as if not quite recognising where they were, looked startled. It was as though the downpour had changed the structure of the place, warped the streets into new and unfamiliar patterns.

Dagmar wasn't quite sure where she was heading. Her feet carried her aimlessly between the puddles of slightly oily water and the small houses. Occasionally the vague smell of cooking drifted towards her. There was no sense of exploration in Dagmar's journey through the cobbled alleyways. Her usual sure step seemed uncertain in the heart of the town.

A group of scarved women had assembled outside one house. She slowed down and one of the women took her arm in a hesitant grip, as if she'd been expected. Without protest Dagmar was steered through the open door. The other women still stood outside, silent as trees. She scarcely noticed the peeling wallpaper, and in the dark and sparsely furnished room, she was confronted by a coffin. It was perched on a table in the centre of the room. Two women in black hovered against the drawn curtains, she couldn't see their mouths. The hand led her towards the open box. She looked. Inside was the shrunken body of an old man, his hollow cheeks covered with an untidy stubble, his eyes weighed down with coins. Dagmar felt marooned and exposed. She continued to stare at the corpse, searching the stranger's wrinkled head for some sort of explanation. She did not know this face. She did not know this family. One of the women in black came towards her.

'It's good of you to come and pay your respects.'

Dagmar remained silent. The hand which led her in escorted her towards the exit, and as she stepped out into the contrasting light, the women in scarves parted to let her through. With a certain giddiness Dagmar walked on down the alley. She knew that they must have mistaken her for somebody else, unless perhaps strangers were shown the dead in Slackhall.

At the bottom of the incline she was faced with a choice of direction.

'Are you lost, dearie?' came the solicitous enquiry. It seemed to Dagmar that the inhabitants of this town kept a peculiar vigil over their broken-down streets.

'Where were you wanting to get to?' persisted the stranger. It was obvious this person would insist on helping.

'The school,' said Dagmar, her choice inspired by the sight of a uniform. The helpful person pondered a moment.

'Well, your best bet would be to go to the market square. It's much easier to get to from there. You're nowhere near it now; you won't find the school round here.' She looked Dagmar up and down. 'I could tell you didn't come from round here. At first I thought you might be trying to find old Mr Robinson's house. God bless him, he's just passed on. Had a good innings, though, seventy-five, and worked in the cotton mill.' She pursed her lips. 'I was just on my way round there, but I thought I'd not go out while it's raining like that. I said to myself, you'd catch your death in that. I've a bad chest, you see.' She paused a moment. 'Are you after a job there, then? The school I mean. You seem to be like a teacher if you don't mind me saying.'

'No,' replied Dagmar, 'I just wish to see the headmistress.'

'Is she a friend?' questioned the woman, and as Dagmar shook her head, she continued. 'Well, she's a bit of a tartar by all accounts; she seems a little too high and mighty.'

'Well, thank you,' said Dagmar. 'I shall ask someone the way at the market square.' She made as if to leave. The woman followed.

164

'I'll show you the way if you like. There's a short-cut through to the square. I can nip round to Mr Robinson's later, he'll not be going far.' She laughed at her little joke.

Dagmar walked along in silence. She now knew the name of the dead man; it disconcerted her.

'Through here, dearie,' cried the woman. Tugging hold of Dagmar's sleeve, she motioned her along a small passageway.

'Bit like Jack the Ripper country through here, isn't it? I wouldn't come through here on my own at night, would you? Not for all the tea in China. There's some funny folk around, that's for sure. I had this woman call at my house today, said she wanted shelter, but I could tell what her game was! She couldn't pull the wool over my eyes.' She turned round to the silent German. 'I said to her, if you don't get your skates on I'll have the police after you. She was plying her trade, if you get my meaning.' She looked round again to see whether Dagmar had got her meaning, nearly tripping in the process. 'Watch your footing,' she cried. 'You could break your neck on some of these cobbles. Somebody ought to do something about it. They'll wait till it's too late, until someone does themselves an injury.' She paused for breath; she wheezed slightly.

'Are you all right?' asked Dagmar.

She smiled up at Dagmar. 'You don't come from these parts at all do you?'

'No,' said Dagmar, a hint of resignation tinging her voice.

'I thought not. You'll find Slackhall a very nice place once you've settled in and got your bearings. See that?' She pointed to the distant twisted roof of the Booths' house. 'That's the only landmark round here. That and the church spire. They own this place lock, stock and barrel. I rent from them. They own the mill and most of Slackhall, too; mind you, that hasn't protected them, though. No. Money doesn't buy everything. Still, there's not much life up there now. By all accounts it seems the old lady's heading for the same place Mr Robinson's just gone to.' She looked round quizzically at Dagmar, her head tilted to one side like some sharp-eyed bird. 'Just listen to me, talking nineteen to the dozen and you not even found your feet here yet.'

She took a shuddering breath. 'Still, you're always welcome at number seven; that's where Mr Wagtail and I live. There's a brew always waiting for any callers, and something a bit stronger if called for.' She gave a little laugh. 'Mind you, if you want to call round, it's better during the day. Mr Wagtail isn't fond of strangers in the evening. Don't get me wrong, dearie, he's not an unfriendly man, just likes to be king in his own castle.'

'Well, that's very kind of you. I shall hope to take you up on the offer.'

'Number seven, dearie. Easy to remember, but best not in the evenings if you follow me; and I go to the market regular every Wednesday.'

Dagmar decided against enlightening Mrs Wagtail about her own residence at the Booths'. She felt no real inclination in ever going round to indulge in idle chatter with her, yet somehow, Mrs Wagtail embodied the thinking of this place. She could act like a barometer. For enduring an hour or so of her grating voice she might find out some useful pieces of information.

'Nearly there now,' called Mrs Wagtail, her voice summoning Dagmar back from the idle calculations.

'It's . . . the . . . red . . . brick . . . place . . . over . . . there.'

Dagmar leant over her, looking into Mrs Wagtail's slightly bloodshot eyes. 'Now, I think you have taken me far enough. It was most kind of you to walk me so far. I'm sure I'd never have found it so easily without your help.' She smiled at Mrs Wagtail, noticing the hairy mole on her cheek, and started to walk towards the school.

The sun broke through the grey clouds, and as Dagmar felt the warmth on her head, she suddenly knew why she had come to this place. It was Ethel Coffin's school.

There was an antiseptic smell about the place which brought back comforting memories of the hospital. The children had already left and the place was silent. In a glass case in front of her were three silver cups. They shone with the sort of gleam which could only be the result of repeated cleanings. Her footsteps echoed along in front of her as her feet marched over the wooden surface. She glanced occasionally through the windows leading into the various classrooms. In some,

exercise-books were propped up on the desk, and black-
boards hinted at the subject taught. She thought more
windows should be open.

Miss Royce heard the approach of Dagmar, and the
occasional pauses which punctuated the progress. She tried to
work out which classrooms the person had stood outside; she
just hoped they had been left tidy. She wondered whether it
were a new parent on the way to see her. She continued
marking the essay in front of her, ticking occasionally in the
margin when she noticed some remark of her own that had
been reproduced. She thought the visitor was now peering
into the geography room, that was always interesting with all
the geological samples laid out in glass boxes.

As inside Dagmar's feet brought her towards Miss Royce,
outside Mrs Wagtail moved off. She had studied the proud
neck of the German with a strange intensity, rather like an
executioner. Inscribing an odd little sign in the silent air, she
gave a small grunt of satisfaction and walked straight past Mr
Robinson's house.

The headmistress removed the glasses which had been
perched on her uncompromising nose. She smoothed down
her hair. As Dagmar's outline became visible, the headmistress called out to her to enter. Miss Royce looked up from
behind her neat desk. She had thought the step to be that of a
man, and now surprised, held out her hand to Dagmar,
wincing slightly at the grip. It reminded her of Miss Blank, the
games mistress.

'Please sit down,' said Miss Royce. 'I'm afraid you've
caught me catching up on some marking, a teacher's day
is never done.' She laughed. 'Now, what can I do for you?'
and before Dagmar could reply, 'Is it about enrolling your
child?'

'Aah, no,' replied Dagmar, and before she continued Miss
Royce interrupted.

'Now don't tell me, let me guess, I'm very good at accents.
You don't look French, it's European though; too guttural for
the divine French.' She failed to notice Dagmar remove the
thin smile which had been pasted to her face. 'Your pronun-

167

ciation would be softer. I've got it, you are Swedish.' She looked expectantly, and realising that she must be wrong, tried again. 'Polish.'

'I am German,' said Dagmar in a flat non-guttural voice. Miss Royce looked momentarily annoyed.

'How interesting,' she said briskly. She could detect all the signs: here was another teacher. 'I'm afraid there's no call for German at this school. This is only a small town and I don't think the governors could be persuaded to add another language to the syllabus. It was hard enough convincing them that French was necessary. You wouldn't believe how philistine people are. This is no place for culture, not at all. I try my best of course. I try to give the pupils a love for the arts, and of course culture.'

She shrugged her shoulders in an apologetic manner. She saw herself as the single beacon of hope in a closed community. She was sure a fellow-teacher would understand this.

'I'm not seeking a post,' said Dagmar. 'I already have a position. I work for Mrs Booth.'

'Oh,' breathed Miss Royce, putting down her red pen. 'Do forgive me. I suppose you are teaching her grandson German.' She noticed Dagmar's shaking head. 'Of course not,' cried Miss Royce. 'What am I thinking about? Mr Pewter teaches him, doesn't he?' She smiled in a knowledgeable way. 'He's a very interesting man, quite widely travelled, you know. We've had him lecture to us a few times at the Women's Institute.'

She stopped, realising that it was probably not necessary for her to have to explain everything to this woman who had also travelled. Perhaps she had found a kindred spirit in the community.

'It must be very difficult to adjust to Slackhall, especially when you are used to places like . . . Berlin.' She breathed the name out as though she alone would be able to understand the wrench it must have been to leave the cafés and galleries. 'Well,' she said, 'just listen to me and I don't even know your name.'

'Dagmar Ehrenhardt,' said the German. 'Please call me Dagmar.' Miss Royce smiled her assent.

168

'Then you must call me Cecilia,' said Miss Royce. 'I must say I do envy you living at the Booths', it's a delightful position. I'd love to see the house, although it's lost most of its former glory. Somehow I think that makes it all the more romantic, to imagine the former greatness. The architecture is a bit of a mishmash, too, some parts are much older than others. I suppose you noticed the entrance-porch was Victorian, but the whole building is on the site of a much older hall. It was burnt down, and part of the present structure dates back to the Reformation. The stones have lived through a lot of history.'

Miss Royce warmed to her subject, taking no notice of Dagmar's cool eyes which were looking out of the window. The headmistress slipped the black patent-leather shoe off her right foot, and flexed it under the table. She felt very relaxed.

'Of course, only the stones were used again from the earlier hall, and no real trace remains of the layout. Do you know,' she sighed, 'the fire took place during the reign of Henry the Eighth, and the original building dated back to the thirteenth century? Dangerous times of course. The fire could have been caused by stray sparks landing on the rushing, and then again it could have been a torch thrown through a window.'

She rubbed the back of her calf with her unclad foot. She was contemplating the possibility of becoming Dagmar's guest, to get inside the Booths' eyrie and see what had been done to the place.

'The banqueting hall was the only part of the structure to have been incorporated down the ages.' She noticed Dagmar yawn.

'Elizabeth the First might have alighted in this very place,' she said. 'Slackhall was even the location of a fight, perhaps skirmish might be a better word. It took place around the area known as Gore Brook, quite gruesome really.' She gave a little laugh. 'Makes you shudder how some places got their names.' She slipped her shoe back on. 'Just listen to me, you can tell I'm a teacher. I am sorry, just an occupational hazard. I delve into local history, you see, any excuse and I tend to launch off thinking everyone will be interested in cairns and barrows and the Wars of the Roses.' She pulled her cardigan

over her shoulder as though she felt a drop in the temperature.

'There is no need to apologise,' said Dagmar. 'It is
interesting to find out more of the history of a place, and
clearly I have come to the right person.' She smiled.

'It's a pity you aren't a teacher,' said Cecilia Royce. 'I could
do with more fresh blood. I'm afraid all the others are a bit out
of touch. I sometimes think that I'm the only modern woman
around here.'

'Yes,' said Dagmar smoothly.

It suddenly occurred to Miss Royce that she still didn't
know the reason for the visit, yet somehow it seemed rude to
ask. It would make it look as though their conversation had
no meaning in itself. Still she couldn't help being curious.

'You are interested in schools?' she probed obliquely.

'Young people are the key to the future,' said Dagmar.

'How right, how right.'

'German youth is aware of its destiny.'

'Putting old heads on young shoulders,' confirmed Miss
Royce.

'We have no problems with under-age drinking,' proclaimed Dagmar, noticing the agitated manner in which Miss
Royce suddenly fiddled with her pen. 'A healthy body gives a
healthy mind.'

'A noble philosophy,' said the headmistress.

'I can see that I shall have to tell you more about Germany.'

'Perhaps I can tell you about Slackhall. In fact,' she
continued, 'why don't you come back to my house. I've some
books on the locality that may interest you, and I'm sure I can
manage a bite to eat, even though domestic science isn't my
forte.'

Dagmar nodded her approval.

As they emerged from the school, darkness was beginning to
fall over the damp town. Gas flames wavered through
steamed-up glass. All over the merry land of England people
were eating, some choked on their food as they tried to read
their evening paper at the same time, the way of the world
sticking in their throats.

'It's getting colder,' said Dagmar conversationally.

170

'Yes, it is indeed,' came the uninspired response.

In fact, Miss Royce was wondering whether she had made her bed that morning, or left an unwashed teacup on the little occasional table. She would just have to whisk it away under her guest's nose. They walked a little further in silence.

As they walked from the narrow streets to the town square, Cecilia Royce made for the monument that rose out of the centre. Dagmar stared nonchalantly at the list of names. Miss Royce suddenly thought how tactless she had been, perhaps Dagmar would feel awkward under the memorial to the dead of Flanders.

'This is one of the highest points in the town. In the Great Flood of 1778, all the people congregated here above the water. All the valleys about were inundated and in one of the old mills there's a flood mark showing how high the water rose.'

'It is always raining about here,' said Dagmar. 'I should think there will be a great flood of 1938.'

'Oh I think that's quite unlikely, the canal's been dredged, no need to lose sleep over that.' Dagmar looked at the sky as though willing it to prove her point.

'I've a feeling we might see more rain,' she said.

'Perhaps we'd better make a move,' agreed Miss Royce. 'This way,' she trilled. 'We are just entering Clarendon Street.'

'Oh,' replied Dagmar, thinking it looked no different from all the others she'd walked.

'This was the meeting-place of some members of the Chartist movement in about 1838. This little cottage housed men who were charged with incitement. Very serious charges. It was all about suffrage, giving men the right to vote.' She used the same voice as that in the schoolroom and Dagmar wondered whether those in the building could hear as well. 'Slackhall has not always been a quiet place, there were mobs who cheered the call to arms.'

Dagmar looked intently at the headmistress. Perhaps the spirit of these people was not as damp as the climate, embers may yet be smouldering. Embers she could ignite.

'What did these chartists do?' asked Dagmar.

Cecilia Royce gave a delighted smile, but decided it was too

171

complicated to explain the five points of the Charter and all the ill will caused by the Poor Law.

'Well, I suppose the Chartists as a whole opened the way for universal suffrage and, of course, they had their members in all towns. In Slackhall, the men charged with riot led a torchlight procession, and it was reported they used some very inflammatory language.'

It would be like a night rally, thought Dagmar. 'The leaders were popular?' she asked.

'Oh yes, I should say so, the whole crowd cheered wildly. They were too wild for the authorities. They were armed as well, and had flags with slogans. "Liberty or Death" was on one, and there were women and children in the crowd marching under a banner; all it said was "Blood". What a thrilling time.'

The German reached out to touch the wet stonework, pondering the events that had once taken place here. She wondered if interest in this type of thing could be rekindled, the hope of a grand alliance trembled through the simple gesture. In the distance a baby started to cry. Having seen Dagmar reverently touch the stone, Cecilia Royce decided on another little detour. They walked away from the Chartist meeting-place, past the cracked and peeling paint of the neighbourhood.

'This,' said the headmistress in a slightly frayed voice, 'is the Mechanics' Institute.' The name was carved into the hard granite over the large door. 'The Women's Institute use it now and the scouts; I learnt to save lives here.'

Dagmar wondered what the Women's Institute was.

'In 1841,' started Cecilia Royce, 'a riot spilled from these very doors, and the Riot Act had to be read out in public. Two troops of Hussars had to be brought in to restore order.' She looked round at Dagmar to see what she thought of that. The German was gazing down the dark street, thinking of how the running feet must have swept over the cobbles, smashing the windows, breaking down the doors. 'It was all caused by a speaker they had. He was talking about the legislative union between England and Ireland. He was Irish, so against it, and as there were quite a few Irish people living in Slackhall at that time because of the construction of the railway, he had plenty of supporters. The locals denounced the speaker as an enemy of the country.' She shrugged her shoulders as though the folly of it all were plain, not only in hindsight, but in 1841 when the factions hurled insults before resorting to bricks.

'The Irish marched the streets with picks and shovels. They shouted as well, "Hurrah for the Repeal. Down with the English", and of course these brawny men didn't just leave it at that. They said they would govern Slackhall, and anyone who wasn't cowering away got a bloody nose. They went up to Slackhall church singing "The Pope shall have his own again".'

'What did the people of Slackhall do?' asked Dagmar.

'Well, they were taken by surprise, but the retaliation was swift and sure. The Hussars were brought in, not to deal with the Irish, but the English. The people of Slackhall raided the Irish quarter; the shanty town they'd set up, smashing the windows, the doors, the people, and what small amount of furniture they had. They gutted the houses. The Irish workers fled on to the moors. They must have huddled in the mist, perhaps it reminded them of the peat-bogs. Still, the railway was built, so they returned, but you'll still find the Irish are hated here. Yet I don't think there will be any alive who could remember it.'

'You have made me see Slackhall with new eyes,' said Dagmar.

'I have to tell you the funniest legend about Slackhall. I promise you it's the last thing I'll mention about the place.' Her voice wavered with suppressed giggling. 'You see the vicarage over there?' Dagmar glanced at the familiar structure. 'Oh, I shouldn't really laugh, but I was just wondering what would happen if it happened today. I shouldn't really, but if you knew the current vicar you would find it amusing.' She paused. 'Have you met Reverend Roe?'

'Yes,' replied Dagmar, not wishing to be drawn on the subject.

'Oh dear,' said Miss Royce. 'Now you will think I'm very rude. Perhaps I had better not say any more.'

'You can't leave me in suspense,' said Dagmar. 'I promise I shall not think badly of you.'

173

'Well, perhaps we'd better move on a little way, not just standing looking at the vicarage.'

Dagmar followed the headmistress, neither of them noticing another figure who had appeared behind them. The person saw how close the heads were and pursed her lips. The two women were sharing some secret, that was for sure.

'It started with the first vicar of Slackhall. His wife was pregnant and when a beggar woman and her children came to the door seeking alms, she sent them off not wanting to have anything to do with them. She called her an old sow with her litter. Of course, they say the old gypsy woman cursed her, put the evil eye on the vicarage for its lack of charity, and the outcome was that the pregnant wife gave birth to a very peculiar-looking daughter. She had a nose like a pig's snout.'

Cecilia Royce started laughing, and Dagmar thought she should join in. 'And, when she grew up, she married another vicar and they say she ate from a silver trough. Her poor mother bought her it.' She laughed even more. 'So, the vicars of Slackhall are not supposed to turn any beggars from the door, or they'll end up with pigs' snouts.'

She clutched out at Dagmar as she screamed with laughter. Dagmar smirked. She thought of the bulging belly of Roe, his white collar, chinless head now surmounted with a pig's snout. Cecilia Royce was gasping.

The noise of the two women had been heard by the approaching figure. Something was obviously very funny. What a way to carry on, thought the observer, making merry in the middle of the street. The figure called out. The voice was that of Dagmar's helper and Sister Ursula's prayers.

'Coooee,' cried Mrs Wagtail, the crazy sound skittering down to the revellers. She decided she would not rush, they could wait for her. She'd done enough running about for one day. They both turned.

'You made your appointment then, dearie?' She addressed herself to Dagmar, waiting for the German to make the introductions. Dagmar failed to respond. 'This your friend then?' she asked.

'Who is this?' asked Cecilia Royce, her height enabling her to talk over Mrs Wagtail's head.

'It's the woman who showed me the way to the school.'

'It's got a name as well,' declared Mrs Wagtail.

'Don't take that tone of voice,' said Miss Royce. 'I'm the headmistress'.

'You could be the Queen of Sheba for all I care,' said the unimpressed Mrs Wagtail. 'I've never seen such a carry-on in all my born days. Such a screeching and a wailing, scarcely human. That's what I thought. Sounded like something had escaped from a circus.' She placed her podgy hands on her ample hips.

'What are you meaning?' hissed Cecilia Royce, not liking this woman one bit and thinking that she had better deal with her here and now.

'What am I meaning? What am I meaning?' mimicked Mrs Wagtail. 'I'll tell you what I'm meaning. Someone,' she said pointedly, 'has been carrying on and cavorting in the street. Acting as though they were no better than they ought to be. Perhaps other folk should know what's been going on. Goodness only knows what nonsense has already been put into them kiddies' heads. What daft ideas will they come up with next? That's what I thought, and now I can see the cause. Why, you should be ashamed of yourselves.' She shook her head.

'Ha!' spat out Cecilia Royce. 'I think, Dagmar, that we are being blackmailed.'

'Blackmail, that's a dirty word,' cried Mrs Wagtail, 'there's no blackmail here. Some people should have their mouths washed out with soap and water.' She looked up at Miss Royce. 'My old eyes nearly popped out of my head. I thought perhaps one of them ladies is having a fit. My heart jumped to think of the shuddering and foaming that was going on. So as fast as my poor legs could carry me, I came rushing to help, but then I saw the smiles and the laughing, and I thought, well, you fooled Mrs Wagtail for sure. You gave her a shock, I'm still not over it, and then in the next breath I hear blackmail. Whatever next?' She looked as though she might finish her performance with tears and opened the dark bag of cracked leather, fumbling about for a handkerchief and sniffing noisily all the while.

She had made the two younger women feel very awkward.

175

Mrs Wagtail had succeeded in becoming the injured party and with a tongue like hers there was no knowing what embellishments might be added for other ears. Knowing she would have to appease her somehow, Miss Royce looked helplessly at Dagmar. After all, the headmistress thought, the woman knew Dagmar, not herself.

'Oh, dear,' said Miss Royce, 'it does seem I was a little hasty in what I said. You see, Mrs Wagtail, when you've got a position to maintain . . . Anyway, I regret very much any offence I might have caused you, especially when you only came to help.'

'Exactly,' said the slightly mollified Mrs Wagtail, 'I only came to give a helping hand and then to be accused of blackmail, and from someone of your standing, well, it's a good job my heart's as strong as it is. A shock like that could have laid me out, and then what?'

'Yes, yes,' said Miss Royce, wondering how far she would have to go to content this tiresome woman. 'Still, we all make mistakes. We should be thankful we realised ours before any harm was done, but I think that there are far worse things going on than we two women laughing in the street. I do apologise if we alarmed you in any way, and if I spoke too harshly, just call it an occupational hazard. I'm afraid I sometimes forget I'm not back in the school talking to naughty girls.' She closed her mouth with the same determination Mrs Wagtail had used on her handbag. She thought she had done more than was absolutely necessary, apologising to this stranger.

'No hard feelings, dearie,' said Mrs Wagtail, 'there's nothing wrong with a bit of fun and games, that's if nothing gets broken.'

'Yes indeed,' agreed Miss Royce, slightly pleased with herself.

'Your pal's very silent,' observed Mrs Wagtail with insensitive accuracy. 'What's the matter, dearie, cat got your tongue?' She chortled at Dagmar's confused expression, and Cecilia Royce joined in, venting some of her disappointment in the conspiratorial joke between the English women.

'Yes, you are quiet, Dagmar, perhaps I've worn you out with the little tour of the town.'

176

'You've been showing her the sights then?' asked Mrs Wagtail. She laughed. 'You should bring her round to number seven, she'd see one of the sights of Slackhall then. Mind you, I can't say Jack would be the prettiest sight she'd see.' She chortled, and dug Cecilia Royce in the ribs. The headmistress gasped, thinking enough is enough.

'Why would a cat have my tongue?' asked Dagmar suddenly.

'Why bless you, dearie,' cried Mrs Wagtail, 'if that doesn't take the cake. Hark to her,' she said to Miss Royce who only just escaped another poke in the ribs. 'It's just a saying. Don't you have sayings where you come from?'

'Of course,' said Dagmar, moving out slightly from the shadow of the headmistress. 'We have many sayings in Germany.'

'Germany,' breathed Mrs Wagtail. 'Well I never, I thought you were Irish, dear. Germany, that's a long way, fancy coming all that way, and now you're standing in the street talking to Mrs Wagtail. Makes you think, doesn't it? The modern world sometimes takes your breath away. I never met anybody from such far-off places before.' She wiped her hands down the side of her coat and proffered one to Dagmar. 'Pleased to make your acquaintance all the same.'

Aghast at the thought of the germs it would contain, Dagmar sought to remove her hand from the vicinity. With a darting movement, Mrs Wagtail grasped the escaping quarry and pumped it up and down, her sly eyes gleaming in the dark street.

'Seems like there's a right old carry-on back at home, isn't there luvvy?' She still held on to Dagmar's hand and pressed it as though in understanding.

'I don't think that much is happening,' said Dagmar tightly, tugging her hand. 'The papers do not always report things the way they are, people can be misled so easily.' Giving a final tug she freed her hand from the grimy embrace and proceeded to wipe it back and forth. Mrs Wagtail smiled at the discomfort.

'Nice material, that,' she commented.

'Oh,' said Miss Royce, 'I think the English press can be

177

trusted, especially the London *Times*, they are known to be very impartial.'

'Well I don't know,' said Mrs Wagtail, warming to the philosophy of international relations.

'Oh no, I do assure you, the press are independent,' replied Miss Royce.

'No, I wasn't referring to the papers, dearie, I don't read that much myself. Now I like listening to the radio, especially if they have a thriller on. I'm very partial to a good thriller, nothing better than a murder mystery to take your mind off things. Do you like thrillers?' she asked Miss Royce.

'I'm afraid not,' she replied through tight lips, thinking it was probably about time they made a move.

'You don't know what you're missing,' persisted Mrs Wagtail with authority. 'You ought to have a listen, they'd probably be right up your street. They keep me on the edge of my seat, good job I've got a strong heart, don't half make you jump sometimes. Still, I've always got a little glass of stout handy, if you take my meaning, just to calm the nerves, mind. I don't hold with drinking just for the sake of it, just an occasional drop now and then. That never harmed anyone, did it?'

'I suppose not,' replied Miss Royce. 'Well, shall we be off then?' she addressed Dagmar.

Dagmar followed her through the hallway, cluttered with haphazard piles of books. The place had a musty smell, and it felt as though the summer had truly gone.

'Please sit down,' said Cecilia, briskly removing a paper from the proffered chair. 'I'll soon have it warmed up in here.'

Dagmar opened the paper, the headlines were about the Sudetenland. She scanned the newsprint; it was in favour of ceding to the Reich. She smiled to think of the foreign journalists sagely deciding Germany should have back what was already theirs. All this mass communication would make no difference. '*Führer befiehl wir folgen!*' this is what had not been realised, '*Führer befiehl wir folgen,*' she murmured.

'I won't be a jiffy,' exclaimed Miss Royce. 'Do make yourself at home.' She smiled nervously and left the room.

178

Dagmar glanced at the dusty spines of the books, and then noticed some yellowing newsprint in a box. She leafed through the cuttings. They didn't tell her anything either, except that a few seemed to deal with accidents of one type or another, mainly individuals struck by lightning, but there was equally a number of recipes cut out from magazines. The ones for cakes made her mouth water, she had a sweet tooth.

'Here we are,' cried Cecilia Royce, 'I hope you are as famished as I am.'

'This seems very English,' said Dagmar laughing and, settling herself into the chintz cushions, she watched as Cecilia Royce slotted one of the crumpets on to a long brass fork and began to toast it in front of the serried rows of small red flames. 'May I wash my hands?' she asked. 'I seem to have got ink on them from the paper.'

'Why of course,' said Cecilia.

As Dagmar scrubbed away at her hands in the bathroom, Cecilia spread the butter on the crumpet, watching it melt and spread on the surface, the oozing greasy yellow slowly sinking into the puckered crumpet. The frenzied rubbing made Dagmar think she was truly cleaning her hands. She rinsed them under the gently steaming hot water, and remembering Mrs Wagtail had shaken her hand, took up the scrubbing brush once more, passing it backwards and forwards over her raw-looking flesh, taking special care with the fingernails, making sure nothing was under the rim. That was the sort of place germs could attach themselves.

The headmistress watched more butter melt into her own crumpet and, with relish, lifted it to her mouth. Her eyes met those of Dagmar as she bit down, the little rivulets dribbling down her chin. She laughed like a naughty schoolgirl and, extending her tongue, licked round her greasy chops. Dagmar proceeded to copy her, laughing as well. The pile of crumpets gradually shrank as the two women gobbled down the succulent textured dough, the only sounds being the occasional gulp, or smacking of lips, a noise which would normally have made Cecilia Royce frown, as would licking her fingers. These she did sitting in front of the glowing red gas-fire, while leaning back and pushing off her shoes, so she could wriggle her toes. As the last morsel of buttery crumpet

179

slid down her well-greased throat, she sighed with contentment.

Dagmar sank back into the cosy chair, forgetting about
Ethel Coffin. She wondered whether Cecilia had a phono-
graph. She would ask her. She would love to sit in front of the
fire and listen to stirring music. As she looked at the serried
ranks of flames, she thought of the fires which forged the
world, of the dwarf smithies where Siegfried's sword was
forged, and she fingered the party button pinned under her
cardigan.

The hooked cross was smooth and cold to the touch. It was
the fire-whisk and twirled the primal substance at the creation
of the universe. Now, as she stared at the fire, she imagined a
huge, flaming swastika, crackling with fire like a Catherine-
wheel whirling round and round. It would whisk up the
undesirables, the condemned, the fools who opposed them.
They would twist and turn in the bright flames, such a fierce
fire would not even leave ashes. She wanted to hear *Götterdämmerung*.

16

William tapped his foot impatiently in the large puddle.

'I'll not clean those shoes,' warned Nanny Bradshaw.

She knocked with gusto on the closed door.

'Ruin good leather,' she murmured.

'There's nobody home,' he remarked.

'She could be at the back,' observed Nanny, knocking once more.

'Perhaps she looked into the crystal ball and saw you were coming.' He laughed.

'Mrs Makin doesn't take kindly to those that laugh at what they can't understand.'

'Well, she's not in.'

Nanny thrust her large face close to the window, screwing up her eyes to penetrate the gloomy interior. She sighed.

'Someone might see you,' warned William, 'being nosey.' He reached out and gave a half-hearted knock.

'She might have gone back to the holy land,' came Nanny's muffled voice, her broad lips pressed flat against the window.

'Let's go,' said William, who was quite pleased that the fortune-teller wasn't home.

As he stepped over the puddle to pull Nanny away from the window, the letter-box on the door clanged open, causing them both to jump.

'What's your game?' came a distorted voice from the black slit.

'Mrs Makin,' gasped Nanny, straightening her hat, 'I've got messages to impart.'

'Peeping and prying through folk's windows,' continued the bodiless voice.

'I told you,' whispered William.

'I need a consultation,' continued Nanny, addressing herself to the open letter-box. She had contrived to push

William out of the way so that she commanded the view, and gave a knowing smile to the narrow opening.

'I've brought William along,' she said. 'He lost his parents,' she proclaimed, 'they're on the other side.'

'Nanny,' groaned William.

'Mind your manners,' hissed Nanny.

'You wouldn't believe what's going on,' she said to the letter-box, 'it takes my breath away just to think about it.'

'Piss off,' warned the voice.

'Mrs Makin!' gasped Nanny.

'Piss off out of it, you big fat cow.'

Nanny stepped back, clutching her chest, pushing William into the puddle.

'It's me,' she cried. 'I know you said not to meddle, but the spirits have come. I need your help, Mrs Makin.'

'Packed her bags and gone,' said the voice.

'Noooo,' wailed Nanny, 'it can't be true.'

'Who are you calling a liar?' came the thrusting voice. 'I could have the police on you, pushing your fat face up to my clean windows.'

'This is the house of Mrs Makin,' declared Nanny. 'I wish to speak to her.'

'Nobody of that name here.'

'Who are you?' beseeched Nanny.

'I'm Mrs Wagtail,' came the voice, 'and you can get your dirty feet off my doorstep.'

The letter-box clanged shut, and Nanny stared forlornly at the grimy door.

'Come on,' said William, 'we don't want more trouble.'

'Who'll help me now?' cried Nanny. 'Gone without a forwarding address.'

He took hold of Nanny and led her over the slippery cobbles. William couldn't help thinking he'd heard the grating voice before somewhere.

'Mrs Wagtail,' he murmured, and glanced back down the street.

At the Coffins', Sister Ursula had just said grace, not noticing that while she thanked God, Ethel was helping herself to a slice of bread. Fanny Coffin had managed to purchase the selection of fruit that her daughter had suddenly expressed a preference for.

Sister Ursula did not think any good would come of giving in to a child's whims. She talked of the periods when she had to fast for at least three days and three nights, directing her comments to Ethel, whose eyes were still focused on the sweet. Fanny Coffin gave little gasps of amazement and wonder at the devotion of her sister-in-law, saying what a good example she was to her little Ethel.

Cecilia Royce was imagining the trips she would like to make with Dagmar to the Midland Hotel in Manchester, where they could sit after walking round the art gallery.

'Lovely,' said Dagmar, and for a second, Miss Royce thought she was referring to her daydream, but as she watched Dagmar lick her sticky fingers, leaving the napkin lying useless on her lap, she knew she meant the cake.

'You are lost in teaching,' said Dagmar. 'Have you never wished to do something else, be something else?'

She stared intently at the headmistress as though willing Cecilia Royce to give some specific answer which would turn out to be the correct one. The smile wavered on the lips of the headmistress as she pondered whether to divulge her secret. Sitting in front of the warm fire, the dark, rainy night hidden behind the closed curtains and her new friend waiting in rapt silence, it seemed the hour for such a confidence to be given.

Her lips struggled to form the words, and yielding to the impulse, she pulled herself from the chair and striding over to the bookshelves, extracted a thick bundle of loose paper bound by a black ribbon. She made as if to hand the precious cargo over to Dagmar, and then, before the German could reach out and take the proffered pile, Miss Royce drew them back to her protective embrace.

'It's my book,' she said, and moved to sit down once more in front of the fire. 'I've never shown it to anyone before, or even told anyone I was writing it.'

She had hoped to be able to tell the life-saving instructor of her secret work, that it would be his grey eyes which would wander with freedom through the paragraphs and chapters of

183

her attempt to summon up the past. She carefully untied the black ribbon.

'May I see?' asked Dagmar.

The inevitable request caused Miss Royce almost to hold her breath. Although she had rehearsed this scene many times in her mind's eye, just as the virgin contemplates ravishment, it was not quite as had been imagined. With great caution she carefully handed over the pile of papers, and it seemed odd to see a head other than that of the instructor bend over her work. She watched as the heavy hands of Dagmar flicked through the pages, and somehow her heart felt resigned to this reality, and the flickering hope that she would get the kind of praise she craved, puttered out like a smouldering candle. By the look in Dagmar's eyes, she knew she was not reading any of it, and she almost regretted letting her see it. The work would mean nothing to her, and she had been a fool to think it would. Miss Royce let her head fall back against the chair.

'What is it about?' asked Dagmar at last, letting the pages fall silently back into place, a few of the corners crumpled where her thumb had bent them back. Without looking down, Cecilia Royce let the question become consumed by silence.

'It's a biography of a man,' she replied. 'He was born round here, but died elsewhere.'

'A soldier, then?' said Dagmar forcefully. 'Did he have a splendid death in a war?'

'He was a judge,' said Miss Royce, scarcely able to keep her voice sounding reasonable.

She just wanted to pick the thing off Dagmar's knee and put it once more on the shelf, to have done with the thing. Dagmar could not see what would be so interesting about a judge. She saw them as scriveners, carrying on the rule of the old order, unable to halt the new. She thought about her pilgrimage to Landsberg prison. She had left her parent's home, and like Gurda travelled across country, passing through towns to the prison in which her Führer wrote his thoughts, and although she was never allowed through, the badge she wore next to her heart had been sent when the tale of the young girl's journey reached the ears of the prisoner. She looked down for the name of the judge.

'Did this John Bradshaw send anyone to prison for their beliefs?'

'He was Lord President of the court which sentenced King Charles Stuart to death, and his was the hand which signed the death warrant.' She paused as she began to warm to her obsession. 'The warrant showed a strong steady hand.'

'He was a hero?' asked Dagmar gravely.

'A hero,' repeated Miss Royce. Her voice echoed with a dreamy resonance. 'A hero to some, and a traitor to others.' She thought of the parish registry which recorded the baptism of the innocent child, and the stark, angry message which had been scratched over it, the single word, 'TRAITOR'.

'It is a tragedy you have written, then?'

'Not a classical tragedy, although perhaps it has the inevitable tragic ending. Yes, I think you can say he had a tragic end, although I feel he wasn't a man for emotions, he had lofty values. Cromwell called him "Honest John Bradshaw" even while they were estranged. A man of values, even if some thought him proud.'

'What was his tragic end?' asked Dagmar, becoming involved, despite herself, in the life of this judge.

'There were no daggers in the back, nothing like that. I suppose the tragedy is that he died while the state crumbled about him and the future he might have supposed, where his tomb in Westminster Abbey would be hallowed for his role in forming the Republic of England, never came about. He was buried with the pomp and dignity he would have liked, but after the restoration of the monarchy, old debts were settled. They took his body, or what was left of it, and hung it from gallows till sundown.' She gave a trembling sigh.

'He was a hero,' concluded Dagmar with passion, 'and I would very much like to read these words that follow his life. He is a symbol to us all. Are there monuments to this man?'

'No,' said Miss Royce, slightly startled by Dagmar's reaction. 'Are you interested in art?' she asked.

'Art is important,' said Dagmar carefully, as though reading from a script with which she didn't fully agree. 'It should inspire people, but that is not always the case.'

185

'Ah,' said Miss Royce, as though she understood everything. 'Tell me, did you see any of the great exhibitions in Germany? There are many galleries in Berlin, or so we are led to believe.'

'I'm afraid I didn't frequent those types of places,' said Dagmar seriously. 'And I lived most of my time in Munich, not Berlin, although I was there for a couple of years before I came to England. It needed cleaning up.' She gave Miss Royce a significant look.

'Well,' said Cecilia Royce, balancing her cup on the arm of the chair, 'I suppose from what you say, it wouldn't be quite correct for an unaccompanied lady to enter those sorts of places. I had heard,' she said, in the hope that she didn't appear too unworldly, 'that Berlin is . . . decadent.'

'Yes,' said Dagmar, 'these sorts of places do not reflect German culture, but it is all being cleaned up, things are changing.' She set her lips in a determined manner. 'There are many of these foreign decadents. We had an exhibition of their degenerate art last year, just to show people that these are the daubs of the mad, they are disturbed.' She leant forward. 'They paint the skies green and the fields blue!' Flinging herself back into the chair, she shook her head.

'You saw them, did you?' asked Miss Royce, suitably aghast.

'Thankfully I did not. They think of themselves as intellectuals,' she laughed. 'The international bankers, the moneylenders, they buy these paintings and so pay for all these pamphlets. They think of themselves as artists, and then spend all of their time writing pamphlets and so-called manifestos. They are all communists.'

'Oh!' said Miss Royce, slightly stunned by this response. She liked to think that she was a modern woman, and although she could not understand all the modern art, the Cubism and the Surrealists, she pretended she could, and would normally have been slightly disdainful of anybody who criticised the current fashion. Somehow Dagmar's raw views overwhelmed her. She wondered whether she should confess that she had never really cared for Picasso, even though she had only seen his paintings reproduced in magazines.

'Berlin has been corrupted by Bolshevism, but it is all being cured.' She leant back once more in her chair.

'I don't think we realise that all this is going on, but I can assure you the gallery in Manchester is quite respectable. It's a municipal building.' Dagmar smiled at the innocence of the headmistress, pausing to take a sip of her sweet camomile tea. 'In Germany, we took things into our own hands. We made bonfires of their degenerate daubs and their useless words. They came in useful for something at least.' She extended her hands towards the gas-fire. 'You could warm your hands on the burning books,' she laughed.

Cecilia Royce gave a worried glance to her own manu-script, and thought that the Germans must not have any magazines to vent their literary criticism. She thought it would be rude to ask if Dagmar had burnt any books. With what Miss Royce could only describe as a smacking of the lips, Dagmar banged the cup back into the saucer, making it look as though she had just drained a tankard of ale. She hoped she wouldn't do that in the Midland Hotel. And then, to the headmistress's horror, her new friend started to croon a song:

> Reject what confuses you,
> Outlaw what seduces you.
> What did not spring from pure will,
> Into the flames with what threatens you.

She tried to smile, but somehow she had the feeling that the expression which was stuck on her face was one of shock. Dagmar seemed to be acting like a drunk. Dagmar grinned and seemed about to burst into another refrain. Miss Royce thought about her neighbours.

'Do you know,' cried Cecilia, 'you're like a breath of fresh air in this town. I confess you have made me feel like a new woman. Dagmar,' she began, 'do you remember that I mentioned that I was a member of the Women's Institute?'

'Ah yes,' recalled Dagmar.

'Well, I'm about to become president of the local branch,' said Miss Royce proudly, sitting a little bit more erect in her chair, and trying to grope around for one of her shoes which she had slipped off earlier.

'This Institute,' asked Dagmar, 'is it like the freemasons?'

'Oh goodness me, no, whatever gave you that idea? The Women's Institute is just where local womenfolk can get together and . . . well, organise things, or rather they didn't really do very much before I gave them a hand, just used to make jams, and do knitting, that sort of thing. Anyway, now it's far more interesting, we have little excursions. The last one was to York.'

'It sounds a very interesting organisation,' remarked Dagmar.

'Well, I like to think that we do our little bit. The point is, we also have guest speakers, and I just thought what a good idea it would be, that's if you're willing of course, if you'd come to speak to my women.' She looked expectantly at Dagmar. 'Do say yes,' she pleaded. 'You'll get to meet lots of the local women, and often the local paper reports on these sort of meetings, so you could get written about as well.'

Dagmar felt that providence had once more laid its hand upon her life. She was becalmed on the outside yet, within, deep currents whirled around. She wasn't thinking of whether to accept or not, providence had decided for her.

'The fee is quite reasonable,' badgered Miss Royce, thinking that she still needed to cajole Dagmar into the decision, 'and you also get a free dinner.'

'These things are not important,' said Dagmar.

'Oh,' said a rather crestfallen Cecilia Royce as she saw her presidency starting with something more mundane like a talk on lepidoptery.

'I accept,' Dagmar cried. 'I shall talk to the womenfolk of Slackhall. We shall have a rally.'

'Well,' said Miss Royce, very relieved that Dagmar had accepted. 'We shall do our best. I'm sure all of my ladies will be most interested. You will be my coup,' she declared.

'I hope they will enjoy it,' said Dagmar. 'I will have a lot I wish to tell them. It will be a joy to fulfil this function for you and the fatherland.'

'Ye-es,' said Miss Royce, tapping her front tooth with a manicured nail as she thought whether they should have tickets printed and posters as well. She could arrange this so not only the Women's Institute's name was made, but her own as well. She would invite all the local dignitaries. After all, Germany never seemed out of the news these days. That should stir up a bit of interest. She could give the introduction, perhaps a little historical background on Germany.

'Well, that's settled then,' she beamed. 'I'll start the ball rolling. Just hold on while I get my diary, then I can give you a rough idea when we can get the hall for the meeting.'

She lurched from her seat, her mind still racing with what she was sure would turn out to be the cultural event of the year in Slackhall. Even her production of *Salomé* at the school paled into insignificance, especially as Roe had stuck his pious nose into the morality of the play.

'It looks as though it will have to be either the twenty-ninth or thirtieth of September, that's if we want to keep it to this month.'

'I wish to talk to the people,' declared Dagmar. 'There are others that will help.'

'That would be nice,' said Miss Royce, 'the more the merrier.'

'Do they have uniforms?' probed Dagmar.

'Who?'

'Your women.'

'Ah no, not unless you count tweeds and twin-sets.'

'We can have flags,' declared Dagmar, 'and we will wear black.'

'Oh yes,' exclaimed Miss Royce, 'it will be thrilling.'

'We will awaken Slackhall,' cried Dagmar, her eyes flashing with little sparks, her convictions bolstered and sutained by the invisible hand of providence.

'Thrilling.'

17

Dagmar moved swiftly through the darkness. As she passed the church her feet instinctively took her to the pavement furthest from the graveyard. Lowering her head so all she could see was the wet shining pavement, she walked oblivious of the muddy water which splashed her stockings and lay in a cold patch at the bottom of her shoes; her toes squelched with every step.

The fears of the dreams and mysteries of Bavarian folklore, the fireside tales of ogres and witches became transposed to the sombre panorama through which she trudged. She had a childlike sense of impending doom, and her senses were tingling, the crunching gravel sent her nerves dancing. With her clenched hand, she formed a gesture to ward away evil, to control her fears. The mists of superstition clouded her blood; she was steeped in the mythic values of her village.

She could see the dark outline of the Booths' house rising up above her. Following the ivy-topped wall, she groped for the door which was set into the crumbling bricks, and went into the garden. The large dome of the dark sky frostily glittered with stars, she was earthbound, trudging miserably through the clinging stalks which grew out of the quagmire into which her shoes sank. The whole place carried with it the odour of decomposition.

As Dagmar's feet became coated with the dark loam of England, it seemed that by contrast her feelings and thoughts were pure German. Her steady stride carried her towards the house, but her mind raced ahead, full of grand designs for the town of Slackhall. In the dark garden she felt a strange sense of desire; as she stalked around the sleeping house, her eyes lit up from within. She thought of John William asleep inside, his lean body trapped within the tangled sheets, and she was swept towards his room by the lustful urge to waken him.

190

She warily made her way through the quiet corridors of the house, and softly, far off, she heard the creak of footsteps. For a minute she listened, and then she realised the sound had come from the room of Elizabeth Booth.

At the foot of the stairs she took a deep breath; she thought she could hear the soft murmurings of prayer. A heavy claustrophobia haunted her slow ascent, her hands sliding along the walls, invisible in the throbbing darkness. She stumbled into the chamber and welcomed the space. Her eyes moved to the band of light which showed clearly round the door. She listened. The sound was not one of inconsolable grief, it had a wheedling intensity. The voice was known to her.

'I was thinking they might have some news for us,' said Nanny Bradshaw. In spite of herself, Dagmar felt a dreadful fascination, and knew that she had stumbled across some secret.

Instinctively she lowered her eye to the keyhole. She could just about see the stooping form of Nanny, who was fiddling with the hand of Mrs Booth, the bulky body obscured much of what was happening.

'It seems to be taking them a while to come through,' said Nanny Bradshaw, and then as though regretting her temerity, she said, 'We shouldn't be impatient, it's early days yet. They've got a long journey ahead of them.' She gave a respectful look to the ceiling. Her body still filled the keyhole, and Dagmar cursed her for being in the way.

The phosphorous moon shone unwaveringly, and beneath its enchanting light a single figure flitted past the stone satyr in the garden. She nodded at it, and then grinned back towards the beacon of Mrs Booth's lighted room, and continued towards the dark wood.

Dagmar's pupils suddenly contracted as Nanny Bradshaw moved. The revelation came. She knew this was no game of snakes and ladders they were playing. Nanny Bradshaw was staring at the board, a sickly smile plastered over her face.

'You'd think Pewter would be only too pleased to pin his

murder on that skinny chicken,' said Nanny. 'Still, the spirits will help us. We'll get rid of that German.'

The words pierced Dagmar like a dart. Her avid eye scanned Nanny Bradshaw, probing the unsuspecting form like a twisting knife. She had discovered a disgusting ritual, some séance. The woman was deranged. The clandestine plot was uncovered and she would be cleverer still. She had always intended to rid the house of the aberration, but had not expected the means to come so readily. Providence was certainly aiding her cause.

She would ensure that John William would make an impromptu visit. She had always feared he would be too weak to take any action on his own, but even he could not condone the use to which the creature was putting his own mother, pawing her with her disgusting hands.

An enigmatic silence had fallen within the bedroom, and the German decided she had seen all she needed to.

'*Judendreck, Judendreck,*' she panted under her breath, as she descended the stairs.

Far away over the fields another figure was contemplating the night. Like ancient mirrors, the eyes of the scuttling figure reflected older values. She spat contemptuously at the times. She stepped into the wood. Deep as a vault the black oaks closed in upon her. The pebble rested smoothly in her crinkled palm and with casual ease she tossed it into the sky. It fell into the tiny stream, the rhythmic lapping which followed the sudden splash soon faded into the darkness.

'So mote it be,' she said.

Mrs Booth's hand made a shuddering progress between the letters. Nanny Bradshaw swiftly licked her pencil and with excited movements wrote down the sequence. She gazed at the word which emerged, and then with cunning looked swiftly around the room. She went over to the door and opened it, sending her shadow over the spot Dagmar had occupied. Seemingly satisfied, she shut it, and went to the silent figure on the bed. She unstrapped the planchette from the wrinkled hand, patting it absently. She lowered her heavy body on to the creaking chair, and looked at the message the spirits had sent. The heavy letters of her own hand stared back; the single word was a conundrum. Nanny decided that the spirits didn't waste their breath. The terse message caused her to shiver, it didn't seem to answer her specific question about where Pewter's body had been dumped. Perhaps they'd got their lines crossed; sometimes the operator did that. Perhaps this wasn't meant for her, but a person unknown. She sighed, and looked down again at the piece of paper which contained the single word, 'Betrayal'.

18

Sister Ursula wafted serenely into the sitting-room. The little changes she had suggested to the layout of the room had all been carried out. Sister Ursula felt that the room breathed new life, as if like St Zenobius she could revive the inanimate by her touch. She sat down regally, and thanked God for another day. She could hear Fanny bustling away in the kitchen as she waited patiently for the arrival of her morning cup of coffee. At the convent, the mother superior would be waiting for her coffee as well.

As Fanny pushed open the door, Sister Ursula was struck with how her sister-in-law always managed to look flustered or harassed. The stray wisps of hair trailed over her thin forehead and Sister Ursula restrained the impulse to brush them back.

'Ah, coffee,' she said, straining to sound pleased. She watched as Fanny poured out the cup, put one spoonful of sugar in, and stirred it without banging the sides as she had been wont to do a week earlier.

'It is very restful sitting here,' she remarked in a conversational voice. 'I've created a little Bethany.'

Sister Ursula smiled through the halo of light at her squinting sister-in-law, thinking that the thin blue-white flesh on Fanny's pinched face reminded her of sterilised milk. It was hard to remember you were a missionary when looking on a countenance like that.

'I hope it's to your satisfaction,' said Fanny meekly.

'You should have sent Ethel with it,' declared Ursula. 'I am already devising the means to humble that girl.'

'I don't think she means to be rude,' sniffed Fanny, 'it's just her way.'

'Her way!' exclaimed Ursula in a stern voice. 'A child of that age should not have a . . . way. You have allowed her to become wilful. She will learn that there is only the will of God, her saviour.'

'Yes,' said Fanny.

'Another thing,' she cried, 'that child of yours is now obsessed with that foreign woman. I heard her with my own ears saying she wished for blonde hair. It would be painting her face next. I tell you, Fanny, you sent for me in time, the child was heading for purgatory.' She crossed herself, and watched Fanny do the same. 'I don't know what possessed you to send for her,' continued Ursula, 'a foreign protestant of the worst kind. I looked into her eyes, and do you know, I knew there was no love for God.'

Fanny shook her head.

With bowed head, Fanny backed out of the room, not wishing Ursula to see the thin tears which were falling for her daughter.

'Humiliation,' muttered Ursula to herself, shifting slightly in the seat, as a heavy iron crucifix that dangled between her legs dug into her flesh.

When she first wore the hidden cross, the sharp edges cut into her thighs as she walked along, the pain suffusing her with religious devotion. In her obsession with stigmata her skin was permanently bruised, and the veined thigh carried the image of the cross. The warm sun lapping her gently made her feel sleepy, and closing her eyes as though at prayer she drifted off to sleep.

Sister Ursula awoke with a jump. She had a falling sensation, and her fingers had clutched the dust-free arm-rests as she had fallen like Lucifer through a blue sky; the face of Ethel floated among clouds like a photograph, and her sulphurous breath enveloped the nun.

The sun had moved its position and she felt a slight chill as though a cold breeze had blown on to her. The door was open, no wonder it was cold.

The hall was empty. A rattling noise disturbed the calm of the hallway. It came from the kitchen, and with every step Sister Ursula took, the metallic clattering became more distinct and fierce. Her hand paused a moment on the door-handle before she opened it with a determined shove.

Immediately she was engulfed in a billowing cloud of hot

steam. She gasped and choked as she tumbled into the swirling vapour. The kitchen was like some Turkish bath, and as the steam condensed on her flesh and slid down like sweat, Sister Ursula made for the Aga range upon which a conglomerate of pans boiled away. She now recognised the sound; an assortment of ill-fitting lids shook as though undergoing a religious ecstasy, jets of white steam escaping in time to the babbling of metal. As though bringing divine intervention, the nun reached out and grasped the handle of the nearest pan, and with a yelp dropped the scalding metal.

With a throbbing hand Sister Ursula raced over to the tap, and thrust it under the cold water. Now armed with a pair of oven gloves, Sister Ursula proceeded to remove the pans, tossing the contents into a heavy pot sink. One had boiled dry and the smell of burned vegetables hung in the air along with the new silence as the last pan was removed and fell quiet.

The nun sank into a sturdy wooden chair. As the air gradually cleared, the throbbing of her hand increased. She wiped the sweat and condensation from her brow and felt she knew what it must have been like for St Cecilia as she was stifled in the steam of her own bathroom. She directed a silent prayer to the martyred saint, and then blew her nose.

She removed the oven gloves. The perfect skin of her right palm had not blistered, but the red patch looked unnervingly like the stain of blood.

A mystical excitement fluttered up in her body like a dove, and she fell down on her knees, her lips moving fervently in contemplation of the suffering of Christ. She pressed her burning right palm against the cool skin of its partner. As her praying hands swayed gently, the enormity of the occasion overwhelming her, she prostrated herself on the stone flags of the kitchen floor, the hard stone piercing her beneath the material of her habit as surely as the spear in the side of Christ.

She swooned in the dream of the Passion and her right hand ached. As the prostrate nun poured out her veneration in torrid prayers, the emotional extravagance which would have been stifled in the convent was given free rein. The hurt in her palm gave her proof of her sacred purpose.

*

196

Just as the recently canonised St Bernadette of Lourdes was the only one to experience the visions, perhaps she would be the only one to understand and see the revelation of her hand. An image glowed behind her closed eyes; the image of the burning sacred heart, the sacred heart which floated in many religious paintings, the heart on fire entwined and bleeding from a band of thorns, this she saw beneath her own ribcage firing her faith.

[19]

William stared out of the window. Although his grey eyes reflected the leaden skies, in his mind he recalled strange, isolated fragments of his past, the gentle smile of his grandmother, her hand holding his. He could almost feel the lingering warmth.

Monotony pervaded the house. Doors would open and close. He had failed to notice the secret comings and goings of serious-faced young men in funereal black. William had avoided the tower in which his grandmother lay. By denying himself the lingering vigil, he hoped to ease the intricate pain of death.

His brooding body stretched itself. Swinging round into the room, William considered for a moment the impulse which had brought him to Pewter's old room. Somehow the tutor belonged to a different life that would only recede when his grandmother who lay on the threshold of death, breathed her last.

'Everybody has to die sometime.' Those were the very words Dagmar had used.

There was a certain impatience in his gait, as though he wished not only to arrive swiftly at his destination, but more, to hasten the inevitable events of the quiet house. It was as if he suddenly became aware of the passing minutes, and the short time he had left before departing to school. The pale autumn light seemed to heighten the melancholic feeling of nostalgia he suddenly felt for the place.

He paused a moment outside a door, and with a self-conscious gesture, patted down his hair, straightened his tie and knocked.

'Come in,' called Dagmar, and checking his tie again, William opened the door. Inside, Dagmar was perched on the bed in a dressing-gown. She had a pad on her knee and seemed engrossed in writing. She didn't look up. As William stood there, he felt slightly embarrassed, trying not to stare.

'No kiss then?' she said. William's cheeks burnt.

'Oh William,' she exclaimed, 'how silly of me!' William noticed the confusion which momentarily spread itself across her face. 'I didn't realise it was you.'

She pulled the dressing-gown together, covering part of her leg that had been exposed. William stood silent and awkward. She smiled at him, but it was clear she had expected someone else.

'Now,' she said, 'what can I do for you?' She closed the pad on her knee.

'Oh, it's nothing,' murmured William in a low voice, just wishing to leave. He turned quickly for the door, but Dagmar's hand clutched him.

'William, William,' the intensity of her voice called him back more than the restraining arm. He turned his grey eyes to look at her. 'What is it?' she continued. 'Tell me, please.' Coming under her spell once more, William wavered momentarily between shouting at her to leave him alone and letting himself sink into the comfort she offered.

'William,' she crooned, sensing that he was close to tears, 'you can tell me.' Hanging on the end of her arm, William collapsed into his sorrow. He stood as the grief racked his body, almost unaware that she had pulled him towards her and was rocking him gently. 'That's better,' she breathed. Sunk in grief, William didn't see the door open and his uncle in the entrance, or the look Dagmar gave him, indicating that he should disappear and leave her to deal with the boy.

'I'm sorry,' William stammered, his voice muffled by the thick material of the dressing-gown.

'Sorry,' exclaimed Dagmar, rubbing the back of his head. 'Don't be silly. What am I here for if I can't help you? I should apologise to you. Everybody has been so involved in sorting out the arrangements for this and that. We forgot that there were others who were being very brave, but might not be able to talk to anyone. No, I am the sorry one.'

She held William's head away from the tear-stained dressing-gown, and smiled into his bloodshot eyes. 'Are we not blood brothers?' she asked, giving him an encouraging smile as he nodded his dumb head up and down. Leading him with the dexterity of a puppet master, Dagmar sat William on the bed and left him for a forlorn moment until she returned with a large white handkerchief, ordering him to blow his nose.

'That's better,' she beamed. William gave Dagmar a weak smile, and then sank his head on to his chest and looked intently at the floor and his gently swinging legs.

'I think what we need,' said Dagmar with some authority, 'is a breath of fresh air.' She paused to look at the unresponsive William. 'What do you think?'

'If you like,' he mumbled.

'Well, that's settled then,' and stepping forward, she ruffled his hair affectionately. 'Still, I can't go out dressed like this.' She laughed. 'You must look the other way like a proper gentleman, while I change.' She tapped him playfully. 'And no peeking,' she commanded.

William continued to stare at the floor and his feet, but with his gently burning ears he could hear Dagmar move around the room. The wardrobe creaked open, and the hangers jostled against each other. Trapped and betrayed by his latent childhood, William felt marooned. High and dry, he sat like an obedient child, while his manhood became unwillingly stirred by the sounds the woman was making. With his head locked into one position, he clung on to the slightest noise. The silence resonated in his brain, and the shuddering memory of Pewter's slides added to the tumult in his mind. The smooth liquid sound of material rustled through the room, whether it was the heavy dressing-gown falling to the floor or the muffled sliding as Dagmar clothed her body, the sibilance resonated and rippled, a serenade which seemed to be arranged and scored to lead the ingenu astray. William, for the first time, heard the secret cadence of women.

'You can look now.' The sudden explosion of her voice seemed dissonant. Dagmar stood in front of a small mirror, her lank hair being brushed vigorously. She turned and gave William another smile.

'Ready,' she said.

The sun was invisible in the flat sky, and it was possible to smell a distant burning as though a farmer were firing the moors. Their feet pressed the newly-fallen leaves into the ground, and as they neared the trees it was possible to see that autumn was coming early, yet the changing shades did not tinge the landscape with richness. It had faded to tarnished gilt and the occasional patch of damp rust, dotted among the dying green.

As they laboured towards the woods, Dagmar appeared unaware of the intense grey eyes which followed the movement of her body under the heavy coat. The aimless route they had taken had unwittingly carried them to the place where they first met, but then the sun had been shining and the grass growing green. Dagmar turned her pallid face towards William, remembering how she had caught him in her arms as he stumbled from these woods. She never had found out why he had been so agitated. Even now he sent the occasional worried glance into the tangle of trees. He seemed afraid, that much was evident from his strained pale face. Thrusting her hands deep into her pockets, she gave him a swift, raw smile.

'Come on then,' she urged, 'nothing ventured, nothing gained. Isn't this what they say?' and, William following uncomfortably after her, Dagmar entered the wood, stepping over the broken branches which seemed to block the path, obscuring its twisting course.

'This is no good,' she muttered, and without a glance in William's direction, she made off on a path of her own making.

'Come on, William,' she called, 'it's much easier this way. There are less things to clamber over.' With the grim determination of Captain Oates, William set off after her, taking the road which offered the least resistance. The untended wood had grown wild to its own design, the younger trees crowding around in spindly profusion.

'A good place for hide and seek,' she said. 'You must have played here a lot.'

'Sometimes.'

'Oh don't be such a spoil-sport, do cheer up a bit William,' she said with some exasperation. 'I don't like to see you like this. Is there something in the wood that you don't like?' Her voice assumed the smoothest tones as she asked the question.

'No,' he said, but his eyes betrayed him as he glanced in the direction of the silent glade in which Mrs Grime lived, and perhaps still did.

'This way,' she said, heading off in the direction of his glance, 'there seems to be a clearing up ahead.'

Dagmar could see that the path she had abandoned also entered the grass, and as her eyes wandered over its destination, they passed over the incongruity as though it had somehow managed to become a part of the place. Yet the image lingered on her retina, and with a startled frown, she returned her eyes to the object William had been staring at fixedly.

'A wardrobe,' she exclaimed, her voice was more surprised than Stanley meeting Livingstone.

She walked over towards it, treading on the scattered stones which had once formed a little path. One of the doors hung open, and cautiously, as though expecting either an unpleasant smell or some wild beast, she craned her neck into the opening. The interior seemed full of sodden rags. A tattered poster advertising some film had been tacked on to the wall, but now hung down lashed by wind and rain. There seemed to be other things hanging from the roof, bundles of leaves or twigs. A broken candle lay in a small pool of water, and as her eyes grew more accustomed, she could make out little bottles which must once have been stacked, but now lay in disarray. There was a partially woven basket. She pulled her head free.

'William, come and look at this.' She spoke in an excited voice. 'Somebody must have lived here,' she stated confidently. 'All their things are inside.'

She poked the outside with her finger, surprised that the varnished surface was still present and that her finger did not sink into rotten wood. She turned, expecting to find William to be behind her, but was surprised to see him standing exactly where they had first entered the place. As he had watched Dagmar make for the familiar landmark, he wasn't quite sure whether Great Granny Grime might not leap out and confront her, but as he saw the open door, he knew that she no longer made her dwelling-place here, and he knew why.

202

Seeing him standing there, Dagmar felt how out of place he truly was. She had never really noticed before. But the silent figure by the edge of the trees was as displaced as some mythical creature. She felt pity for someone who would never belong. Like the fabulous cockatrice, William stood apart, a plumed serpent to be spurned by the reptiles and the taloned birds. Then she thought she had the answer.

'Is this your secret hiding-place, William?' she asked, thinking the abandoned wardrobe a perfect place in which to construct an imaginary world. He shook his head, still unwilling to venture from the shadows of the sheltering trees. 'There are things inside,' she repeated. 'Somebody must have used it. It must have been the hiding-place for someone.'

She stopped for a moment, realising she had not even questioned why a wardrobe lay in the midst of a wood. Turning to look at it, her eyes widened at the mystery.

'Somebody did live in it,' said William. 'She found it, just as I did, and she lived here, or used to . . .'

'Used to?' repeated Dagmar, questioningly.

'You said it was deserted,' said William, sounding a little unsure, as though perhaps Dagmar had made a mistake, although he knew this could not be.

'Nobody could live here. Not,' she added, 'unless they used it as a hiding-place.'

'I don't think it was a hideout, not then anyway. She was all alone in the world.'

'Some people are always alone,' said Dagmar, finding it a strain to carry on the conversation with the broad patch of grass between them. 'It's not healthy to be alone. It is better to be part of the crowd.'

'She was my friend,' said William.

'Friend?' came Dagmar's incredulous voice. 'How can someone who lives here be your friend? Did you report this to your uncle?'

'No,' he said, 'she wasn't like that. We were friends, friends . . .' His voice trailed away as though he were doubting his own beliefs.

'Friends,' pounced Dagmar. 'What did she do, this friend of yours?'

'Made things. Oh I don't know,' he said in a frustrated voice, 'medicines and baskets, to sell to people.'

'A gypsy,' gasped Dagmar, 'a gypsy,' and at once she looked down at her hands. 'They carry disease,' she cried at William. 'Surely you knew this. They go from place to place carrying their filthy habits and diseases with them.'

'Well, I don't suppose she washed much, but I . . .'

'Water,' screamed Dagmar, interrupting William. 'Find me some water.' He remained rooted to the spot, wondering what on earth was the matter. 'Water,' she shouted, and grasped hold of William.

'All right, all right,' he stammered, 'there's a stream not far away,' and rubbing his arm, made off towards Gore Brook, Dagmar striding after him. The once dry bed now ran with tumbling water splashing over the green slimy stones.

With one leg still on the bank, she straddled part of the Gore Brook, and thrusting her hands into the frigid water, let it flow over her flesh. Intent on what she was doing, she ignored the presence of the puzzled boy who watched as the first woman he had loved scraped her hands in the gravel which lay at the bottom of the stream, as though she were trying to shed her skin like a snake. Still massaging the life back into her hands, Dagmar looked towards William, who, she realised, was standing a safe distance away.

'I thought I ought to wash my hands,' she explained, laughing slightly as though it were really a little eccentric foible, 'one never knows – '. She looked down at her hands, leaving the sentence unfinished and its strange meaning hanging between William and herself. 'You know,' she continued, 'your uncle thinks a lot of you.' The change of topic left William feeling more bewildered. 'We both think a lot of you,' she corrected herself, emphasising the plural. William suddenly realised whom she had been expecting. It was his uncle. Thinking that perhaps she had said enough, Dagmar got to her feet.

As they walked along the banks of Gore Brook in silence, William was beginning to feel the terrible solitude of one who loves,but is not loved back, the emotions trickling like sand into the desert.

'Have you heard of the Women's Institute?' asked Dagmar.

'Yes,' said William sullenly.

'Well guess what,' she said, continuing before he could attempt to guess. 'I have been asked to speak to them. What do you think about that?'

'When are you giving your talk?' He hoped it would be after he had left for school.

'No date has been fixed yet. I think they are going to ask many important people. Of course, you must be there: you would be my guest of honour.' She looked at him expectantly.

'I thought my uncle would be . . . your . . . guest of honour.'

'Haven't I just asked you?' she said forcefully.

'But school,' he began.

'School is not a prison; you can get out. We shall make arrangements; that's if you would like.'

'Oh yes,' he cried, forgiving her in an instant, his flushed face grinned at her. 'Are you going to liven those women up?' he joked to her.

'Oh, I should say so,' she exclaimed, her pale face remaining impassive. 'I shall offer them not emancipation,' she confided, 'but redemption.' Nothing softened in her face, as she looked into the laughing eyes of William.

'Where are we going?' she said, and linking her arm with his with delightful abandon which sent his blood racing once more, she pulled him on.

Dagmar now thought she had sorted things out with William. This was the little chat she had been planning for some time. She knew he would see things her way and gave his arm a little squeeze. William thought the pain was worth it.

'Where are we?' she asked. 'Is this still your land?'

'Yes,' he said, for the first time feeling proud of his family, 'and this is called Gore Brook, and we're heading for Red Beck.'

'Gore Brook, Red Beck,' murmured Dagmar, as though fascinated with local names. 'I've heard these names before.'

'Perhaps it was on a map,' offered William.

'No,' said Dagmar, clicking her teeth with annoyance. 'I

have it!' she exclaimed, remembering Miss Royce telling her the local legend. 'This is where the soldiers were betrayed.'

She stopped walking, looking around at the silent trees as though they would proffer a clue. The tug of battle made her walk further up towards the source of the cascading water.

'How do you know?' cried William, struggling to keep up with her long strides.

Ignoring his question, Dagmar paused again, looking down into the troubled waters named for the blood which once flowed into them.

'You can feel it,' she said, and extended her hands into the air. 'It's all around us, can't you feel it too?'

William stuck his head out further into the air, hoping to catch a wisp of whatever Dagmar was feeling. He thought he could feel a slight breeze. Lowering her arms slowly, she suddenly shot the right arm forward again, the jerky reflex reminding William of when Dr Baldwin tapped the nerve under his knee with a rubber hammer. Dagmar saluted the dead.

'Thank you, William,' she ejaculated, 'thank you.'

With his neck still craning out, he smiled with pleasure.

'You know,' he confided, 'I've seen the river run dry.'

'Have you?' said Dagmar, only remembering the tale of unjust betrayal and forgetting the curse. 'That must have been interesting.'

'We-ell yes, I suppose so,' said William, feeling disappointed, 'but I looked into it . . .' he nodded at her meaningfully, 'you know . . .'

'Well I don't think I'll get to see it dry, it never seems to have stopped raining here. I knew England was wet, but this . . .' she laughed, and having lost the moment, William did not boast to Dagmar about the curse, she would think he was showing off.

'No,' he agreed, 'I don't think it will run dry for a while.'

The sibilance of the water grew fainter as the two of them made their way out of the wood until they emerged into the hush of the tangled gardens, yet William would have sworn that deep within his ear, the resonance of the stream could still be heard, as if, like a secret shell, the boy could sense Gore Brook.

It was no mere chance which caused Nanny Bradshaw to be pressing her florid face against the cool glass of the window; she had just received a nasty shock. With eyes as round as a sugar-plum, she had listened as John William spoke to his mother, telling the unresponsive figure how his life now had meaning, and that he knew that if she could speak she would give her blessing. She closed her eyes against the hard glass, trying to push out the voice which had the consistency of molasses but the bitterness of wormwood to her ears. What the old lady must be thinking didn't bear thinking about. It was now up to her to expose the flibbertigibbet. She opened her eyes, now as hard as boiled sweets, and what she saw from the window set her teeth on edge.

'William's with . . . her . . .' she said out loud so the figure on the bed could hear. 'If he can spare the time to see the likes of her, he can come and see his grandmother, that's for sure.' Pulling herself away from the vantage point, she lumbered over towards the bed. 'Don't you fret yourself,' she said. 'I'll put him straight on a thing or two, or my name isn't Dorothy Bradshaw.' She reached down and gave Elizabeth Booth's hand a reassuring squeeze.

'I shall have to put my thinking-cap on,' she said. 'There will be a reckoning, that's for sure.' She sucked thoughtfully on her teeth.

'She's a cunning one, though,' she said, 'but we'll be more cunning still. We're not beat yet though, not by a long chalk. We have friends,' she said, 'friends in high places.' She looked up towards the dark ceiling, bestowing upon it one of her ghastly smiles. 'There's work to be done, if you get my meaning.' She winked into the blind eye, and as though it were her own private mirror, arranged her grey hair before leaving the room.

William was in the library when Nanny Bradshaw finally tracked him down.

'What do you want?' he asked, looking up from his book.

'What do I want?' she mimicked. 'What do I want? Well we've got very high and mighty recently.' She placed her hands on her hips and gave a mocking bow. 'Very high and

207

mighty. I wonder why that is?' she mused. 'Perhaps it's the company you've been keeping lately.'

'I'm busy,' he said brusquely.

'What, too busy to spare time for your old Nanny? Perhaps I'd better go back to your grandmother and tell her.' She turned with excruciating slowness.

'All right, all right,' he shouted. 'You don't frighten me any more,' he added defiantly. She gave him a smile that would have chilled the hard earth.

'You and I must have a little chat,' she said, and briskly pulled up a chair. 'Your grandmother knows I'm here,' she added, noticing how he flinched every time she used the word. That would be guilt, she thought. 'We talked it over,' she added, 'your grandmother and me.' He twitched again and looked puzzled. She almost laughed.

'She can't,' he began, his voice trembling.

'Oh,' she interrupted, raising her eyebrow, 'and what do you know about it? Have you read it somewhere in one of your books? It can't be through any visits you've paid to your grandmother, can it?'

'You don't understand,' he protested.

'How could I? I'm not the one with the education; I'm not the high and mighty William Booth. Oh, no, I wouldn't presume to understand, and now you're going off to a big school. That should suit your big ideas.'

'It's not like that,' he pleaded. 'I love her.'

'Who,' cried Nanny Bradshaw, 'that German? You should be ashamed of yourself.'

'No, no,' he sobbed, 'it's Grandma I love, it's her.' He started to cry.

'You needn't waste your crocodile tears on me,' cried Nanny Bradshaw. 'Love now, is it? Well a funny sort of love if you ask me, ignoring your poor grandmother, going off on picnics and what have you, smiling at that flibbertigibbet.'

'We had no picnic,' he sniffed, 'and she's not like that. You don't understand.'

'Of course not,' snapped Nanny Bradshaw, bringing her head closer to his, 'there's such a lot a poor old simple soul like me couldn't possibly understand. Not when we've got someone of such learning.' She slammed the book closed, making William jump. 'There's not much your old Nanny knows really, is there? I just get on with my job, without a word of thanks, mind you. If anything needs to be done, there's always Nanny isn't there?'

She banged her hand on the smooth leather cover of the book, causing William to jump again. 'What I do know,' she persisted, 'is that there's trouble brewing, and there are those who are going to get their come-uppance. Oh yes, I might not have the book learning of some people, but I know what's what.' She pursed her lips. 'That woman,' she said, 'that's what your grandmother called her, "that woman". She didn't care for her at all, and still doesn't, she doesn't belong in this family, that's for sure. She called your gran a poor creature.' She nodded her scandalised head up and down. '"A poor creature", that's what she said. I told her straight, there are no creatures in this room. She's a lady your grandmother, and that trollop's not fit to breathe the same air, never mind think that she can look after her. All she wants is to pack her off to a hospital. But she'll be laughing on the other side of her face, I have evidence. Her best bet would be to pack her bag.'

'But,' began William.

'But,' cried Nanny Bradshaw, jumping to her feet, 'there are no buts. She's been cunning. I said to your grandmother, she's got cunning that one, but there's evidence that she didn't plan on. Some people have been on to her little game from the start. She's got her eyes on this house, she's got covetous eyes. And you,' she spat out, 'you have been a fool, taken in by a simpering smile, just like that uncle of yours. She's a shameless strumpet.'

'It's a lie,' he cried, 'a lie.'

He knocked the book off the table so it clattered on to the floor and, burying his head in his hands, he cried like a little boy. Nanny Bradshaw looked down on her handiwork. How like a little child he was. She would forgive him being rude to his old Nanny. She would go over now and wipe away his tears of shame and guilt.

'Come on, come on,' she cooed, 'you can't see your gran looking like that.'

*

Elizabeth Booth had grown used to the drifting quality of her days. She hadn't even noticed that it was a while since William had been to see her. She thought the little boy was like his father. She kept seeing him standing at the foot of the bed and thought she would smile at him, but her face remained still. She wondered if she should do some baking. She liked to do that sometimes; go down to the kitchen and for a surprise make them all a pie. The little boy was there again. She smiled at him and wondered if he would like a pie. She asked him. What a funny little boy, she thought, and reached for the flour tin, and with the heavy bowl, started to mix the pastry.

'She's so still,' said William, 'you can hardly see her breathing.'

'She understands every word, though,' said Nanny Bradshaw. 'You can tell when you look into her eyes.' She leaned over and nodded at Mrs Booth.

'She's pleased to see you,' she informed William.

'Hello,' he whispered.

'You've got to speak up a bit,' instructed Nanny Bradshaw. 'I've been telling William,' she bellowed, 'what that skinny chicken has been up to. He's on our side now. Shall I tell him about our guide?' she asked, and leant over to look into the glazed eyes.

'Do you prefer apple or gooseberry?' asked Mrs Booth, and laughed when the little boy said he wanted both. 'Goodness,' she cried, 'that will be a funny pie,' but went on to make it nevertheless.

'She doesn't mind if I tell you.'

William glanced at his grandmother. He had tried to see whether there was even a flickering of her eye, but there was nothing. He gave Nanny Bradshaw a puzzled look, as she gave Mrs Booth a knowing smile.

'We get messages,' she said.

'Messages,' repeated William dully, suddenly feeling very tired.

'Yes, from the other side,' she breathed, 'from Pewter.'

'Pewter,' gasped William. 'Where is he, where is the postmark from? I must get in touch with him.'

'Bless me,' laughed Nanny Bradshaw, 'it's only your grandmother who can contact him, you silly goose. Pewter's

210

in the spirit world, you can't post any letters from there.'
She rubbed her sides from the trembling laughter, hoping
that Pewter didn't think she had been rude. 'He knew I was
going to put on a good spread for him,' she said in a
meaningful voice, thinking it would do no harm to remind the
tutor.

'He's dead then?' asked William, who no longer knew
whether he should be surprised or not.

'Murdered,' she whispered.

'Murdered,' gasped William. 'How?' he asked, seized with
gruesome fascination.

'We don't know,' replied Nanny Bradshaw, 'but there's
them that do,' she added significantly. 'Spying,' whispered
Nanny Bradshaw, looking round as though she expected that
someone would be trying to listen in.

'Golly,' he breathed, thinking of all the times he had taken
the tutor for granted, and all the time he was a spy, just like
some glamorous film star. 'Who did he work for?' he asked.

'Your grandmother,' said Nanny, not really wanting to get
into a discussion of the ins and outs of Pewter's life.

'No, who was he spying for?'

'That doesn't matter,' she said importantly. 'All this
chitter-chatter is getting us nowhere. What we want is the
miscreant. Pewter must be avenged.'

'But he's dead,' said William, still not understanding.

'Yes, that's right,' frowned Nanny Bradshaw, 'haven't I
just explained that to you? How else could your grandmother
get the messages?'

'But that's it,' cried William. 'How can she get messages
from someone who's dead?'

Nanny Bradshaw gave William a long look. It seemed to
her, William hadn't been listening properly.

'She's a natural,' she explained. 'I found out of course, but
it's your grandmother who's the medium. I just help a bit,
although we haven't had any ectoplasm or anything like that.
I'm writing it up,' she confided, 'she will be a sensation, that's
for sure. I only wish Mrs Makin could be here to see it.'

'I don't understand,' said William, glancing at the figure on
the bed.

'William,' came back the exasperated Nanny Bradshaw,

'how many more times before it sinks in? What we should be concerned with is unmasking the murderer, or should I say murderess?' She leant over towards William. 'It's the German.'

'Dagmar,' cried William, as though he were calling out the name in a nightmare.

Nanny Bradshaw laughed. 'There's a turn up for the books,' she said, 'and it was old Nanny who saw through her tricks.' She folded her arms proudly and sat back in the chair, a contented expression resting on her face.

'They'll hang her by the neck,' she concluded with relish. 'She'll swing on the end of a rope for what she's been up to.'

'No,' exclaimed William, covering his ears. 'No, no, no. She'll curse you,' he cried, 'if they hang her, she'll curse you, and then you'll be cursed just like we are.'

'What are you saying?' said Nanny Bradshaw, and reached out with her heavy hand to grasp William's wrist. 'What nonsense are you talking? Who told you about a curse?' She tightened her grip on William, her fingers biting into the thin flesh around his wrist. 'You know nothing,' she spat out. 'Nothing. You weren't even born. Fancy talking like that in front of her,' and she gave his wrist a vicious twist. 'Don't you take any notice of what he says,' she said to the figure on the bed. 'He's an ungrateful little sneak,' she added, giving William a glowering look. 'We'll get justice; we'll bring the guilty to account; there are those who demand revenge.'

She swung round on William, who was still rubbing his wrist. 'The last message warned me,' she cried, 'but I didn't heed it.' She extended her arms into the room in a gesture of supplication. 'I'm sorry, Pewter, forgive me, forgive an old woman's soft heart. I thought he would understand, I thought he would help.' She looked disparagingly at William. 'He loved me,' she sobbed. 'I was his true love and I'll have my revenge. He said betrayal, that's what he said, but I never thought it would be you. How could you?' she cried. 'How could you betray your grandmother and your old Nanny?'

'I'm not betraying anyone,' shouted William. 'You can do what you like. You're mad, and I don't want anything to do with you. You can go to hell for all I care.' Flinging himself from his chair, he dashed past Nanny Bradshaw and left his grandmother's room for the last time.

'Do you want another slice of pie dear?' asked Mrs Booth, knowing full well that little boys could never resist another slice of pie. She smiled when he said yes.

'Agnus Dei, qui tollis peccata mundi: miserere nobis
'Agnus Dei qui tollis peccata mundi: miserere nobis
'Agnus Dei qui tollis peccata mundi: dona nobis pacem.
'Kyrie eleison
'Christe eleison
'Kyrie eleison,' chanted Sister Ursula, missing the voices of her sisters, and the echo of the chapel. The candles she had lit flickered slightly from the exhaled breath of her praying. It was still dark and the private matins she performed took their text from her own favourite liturgies.

'Sanctus, Sanctus, Sanctus Dominus
'Deus Sabaoth. Pleni sunt caeli et
'terra gloria tua. Hosanna in excelsis.
'Benedictus qui venit in nomine Domini.
'Hosanna in excelsis.'

A secret thrill passed through the nun's body: she wondered whether it might be the Holy Spirit. Perhaps a flame glowed above her head; if she opened her mouth, she might speak in tongues. She gripped her hands in ecstasy, wincing slightly as her right palm still pained her. The pain was the proof, she could share the suffering; her eyes glowed in the candle-light. Her back was rigid as she knelt in prayer, as though like St Simeon the Stylite, she were on a pillar, oblivious to the secular world, and had to be careful not to tumble from the heights. However the illusion soon vanished as she prostrated herself on the floor, something which the pillar ascetics would have been rash to attempt.

Although she had been fasting, Ursula felt she was gaining in strength for the fight ahead. She just wished she hadn't developed the sore throat. When she woke in the morning it was as if, like St Berikjesu, someone had been pouring burning pitch down her gullet. The house was damp, she concluded; the fireplace in her room had been boarded over, she felt it very short-sighted of Fanny and Wilfred. It was strange, she thought, how when at prayer her mind separated, one half slipping away slyly while the other didn't notice. She decided that she would beg forgiveness for such a tendency, although perhaps God found it endearing. With her nose resting on the carpet, Ursula could smell the dust.

She decided she must write to the convent. Sitting up abruptly, she sneezed, and as the candles extinguished themselves, the room was cast into the darkness of purgatory. Fumbling to find the matches, Sister Ursula relit the three candles grouped around the chipped statue of the Madonna. Searching through her case, she found some writing-paper, and picking up a pen she started to compose a letter to the mother superior.

She decided to refrain from mentioning the miracle which had occurred. Looking down at her injured palm she realised her intercession would come from higher than any saint: her raw palm would redeem her. She told the mother superior that she knew God was looking over her actions, but hoped the sisters would pray for the success of her endeavours, and then she would come back to the convent with an easier heart. She decided she didn't like the life outside. She chose not to mention the wireless.

She put down her pen for a moment, imagining what it would be like to sit as mother superior. You had to admit Sister Barbara wasn't as young as she once was. She finished the letter with the express hope that Sister Barbara was keeping well, and that she wasn't overtaxing herself. She had to be careful at her age. With a flourish she signed it, her extravagant hand almost covering half a page of paper. Stiff necked, Sister Ursula sat back in the chair facing the blank wall.

The light gradually grew as dawn broke, but Sister Ursula never looked out of the window to see the beauty of it. She heard Fanny and Wilfred stirring. If she wasn't already awake, there would have been no doubt that her brother's early morning hawking would have woken her as surely as the point of an arrow. The mattress in their room creaked as

215

though it had been holding some great weight. The intimate sound made Sister Ursula reach for her rosary.

The morning shift was on its way to the mill, and through the glass of the window a second series of noises assaulted the nun. The heavy footfall of men, and the occasional joke or ribald remark filtered from below like the unwholesome smell of an open drain. And now the pipes rattled away with brazen and cavalier abandon, insensitive to the presence of a bride of Christ.

Sister Ursula disliked using the bathroom. The tiles seemed to magnify whatever noise was produced, informing anybody who was in the proximity of the exact nature of the proceedings and the lack of ventilation meant that any odours would remain as a testament of the whole unsavoury business. Whenever a call of nature made such a pilgrimage necessary, she checked first to make sure that nobody was in the vicinity either to observe her entrance or exit. As soon as she was in the bathroom she would spin the taps to start the rushing water swirling round the basin, in the hope it would drown any further noise. Then she flushed the toilet before she even used it. This ritual cleansing continued as she wiped down the toilet seat. Once at the convent she had leapt up from the seat as if scalded, feeling the dull heat of whoever had last been there. The sensation had so sickened her, that the desire to void her bowels disappeared, and her rigid body denied itself the natural function as long as possible. The nun was constantly constipated.

Ursula was the cause of Fanny Coffin's pursed lips. She berated her husband about the strain of complying with the whims of the nun. It just couldn't go on, she said. Leaving trays of food outside the locked door, and finding that they hadn't been touched; it was a scandalous waste of food. For all she knew, it could be attracting mice and rats into the house, and then where would they be. She slumped down into the chair, the thin veins standing out on her thin arms and neck. Wilfred's teeth snapped down on a dry piece of toast.

'It's up to you,' she said, watching as he reached into his waistcoat pocket.

He extracted his fob watch with excruciating precision and

proceeded to wind it up. Although she closed her eyes, she knew that as he finished the winding he would lift it up to his ear to hear its steady ticking. He would slowly lower it, check the face, and then drop it into the snug pocket where it would nestle in the material worn by this daily occurrence into a shiny patch on his pocket.

'Any more toast?' he asked.

'Wilfred,' she screamed. 'Haven't you been listening to a word I've said? You must go and speak with her, she'll listen to you. It just can't go on.' She hid her head in her hands. Wilfred Coffin dabbed his lips nervously with the clean napkin.

'I'll be late,' he mumbled, fumbling for his watch.

He felt the strong sensation he was about to fall. Synchronously, Fanny slipped to the floor. The time shown for this event on the dangling watch was six forty-six.

As Wilfred turned to reach his stricken wife, the chronometer swung and its movement was frozen as a permanent record for posterity, as the face smashed against the side of the table. Now time was both interminable and ephemeral, as though in smashing the clock, he had fragmented not just the face, but jumbled the hours, minutes and seconds of existence. There would be no comforting chimes to signal the course of the hours and the passing of the days.

He looked into the face, which had grown through the years more and more like his own, as though their twin natures in order to co-exist had begun to redistribute the very flesh, so husband and wife resembled each other as though they had sprung from the same egg. With the broken watch dangling from its chain, Wilfred peeled back his wife's eyelid, and it might have been as if he were revealing his own tear-stained orb.

'Fanny, Fanny,' he sang, as though like Orpheus he was trying to summon her back.

He brazenly stared at his true love. It was the worst thing that had ever happened to him, worse than the first day he started work, when as initiation, cold, heavy dark industrial grease was smeared on his crotch. Dragging her from under the table on which lay the remains of the breakfast, Wilfred, his thin chest heaving in and out, started to cough. He spluttered away from his prostrate wife, and the familiar sound worked its magic; her eyelids twitched back to the siren call of his wretched chest.

'Goose grease,' she intoned in sepulchral tones.

'Fa-anny,' he gasped out, the surprise making his heart jolt, only adding to his own incapacity. Yet to the recumbent Fanny, he might just as well have been decked out in a shining armour. He was her rescuer, her hero.

'Would you like some more toast?' she asked meekly, thinking with shame of the manner in which she had rebuffed his earlier request.

But Wilfred was too overcome to answer. In fact, he was now becoming the cause of alarm, and struggling to her own two feet, Fanny allowed Wilfred to collapse into the very spot that was still warm from her own flesh. His shoulders trembled as though they carried the weight of the world. Fanny Coffin looked round in vain, there was nobody to help. Upstairs Ursula sat in silent contemplation, and in her tousled bed, with mouth agape, Ethel dreamed of heaven, her shuddering breathing sounding unnervingly like snoring.

With the jerky movements of some automaton which was winding down, Fanny Coffin left the room. Slices of toast covered with a heavy layer of goose grease floated in front of her. She closed the door so Wilfred wouldn't be lying in a draught, and went to the kitchen. Now she bustled round as though an invisible hand had wound her up, reaching for the bread, cutting thin slices, making ready to toast them. The shrine to Ursula's revelation had its first devotee.

As the pile of toast grew like a replica of the Tower of Babel, the warm bread exuding its own special message, Fanny searched in the pantry for the jar of goose grease. The fetid odour filled the kitchen as she unscrewed the lid. The compound she usually smeared on Wilfred's white, hairless chest, was now spread like a succulent jam over the waiting toast. Arranging it on a place covered with a clean doily, she paused a moment as she considered whether she should have put the kettle on. The goose grease gently melted, sliding over the bread, and congealing in oily streaks on the plate. When the first piece of toast was lifted, the rest would follow suit; they were stuck together by the yellow fat.

218

As Ursula started to pray, Fanny lifted the first piece of toast to Wilfred's silent lips, and as her hand trembled the other pieces tumbled as gravity took hold, landing on Wilfred's suit.

'Oh dear,' exclaimed Fanny, holding on to the listless head, which was also subject to the laws of nature. As she removed her hand to start picking off the slices of toast, Wilfred's head fell back impelled by the slowly rotating planet. What was clear, was that Wilfred would not be going to work that day.

Weeping, Fanny Coffin rushed upstairs to Ursula. As she hammered on the door, she never heard Ursula command her to enter. Gripping hold of the handle and shaking it in her desperation the door clicked open and she stumbled into the serene presence of her sister-in-law. Seated in a chair, her arms devoutly crossed over her chest, Sister Ursula resembled the calm Madonna in Fra Angelico's *Annunciation*, composed for any news the angel might impart. Perhaps even the Madonna's mouth might have been forgiven a little twitch of distaste if she had the dishevelled form of Fanny Coffin break into her reveries. Her apron had become unfastened and her hair was in a veritable frenzy. Beneath her wimple, Sister Ursula's scalp prickled in protest. Even St Perpetua had managed to tidy her dishevelled hair in the arena while the wild animals roared. Surely it wasn't asking too much for Fanny to at least make an attempt.

'It's Wilfred,' cried Fanny.

Sister Ursula shifted slightly in the chair, and smoothed down the perfect creases in her habit. She liked how the material fell in even folds. God's perfection could be found in simple material, his harmony spread over the world.

'He's dead,' keened Fanny, collapsing like a broken puppet, clutching at Ursula's peerless habit. Her greasy hands left blotchy marks as she scrunched the material in her feverish hands. Reaching down, Ursula plucked the hands away.

'Nonsense,' she said, as though she too could be aware of the falling of the lowliest sparrow.

'He is, he is,' persisted the distraught Fanny.

Rising as the occasion demanded, Sister Ursula almost

219

floated from the room, as though the fasting had made her defy the gravity which had grounded her brother. Fanny never felt the brush of Ursula's habit, and would always swear that Ursula had levitated. And so started the elevation of Ursula in the mind of her sister-in-law, who would in later years, after Ursula's death, campaign for the miracle to be recognised. As she never saw Ursula arrive at the side of Wilfred, the papal authorities were understandably reticent about confirming the resurrection of the dead man, who after all, might not in fact have been dead.

It was perhaps just as well that Fanny did not witness Ursula standing over the wheezing form of Wilfred. Indeed, had the seventh trumpet given its final peal, the face of judgment would not have had a harsher aspect. The shock of seeing Ursula looking down on him like the angel of death she used to play in her childhood, caused Wilfred to cease his coughing. He cringed under her apocalyptic gaze. Sitting up, he suddenly wondered whether this was the time to have the talk with Ursula. He had hoped to rehearse it in front of a mirror. He cleared his throat nervously. Fanny had said it was up to him.

'Don't start coughing again,' warned Ursula, mistaking the clearing of the throat. 'Have you been praying to St Blaise?' she asked, her eyes combing him for the answer.

'Wilfred!' screeched Fanny, who had just arrived. A shard of glass from the watch-face entered her foot, but she was so overcome that she didn't notice. It was Wilfred who exclaimed, 'Ouch.' After hugging Wilfred and the toast, Fanny eventually turned her tear-stained, but awestruck eyes to the standing nun.

'You are a saint,' she stated, and Sister Ursula changed her expression at once from a brooding incomprehension to a beatific smile. It gently played round her lips, capturing those many moods that a martyr must experience. It was indeed a subtle self-sacrificing smile, one Reverend Roe would have recognised, and most jealously, since he had not perfected one for himself.

'A saint,' persisted Fanny, 'and you,' she said, hugging Wilfred, 'are as lucky as Lazarus,' although it had to be admitted that he did not feel that lucky, wincing with pain from the glass in Fanny's foot.

220

'She flew to your side,' said Fanny literally. Wilfred wondered whether he should mention the glass, he didn't want it to go septic.

'It's been quite a morning,' was all that Ursula said, a comment that had been echoed by others that very day.

The thirteenth of September was indeed not a very auspicious date. The unlucky number stared up at Neville Chamberlain as he prepared himself for the first aeroplane journey of his life. Closing his diary with a click, the prime minister stared out of the car window on the dismal drive, contemplating a flight of a very different kind from that of a levitating nun.

It was also the day on which Wilfred Coffin failed to turn up for work for the first time in thirty years. At the mill, consternation reigned. The office staff were in as much disarray as his broken watch. Cups of tea were brewed, invoices lay untended, typewriters were silent, and hushed voices considered what ought to be done. One junior piped up, suggesting a search-party be formed and the canal dredged. Miss Boothroyd broke down in tears, and the blushing boy was sent on an errand to prevent further upset. Miss Boothroyd said not to be too hard on the junior, a certain Master Dickinson, who she thought to herself had such a clean white smile. It was the empty hat stand, she explained, which had upset her, pointing like a finger into the guilty souls of the office staff.

At that very moment Wilfred Coffin was seeing another finger, that of his sister. The nun stood in front of the twin beds, which held the twin frames of Wilfred and Fanny Coffin, and the finger was wagging. Having forgotten her own undertaking about obedience and the sin of pride, Sister Ursula was laying down the law to her captive hosts. She expected the compliant patients to obey the régime she was formulating with the most basic medical knowledge of feeding a cold and starving a fever. Sister Ursula decided to alternate the treatment, feeling whatever affliction the two patients had contracted would succumb under the prophylactic diet. With her palm gently throbbing approval, she would

221

perfect the nostrum: there would be a transfiguration. She placed a leather-bound Bible on the small cabinet separating the beds and then left the room.

As the Coffins cast guilty glances towards the silent book, the office staff also avoided looking at each other, and another complicity arose in the stumbling way they all began to speak at once. The babel of voices broke the guilty silence in which so much had been left unsaid. Making up for time, they outdid each other in the praise they heaped upon the unsuspecting head of Wilfred Coffin. To say he was a good man was not sufficient.

'He was a perfect gentleman,' said Miss Boothroyd, lowering her eyelids quickly to avoid those of Mrs Potter to whom she had once confided the false tale of Wilfred Coffin's wandering hands. She told of how the inexperienced manager pinched her behind, let his hand stray to her fat knee, and of how he asked her to sit in his lap. Mrs Potter had been aghast. She did not pause to think of how the ample frame of Miss Boothroyd would have been liable to snap his legs like dry twigs if she had succumbed to this suggestion. A dirty old man is what they had called him, a debauched thrill-seeker. In short, they had concluded he was a pervert.

Mrs Potter, not to be outdone, called him a model of virtue. The treacly tones of Mr Grundy joined in and instead of the whining jealousies he usually muttered about Wilfred Coffin, he spoke in a clear voice about how he was the salt of the earth, a pleasure to work for. Wilfred Coffin's subordinates filled his office with sanctified talk, remembering little deeds which they spoke of in hushed tones as though forging myths for the future. A good sort; a brick; a trump; the praise echoed round the office, and as the general sound faded, a single word lingered, a 'saint'.

What Ursula pursued so energetically had been bestowed, in name only of course, on her indifferent brother. Had she known of this, her eyes would have blazed with the fire of the Inquisition, although perhaps she would have taken comfort in the tendency of the Church to frown upon the dual canonisation of siblings, a notable exception being St Benedict and St Scholastica. Ursula would not have wished to emulate them; she would keep the glory to herself.

222

Oblivious to the sobriquet, Wilfred Coffin and his wife heard simultaneously the approach of Ursula. She carried in her hands a small enamel bowl filled with scalding water and Dettol. The antiseptic smell caused Wilfred's nose to twitch, and his throat tickled with an incipient cough. He knew with dread certainty that Ursula had come to remove the splinter of glass from Fanny's foot, and his hands clenched white under the sheets.

'This won't hurt,' she commanded, and taking a pair of very hot tweezers, probed around in the small wound.

The only ones who were unaware of Wilfred Coffin's mysterious absence from work were his employers and his daughter. The former were about to be consulted by Mr Grundy, and the latter, presently dreaming away in bed, was about to have a rude awakening.

Ethel Coffin was having an interesting discussion with an angel who bore a striking resemblance to Dagmar Ehrenhardt. You had to have blonde hair explained the angel, to be one of the chosen few, and it seemed a good complexion would also count for a lot. While Ethel sat on a pink cloud pondering this revelation, her aunt entered the bedroom in which her corporeal body lay snoring in bed. There was a heavy, musky odour of unwashed girl which assaulted the nun's nostrils, and this had a strangely narcotic effect. Ursula found her eyelids becoming heavier and heavier, the resonant snoring of the shadowy mound on the bed began to mesmerise her. She felt as though her head were being pressed into a soft substance. Sleep was taking hold of her like a hug from a fat person.

Ethel rolled her great head from side to side, as though slowly shaking away the drowning sleep, and with a huge yawn she suddenly sat up in bed. She watched from the warm bed, her round eyes staring through the shadows as though seeking to divine the meaning of the nun's presence. As she gradually became bored with glaring and occasionally putting her tongue out at the taut figure of Sister Ursula, she heaved her trunklike legs out of the crusty sheets. Robed in a voluminous nightdress, Ethel billowed towards her aunt like a schooner with sails at full rig. The nun's palms glowed in the dark like a beacon or lighthouse by which Ethel could chart her course, but instead of sharp reefs piercing the hull, Ethel trod on the shard of glass sticking up from the damp carpet where the contents of the bowl had fallen. Ethel screamed and her voice echoed around Sister Ursula like a landslide, and in their bedroom, the faces of her parents blanched at exactly the same moment, and their hair now suddenly prickled and started to stand on end.

It also awoke Sister Ursula. In the blink of an eye, she saw Ethel jumping up and down on one foot, moaning like a stricken animal. She struck Ethel a stinging blow across her cheek and Ethel sank to the floor. Striding past the slumped figure, Sister Ursula yanked open the curtains, letting the morning light into the stale room. It was then she became aware of the ululations coming through the thin walls. In discordant harmony, Mr and Mrs Coffin keened for their injured daughter. They were sitting up in bed, their heads wobbling as though palsied, their white hair flapping in time.

Leaving Ethel, Sister Ursula made quickly towards the dreadful sound. The nun's footsteps were accompanied by the sound of breaking glass, as the Coffins' voices reached a certain pitch. Houses all down the road were filled with the glittering crescendo of shattering glass. Windows exploded; vases cracked, spilling water with flowers, as the Coffins' cry resonated through the air. Sister Ursula felt her fillings ache within her mouth. Her bones rattled as she tried to steer herself towards the Coffins' bedroom. The glass lampshade exploded above her head.

In another country, at another time, another people, of a different faith would also lament. The Coffins cried out fifty-seven days before the other voices would cry to the baroque sound of broken glass, while burning synagogues warmed the autumn night, the flames reflecting and glowing in the crumpled shards of plate-glass windows. The mounds of glass would sparkle in the cool, clear air, like chandeliers in the very streets on Kristallnacht. And so, bereft of time, the Coffins knew of the darkness to come; felt the destruction which would shatter more things than glass. Civilisation would be broken into a thousand pieces, and they closed their mouths at exactly the same time.

That was how Sister Ursula found them, sitting up in bed

with wide staring eyes, these unlikely witnesses to the misery and the darkness, surrounded by piles of broken glass, and the broken watch which lay on Wilfred's open palm. Sister Ursula added herself to the tiny reflections moving among the pieces of broken mirror in this hall of ice the Coffins had created. However hard she tried, Ursula could not get them to speak.

It was, in short, a miracle. It might have been the first miracle that had occurred in Slackhall since the reverend's wife fell victim to the gypsy curse and gave birth to a strangely featured daughter, but the phlegmatic dwellers did not like to have miracles or mysteries occur at such short notice. As the scale of the phenomenon became apparent, reporters arrived from the local newspaper, even one from Manchester was despatched. By the time he arrived, the broken glass had been swept from the roads, but it still lay in tidy heaps.

Of course, various theories were in circulation as to the cause. Some people favoured the view that it was the communists, others thought that it could be the blackshirts. Still others, smarting under old prejudices, felt it could be the Irish. Although the town sought to pin the blame on somebody, it had to be said that the police did not have much evidence to go on. There were no bricks to examine, as none had been hurled through the windows. There would have to have been a small quarry full of bricks to have smashed so many windows, and as Inspector O'Connor stated, that did not explain the damage wrought inside the houses.

There were, of course, those that murmured that the inspector was not likely to probe too deeply into the Irish connection, not with a name like his. Nobody suspected the Coffins. Nobody gave their house a second glance, and although Inspector O'Connor kept the file open, the morning of the broken glass was never explained and gradually the incident was forgotten.

Ethel was sitting on the floor, sharing it with the odd pile of fragmented glass. A cool breeze was blowing through the house, entering through the gaping windows. Sister Ursula allowed herself a despairing sigh. Ethel's nightdress rustled in the breeze, yet she didn't appear disposed to move herself from the draught as the chill air turned her ears red. The thin

225

sliver of glass from the timepiece stuck out of her foot as though still attempting to carry out a time-keeping function, now casting a small shadow as the sun's rays caught it.

Sister Ursula's feet crunched over a pile of pulverised crystal. Oblivious to the dangers of also having glass embedded in her foot, the nun approached Ethel. She could hear the voices outside, as the neighbours talked about the strange occurrence. The nun thought it sounded as though there was a party going on. She looked out of the broken window, down on to the heads below, and clicked her tongue. She couldn't see the faces; couldn't see their mouths; but she could hear them, talking, talking. She wondered if anyone had heard the noise. Nobody seemed to be looking at the house, and so far no one had started to clear the street. The landscape of grey walls, grey stone and grey people was littered by the flashing, glistening scatterings of glass. The myriad surfaces reflected a message, a strange semaphore which was ignored.

Turning her back to the window, Sister Ursula didn't think of the freedom she now had to rearrange the furniture. Her mind rested on Ethel. Everyone has their own Calvary, she thought. Nobody had looked at Ethel the way her aunt did for such a long time, and yet the fat girl did not shift. It was indeed the nun who recoiled slightly as if her probing eyes had been pressed back by the doughy skin.

There was something overripe about Ethel, as though her skin had been filling up and soon it would split open. Staring down at her niece, she felt another hand was at work here. In the periphery of her mind, she could see the red letters which spelled out the frightful truth, but she pushed it away. Yet the terrible thought became lodged: her niece was possessed by the devil.

Her Christian duty flared up within her. The child, for whom she cared not a jot, became the most important thing to Sister Ursula, not only a test of her own sanctity, but of Christ's. Before she had time to exchange a word with Ethel, her attention was diverted by the heavy rapping of somebody on the front door. It was a long time since Sister Ursula had answered a door, and what made it worse, was the fact that nobody was expected.

'Hello,' said the person on the doorstep. Sister Ursula did

226

not respond. 'It looks as though there has been an explosion,' said the caller, indicating the wrecked windows and broken glass strewn about. 'The whole town is like that. It's been very strange walking about, with everybody looking at you with suspicion. They will have to find the culprit,' she stated with authority. Sister Ursula raised her eyes towards the sky, as though indicating that God moved in mysterious ways, although still no words escaped her stern lips. 'We had a phone call,' explained the caller, 'about Mr Coffin. I wondered whether he was ill?'

'Ill?' repeated Sister Ursula. 'How did you know? Who phoned you?' She thought this inexplicable piece of knowledge should not be spread about the streets.

'Why, his subordinates. They were worried and rang the house. I thought I would kill two birds with one stone.' She gave a small laugh as though she had said something rather clever or witty. 'I think that is the way you say it,' she smiled.

'Thank you for your enquiry,' said Sister Ursula, feeling that somehow it was not the time or place to stand talking on the doorstep. 'I shall pass it on to Wilfred.'

'You don't remember me,' said Dagmar, trying to stand so the sun shone on her fair hair.

'The Austrian nurse,' exclaimed Sister Ursula under her breath, but Dagmar's keen ear picked up the mistake.

'German nurse,' she corrected. 'I thought perhaps I might be allowed to see Ethel.'

A few people were still gathered around in the street, and the tinkling sound caused by their sweeping brooms had fallen silent. They stood with idle hands, but, suspected Sister Ursula, not idle ears. She stepped back into the shadowy hallway, and motioned Dagmar inside. She saw the nurse was staring at the small piles of glass that still littered the hall.

'Do be careful,' warned Sister Ursula, fearing another accident.

'Perhaps it was an earthquake,' suggested Dagmar, 'although I didn't feel the earth move beneath my feet, did you?'

'I think I did,' lied the nun, clutching her slightly throbbing hand behind her back. 'That's what happened, and perhaps it is a judgment, a warning.'

227

'Did it frighten Ethel?' probed Dagmar.

'She slept right through it,' said Ursula, 'she's still sleep-ing.'

'That is not good for a young child,' stated Dagmar.

'She's got a cold,' fibbed Sister Ursula. 'I thought it would do her good to have a bit more sleep.'

'And Mr and Mrs Coffin?' asked Dagmar, moving slightly towards the bottom of the stairs.

'Colds,' stated the nun emphatically, not missing Dagmar's shifting position.

'Perhaps,' started Dagmar, reaching out for the banister, 'I should take a little look at the patients.'

'Too kind, too kind,' said Sister Ursula sweetly, interpos-ing her body between Dagmar and the stairs. And then, as though oblivious to the dance they had been conducting, Sister Ursula gave a little gasp. 'Oh how selfish of me,' she exclaimed, 'taking advantage of such a kind heart, that would never, never do.'

'It is no trouble,' smiled Dagmar.

'Of course it isn't, my dear,' replied the nun, 'but I really can't allow it.' She swept her arm down, and snaking it through Dagmar's, she led her away from the stairwell. 'No,' she continued, 'it just wouldn't do at all. How could I forgive myself if you carried the germs back to the old dear, or even came down with the cold yourself. Really it would be so, so selfish of me,' and as she saw Dagmar was going to open her mouth in protest, she gave a little laugh. 'Now, now,' she said with mock severity, 'I'll hear no more about it.'

It was the first time she had ever had to entertain a Protestant, and it made her uneasy.

'Tea with milk?' she asked and wondered whether they drank milk.

Moving her head slightly, Dagmar tried to use the nun as a shield from the sun, and with hesitant fingers she reached down for her wicker basket. Before replying she pulled forth a little sachet which she used for herbal infusion.

'Would you mind?' she asked, holding the packet out. It was with a hesitant hand that the nun received it.

Moving into the kitchen, Ursula almost forgot the genuflec-tion she had decided to bestow on the hallowed place, the

228

scene of her revelation. She left the door ajar, so that she could see if the nurse entered the hall. She could sense the strong will of the German, and with her Lutheran ways, she would not put anything past her. She looked down at the sachet that lay in her palm, and with a certain relief dropped it into a waiting cup. She then rinsed her hands under the tap, unsure whether she had committed a venial sin in handling the acrid potion. She wondered whether all members of the Protestant church drank this devil's brew. She stirred the spoon around, making sure it did not bang the sides of the cup, and kept pulling it out to look whether the silver was becoming tarnished. With great care she placed the cup on a tray, and as far away as possible she set her own cup.

As she entered the room, her eyes fell on the empty chair standing in a shaft of sunlight and the pleasant expression she had been wearing, slipped off her face.

'The sun was in my eyes,' said Dagmar, and as the surprised nun wheeled round in the direction of the voice, it was too late to mask the mistake she had made in thinking Dagmar had been stealing from the room. The smile she tried to direct at the German's knowing eyes, wavered slightly.

'You gave me a little shock, my dear,' as she strode quickly over the carpet. Her briskness attempted to hide her embarrassment. 'That cup rattles like my old bones,' she laughed.

'You don't look that old,' said Dagmar bluntly. Sister Ursula thought flattery will get you nowhere, although she would admit to having a good skin. It was Sister Ursula who now had the sun in her eyes, and she tried to give the impression that its glare did not affect her, although her eyes had narrowed to thin slits.

'Ethel seems to think a lot of you,' she said to the shadowy figure of Dagmar. 'Strange, don't you think, after only one meeting, unless that is,' she added, 'you have been seeing more of my niece than we know.' She took a steady sip of her tea, and her nose twitched slightly, as a faint whiff of Dagmar's drink came to her. 'Have you?' she persisted.

'Have I what?' asked Dagmar innocently.

'Have you been meeting Ethel, outside this house?' She rested the cup and saucer on her still lap.

'Oh no,' protested the nurse. 'I merely saw the poor child

229

the once, although I would like to see her again. It was her mother who asked if I could help the family.'

'Well,' said Ursula in dulcet tones, 'her mother and father asked me to try and help and, after all, we only want what is best for Ethel.'

'Of course,' replied Dagmar. 'There is some history in the family, of this sort of . . . malaise?' she asked.

'History,' repeated Ursula in a strangled voice.

'Yes,' said Dagmar in a soothing voice, 'of mental troubles.'

'Certainly not,' exclaimed the nun, 'not on her father's side of the family.'

'Ah aaa,' said Dagmar knowingly. 'No offence.'

'Of course not, my dear,' replied Sister Ursula, gathering her anger into an equally sugary voice. She leant forward and tapped Dagmar on the knee, holding her breath as she did so, against the stench of the German's drink.

'It's not the child's fault,' she continued. 'It has never had proper instruction.' She gave a big sigh. 'But now her aunt is here, I shall with God's help of course, heal the child.' She tapped Dagmar once more. 'I have never seen a child behave in such a way. Her teacher has a lot to answer for, at least on judgment day. I said no good would come of sending the child to a Prot . . . Oh dear,' she gasped, 'I'm sorry, my dear, I hope I haven't insulted you. It's just that our ways are different, and it doesn't do, doesn't do at all.' She took a quick sip of her drink, feeling quite pleased with the way she was handling this. 'I know you understand, you have such an understanding face.' She leant forward again, and squeezed Dagmar on the knee. 'Shall we say no more about it?' she said.

'About what?' asked Dagmar.

'Now, now,' admonished Sister Ursula as though she were dealing with a novitiate. 'You are not a Roman, my dear, and it just wouldn't do. The child must be given a firm hand now, taught our way. Why, it makes my blood boil to think of how that headmistress treated Ethel. She's lucky her pupils don't do her a mischief. St Cassian of Imola, that holy man, was stabbed to death by his little heathen pupils with the iron nibs of their pens.' Ursula's eyes had a faraway look. 'Well, I mustn't keep you,' she said then, as if interrupting herself. 'I'm sure you must be very busy. I've probably kept you far too long anyway.' She got to her feet. 'And just look at all this I have to do.' She motioned to the scattered glass from the imploded window which had rained down on to the carpet. She held the door open for Dagmar.

'I'm so glad we had our little chat,' said Sister Ursula. 'We all want the same thing, isn't that so?'

'Certainly,' said Dagmar, glancing vainly up the dark stairs.

'So nice meeting you,' said Ursula, opening the door.

'I nearly forgot,' exclaimed Dagmar, and reaching into the wicker basket, pulled out a brown-paper parcel. 'Some fruit for Ethel,' she explained.

'Oh really,' protested Sister Ursula, 'I'm sure that wasn't necessary, my dear. Do keep it for yourself, or perhaps the old lady would like it.'

'No, no,' persisted Dagmar, who had managed to open the door more widely than the nun wished. Sister Ursula had a clear view of the heads which turned at the sound of the German's voice. 'They are for the child,' cried Dagmar. 'Surely you cannot object to that?'

'Why of course not,' said Sister Ursula, her voice matching the volume of Dagmar's. 'I should be delighted to accept your kind gift,' and she snatched the package from Dagmar's hand.

'Goodbye, then,' said Dagmar. 'No doubt I shall see you again.'

'I shouldn't think so, my dear,' replied the nun, in a quieter voice. 'Oh no, I don't think so somehow, not after today. I thought we sorted that out in our little chat. Goodbye, my dear,' she stated with a note of finality, and swiftly closed the door.

A look of distaste swirled over the nun's face, and she lifted the paper bag to her nose and sniffed. A fresh citrous smell met her open nostrils. It was fruit after all. She opened the rustling bag and looked in. There were a couple of oranges, an apple, a few grapes and a pomegranate. Far too extravagant, thought Sister Ursula.

Dagmar turned on her heel and walked away, a smile playing on her thin lips as she stepped round the piles of glass, and from the eyrie of her gaping window above, the round

231

eyes of Ethel followed the blonde head down the road. Her nightdress billowed around her. She didn't feel the cold. The white figure appeared to be frozen in this attitude, not even turning her head as her aunt entered.

'Ethel,' commanded Sister Ursula, 'come away from that window. Have you no modesty? Goodness knows how many people have seen you.'

She paused a moment, waiting for the girl to do as she had been told, and then remembering how she had left Ethel slumped on the floor, wondered whether the girl was sleep-walking. She clutched at her thin chest, realising the drop outside the window. The cold air blew through the gaping hole as if to remind the nun of the danger.

'Come away, my dear,' she said in a more reasonable tone. 'You must be getting very cold. Your aunty will go and make something warm for you, so come away dear.'

While she had been talking, she had been creeping as softly as frost over the floor. With great caution she reached out to get hold of Ethel's fleshy arm. The strange feeling of vertigo persisted, even though both her feet were planted firmly on the floor. Somehow she had interposed herself between Ethel and the window, and could feel the frigid air waft the back of her legs through her habit. She was pressed close to her niece, and the blank, expressionless face frightened her. Whatever she was seeing, it wasn't the worried head of her aunt.

As she steadied herself, Sister Ursula slowly released her meagre grip on Ethel's arm. She had felt the unnatural cold which emanated from the girl. She looked down at the hand which had been holding on to Ethel. Her frozen fingers painfully unbent themselves, the joints red and raw, until the palm lay exposed. Where once there had been a mark, there was creased skin and nothing more. The nun gasped. For a moment, she thought perhaps she was looking at the wrong palm, but as she slowly decided to believe her eyes, she stared in horror at Ethel.

'What have you done?' Her desperate hand flew out and struck the uncaring flesh of the girl. 'Damn you, damn you,' she screamed, oblivious to the small collection of passers-by who stopped in their tracks to watch the unfolding story in the upstairs window. 'He has forsaken me,' she sobbed. 'I have sinned mightily, and am cast down.' She swayed with mounting hysteria. 'Forgive me, forgive me,' she screeched, 'I know not what I have done.' The awkward phrases spilled from her spittle-flecked lips, and still Ethel stood impervious to her aunt's display. On the street, the people had clustered together.

'It's a nun,' said the first voice.

'She's fighting somebody.'

'She is drunk,' interrupted the third voice.

'It's a sin,' came a woman's voice.

'Drinking?' questioned the first.

'No, suicide! She's going to throw herself out of that window.'

'Nonsense,' replied the first voice, 'I was here first. I saw it all. There was a white figure, or a sheet hung up, it was difficult to tell.'

'Aha,' said the woman's voice, seizing on this uncertainty. 'She was probably covering the window with a sheet, and then decided to throw herself out. I've heard of that type of thing before.'

'Jesus Christ Crucified,' screamed Sister Ursula, causing the voices to fall silent.

Her hands ceased pummelling the unyielding body of Ethel. In a paroxysm of grief she wilted like a stricken flower, and as her cowled head hung low, the ground below swam into view. The sharp slivers of glass glinted in the bleak morning. Her breathing fell silent as her eyes gazed at the dizzy drop beneath her. The nun found out she couldn't close her eyes to the beckoning ground. With great effort she moved her eyes downwards to the clustered heads. The enticing hole seemed nearer, as if she had lost her grip, not just on Ethel, but on the information her eyes sent to her frenzied brain. She reached out slowly to feel whether or not the hole was an illusion conjured by the devil. She knew of his tricks to confuse the mind, lead the righteous from the true path. Her hands met unresisting air, and below a woman screamed.

The sound pierced Sister Ursula, whose arm swayed from the jagged hole. She tried to steady the shaking that surged through her body.

'She's going to jump,' shouted the woman. 'Somebody get

the police, somebody call an ambulance, it's just like that actress. She jumped as well.'

'Shut up,' came the other voices in unison, as though they were complaining at the cinema or a theatre when somebody was making too much noise with toffee paper.

Sister Ursula could feel her hidden crucifix rubbing against her trembling thigh, and prayed to the eleven thousand virgins to aid her at this moment of peril. If they sighed in unison, the sweet breath they exhaled would have suspended her in air and her resolve hardened when she heard a gratingly familiar voice drift up to her ears.

'What's going on then?' asked Mrs Wagtail.

She had prowled around the confused streets, peering through the broken windows, taking the opportunity to have a look in the houses where the occupants would show her what precious crystal objects had broken. She had shaken her head, and sometimes when nobody was looking, had taken some powdered glass and swiftly deposited it in her creased, black handbag. In the same way, she kept her eyes peeled for any nail parings or stray hairs or threads from clothes. These went into the bag as well. If anybody saw her cracked nails straying over the material on a chair, she would give them a little ingratiating smile. 'Lovely fabric,' she'd say, pulling away little fibres which caught on her corrugated skin. Only glass and crystal, that had been the strange thing, not pottery, not stuff made from clay and earth. She pondered on this as she tramped the streets. She knew the properties of gems and precious stones, but glass, that was a puzzler. Perhaps, she thought, it would just be like crystal. It might induce sleep and pleasant dreams, even visions.

She was slightly out of breath when she pushed herself into the small crowd, who parted as they saw her brush up against them. The woman who had screamed and had once read of an actress throwing herself out of a window felt uncomfortable standing next to Mrs Wagtail.

Sister Ursula looked down and caught sight of the strange individual whom she had included in her prayers since her first day in Slackhall. As their eyes met, the figure below gesticulated wildly with her hands. The nun closed her eyes and groaned. At the convent, her sisters would be gliding

234

through the cloisters with their breviaries in hand, and here she was suspended over a street of staring eyes.

'This is a strange how do you do,' muttered Mrs Wagtail. 'Is she trying to top herself? She called round my place once, without a by your leave; tried to force her way in, too.' Nobody reacted to her comments. 'She's got bad inclinations,' she stated knowingly. 'She must be wanting to repent.'

'She did scream out something about forgiving her,' said one of the men.

'Well, forgive and forget,' said Mrs Wagtail, 'that's my motto. This one here's a Jehovah.'

'Jehovah!' exclaimed the woman, 'you must need some spectacles. That's a nun, or somebody dressed up as a nun. It could be another actress in a costume.' As she caught the eye of the man wearing the nice tweed coat, she simpered.

'I'll go and get the police,' said the man in the tweed jacket.

'Oh yes,' replied the woman. 'We'll wait here.' She meant she would.

They followed the solid figure as he dashed in what the woman thought was an athletic manner up the street. As nothing seemed to be happening at the window, she opened her neat little handbag, pulled out a small compact, and opening it, gave her face a swift once-over. As she scrutinised her features, she didn't notice Mrs Wagtail removing a stray platinum blonde hair from her shoulder and deposit the dyed hair into her own bag, muttering 'floosy' under her breath.

A strange stillness had settled on Ethel's bedroom. The sister of mercy stared out into the benumbed form of her niece. Satan has her in his power, thought the nun. With cold certainty, she knew her life could be lost, her ending providing a spectacle for those below, like a crowd at an amphitheatre . . . watching, watching.

It was her good nature, she decided, that had put her in this unfortunate position and, of course, there would be those who could profit by a nature such as hers, Sister Agnes for instance. For all her stupidity, the nun was a senior member of the convent and, of course, a possible rival if anything happened to Sister Barbara, and there had been that rumour about the trip to Rome.

The abyss yawned beneath her. The merest pressure from

Ethel could send her tumbling from the broken window, out of this world into the next. She wondered how long it would take a priest to arrive to administer the last rites. She shuddered, the movement sending one of the remaining shards of glass tumbling down. As it crashed, Mrs Wagtail had made her move.

As she closed the Coffins' front door, she gave a little smile of triumph. Stepping into the lounge, her eyes fixed on the crucifix. Her hands roved over the chairs, occasionally picking up the detritus of the Coffins' lives. Her black bag hung open, as it received the flotsam into its dark depths.

As her beady eyes fell on the used teacups, they betrayed an inner excitement, as though this was something she hadn't even hoped for. She wiped down her hands on the side of her greasy coat before she reached out to take the innocent piece of Worcester. She lifted it to her face and inhaled the faint lingering smell of Dagmar's herbal infusion. Her tongue dipped into the depths and probed around like a flat worm.

'Mugwort,' she said. 'Mugwort, rue, wormwood and betony.'

She sniffed the cup again, and without more ado dropped it into her bag. This cup, she decided, was full of bitterness, blood and intoxication. With a sly glance at the only other occupant of the room, she left. As she passed the kitchen, she paused for a moment, as if she had just remembered something she had forgotten to do, or had walked into an invisible line.

In the empty hall she made a peculiar little detour, sliding along the wall like a small forlorn spider, having strayed from its own web and unable to spare the time to weave another. As she reached the bottom step, her breathing was very heavy, and little drops of sweat beaded her forehead. Rooting around in her pocket, she brought forth a tattered scarf and dabbed her forehead, then fished around and pulled out a rag-eared pack of cards which also looked as though they had seen better days. With a dexterity that belied her old rheumy fingers, she shuffled the pack, mouthing something silently under her wheezing breath. Mrs Wagtail studied the tarot cards for a few moments. Occasionally glancing upstairs, she sighed, and then, with equal rapidity, mixed the cards up as if

236

wishing to erase the unique pattern they had made, obscuring whatever messages she felt they contained. She stuffed them back into the mouldy depths of her pocket and with a grunt of effort she pulled herself upright, to make her way up the stairs. By the time she reached the top, her chest was heaving and she clutched on to the banister as she paused for breath.

Sister Ursula had thought she had heard somebody coming slowly up the stairs; the excruciating pause between each ponderous step set the nun's teeth on edge. She wondered whether her ears were deceiving her. She could no longer tell. It was a few moments before she realised with a start that somebody had entered the room.

She heard herself asking, 'Who's that?'

'*Tu qui es praeter omnia,*' muttered a voice.

'Wilfred?' asked Sister Ursula. 'Fanny?'

'*Caveat; caveat, caveat,*' came the voice, chanting slowly and surely.

There was a scraping sound and Ethel shuddered, her body turning full circle until Sister Ursula was given a momentary view of the intruder. At the same instant she realised who had entered the house. She discovered that she was no longer pressed against the window, and the demand for an explanation died on her lips.

'*Omnia in Duos: Duo in Unum: Unus in Nihil ut erat est erit in saecula Saeculorum,*' murmured the voice, keeping the pitch so low it was difficult to divide the words. It was no benediction that the nun had ever heard before. Still she remained silent, watching the back of her niece slowly move away into the centre of the room.

'As above so below,' said Ethel.

'I should think so,' said Sister Ursula, unable to restrain herself any longer.

'As above so below,' shouted Ethel, her voice assuming a curious masculine depth, as though it were breaking.

'I hope you are going to apologise,' said the nun. 'I won't put up with this type of behaviour. Goodness me, you are a lucky girl,' she said to the back of the heavy nightdress, 'a lucky girl not to find yourself in serious trouble. What if your aunt had fallen from the window, what then?'

'El, Elohim, Elohe Eoba, Sabaoth, Turiel Seraphiel,

Uriel, Anael Theiron, LA! AL! LA! AL!' croaked the hidden figure, and then before Sister Ursula could direct her attention to Mrs Wagtail, Ethel's body doubled up, and she made a retching noise.

'Not in the bedroom,' cried the nun, forgetting that she still hadn't moved from the window. It was too late, Ethel was being sick all over the carpet. 'Oh Ethel,' Sister Ursula said, 'how could you, how awful.' She couldn't imagine how she would bring herself to clean that up.

'That's right, that's right,' cajoled Mrs Wagtail, moving over towards the sweating girl, who was moaning slightly.

'My foot hurts,' complained Ethel.

'That won't be the only thing,' said Ursula fiercely. She had just found out that her habit was caught on a sliver of glass, and in pulling away she had heard it ripping through the material.

'Now look what I've done,' she said petulantly. 'This is all your fault.'

'I'm ill,' declared Ethel. 'I've been sick, you should call the doctor.'

'No need for that, dearie,' interjected Mrs Wagtail. 'I'm here now. You don't want no smelly doctor probing and pushing, sticking his nose in. Mrs Wagtail has something in her bag. That will do the trick.'

'I beg your pardon,' said Sister Ursula, aware once more of the stranger's presence. 'I am this girl's aunt. I shall say what is to be done, or what is not to be done.'

'I'm dying,' wailed Ethel, fearing that this time she might not be reborn.

'Tsk, tsk,' muttered Mrs Wagtail, and poked Ethel under her wobbly chin.

'Honestly,' began Sister Ursula, and then she heard somebody running up the stairs. She fell silent. The door swung open and there stood a policeman and the man in a tweed coat.

'This is a farce,' declared the nun, feeling slightly hysterical.

'What's going on then?' demanded the red-faced constable who had run all the way, and felt in no mood to be informed that this was a farce. He had expected to see a body, a body

238

hanging out of the window. 'It's a serious matter to waste police time,' he informed the room. 'There's been some funny goings-on in the town. Important investigations are under way, and I want to know exactly what's been going on here.' He eyed them all sharply as though they were all suspects.

'I'll be off then,' said the man in the tweed coat, thinking that he didn't want to get more involved.

'Oh no you don't,' said PC Bowles, feeling rather hot despite the cold air rushing through the broken window. 'It was you summoned His Majesty's constabulary. I shall have to be taking statements all round.' Slowly he unbuttoned his breast pocket, and pulled out a rather shiny-looking book. 'You may be called upon to testify,' he warned. 'Let's start from the beginning then,' he said. 'Name first.' He licked the bottom of his pencil in a thoughtful way, and steadied it on the pristine page.

'This is ludicrous,' stormed Sister Ursula. 'You must get out of this house immediately.'

She waited for her instructions to be acted upon, but instead of respectful movement, all that met her astonished eyes were the incredulous eyes of PC Bowles, Mrs Wagtail and the man. Ethel was examining her podgy foot.

'Did you hear me?' she asked, her voice sounding shrill. 'There are sick people in this house. You must leave at once.'

'Sick people,' repeated the policeman slowly. 'Nothing contagious, I should hope.' He sniffed, and looked about him.

'Get out,' screamed Sister Ursula.

'She the actress then?' asked the policeman, jerking his thumb in the direction of Sister Ursula, who felt that she might faint any second.

'Jehovah,' interjected Mrs Wagtail, afraid that she might be forgotten.

'Don't blaspheme,' said the nun automatically. 'I want your name and number,' she said to the policeman, and then immediately wondered what on earth had made her ask such a thing. Mrs Wagtail smiled, this was better than listening to a radio play.

'Now then, now then,' said PC Bowles, feeling that all this

239

had gone far enough. 'I shall have to ask you to accompany me to the station if I don't get any co-operation.'

'It's a fair cop,' she replied, and then threw her hand up to her mouth and gasped in amazement at the alien words which had spilled from her lips a second time. She looked at the red face of the policeman, and swiftly closed her eyes, praying to St Dympna; she was convinced she was going mad. She never heard the snickering of Mrs Wagtail. When she felt the hand of a man on her body she screamed, 'Profane, profane.'

'I've cut my foot,' declared Ethel. 'I might bleed to death.' She raised her bovine eyes. 'And I'm hungry,' she shouted.

'Is this your daughter?' asked the policeman, still holding on to Sister Ursula.

'I'm a nun,' she screamed, feeling that reality was melting away into some sort of parody. She felt the policeman slacken his grip. 'I am Sister Ursula,' she added with some dignity. 'I am not to be handled,' she declared, as though she were breakable cargo. 'And I refuse to participate in this any longer.' The policeman looked at her closely, and then felt his throat begin to tighten up, as he believed her. He coughed nervously.

'I'm sorry ma'am,' he muttered. 'I was given misleading information.' He cast a baleful look at the man in the tweed coat. 'I was given to understand an actress was threatening suicide. I'm sorry to have disturbed you.' Sister Ursula gave a brief half-forgiving smile, and then resumed her stern countenance.

'I shall overlook it this once,' she added magnanimously.

'It was a domestic dispute,' said Mrs Wagtail. 'You don't want to get involved with that, luvvy.' She smiled at the policeman. 'I always like a man in uniform,' she added.

'And who might you be?' asked PC Bowles.

'Mrs Wagtail of number seven, a friend of the family.' She poked Ethel in a motherly way. 'Having no children of my own, she's like a daughter to me.' Sister Ursula gaped in disbelief.

'You have children,' she stormed. 'I know you, you are to

240

blame for all this,' and she made a gesture to encompass the room, and implied things beyond the room.

'Why bless you, dearie,' laughed Mrs Wagtail, 'whatever next.' She turned to the policeman, and with a surprisingly strong pull, yanked him closer so she could whisper, 'It's all been too much for her. You just leave her with me, and she'll be as right as rain.' She prodded him in his side, as though feeling the quality of a joint of meat. PC Bowles jumped. 'You're a twitchy thing,' she remarked. 'Could do with a good steak and kidney pie as well, by the look of you.' She gave him a knowing wink: 'You call round any time, although Thursdays is meat and kidney, with lots of gravy,' she added, licking her lips, and then reaching forward, deftly removed a stray hair from the policeman's jacket. 'Tut, tut,' she said, 'that will never do.' PC Bowles blushed.

'We'll be off then,' Bowles stammered, glaring at the man in the tweed coat who felt rather awkward and cursed the woman in the blonde hair who had suggested he go off to the police.

Mrs Wagtail dashed over to the window to wave at the departing men. Sister Ursula pointed her finger, as though, like the hand which wrote for Belshazzar, she could humble Mrs Wagtail's insolence and number the time in which she had to endure the dreadful woman's presence. It seemed to Sister Ursula that the lopsided head could not discern the writing on the wall.

'Let bygones be bygones,' instructed Mrs Wagtail, brushing past the pointing quivering finger.

'Out,' stormed the nun. 'Out! Out! Out!'

'Calm down,' commanded Mrs Wagtail, and as the refrain ceased upon the instruction, the little woman turned to squint at Ethel.

'Go and get some hot water and a mop,' she instructed, and without a single word of protest, the nun found herself obeying. Her limbs moved towards her kitchen, and her own behaviour seemed without rhyme and reason. She would rather have obeyed the Borgia Pope, Alexander VI. Sister Ursula decided that she would confront the woman, demand that she should leave these walls. It wasn't an easy task, climbing the stairs with the awkward bucket.

241

'You took your time,' observed Mrs Wagtail. 'It's not been very nice having to sit here next to that.' She motioned to the vomit. 'Better clean it up at once.'

'Clean it up,' repeated Sister Ursula disconsolately.

'It smells,' said Ethel. 'Makes me feel sick.' She sniggered at the joke.

The nun banged the bucket down, the room filling with a metallic retort. Mrs Wagtail eyed it suspiciously.

'That's not iron, is it, dearie?' she asked cajolingly.

'I have no idea,' replied Sister Ursula swiftly. 'If you are so bothered, take a closer look.' She pushed it towards Mrs Wagtail, who flinched slightly. Sister Ursula turned to Ethel. 'I think that you are big enough to clean up your own mess.' She thrust the mop at the bewildered girl, who looked round at Mrs Wagtail as though seeking intervention of some sort.

'I've been exercised,' said Ethel proudly, not quite sure whether it was as grand as being reborn. Mrs Wagtail laughed nervously, and prodded the bucket with her toe.

'Tin,' she exclaimed, and at once jumped down from the bed upon which she had been sitting.

'Exercised,' said Sister Ursula cautiously. 'I don't think that was very wise after just being sick. You have to be very careful or you might pull a muscle.' She eyed Mrs Wagtail as though she had discovered the old woman was feeble minded. 'I shall call the doctor to examine my niece. I just hope there is no danger or explanations might be sought.'

'No need for a doctor,' said Mrs Wagtail, 'though to my mind, the best cure would be trepanning.'

'What's that?' asked Ethel, examining her foot.

'Speak when you are spoken to,' snapped Ursula.

'Cheerie-bye, then,' said Mrs Wagtail, so suddenly that the nun gasped.

Tipping her head from side to side in an animated manner, Mrs Wagtail gathered up her long coat and stepped over the bucket showing a pair of thick woollen stockings in the process. Sister Ursula crossed herself as the little woman brushed past and in the doorway Mrs Wagtail paused.

'The Lord gave and the Lord hath taken away,' she said, smiling insolently.

As Sister Ursula reeled from the blasphemy, Mrs Wagtail closed the door, sealing in the nun, and muffling the horrified shriek.

[21]

While her ex-pupil became aware of a hollowness within her, Cecilia Royce was becoming full of a dangerous excitement. Her eyes which once gleamed with bookish lore, were now transfixed with another obsession. Miss Royce had been snatched from her circumspect life by the intoxicating and exotic presence of the German fascist.

The dullness of her uneventful days was to change, and she bustled around her room, removing all the books which might compromise her new zeal. She paused to wipe her sweaty brow, and as the doorbell rang, she seemed to sway to the door with a drunken rapture.

On the doorstep stood three young men. She felt her blood throbbing, reverberating through her body, and thought of how one of the men resembled the life-saving instructor, and as his arm was raised stiff and muscled, she imagined herself hanging from the black clothed salute.

'There's been trouble in the town, Miss,' said one.

'Trouble?' she gasped.

'Broken windows and such. We thought we'd check.'

'Probably the communists,' exclaimed the one with the black shirt.

'Probably,' agreed the headmistress.

'Hard and humble tasks,' groaned Sister Ursula, flailing her rosary beads back and forth over her crouched back. This impromptu scourging ceased when the nun realised she was not alone.

'Mortify the flesh,' Ursula said, 'to cleanse the spirit.' She struggled to her feet.

'You will learn the catechism,' the nun exclaimed, 'but first you must clean up that mess.' She raised her eyes and pointed in the vague direction of the pool of vomit.

'Can't I have something to eat first,' pleaded Ethel, 'I'm empty inside, all holy.' She saw her aunty gasp, and wondered what was wrong now.

'Don't let me hear you blaspheme again. You should say twenty Hail Marys for that.'

Ethel realised that she wasn't going to get food until she complied.

'Look,' cried Ethel, bending forward and inspecting the floor, 'there's all bits and things in my sick. I must have lost them from inside.' She felt her corpulent belly. 'All my workings must have shot right out of my mouth.'

'It is not very ladylike,' remarked Sister Ursula, 'to stare at something like that.'

'I'm unstuck,' wailed Ethel. 'I can feel it all wobbling about inside. All my pins have come out, I must be broken.'

The pool of vomit had been disturbed by the mop and smeared about the carpet, and just as the nun was about to avert her gaze, she noticed something glinting in the regurgitated contents of Ethel's stomach. Caution thrown to the wind, she bent down to see what had caught her eye, and suddenly became aware of a sprinkling of glinting points. Needles and pins. It was as if the contents of a sewing basket had been tipped out, and as she tried to think of some explanation for the strange objects, she noticed little slivers of broken glass sticking out of the vomit as well.

'My seams have split,' declared Ethel. 'I'm all undone.'

'What silly trick is this?' declared the nun fiercely, taking hold of Ethel's arms and shaking her. 'Why did you put all these things on the floor?' she demanded. 'Did that woman tell you to do this, throw all these things on the floor and make a mess? Tell me.'

'She did it,' declaimed Ethel, clutching at the proffered betrayal. 'She did it, she did it.'

'I thought as much,' said Sister Ursula, feeling satisfied that she had got to the bottom of the mystery. The trials and tribulations she decided, were a test of her true faith. She would make Ethel kneel with her. The stains of that Protestant school would be wiped clean.

'You may report to me when the room is spotless,' she instructed.

By the time the smell of food cooking drifted up the stairs and wafted into Ethel's room, she had finished clearing up. As she burst into the kitchen she could hardly speak for the saliva which flooded her mouth.

'Eggs, bacon, tomatoes and mushrooms.' She dashed the words out as though the quicker they left her mouth, the sooner their corporeal counterparts could take their place.

'Now, now,' interrupted the nun, deftly turning the sizzling bacon, 'I think you've committed a venial sin.' She eyed Ethel for a second before turning her attention to the frying-pan. 'Do you know what that is?'

'Yes,' mumbled Ethel sullenly, thinking there didn't look to be very much bacon in the pan.

'Well that's a relief,' said Sister Ursula sweetly. 'What is it then?' She turned to look at Ethel, widening her cold eyes, and making Ethel feel uneasy.

'The bacon's going to burn,' she said hopefully.

'Then we shall have burnt offerings,' countered Sister Ursula coldly. 'That will be a little penance.' She gave Ethel a sweet smile. 'And what is a venial sin, my dear?' she persisted.

Ethel felt red and stupid, and bit her fleshy lip as though to gain inspiration and sustenance at the same time.

'Don't do that dear,' said Sister Ursula, making Ethel go even redder. 'Now, what about that little question then?'

'It's hard to explain,' attempted Ethel. 'You just know, that's all.'

'You do, do you!' exclaimed Sister Ursula. 'Pride, that's a venial sin. And it could be worse; giving way to your pride may lead on to further temptations from the devil, then you are lost.' She folded her arms, and stood as remote as a carved statue. 'You are my mission,' she declared. 'I see that now, as clearly as we can see Our Lord's five wounds, and his sacred heart.' Ethel watched cautiously as her aunt crossed herself, and with a hesitant hand she did the same. 'Good, good,' beamed Sister Ursula, 'but with the right hand, my dear.' She smoothed down her habit and tipping the food uncere- moniously on to a plate for Fanny and Wilfred, she glided out of the kitchen.

Ethel cast her own eyes round the room, a guilty smile

246

passing briefly over her droopy lips which trembled with anticipation. As her chubby fingers salvaged the crisped rind from the grey fat which congealed around the frying-pan, her senses sang the praises of this portion of the pig. She licked her fingers with relish, and scooped up more of the fat with prodigal ease. She liked the feel of her fingers slipping and sliding through the grease. Soon the pan was scraped clean. She burped, the hot breath smelt of cooking fat, and singed flesh.

A brown bag lay nonchalantly on the kitchen table. Ethel burped again. As her voracious gaze fell on the bag, the juices of her stomach simmered away rapaciously and her hands were unable to resist touching it, crinkling its surface, as her fingers moved delicately, moulding themselves to the hidden contents.

She caressed the bag gently, jostling the tender fruit beneath, feeling the grapes giving beneath her probing fingers, and sensuously stroking the larger bodies as the libido of her stimulating appetite took over. Her impatient movements tumbled the contents on to the table top, and with surprising swiftness her hand darted out to prevent an apple falling to the floor and bruising its tender surface.

A pomegranate lay tantalisingly among all the familiar shapes. She didn't know what it was. The strangeness intrigued, tempting her hand to pick it out above all the rest. As this symbol of immortality lay in her chubby palm, she could have been posing for a Renaissance painting, her cherub hand standing in for the baby Christ.

The iconograph was broken as with ungainly motion she raised it to her nose and sniffed the hard surface. She placed Dagmar's gift on the table and went in search of something to cut it open. Ethel knew where the knives lay. So the pomegranate didn't roll about, she placed it on a white cloth, which she smoothed down with an intense look.

Somehow Ethel believed the unnatural fruit would have strange properties. Her fingers palpated her greasy cheek; this could be the very thing to improve her complexion. She tossed back her hair, which fell limply into place and ran the sharp blade experimentally over the unorthodox gift. Her tongue stuck out with concentration.

247

The bright blade cut through the pomegranate, the thick juice oozed out, and Ethel dropped the blade. It was as if the monstrous fruit bled. A red stain spread beneath the two segments and formed a strange shape, like a fragment of a map, the boundaries of which expanded as more juice soaked into the white material.

The exotic interior lay exposed. The core of the fruit glistened as its secret folds were probed by the girl's eyes, and still it bled. A strange fragrance had been released by the passage of the sharp blade. Ethel wet her finger in the blood-red juice. She dabbed a little round her face thinking it might seep into her skin, leaving it as smooth as Dagmar's. With great delicacy Ethel removed a single seed from a palpitating interior. She lifted the finger to her mouth and the seed swirled in the moist folds of her jaw for a few seconds until she swallowed and sent it on its journey through her body. A subtle flavour had popped inside her as she crushed its firm surface. As she reached down for one of the halves, intending to sink her teeth into the serried layers, the fruit went spinning from her hand.

Sister Ursula knocked it to the floor, drops of red splashing from the crushed segment as though blood had been spilled on to the tiles.

'Wicked, wicked child, you are heading for purgatory,' she hissed.

Like Persephone, Ethel Coffin had eaten a single pomegranate seed. Demeter's daughter had eaten in the world below, and for one-third of the year she lived in the dark realm of Hades, for then it was winter, the trees stark and all seemingly dead in the world.

It was indeed a fruit with strange properties.

The busiest people in Slackhall over the next few days were the glaziers. Like rats to Hamelin, they came in droves: fat ones, thin ones, old ones, young ones, and soon the gaping holes which let the cold, autumn air into the houses were once more covered by glass, to keep the inside in and the outside out. With every window replaced, a sense of normality began to take over, and people sank into the security of their own homes, and the shared experience somehow became a subject which they preferred not to discuss, and children soon found out that they were sent to bed without supper if they asked too many questions. It was natural that it should be Dr Baldwin who first became aware of another strange epidemic which began to affect the townsfolk. Of course, Slackhall had its share of illnesses; there had been an outbreak of diphtheria, the usual measles and chicken-pox, but this was an epidemic of accidents.

It was as though the people had suddenly become clumsy and careless, and the numbers kept the good doctor's feet walking the streets. The glaziers got to know his compact form and would nod at him, and be greeted in turn by his awkward, barking laugh, which became familiar all over the town. Sometimes he had to visit every house in a street; it was as though there had been a collective failure within the people of Slackhall.

Meanwhile, the seven-hour flight of Neville Chamberlain to Herr Hitler's eyrie at Berchtesgaden was completely overshadowed by the strange happenings in Slackhall. Only the glaziers showed some interest due to the account of the very large windows the German chancellor had installed in his country retreat. As the Führer tried to point out the scenery through the cloud and mist to the tired old man, he gave the dimensions of the largest window ever constructed. The glaziers imagined the tricky business it must have been to put in place, and the amount of putty that would be needed.

The contagion which dispersed its unorthodox symptoms throughout the town was difficult to treat at source. It had started in little niggling ways that even Dr Baldwin was not aware of. When milk was poured into the morning cups of tea, it was found to have gone sour. The local farmers shook their heads and assured their customers they had not been given old milk. Clean brown shells would be broken to find rotten eggs; after a morning's baking all that was removed from the oven were shrivelled black cakes.

These natural disasters were the annoying precursors to the spontaneous catalogue of mishaps which started to befall the people of Slackhall.

At first people might have noticed a spontaneous twitch of a limb, and perhaps an uncomfortable attack of pins and needles. The people of Slackhall would not pay out hard-earned money for such trivial things, and the memory tended to be obliterated by the subsequent mishap. Although the glaziers brought with them a higher proportion of ladders under which the population had to avoid walking, the bad luck which started to plague the town had to be caused by more than this.

Dr Baldwin was inundated with patients. Twisted ankles, sprained wrists, broken bones, slipped discs; healthy bodies had to be swathed in bandages and plaster of Paris and Dr Baldwin's hands began to grow callouses as he slapped the casts into place.

Although he felt within his own bones that something unwholesome was happening, he sat at night in front of his fire, musing over a glass of brandy. He was a scientist and came to the conclusion that he was overworked and lived in a town bedevilled with clumsy people. The good doctor went about his business restoring health as best he could and began to welcome those patients who came with what he saw as healthy sicknesses. Vomiting, diarrhoea, blood pressure, shingles and even ringworm brought a light to his jaded, plaster-of-Paris eyes.

One poor woman stuck in his mind. Somehow he associated her with the accident victims, although she hadn't slipped and hurt herself, or dropped something on her foot, or even burnt her hand while cooking. Her symptoms seemed to be more of a genuine medical disorder. She had developed a type of alopecia; her peroxided hair had begun to fall out in huge tufts. She wore a smart, if bright, silk scarf reeking of perfume, which covered her shame.

At first he thought that her brittle hair, which seemed like spun glass and snapped at the merest pressure, had been affected by the peroxide. She had admitted that she was not a natural blonde. He smiled into her brown eyes and advised her to discontinue the use of the bleaching agent. He tried to assure her that the hair would grow back. When next he saw her, she was nearly bald. Her red eyes brimming with tears stared at him, shining with hurt for the failure of his diagnosis and his inability to provide a cure. Not only was her pate bereft of hair, but the skin had begun to itch, and the red swellings had developed into ulcers, her heavily made-up face capped by a dome of running sores. He lowered his scientific eyes, and his stethoscope hung shamefully around his neck while the woman sobbed quietly. He arranged for her to go and see someone in Manchester, but the appointment was never kept for in the dark despair of night she hanged herself. As she kicked the chair away, she thought briefly of the film star she had once read of, who had also killed herself.

Reverend Roe strode about the town like a black shadow, occasionally acknowledging Dr Baldwin, but walking briskly past the practitioner in case he should ask about Roe's wife. He even stepped under ladders with impunity. Nobody seemed to take much notice of another little figure which darted around. She kept clear of the glaziers' ladders, and her heavy, black bag swung merrily in her hand. For no apparent reason she would begin to chortle, the laugh winding through the empty streets.

Another effect of the series of calamities was the gradual diminution of the number of able bodies who could operate the looms. From the deafening clacking of shuttles whirling back and forth, the sound had spread thinner than the cotton produced as more and more machines fell silent. Light no longer poured from the factories on the early mornings, and

251

the chimneys did not smoke; neither did the familiar smell of the dye-works drift over the town, turning the sky to whatever colour was being produced, tinging the nostrils of those who breathed deeply, the darkest indigo, the brightest red.

Those who were away from the carding room coughed even more, their lungs craving the air filled with cotton seeds and fibres as they worked the raw cotton bales into thread. Even the followers of General Ludd who vowed to smash the machinery, had not caused the mill to fall so silent. The idle hands in Slackhall fidgeted and tapped impatient fingers. Like the British delegation in Germany, they had trouble whiling away the fruitless hours and stared glassy-eyed at nothing in particular.

[23]

The singing died away unevenly; some voices sustaining the last note while others broke off suddenly.

He closed his mouth with an abrupt click. Over the years he had become adept at miming the various hymns. He walked over towards the pulpit, and as the shuffling and coughing carried on, he turned to face the congregation. It seemed to him that this national day of prayer had certainly packed them in. He smiled inwardly at such complacency as he rubbed his hand along the polished wood of the lectern.

'We are gathered here,' he began, 'to pray together for peace within this troubled world.' He paused a second as another coughing fit started up.

'Our prayers go out to the world leaders who have been talking together. To the British Prime Minister, Neville Chamberlain, to the German Chancellor, Herr Hitler, the French Prime Minister, Edouard Daladier.' Roe hesitated a moment. 'We applaud these men of peace who struggle to prevent bloodshed. Perhaps we should also remember in our prayers those brave men who laid down their lives in the Great War.' He leant forward slightly. 'They died so that we might live.' He listened to the echo of his voice dying away into the shadowy corners. 'That was the war to end all wars,' he said, 'and there are many among us who can remember those dark days. We pray never to see their like again.'

The morning sun suddenly broke through the heavy clouds and rays of filtered daylight played over the congregation, a kaleidoscope of blues, reds and yellows flowered on the assembled heads as the coloured light warmed them for a brief few seconds. The startling beauty of the flaring colours made Roe catch his breath, and he gave an intimate little gasp.

'God,' he said in a choked voice, 'will not abandon us. God

·253

is everything.' His voice thrilled to the adoration. He had seen the presence of God in the coloured light and as it washed over him he felt forgiveness and not condemnation.

'We are weak vessels,' he preached, 'easily led.' He glanced into the crowd, and thought he heard a trembling sound, like a suppressed laugh. The sitting bodies shuffled silently as his eyes swept over them. He leaned forward as though trying to gauge the mood, like a lookout in the mizzen, sniffing whether there was stormy weather ahead.

'Let us pray,' he intoned, closing his eyes. He fell silent, and a mumbling whispering filled the stone place. Reverend Roe began, 'Our Father, who art in heaven . . .' but the inner voice fell silent. He suddenly thought about Georgette and her long hair, and her smooth hands and knowing smile. He stood in front of his congregation and dreamt about his mistress. 'The kingdom come, thy will be . . .' He wondered where she was now, what she had spent the money on . . . the money she had received for sacrificing their child. He was glad the countless eyes were closed. 'Give us this day our daily bread, and forgive us our trespasses . . .' He hoped there hadn't been much pain. Behind the mask of the praying face, the reverend saw blood spurting, the colour of her fiery hair. He fought against the terrible anguish that washed over him like the blood of the innocent. He had been helpless, and she gave birth to his dead child. The spectre of that death would for ever haunt him. 'For thine is the kingdom . . .' There had been no kisses of farewell, just the brown envelope stuffed with the payment. His hand had trembled as he pushed it through the door. The door through which she went with her pale hands crossed over her swelling belly. He had never seen her emerge, light and pale as a ghost, her eyes dry and shining, her cheeks flushed red . . . red as the blood of the dead child. 'For ever and ever . . . Amen.'

The words hung trembling in the air.

'Amen,' mouthed Roe.

His sickened eyes wearily opened, and although he felt the weight of the sun's rays and the dazzling coloured glass, his sudden joy was under lock and key.

The congregation waited.

He looked into the indifferent bodies. This was all he had

254

left. This was the choice he had taken, and like Peter returning to Rome, the consequences stared him directly in the face.

With a dry heart, he pulled himself upright. He would not allow anyone to see him suffer. He stared directly into the yawning mouth of a parishioner. It was like the gaping abyss of his personal hell.

He opened his own mouth, and the sterile voice fell out:

> The wolf also shall dwell with the lamb,
> and the leopard shall lie down with the kid;
> and the calf and the young lion and the
> fatling together; and a little child shall lead
> them. And the cow and the bear shall feed;
> their young ones shall lie down together;
> and the lion shall eat straw like the ox. And
> the suckling child shall play on the hole
> of the asp, and the weaned child shall put his
> hand on the cockatrice's den.

All over the merry land of England the people prayed that day for peace . . .

It was the feast day of St Thecla, and Ursula wished to celebrate the virgin martyr's death. Provisions had fallen quite drastically. Her régime, of one day cooking anything she could lay her hands on and the next day providing cups of water, seemed to be having an unexpected effect on Fanny and Wilfred.

They had still not spoken; they were frozen with an awkward stage-fright, and despite all the cajoling the nun could muster, their lips remained clenched. At first she thought they might have taken a vow of silence, dedicating their voices and the bitter-sweet practice of communication to God, but no such zeal shone in their eyes, and pious habits had not been maintained in this house.

Their mouths opened in strange synchronicity to pile in the food, or to sip the water, and it made Ursula dizzy to watch the perfect timing. Even the angle with which the knife and fork were held was exactly the same. The room also seemed to be becoming dimmer. Although Ursula brushed away such fancies as a trick of the light, she would enter the room with a tray and cautiously glance at the beds. She knew their static forms were lurking within the sheets, but it was often difficult to make out their presence. Again she blamed it on the light, and determined to take down the net curtain. When at last she did take down the fragile netting, she had a shock; trapped within their beds, subjected to alternate days of gorging and fasting, the results of her nursing lay before her.

It was clear that both their bellies had ballooned. The mounds could be seen, shielded by the blankets, but worse than the slight corpulence was the state of their skin. Like Pacific salmon at the end of spawning, the Coffins looked as though whatever journey they had made, had gone way beyond mere exhaustion. Their outer surface had turned scaly.

The Coffins became to Sister Ursula an outward manifestation of the state of their daughter's soul; it was clear that Ethel was damned, and her poor parents were suffering on her behalf.

At night Ethel lay as stiff as a statue. Yet within her a small kernel seemed to be forming, as though the pomegranate seed had lodged within her intestines, and like an irritant grain of sand in an oyster, a small hard core was forming. At this stage, it was too early to say whether it would be a shiny pearl, but whatever it was, it was growing.

Sister Ursula took Ethel with her to the market, she was determined they should have fish on Friday, and she felt that greens might improve both Fanny and Wilfred.

'I need some greens,' explained Sister Ursula to the greengrocer, 'for medicinal purposes.'

'This is the place then,' replied the greengrocer, thinking that there must be something wrong upstairs with that one, asking for greens, and having them staring her straight in the face. The girl didn't look a full shilling either. 'Them cabbages are nice and firm.' He nodded in their direction. Sister Ursula blanched slightly as she looked on the unfortunate vegetable.

'I couldn't possibly,' she stammered. Even if she knew the cabbage could have saved the lives of Fanny and Wilfred, she could not have made her hands touch the favourite vegetable of the Emperor Diocletian. She knew that some Catholics ate them, but not in any kitchen she ran.

'There's nothing wrong with them,' he said in a voice which was rather too loud for the nun's liking, and what was worse, he picked up one of the diabolical things and thrust it towards her.

'No thank you,' said Sister Ursula weakly, deciding that she had endured enough for one day, and taking hold of Ethel who had started to watch a woman make a toffee apple, left the market.

The Booths were also having fish. William was to set out for school on the next day and found he could not settle down to doing anything. Since the outburst with Nanny Bradshaw a

257

mutual silence had fallen between them. It was heavy with bitterness, and William looked forward to escape. As so often in the past, his feet brought him to the large kitchen, and although he did not seek the warmth of the fire, he stood in the shadows and watched Cook preparing the food. Several fishes were lined up. Their bodies flashed in the firelight, and when Cook took hold of one, it seemed as though it was still alive, as it slid around in her raw hand. He watched as the pale bellies were slit open and the guts spilled out. Cook rinsed the fish and took a sharp knife to scrape away the fish's scales which began to fall, although some stuck to the blade. The rasping sound set his teeth on edge, and he wanted to tell her to stop. He had no explanation for this sudden feeling of empathy for a dead fish which was shedding its shiny scales. He watched for a few moments longer, and then turned his back on the kitchen. Somehow, he knew he would not feel hungry when the cooked trout was placed before him.

He trailed along the corridors, his shadow dragging behind like a ghost of his childhood. That night he had a strange dream. It was a vision of a bed, a bed with tousled sheets as though a peculiar fight had taken place on their surface. There were damp stains which proclaimed the pressure of bodies; somehow he knew they had been naked bodies. His mouth had been dry, and then, just as suddenly, he had been under the bed, a darkened lair. At first it had been warm and safe, and then a cold desperation blew round him, and above his head the bed heaved and shook, and he knew he was trapped. He lay there afraid of being discovered, and yet fascinated by the sounds he heard. He couldn't make out the whispered words, but he knew the voices. It was Pewter and his grandmother, and then he heard their words. They had been talking about being dead, and he had gasped as the bony fingers curled round his ankles and tried to pull him from the darkness, and he woke shouting, 'No, no, no, no.' He wondered what had made him suddenly think of that, as though he were striving to find meaning in anything that happened to him in the last few hours before his departure. At the bottom of the stair-well he almost ran into Reverend Roe.

'William,' beamed the vicar, 'just the chap I have been

looking for. We always seem to meet when we are going in the opposite direction.' He took hold of William's shoulder. 'Shall we go somewhere a little more private?' he said, and deftly steered William down the corridor. The door didn't close properly as the wood must have warped, but the reverend struggled for a few minutes before giving up.

'You are leaving my little flock then,' said Roe, trying to sound woeful.

'Yes,' said William, hoping that if he remained relatively uncommunicative, Roe would take the hint and think he was upset and wanted to be on his own; which last was true.

'You'll have to be more talkative than that at school,' instructed Roe. 'I warn you, William, you must try and fit in with the crowd. They don't take to silent types at school. I remember my place, not as good as the one you are going to of course, but they made life hell for one quiet chap; I wouldn't like to have been in his shoes.' He coughed, and as William looked up at him, he was suddenly sure that Roe was talking about himself. 'Just between you and me,' winked the vicar, as though confiding something man to man, 'some of the other chaps passed water on him.' The vicar shook his head. 'They were expelled, some of them; went too far, too far.'

William watched as the vicar felt inside the breast pocket of his bulging waistcoat and pulled something out. As he realised William's eyes were following, the vicar looked embarrassed and awkward. He tried to conceal the paper in his palm and coughed nervously.

'Still,' he persisted, 'I should think that you'll be pretty quick at spotting what is what. It will do you a world of good to be mixing with other . . . er, young men,' he laughed. 'You all grow up so quickly these days, you'll no doubt be towering over your old vicar when you come home for hols. Still, you don't want to be listening to an old buffer like me, do you?' The laugh didn't arrive as the vicar stared into William's impassive face. Almost insolent, thought Roe to himself. 'Well, I won't keep you then William,' he said, and moved away from the door.

William tilted his head on one side, in what Roe thought was a very knowing way, and then slowly getting to his feet, he made to leave the room.

'Almost forgot,' said Roe, as William opened the door, 'thought it the right thing to do,' he explained in a confused way, and thrust the piece of paper towards William. 'Hope you don't think I'm being out of order, but it's better to be safe than sorry; people can be quite rum at school.' William took the proffered piece of paper, determined not to look at it, not under the nose of Roe at any rate.

'Good, good,' breathed Roe, and squeezed William's shoulder. 'Just a bit of advice. I'm sure it wasn't necessary, though,' he added and held his hand out, but William had already left the room.

He looked down at the piece of paper and, glancing at it briefly, it seemed to be three references to the Bible, all the Old Testament, Genesis.

He nearly scrumpled it up, but his nagging curiosity got the better of him, and he made for the library, and as he quietly shut the door behind him, he felt a solitary excitement. He knew Roe would know what he would be looking at; again he almost decided not to look. The empty library seemed to induce a caution into his movements, and as his fingers closed around the thick spine, he somehow felt he was tempting providence. If this had been meant as a pitfall he had fallen into it.

Smoothing out Roe's piece of paper, he looked at the references: Genesis XVIII and XIX were the first. He turned the pages; whisked past the creation of the world, the planting of Eden, the forming of Adam and the taking of the rib; stopped at the fall, and read down: 'for dust thou art, and unto dust shalt thou return'. The clever little smile he had been wearing froze on his face. He glanced over his shoulder. He knew he was being stupid; it was just a book. He just thought how he wouldn't have waited for Eve to take the apple, he'd have bitten into it first, then briskly turned over the page and shrugged his shoulders up and down as though trying to turn them into nascent wings.

He paused a moment before turning more. There was an illustration of Noah's ark perching on Mount Ararat with all the beasts. He felt himself perched on some lonely summit as well and suddenly felt in danger. He covered up the pages with his hand; it was so quiet in the room it made him feel uneasy; he was being a fool. He was covering the glory of God with his hands made from dust. He snatched them away as though the page was white-hot. And then he put them back again. Tentatively, he played the game of peekaboo, and then laughed. No lightning had struck him; they were words after all. Somehow he felt cleverer, as though he had been the first to realise this and flirt with impiety.

Swiftly now, he turned to the relevant section, his finger tracing down until it found XVIII and under the strange heading, 'Cities of the Plain', he read on. The fall of Sodom and Gomorrah, where it seemed not even fifty righteous people lived. Although he read it again and he imagined he grasped its meanings, thinking that there must be a wonderful religious message, he determined to keep the little note to remind him of the section. He wouldn't admit that the importance was hidden from him. Genesis XXXVIII,9 was the other reference. William idly turned to it, thinking of poor Lot's wife turned to a pillar of salt, and his dry eyes ran down the side, found the place and read.

'What's this,' came a sardonic voice, 'has the little pagan found religion?' William tried clumsily to turn to a different section of the Bible, but he knew his uncle would have seen the convulsive movement, as though he were trying to hide something.

John William covered the distance between the door and the table so slowly, William thought he would never get there. His uncle's eyes fell on Roe's slip of paper, and extending an elegant finger, he disdainfully turned it, so he wouldn't have to twist his head to read it. He smiled at William.

'Who would have guessed it,' he mused, 'a theologian within the family. Have you perhaps found your vocation in life, after being a lazy dreamer for so long? You'll have to remind me,' he drawled, 'I'm afraid I'm not so well up on the Holy Book as you. What's of such interest in these sections?' William stared at his uncle's black shirt which showed up dandruff at the shoulder. 'I see,' said John William, 'in that case, I shall just have to look for myself,' and he pulled the book from under William's hand, and started working backwards until he reached Genesis.

'Let's see,' murmured John William, 'Genesis thirty-eight,

verse nine.' His manicured fingernail left a tiny indentation on the thin paper as it ran down the numbers. He smiled and read: 'And Onan knew that the seed should not be his; and it came to pass, when he went in unto his brother's wife, that he spilled it on the ground.' He stopped, and raised one eyebrow, 'lest he should give his seed to his brother.' William tried to stop his cheeks from going red, but the more he tried, the hotter he became.

'And what delights do Genesis eighteen and nineteen hold?' continued John William. 'What little gem of wisdom have you uncovered there I wonder?' He turned over the pages, and then scanned a few lines. 'Sodom and Gomorrah,' he laughed, and shut the book, and gave William a charitable smile.

'Well, well, well,' he sneered. 'Oh, don't worry, I shan't tell. I wouldn't want to spoil the spotless record of innocent William; but using the Bible for licentious purposes!' He sat down on the table and William wished with all his heart that something dreadful would happen to the sneering head.

'Onanism and sodomy,' laughed his uncle, 'not very healthy, what shall we say, interests, for a . . . boy of your age.' He placed one foot firmly on the seat of the chair next to William, who shifted uncomfortably.

'You won't find what you're looking for there. If it's excitement you're after, there'll be plenty around.'

William remained resolutely silent.

'You'll go blind,' his uncle laughed, 'that's what I was told.' He laughed again, and reaching out his hands, made groping movements mimicking the sightless. 'Still, a word from the wise; I wouldn't let old Thrasher know you went in for that sort of thing.' He smiled at William's incomprehension and laughed. 'Your headmaster!' He prodded William with his foot. 'What Thrasher hates more than anything,' he declared, 'is depravity, and he knows young boys. He was always sneaking about prying into dark corners. He used to sniff the air, and then grab hold of somebody's hands and sniff them.' He laughed. 'That was it then, pulled by the ear by his good hand, and off for a proper caning. Everybody got thrashed.'

He suddenly reached out and took the piece of paper.

'Perhaps,' he said slowly, 'I'd better look after this.' As

262

William reached out to snatch it back, his uncle raised his arm and let the paper dangle there, out of William's grasp. 'One boy,' reminisced John William, 'was beaten so severely, he had to be taken to hospital, but his parents never took the matter further, old Thrasher just kept on. Mustn't have wanted the publicity, the parents I mean, although everybody knew.'

'Knew what?' asked William, and immediately cursed himself for breaking his silence.

'Aha,' gloated John William, 'thought that might interest you, but such innocence, William!' In his seat, William shifted his gaze away from his uncle's watching eyes. 'Sex, of course.' The word hung in the air, while William lowered his eyes and knew that his uncle was watching him. 'Tremaine was beaten for buggery. Takes two, of course!' His laugh somehow appeared coarse and animalistic in the empty library. 'The English master was sacked and perhaps the police were involved, although I can't remember now.' He popped the betraying piece of paper into his pocket. 'Well,' he said, 'I won't disturb your study any longer.' He gave a sardonic smile. 'But you should get more fresh air. All this . . . research is making you pale.'

He laughed, and the sound continued as he left William sitting alone in the library, his ears burning with humiliation.

[25]

'Good heavens man,' snapped Dr Baldwin, 'this is ludicrous.'

'Heaven,' said Reverend Roe smoothly, 'has no place in the matter.'

PC Bowles shifted uneasily. He couldn't really see why the law had to be dragged into this. He would far rather be having a word with Bob, the gamekeeper, about the trouble with poaching. You could always be sure of the offer to wet your whistle, and sometimes the odd rabbit was slung over the back of his bicycle, as he waved cheery-bye.

'This is 1938,' persisted Dr Baldwin, 'not the dark ages. Good grief man, where's your Christian spirit?'

'I think,' said Roe, fingering his white collar, 'my Christian spirit is not the issue, nor in question,' he added, turning to PC Bowles who coughed. 'As if it wasn't bad enough, the woman was a suicide.'

'A lot of it about,' interjected PC Bowles, who fell silent at a glance from the vicar.

'If I may be permitted to continue,' said Reverend Roe, 'not only was this . . . patient of yours,' he smiled acidly, 'a suicide, I also have reason to believe she was a woman of dubious character.'

'She was a good sort, though,' persisted PC Bowles, remembering the few times when he had had cause to conduct her home slightly the worse for drink. She'd lean her warm heavy body against him, and tell him how strong he was, what a big boy he was. He found himself blushing.

'Police Constable Bowles,' said Reverend Roe, enunciating every word slowly, 'I will not change my mind. If the coroner's inquest pronounces a suicide, which I don't think is in dispute, I will not allow her to be buried in the churchyard.'

'Deny her a Christian burial,' stormed Dr Baldwin, 'you'll

264

not hear the last of this, Roe, I shall go and see the bishop.'
He glared a moment at the two men, and stalked angrily from
the church.

'Men of science, men of science,' Roe sighed, 'very
temperamental, wouldn't you say so Bowles?'

'Very likely,' he said without looking at the vicar, and
wondering whether it was the pox that Mary Leech had
caught, all those sores on her head and no hair. 'Is that all?' he
asked, seeking dismissal from the vicar.

'Of course, of course,' said Reverend Roe, trying to make
his voice sound lighter and less troubled, 'it was very good of
you to take the time. I fear the good doctor is overtired: very
demanding profession.'

'It is that, sir,' said PC Bowles, and clicking his
feet together, started to walk up the aisle, running his red
hand through the stubby thatch which covered his solid
head.

'Ah, ah, Bowles,' called out Reverend Roe, unable to see
the silent curse that was on the policeman's lips. When he
turned to face the vicar, his face was impassive.

'You said there was a lot of it about,' said Roe.

'Beg your pardon, sir,' said Bowles, not grasping what the
vicar was going on about.

'Suicides?'

'Begging your pardon,' said Bowles, 'just a turn of phrase
really. I was just referring to another incident.'

'Aaah,' said Roe, wondering why he hadn't heard about
another suicide, 'how distressing for you.' He gave the
policeman a concerned look, and PC Bowles felt embarrassed
that he'd said damn under his breath when Roe called out to
him. He wasn't such a bad old stick.

'Yes,' said Roe, trying not to sound too eager.

'Well,' repeated PC Bowles, 'I'm not supposed to discuss
incidents, but seeing as how this is sort of a religious matter, I
don't suppose it would do no harm. Just between you, me and
the four walls mind.'

'Of course, of course,' said Reverend Roe, tapping the
side of his nose in a manner he had once seen in a gangster
film.

'Well, I can tell you it was a strange do.' He shook his head.

265

'We were rushed off our feet that morning. It was when all these calls came in about ruffians smashing windows.'

PC Bowles then proceeded to retail the story of the actress-nun, Mrs Wagtail and the fat child, while Roe rolled his pious eyes. Along the way, he recalled Mary Leech outside the building in question. Roe took it all in with pale intensity. Things were getting no clearer in his mind.

As soon as PC Bowles had shut the heavy, latched door, Reverend Roe pulled out the note from his pocket and swiftly moved into the robing room.

'Dear Reverend,' started the scratchy writing which was tiny and jumbled, 'acts of filthy indecency have been going on, right under our noses, and by them as should know better, if you get my meaning. Certain correspondences have fallen into my hands; by rights some of them belong to you.' Roe felt his hand tremble and heavily, he sat himself down. 'If I were you,' it went on, 'I would not let a trollop that has recently done herself in get buried in your church. She was a shameless strumpet and got what she deserved. She will burn in hell.' Roe rubbed a trembling finger over his sweaty brow. 'If you know what is good for you, a certain floosie's letters may be obtained.' That was all it said, apart from the signature, 'Mrs Wagtail'.

He couldn't see what this person had to do with everything, perhaps she was a procuress. The stupid Bowles had probably been duped by this woman; there must have been an orgy; somebody must have the fetish for dressing up as a nun; this Wagtail must be a brothel-keeper. It wouldn't take much to pull the wool over that idiot's eyes. The actress was probably just picking up a bit of extra cash. And with Mary Leech outside, that confirmed it. She was probably on the look-out, another of Wagtail's whores.

He folded the paper up; he would burn it. He couldn't ever remember writing anything to Mary Leech; in fact, he knew he hadn't. It must have been something the stupid girl had done herself, and now her madame thought she could get a bit of extra cash. On top of that, the girl seemed to have died of the pox. He went into the church where a little woman knelt at the altar. Brushing down his jacket, he gave her a beatific smile and tried to avoid looking at the light which was creeping through the stained-glass windows. He pulled out a dead flower from the altar display, and Mrs Wagtail smiled back at the unsuspecting vicar.

[26]

While the glaziers handled the fragile substance that was their livelihood, replacing those parts of Slackhall that had been shattered, there were other fissures which were beginning to appear that putty would not fill. Following the plague of accidents, the residents moved around with silent caution and frowned at anyone who spoke above hushed tones. A quiet expectancy filled the town. Then the ladders of the glaziers were put to a nocturnal use and a gaudy series of posters appeared all over the town like some strange flora which had burst upon a dull world.

Miss Royce was proclaiming her meeting and had employed the showmanship of the circus. Her poster flashed with primal hues, incongruous against the grimy walls and oblivious to the cracks it hid. Nobody had heard the hands which pasted and stuck the posters throughout the town. The secret army of the night caused the bewildered townsfolk to shake their heads with wonder.

And what was the message? It was more like a summons; a gaudy imperative which assailed from every corner, every wall and even from trees. The letters had been printed on a background of searing red. The first letter of each word was yellow. Every second letter was the piercing blue of Aryan eyes. Words which had a third letter, had it printed in green. The colour which should have nestled in between blue and yellow in the spectrum, had been shifted, and the pure and virile colour stood out like a judgment. The fourth letters were white, the reflector of all colours. In some parts the shade of mourning, but in the poster it shone like virgin snow, dazzling the eyes. As though after the perfection of the white the printer had lost all inspiration, the rest of the letters were black.

The posters mesmerised the eye; people stood as if hypnotised, and when finally they made room for some other inquisitive body, they wandered away with a dazed expression, like victims of shell shock. After they had read the poster, the words nestled like a virus, to be spread in the gossiping excitement which now gripped the town. Caution was flung to the wind as voices began to regain their old volume; plans were made as to how those encased in plaster could be transported to the meeting. They would have hobbled there if necessary, such was the impact of the advertising campaign.

For the remaining time that the town was still littered with leaning ladders, people walked obliviously under the wooden structures. The glaziers shook their heads at the bad luck which was piling up around them. Their ladders carried them not, like Jacob's, to heaven, but to the hearts of the people. Houses were exposed to their steady gaze, and although the sights carried with them the burden of the confessional, the glaziers had evolved a code of silence. No confidences were broken by the glaziers, but they developed the knack of sifting through the lives of those they saw through the broken windows.

As Nanny walked back to the house, she passed several posters. These bright lesions which had sprouted over the surface of the town had been diagnosed by the glaziers as the first tell-tale symptoms of a disease which could lay the town low, and spread to other parts of the country. Although what ought to have been prescribed was a strong emetic, the strange prescription which would flutter in the hands of the prime minister would only turn out to be a placebo.

'Another calamity,' muttered Nanny Bradshaw, pushing her way through a group of people staring at the summons to the rally.

In the deep pocket of her winter coat lay the letter which she had addressed to the inspector of the police. She nodded in a satisfied manner, listening to the dull thud her evidence made as it slipped from her fingers into the depths of the post-box.

'Like rats in a trap,' she whispered, and trudged back

269

towards the house, sniffing in a knowing way at the gaudy posters.

The little figure of Mrs Wagtail stalked her from the church, and as Nanny entered the Booths' house the furtive form smiled and nonchalantly pulled at the corner of one of the posters, observing to a passer-by that 'they brighten up the place a bit.'

'Is that you, dear?' called out the voice of Roe's wife. He quelled the urge to shout, 'Who do you think it is?' and instead called, 'Yes.'

'Have you had a nice day?' she trilled. 'I'm afraid I've been very lazy, I haven't done a thing.' She emerged from the sitting-room, and smiled at her husband.

'The doctor said you must not fatigue yourself,' replied Roe, standing still until he could make out the destination of his swaying wife. She barred his way, and he could smell alcohol.

'You're not angry with me, are you?' she pouted. The protruding bottom lip quivered, indicating the imminent deluge. 'Please say you're not angry; don't scold me. I'm sorry, I'm sorry.' She clutched his arm, as if to steady herself. With a look of utter revulsion, Roe pushed her back, but still she clung on to his arm.

'Leave me alone,' he sobbed, and she laughed; and such a laugh, as dry as old bones.

Her barren scorn was flooded with her hatred. His colourless wife, who hid behind the cloak of despondency, no longer flinched from his gaze, and she, too, waved a piece of paper in her unsteady hand and he knew the writing. Mrs Wagtail had written to his wife as well. Her moment over, she collapsed like an anemone, her hard laugh dissolving into drunken giggling, her resolve swept away on the tides of sweet sherry. She rolled her eyes in a devil-may-care way, and slumped against the wall. Taking a deep breath, Roe straightened down the jacket she had pulled awry.

'I'll take that,' he commanded, holding out his hand for the piece of paper. She looked up at him, with a sly little smile.

'It's mine, it's mine,' her shrill voice echoed, and Roe

270

looked round to make sure the door was closed. Even so, he wanted to get her out of the hall.

'Will you take me out for dinner?' she asked suddenly, a dreamy expression filling her face. 'I should have melon,' she declared, 'and then pigeon; braised pigeon. They have to smother them you know, press down on their little throats, just so we can eat them. I could dress up, make myself look nice. It's so long since I've had occasion to dress up, perhaps I'll get Bethsheba to open the wardrobe and bring my gowns out for an airing. I might buy a new dress, I don't want to look old fashioned.' She steadied herself slightly, but still held the hand containing the letter behind her back.

'Shall I help you into the sitting-room?' he asked, looming over her, and trying to grasp her thin shoulders.

'Oh you are terrible, just like a fierce animal,' she giggled, and fell limply against his body. She tried to burrow her head on his chest.

'Are you going to give me the time of my life?' she asked.

Roe looked down into her glazed eyes and wondered where she had learned to talk like that. His questing hand could not make contact with the little piece of paper, and so he lifted her like a mannequin and carried her. A fire was roaring in the grate, and Roe deposited his wife in the chair.

'Where is Bethsheba?' he asked her lolling head and the eyes which now looked dead. He repeated the question. Florence Roe swept out a jerky arm and shrugged her thin shoulders. 'That's no answer,' said Roe.

'Looking,' said Florence abstractedly.

'Looking for what?'

'Something I mislaid,' she said, in an irritated voice. 'Questions, questions, questions.' Her fingers twisted each other in an excitable way, and Roe saw the paper lying on her lap.

'Would you like something nice to drink,' he asked, keeping his eyes on the paper, 'a little pick-me-up?' She stirred sluggishly in the chair.

With a steady hand, the vicar poured out a generous measure of gin. He held the glass out to her and saw her lick her trembling lips.

'Ah, now,' said Roe, just lifting the glass out of her reach,

271

'what do you say now?' He gave her a stern look. 'Naughty girls don't always get what they want,' he said. 'What's that little word I want to hear?' Her hands clawed at the empty air.

'Please,' she sobbed, and as Roe let her fingers curl round the glass tumbler, he triumphantly yanked the piece of paper off her lap. The gin was already flowing into her open mouth.

'That's a good girl,' he said, and turning his back, without even reading it, he threw the paper into the fire, and watched with satisfaction as it curled up and burnt.

[27]

As Mrs Wagtail's little note was feeding the flames of Reverend Roe's fire, Cecilia Royce was taking a little break, a well-deserved break she thought to herself, as she naughtily dipped her biscuit in her cup of tea.

A corner of soggy biscuit broke off and dropped to the bottom of her cup, but she didn't mind, it seemed nothing could spoil her day. All the broken windows had been mended and there was no chance that her girls would come down with colds or flu. She smiled to herself. After the speech she would be quite a figure in the community. She had nailed her colours to the mast of the modern world. She looked down at her watch. The school governors would be arriving in a couple of hours; she'd finish her tea, and then give a quick inspection of the school, just to make sure everything was shipshape. There was a knock at the door.

'Enter,' she said, popping the remains of the biscuit into her mouth. Her secretary, Mrs Withington, bustled into the room.

'There's a gentleman who wants to see you,' she said. Cecilia Royce didn't open her mouth because it was still full of the biscuit. She gestured to Mrs Withington to let the person enter, but the secretary still stood there. Miss Royce swallowed the biscuit.

'A gentleman of the law,' breathed Mrs Withington, with a hint of scandal in her voice.

'Well,' snapped Miss Royce, 'don't just stand there, show him in.'

She clapped her hands briskly as though she were in class, and with a sullen look Mrs Withington went out. Miss Royce could hear her telling the policeman to follow her. As PC Bowles entered the room, she stood up and extended her hand. He looked awkward, stopped midway in his salute, and

273

instead, grasped her hand and shook it firmly up and down. It made her feel quite giddy, and she was thankful of the chair as she sank back down into it. Mrs Withington still hung around the open doorway.

'That will be all,' called Miss Royce, wincing slightly as the door banged to. The policeman still stood in the centre of the room. He cleared his throat, reached into his breast pocket and pulled forth a little book. Miss Royce thought it was all charming.

'Miss Cecilia Royce?' he asked.

'What a lovely deep voice you have,' she said, 'very authoritative. At a girls' school you tend to forget the sound of a man's voice; the higher octaves are all that your ears normally receive. It's like a tonic,' she declared, and gave him a smile. 'Have you ever thought of a stage career?' she asked. 'I know it's very forward of me to say so, but I think you would be splendid, and being a modern woman, I just come right out with what I'm thinking. Terrible, isn't it?' she laughed, and opened her mouth in a theatrical mime of horror.

'Miss Cecilia Royce?' he asked again.

'That is me,' she squealed, 'I am she. Have you come to arrest me?' she asked coquettishly.

'You are the headmistress of St George's school for girls?'

'Are you asking or telling?' she teased, noting the blush which started to creep up from his tightly-buttoned collar.

'I'm sorry miss, but I'm only doing my duty.'

'Goodness,' she exclaimed, 'that does sound serious. Have I been spotted robbing a bank?'

'May I ask whether you are aware of certain posters which have appeared all over the town of Slackhall?'

'Oh rather. Aren't they splendid? I'm expecting quite a turn-out; of course, some people have special invitations.' She looked at him as though considering whether he should be a lucky recipient of such an honour.

'Did you put these posters up yourself?' he asked. She wondered whether all the questions were written down in his little book.

'Certainly not.' She was beginning to think that he was a little immature. He looked very young, but that meant when

274

you thought policemen were getting younger, you were getting older.

'Do you know the person or persons who were responsible for sticking the posters up?'

'Not personally.'

She decided she would not ask this rude young man to sit down. She had been wrong about his figure as well, his shoulders sloped, not like the life-saving instructor's, and the policeman had a weak chin. She could see that he had cut himself shaving. She wouldn't offer him tea either.

'Would you mind giving me their names and addresses?' He brought forth a little pencil and licked the end. Just like a tradesman, thought Miss Royce.

'I've no idea, young man. You shall just have to enquire elsewhere. I suggest you ask Miss Ehrenhardt, the speaker. They were some acquaintances of hers.'

'How do you spell that?' asked PC Bowles.

'A-c-q-u-a . . .'

'No, the lady's name.'

'Ah,' said Miss Royce, 'I thought this was going to have to be a spelling lesson. I thought perhaps acquaintance was a word you wouldn't have learnt. I think it's spelled E-h-r-e-n-h-a-r-d-t.'

'Thank you,' said PC Bowles. 'Would you happen to know whether these persons unknown were perhaps blackshirts?' He looked her carefully in the eye.

'Blackshirts?' she said faintly. 'It's a lie. I think you have been sent on a false errand, misled by evil gossip.'

'You have heard this gossip yourself?' he asked.

'No, no, I just presumed that's what had happened.' She watched him write something down. 'What are you writing down?' she asked, and as he looked up at her, she straightened her back in the chair. He wrote something else.

'This speaker, Miss Ehrenhardt, where would I be likely to find her?'

'She's an employee of Mrs Booth.'

'She'll be at the factory then.'

'Oh, I shouldn't think so. She's a secretary, well a nurse really, but for some reason she's acting as secretary.' She stopped and wondered whether she was giving away too much information.

'How long have you known Miss Ehrenhardt?' he asked.

Miss Royce began to wonder where all this questioning was leading. She was not accustomed to having a rude young policeman interrupt her afternoon break. She wondered whether she should refuse to answer any questions until her solicitor arrived. She knew this was what people said, because lately she had been listening to the late-night 'who-dun-its', curled up in front of the hissing gas fire. She realised she didn't have a solicitor, and PC Bowles was still waiting.

'Not very long,' she admitted, 'but she has become a close friend. Why are you asking all these questions?'

'I'm only obeying orders, miss. I'm sure there's nothing in it, but complaints have been made, and information received.' He turned over the page in his notebook.

'Have you ever come across a Mr Pewter?' he asked.

'What complaints?' demanded Miss Royce. 'I suppose this is all to do with that girl's aunt. I tell you, she's a fanatic. I don't call it normal, shutting yourself away like that. Why, they have no idea of the modern world and its problems. The girl was a disruptive influence, drinking alcohol at school. I had no other alternative except to expel her. I had to think of the school as a whole.'

'What girl is this?' he asked.

'Haven't you written anything down? The girl is Ethel Coffin. She's the niece of this person who has made the complaint.'

'Ethel Coffin,' he repeated in a bewildered voice, and then it clicked; the nun was called Coffin; talk about a lucky break, he thought to himself, something big was going on here and he was on to it.

'Is that all?' Miss Royce's forehead was creased, and she could see the debris of the soggy biscuit lying at the bottom of the teacup.

'I'm afraid that you have made a false assumption,' said PC Bowles, sounding quite pleased that he'd got one over on this school-ma'am who thought she could give him a spelling lesson. 'The complaints did not come from the Coffins. Although I can't divulge the source, I think you should know, that whoever was responsible for sticking those posters up all over people's property could be in serious trouble. Permission was not given,' he declared, 'and we have reason to believe that there might be trouble at the meeting, a possible breach of the peace.'

'Breach of the peace,' gasped Miss Royce, becoming aware that the sound of the typewriter had fallen silent in the next room. 'At a Women's Institute meeting!'

'Have you ever attended a meeting of Sir Oswald Mosley's British Union of Fascists at the Free Trade Hall?' he asked.

'I fail to see,' she began, and there was a knock at the door. 'Enter,' she called.

'Sorry to interrupt,' said Mrs Withington, 'I thought you'd like to know that Councillor Drinkwater has arrived.'

'Ah,' she said, trying to think which was Drinkwater. They all seemed to have flabby, port-red faces, and all of them misogynists. How they must have wished they could appoint a man to run a girls' school. 'Perhaps you'd be good enough to arrange some refreshment for him and tell him I'll be there shortly.'

She stared at the impassive head of PC Bowles. He waited until Mrs Withington left the room. Miss Royce could not imagine that her secretary would lose this opportunity to mention that the reason for her delay was the arrival of a policeman.

'I hope you realise,' she said bitterly, 'that you have placed me in a very awkward position.'

'I don't believe you've finished answering my last question.'

'I really don't think I can help you any further.' She gave him a wintry smile, but her fingers trembled under the table. He stood for a moment, flicking back the pages of his little notebook, then he looked up at her.

'Did you say you knew a Mr Pewter?' She could hear a few muffled voices in the room outside. She felt slightly trapped.

'I believe,' she said in unguent tones, 'that Mr Pewter spoke twice to the Women's Institute, once about Japan, and I'm afraid I can't remember what the other lantern lecture was about.' She was beginning to feel exhausted.

'Are you aware of any involvement of the blackshirts in

distributing the posters?' he persisted, in a voice which she thought needn't be so loud.

'None: if I were, I would have told you.'

'Well, as I say, I'm only doing my job. You can never tell you know,' he added in a warning tone. 'Until I joined the police, I wouldn't have believed half the things that go on.'

'I'm sure the whole town is grateful for the work you do,' she said smoothly, and got to her feet to show him to the door.

'We just don't want no riots like there was at Earls Court in July.'

'Earls Court?' She was confused again.

'The blackshirt demonstration,' he explained. 'People don't want to be replacing all their windows again. Somebody will have to foot the bill next time,' he added ominously. She shook her head at these oblique revelations, hoping that it was the correct gesture to give, and as she opened the door and was confronted by the eyes of the governors and the simpering smile of Mrs Withington, she wanted just to slam it shut again.

28

'Nights drawing in now,' observed Nanny Bradshaw, standing in front of the window and obscuring what little light was left. 'They've gone off to that meeting,' she confided, 'there's just you and me in the house.' She turned to the bed and smiled at the shrunken form within. 'I've cooked her goose, cooked it good and proper. All the information is in the hands of the authorities.'

She thrust a large hand into her dress, and with a good deal of wriggling adjusted the stays in her corset, oblivious as to whether Elizabeth Booth minded such a display. Elizabeth Booth was singing to herself in a lisping, lilting voice, the voice of a five-year-old. No sound escaped the dry, cracked lips.

'I thought we might be in for a bit of rain,' confided Nanny Bradshaw. 'That would have dampened their spirits.'

> Little Bo Peep
> She lost her sheep
> And couldn't tell where to find them.
> Leave them alone!
> And they'll come home,
> Dragging their tails behind them.

Elizabeth Booth giggled. The jingling rhyme danced around her mind like the wagging tails of the lambs, their white coats gleaming like the Lamb of God. She was waiting for her saviour.

Nanny Bradshaw bent over Elizabeth Booth, casting a shadow like a cumulus, her thick hands pressed tenderly on those of her employer.

'I thought she might as well be hanged for a sheep as

279

for a lamb. We'll be shot of the skinny chicken once and for
all.'

> Little Miss Muffet
> Sat on a tuffet,
> Eating her curds and whey,
> Up came a big spider,
> And sat down beside her,
> And frightened Miss Muffet away.

Elizabeth Booth fell silent, her little tongue sticking its pink tip
experimentally into the dark bedroom. She wished she hadn't
sung that one. In the laudanum silence she could hear the
creaking of the big, fat spider; the dark shadow of its bloated
body swung over her. Her tongue scampered back into the
warm sanctuary of her mouth, and her round eyes probed the
gloom. She could hear the creak, creak of the spinning wheel;
the groaning spider was spinning a sticky web, the thick
glutinous threads were floating all around the room. One
landed on her hand, sticking to it. She trembled in her bed.
She had watched spiders at work. She had called the spider,
and now it sat down beside her.

'I'll have to get Mrs Higginbottom to check these stays.
There's more whalebone in this corset than Jonah saw,'
complained Nanny Bradshaw as she slowly sank her girth on
to the bed, her corset creaking and scraping.

'Got the trembles, have you?' said Nanny Bradshaw. With
one heavy finger she started to stroke Elizabeth Booth in an
obscene parody of an adult chucking a baby under its wobbly
chin. 'Is there a message coming through, then?' she asked,
continuing the motion as though trying to coax ectoplasm up
from her throat. She considered getting the ouija board, but
she felt too comfy. Whoever it was, she thought, if it was
important they'd be back.

'What about a go at rapping?' suggested Nanny Bradshaw.
'You call them, and I'll explain the ins and outs to whoever
comes from the other side. It'll save my old body the journey
for the ouija board. How about it then?' she asked to the
static head, and shifting her position slightly, the whalebones

280

in her corset snapped and rapped as though a whole crowd of spirits were trying to communicate at once. 'It was those Fox sisters who started it all,' explained Nanny Bradshaw, 'they had an invisible rapper, and it was the kiddies who first got the spirit copying their little snapping fingers, like a game. Oh yes, it was a sad case. The rapper was a murdered man, could find no rest, his poor bones just dumped in the cellar, just like Pewter. He had no home to go to. It was a new idea at the time, a bit of a step up from the crystal ball.'

> Humpty Dumpty sat on the wall;
> Humpty Dumpty had a great fall;
> All the king's horses
> And all the king's men
> Couldn't put Humpty Dumpty together again.

Elizabeth Booth sang to keep the spider at bay. Let Humpty fall into the abyss, down the dark well, she would sit very still on the wall, hardly breathing at all.

'I don't hold with that nonsense about cracking toe joints, and nobody could accuse us of fraud. I don't reckon it's possible for a body to crack their toe bones, not under a pair of shoes.'

> Pat-a-cake, pat-a-cake, baker's man!
> Bake me a cake as fast as you can!
> Pat it and prick it and mark it with P!
> Bake it in the oven for baby and me!

Elizabeth Booth chanted in a hushed little voice, balancing on top of the wall, and singing in time to the clapping hands, beating out the rhyme in a ceremonial rhythm. She thought it was her mummy behind the wall clapping her hands in time; crack, crack, crack.

'These stays,' moaned Nanny Bradshaw, and then she fell silent as she heard a scraping sound as though furniture was being moved, and then a knocking, a banging thump. The wished-for rappings scuttled across the ceiling, like a trapped rat in the loft.

281

'My poor old heart,' gasped Nanny Bradshaw, rolling her eyes around the shadowy room. Her hand instinctively sought the unresponsive palm of her employer and she sat for a moment quietly on the bed.

'One rap for yes, two for no,' came her quivering voice, then she added 'if you please.' Her fingers were rubbing the still hand back and forth, as though in soothing Elizabeth Booth she was doing the same to her thumping heart. 'Is that Pewter?' she asked. 'This is Dorothy,' she nearly said, your Dorothy, but thought that perhaps it wasn't Pewter.

She fancied he might be at the meeting, watching his murderer brought to justice. The dark room was silent except for the slight creak as her stomach heaved itself like bellows inside the casing of whalebone. Her heavy mind ruminated the possibility of a materialisation.

'I'm ready,' she warbled, 'reveal yourself to me.'

Then inexplicably she closed her eyes, squeezing them shut tight, so not a chink of the gloom entered. Behind the scrunched-up eyelids her excited eyeballs danced around with impatience, and then she opened her eyes wide. Her expression held an expectant sense of wonder, as though she had anticipated she would be staring at the bright air of heaven, some marvel to match the greatest achievement of nature. The dark silent room met her probing eyes. There was no glimmer from a visitation, no apport to gasp at, just the night drawing in, for summer-time was due to end the next day.

Realising she still had hold of Mrs Booth's withered hand, she dropped it unceremoniously back and levered herself off the bed. The spirits were mocking her. She hadn't checked her horoscope that day, she'd admit to that, but what with the nuisance of making sure they all had their gas-masks, and filling out the forms for food ration cards, she'd not had the time. She should have got her priorities right. All this panic had messed up her chances of seeing a ghost. The planets might have told her that she would be denied this chance, it wouldn't be the cusp she thought to herself, and she'd heard the rapping, as clear as anything, the cherished memory echoed in her mind.

*

Hickory, dickory, dock!
The mouse ran up the clock;
The clock struck one,
And the mouse ran down,
Hickory, dickory, dock!

Elizabeth Booth had felt the big chime of one. It shook all along her spinal column, and the spider had jumped away. 'Hickory dickory dock,' she sang.

Nanny Bradshaw opened the window, wondering why she had been forsaken. She gazed disconsolately into the shadowy garden. The light of the town could be seen; all those people seemed so far away. She had a sudden notion to put on her hat and coat and take a little walk into Slackhall, and watch while the authorities acted on her tip-off and raided the meeting.

She thought of William. He was as distant as any of those houses; he might as well be in a foreign country. As her disappointed eyes stared into the clinging darkness, William made the transition in Nanny Bradshaw's mind to one of the departed. As surrogate mother, she felt a numb despair. Her body was held in the febrile light of the room, but her head was lost in shadows. Like Madame D'Esperant, it looked as though a vital portion of Nanny Bradshaw had melted away into thin air. A rustling from the bed brought her from the dark reveries and her head reappeared inch by inch as she manoeuvred herself back into the room. The rustling had quietened, and in the heavy silence, Nanny Bradshaw felt a presence. It pressed down in the hushed, malodorous air. She felt a prickling fear; the warped structures of the room seemed to quiver and close in upon her. She thought of all that the stones must have witnessed.

The light of the town which had called her now seemed further away, the few candles which lit the room had burned low and swirls of dark vapour trailed a burning smell into the air as they puckered out. Nanny Bradshaw looked at the bed. The heavy hangings seemed to have been carved out of the very shadows, and like some effigy lay Elizabeth Booth. Whatever rogue movement had caused the rustling had now ceased.

283

She gave a start which sent the candle flames dancing as an owl's sudden cry sliced through the still air. Her heart pattered like the small creature who was the quarry of the curved beak, and she placed her palm on her chest, to steady her nerves. Mrs Booth hadn't stirred at the cry, but Nanny Bradshaw leant over her and smoothed down the blankets until there was a palpable calm in the room, which belied the feelings which were racing through Nanny Bradshaw's old frame. In the moonlight she once more took the hand of Elizabeth Booth. Despite the creases of age, it was a hand that did not bear the marks of work. It nestled like a featherless fledgling in the roughened nest of Nanny Bradshaw's hand; a hand which had dealt with the housework, had overseen the kitchen and punished and trained the children, while Elizabeth Booth had flitted through the spacious rooms, not even stirring the dust, for Nanny Bradshaw had seen that there was none to disturb. As she looked down at the captive palm, she thought of how the years had changed things. The dust which had once been vanquished, now ruled the house, coating everything in its fine mantle, moved from one surface it would reappear elsewhere. In the silver moonlight, the dust glistened like frost; an unfeeling shroud covered everything.

'Ah well,' she sighed, 'I'm not getting anything done just standing here with you.' She patted the hand gently in a resigned sort of manner. Whatever she had set in motion was now beyond her influence. 'You don't have any trouble dropping off to sleep do you, my dear,' she said, placing the captive hand once more on the bedspread. 'I think I shall take a cup of Allenbury's diet. That should send me to the land of nod sure enough. I could do with an early night.'

She went over to the candles which flickered wildly at her approach as though aware that she would snuff them out. Slowly and methodically she licked her thumb and one finger and clenched them over the shrinking flames. A single candle she kept alight as it had nearly burnt its course and it seemed to burn all the brighter for the loss of its companions.

Nanny Bradshaw rubbed at her corset, thinking of the relief of unhooking it and warming her hands on a mug of Allenbury's diet. The prospect became the only thing to fill her mind, and with this single purpose she left the room.

A dull scuttling passed over the ceiling, and the candle flame burnt brightly, seeming to lengthen on the dark wick. Wrapped in bed, Elizabeth Booth drifted in her own world, the scents of different times wafted along under the nose of her memory which served her now like a recycled dream, as though, like the different bands on the crystal set, fragments of life moved with rapid succession, snatches of sound faded in and out like some conversation she wished to eavesdrop.

'Goodnight, darling,' said her mummy, tucking her up tight in bed.

'I'm the one you want,' said her husband, his heavy body pushing her tight into the bed.

'Just one more push,' said Nurse Bracewell. 'That's the ticket,' she cried. She could feel her body opening on to the bed.

'That's right, that's right,' came the lulling voice. 'Ah, my dear, don't let your heart break,' but she pushed her sobbing head deep into the comforting bed which for evermore would be half empty.

'This won't hurt,' said Dr Baldwin, but it always did, and she flinched, pressing the rest of her body into the bed as the needle entered her arm.

'I love you,' cried William, flinging himself on to the high bed.

'The dead will claim their own,' cried the red-headed maid.

'Amen,' intoned Roe, towering over her. He pressed the chalice to her lips and the bitter wine of communion filled her mouth.

'What if she's dead,' exclaimed Dagmar to herself.

'I think we'll just have to wait and see,' said the distant voice of Dr Baldwin. She tried to steel herself for the needle, but none came.

'There's no telling what revelations will come,' whispered Nanny Bradshaw.

'Goodnight, darling,' said her mummy, tucking her up in bed.

She liked lying warm in bed while the rain drummed on the roof, or the wind howled through the rafters; a pleasant drowsiness brushed over her like a shadow, yet there was no rain, and no howling wind outside the house. A distant rustling scraped above her head, as though something were trapped in the attic. It scuttled back and forth.

One hard winter, the attic had become a veritable aviary. The drowsy warmth of the chimney had attracted the birds, and from the harsh cold they fled, perching on the heavy beams and the old crates and trunks which littered the cavernous shelter, and a heavy must emanated from the excrement which whitewashed the attic. Starlings, sparrows, blackbirds, blue tits, robins and even a missel-thrush found their way into the abandoned region, and devoured the spiders, whose realm it had once been. They found their way in, but whether it was the creeping warmth which dulled their wits, or the diet of spiders which distracted their navigation, none found the way out. The attic became an ossuary for the birds. The reek caused by their dead bodies eventually filtered down into the house, and as the attic was unlocked, the breath of decay oozed out, and the lamp showed the phosphorescent glow of white, as though snow had fallen in the gloomy place.

> Little Jack Horner
> Sat in a corner,
> Eating a Christmas pie.
> He stuck in his thumb . . .

She fell silent as though trying to remember the rest, but really she was listening. Her pink tongue emerged with the concentration. When Mummy and Daddy had gone out, she would always try and stay awake, waiting till she heard them return. It didn't matter that she was called a sleepy head the next day, she liked to listen to their warm voices drifting up the stairs to the nursery. Sometimes Mummy would come up, and give her a little kiss and put out the bedside light. She would watch her through her eyelashes, hoping that her sharp little eyes wouldn't be noticed. The light was glowing bright; it was a red glow behind her closed eyelids, like a distant bonfire. She kept them shut and used her ears.

Something had flown in through the open window. She

could hear it banging around the light; a stray insect had been attracted by the little beacon, and its hard little body crashed into the walls. She opened her eyes and the candle went out. Now nothing looked familiar. She wondered where her toys were; the room was all wrong. The probing eye of the moon made her shiver. It could be a moth, fluttering just above her, with dusty wings. Her eyes strained to see a shadowy form, but all she could see was the night. The insect seemed to be coming closer, the noise transfixed her, and she trembled for the expected contact of fluttering wings and twitching legs. The sounds began to swamp her and in a game of hide and seek, the insect moved closer. She felt the trembling breath of its wings and swiftly clamped her eyes shut, for fear of it darting into her straining pupils. Nearer and nearer came the thudding body; louder and louder thudded her own heart. She tried to remember another rhyme; she wanted to open her eyes, watch it, but she couldn't.

> He stuck in his thumb
> and pulled out a thumb
> and swallowed it whole . . .

'No,' she cried, 'that isn't it,' and she opened her mouth wide to scream, and in went the fluttering wings. All sound died in the throat, eaten up by the beating wings. She lay there feeling the insect flying down her throat, now it was in her chest, its wings beating, beating, beating.

> Old Mother Hubbard
> Went to her cupboard
> To get her poor dog a bone;
> When she got there,
> the cupboard was bare,
> And so the poor dog had none.

The beating died away, crumpling into the moonlit room.

William couldn't get to sleep. The radiator hissed behind his head, and it sent its warmth into the dormitory filled with the snuffling, twitching boys. The usual chatter had died quickly, Mr Frazer had warned them about noise as he made his round, sending the probing beam of the torch into dark corners. The staff were going to celebrate, and would not take kindly on this important occasion to have to come back to the dormitory to deal with any disturbance. They could see his mouth moving as he gave the pronouncement. As if displaying himself as he spoke, he turned the torch on to his shadowy head so it was lit from underneath. The spotlighted head mouthed away about historic occasions, and that some Eton boys had met the prime minister at the airport and had sung 'He's a jolly good fellow'. They had set an example to all their peers. They were the representatives of the generation that had most to gain from the new peace in Europe. William guessed that the head would spend some time talking in similar terms before they could begin the lumpy porridge at breakfast.

He heard Middleton turn over in the bed next to his. He closed his eyes and tried to concentrate on the natural task of falling asleep, but the more he thought about it, the harder it became; he was too hot. He considered the prospect of being allowed to move his bed, but however his mind set the scenario, he always ended up being thought of as namby pamby and soft, a label which was already hovering over him.

The initiation on the first night he had spent there had not been a success. As the strange hands pummelled him from the dark, they had expected to be met with a struggling form, or one that cried. William didn't lift a finger, and as they pinched and pulled his pliant body, the enthusiasm drained from the attackers. It was not sport to savage a dead thing, and as he didn't sob into his pillow, they couldn't figure him out, and although he never knew those who had set about him, the tale had gone the rounds. If not exactly shunned, nobody sought him out. All the new boys had written letters home except for him. Mr Frazer had spoken to him about it, and gave him a strange look which was perhaps to become his lot in life. He had to write home, that is what Frazer said, and to stop feeling sorry for himself.

Middleton turned over again, and William opened his eyes.

The little locker that stood beside his bed was bare, the picture which had stood next to his bed at home haunted his sleepless eyes. Nanny Bradshaw had packed it, but in hot embarrassment he hid it back in the trunk which was taken away, carrying the hidden picture of the crucifixion.

He closed his eyes again, and turned over. The slightest sound seemed to be magnified. He rolled his head on the pillow until when he opened his eyes once more he was staring straight ahead at the foot of the bed, and it was a moment before he had the sense to realise someone was standing there staring at him.

'What?' he cried, and Middleton woke too.

'Can't you shut up,' he said to William. 'Having a nightmare were you?' he sneered. 'You sounded like a stuck pig, Booth,' and with another grunt he turned over again. William continued staring at the bottom of the bed with a morbid fascination.

There was nothing there now, but there had been. A little blonde-haired girl had been standing there, and to his ears came the lilting voice reciting Old Mother Hubbard. It had seemed perfectly normal for the girl to be standing there, and he had smiled at her until his growing sense of wonder caused him to cry out. He knew it wasn't the daughter of any of the school's staff. There was something uncannily familiar about her smiling little face, and it was only a week later when he saw an old photograph of his grandmother as a little girl that he recognised who it was. The apparition was the last view of his dead grandmother and he didn't even recognise her.

William was not the only person to be visited by the figure of the little girl. Twice more she appeared, and it was only William who knew it was a ghost. The little girl reciting a hushed poem looked up at the platform upon which Dagmar was speaking. Whatever chains were holding her to the earth made her wander in strange locations, a young girl in a boys' dormitory, standing as Dagmar was given a standing ovation, and then watching from the crowd in Downing Street as Mr Chamberlain stood there amid the popping flashbulbs, listening to the cheers and the relief as after a busy day he said, 'It is peace in our time'. Mrs Chamberlain smiled down at the blonde-headed girl, who really shouldn't have been up so late, even though it was only seven o'clock.

There were no shooting stars that night, no other omens which could foretell the future, save the strange trinity of appearances, and they didn't change the world. Whatever Elizabeth Booth was up to it was lost in the excitement of the hour, and nobody could care less whether the cupboard was bare.

29

She laughed noisily as the champagne surged out of the glasses and over her trembling hands which tingled with the tiny bursting bubbles. Her tongue darted out, and licked the spillage.

'A toast,' said John William, taking one of the glasses from her hand. He held it up into the light, the steady spires of escaping gas writhed away, imitating a boiling liquid. 'To the future,' he said, and placed his lips to the glass and drank deep.

The cool champagne slid icily down his throat. Dagmar watched from under heavy lids, and then took a cautious sip. He poured, white foam overflowing once more so that the carpet absorbed the rich scent of alcohol. He ground his foot into the damp patch.

'Just this once,' said Dagmar, holding out her glass. She would not however take a cigarette or the suggested dance round the heavy carpet. 'You think they liked it then?' she asked.

'Liked it,' he slurred, 'they loved it, you were very good.'

'Very good, what does that mean?' she demanded.

'Well, excellent then, if you prefer.'

'It is not what I prefer. Do you think they understood me?'

'What does it matter?' He gave her a lopsided grin, and moved towards her.

'Of course it matters,' she snapped, making sure that the table lay between them. She put down her glass.

'How should I know, darling,' he took another sip, thinking what a damn fine woman she was; pure woman, there was no doubt about that.

'You were there, you were listening.' She eyed him sharply. 'You were listening?'

'Of course, of course, every golden word.' He put out a

291

hand to steady himself against the table. 'Strong stuff that,' he laughed.

She paced over to the window and pulling the heavy curtain aside, looked out into the dark, her stern reflection caught by the glass. John William looked at her as she stood in contemplation, her fine white arms folded. She had been so gay a moment ago, and now somehow the mood was changing. He looked at the nearly empty bottle which hung from his hand and considered breaking open another.

'Another toast,' he suggested. She stared out of the window. He felt her reflection was piercing him and consoled himself with draining the glass.

'There were six million unemployed,' she mused. 'They did not seem to understand this, or the cruelty of that treaty signed in the hall of mirrors. They could see their own reflections in Versailles, and still they all signed with broad smiles.'

'What?' asked John William, venturing a small smile himself. She turned with a sigh.

'It suits you,' she said, the planes of her face softening slightly.

'Suits me?' He looked puzzled. Just like a small boy, she thought to herself.

'Black,' she smiled, and held out her hand to him.

'Quite a crowd you pulled,' he enthused, grasping hold of the hand and the change in mood at the same time. 'Want some more?'

He waggled the empty bottle back and forth. She shook her head. He thought her neck was graceful.

'Not cold are you?' he asked, wanting to warm her pale flesh, as the alcohol warmed him, from the inside.

'When I said I wanted them all to come to Germany, I meant it, but they laughed. They must see we are all the same. Soon there will be no differences.'

'They loved you,' he said, relishing the words, and lingering over the heavy languorous sound, 'lo-oved you,' he repeated.

'They laughed,' she persisted, pulling her hand abruptly from his.

'Not at you,' he laughed himself that she misunderstood

292

them so. 'They loved you,' he repeated. 'Look how they clapped you; they stood and clapped you.'

'Yes,' she said quietly, her eyes suddenly shining with the memory, 'yes they did.' She had never thought what it would be like to look down on all the faces, see the eyes staring up, pinning you to the spot. She wanted it to go on and on. 'But the announcement,' she said, remembering Cecilia Royce's call for silence.

Telling those who didn't know of the new understanding, about the paper which bore the names which fluttered its contents in the English wind, and then she read it to them. Was that when they stood up and clapped even harder? She saw them standing up, her memory's eye passing over the blonde-headed little girl among so many taller ones. She was more concerned with how the clapping rose and fell.

'You made quite an impression,' he said.

'You are sure?' she asked.

'Positive,' he declared, edging himself round the polished table. 'That Raymond chap came up to me. You know what a bigwig he is, knows Mosley himself, helped set everything up. He said you were an asset. Those were his words, an asset.'

'Perhaps the news will get back,' she said, her eyes clouding with a secret faraway look, 'after all, they married at the Goebbels' house.'

'Not everybody is supposed to know that,' he said. 'You didn't mention it to anyone else, did you?'

'No,' she said sharply, the abruptness shattering her daydreams of a second wedding with such illustrious guests and her all in white.

'I thought it was a clever move to get them to send that telegram to the embassy, giving our wishes for a speedy recovery to Field Marshal Goering. Bet he wishes he could have taken part in the chinwag.'

'Chinwag?' asked Dagmar.

'You know, all those meetings and what not. I think I'd rather have a tricky lymph duct, or whatever it is.' He smiled. 'Especially if you would nurse me.' He yawned, and raised his eyebrows slightly. 'Must have gone to my head,' he joked.

'There is plenty of room.'

293

'Charming, as usual,' he grinned, 'do you remember when we first met?'

'Of course, you opened the door to me.'

'No, not then.' He ran a finger over her bare arm. 'By the old pond, you know, you were like a wild thing.'

'I still am,' she laughed, and swiftly pinched the hand which lay on her arm.

'Ouch,' he cried, pulling away. 'The fool doth think he is wise, but the wise man knows himself to be a fool.'

'Bravo!' she cried.

'Shakespeare, I'm afraid,' he laughed. 'Had to learn lots by heart.' He bowed to her, placing a hand over his own chest, above the pumping organ.

'Ah well, at least there is one lesson you have learnt well.' She gave him a hard look. She walked to the door and, opening it, turned to wait for John William.

Like a sleep walker he followed her, and as they reached his room, there was surprise that it was his door they were standing in front of, and with the certainty of a repeated dream, he saw her cool white hand reach out and grasping the handle, open the door and slide into the gloom within.

His eyes were riveted by the tantalising gap through which Dagmar had disappeared. He listened at his own door, eavesdropped through the dim light and trembled as he heard the bed creak with voluptuous sighs as it took the weight of a body. His legs prolonged the pleasure, refusing to carry him over the threshold.

Finally his legs sliced through the air, and he closed the door softly behind him. He felt the hard wood pressing against his back as he leaned against it like a weary soldier. He could see nothing. As he stilled, he heard a slow creak as Dagmar's body shifted slightly in the bed, more sweet than the song of the siren. He swam through the darkness to be consumed upon the rocks. As with the efficient hand of a nurse, she disrobed him, he thought how strangely cold was her body, yet the heat of his own prevented him from shivering, and like a child about to go to sleep, he closed his eyes. He felt her chill breath rustling next to his ear.

'So we seal the pact,' whispered Dagmar into his receptive ear.

As an uncaring river flows over the troubled body of a suicide, so she let him enter her. His eyes remained clamped shut. So tightly were they sealed that a single tear could not escape. But beneath, his eyes watered, until at the final moment his senses gave way, and before his body slumped above her, a single warm tear rolled down his cheek.

As the tides of sleep took over, the tracks of the tears were lost and in her empty tower, the temperature of his mother's body had dropped several degrees. As cell death took place, the blood began to discolour the joints of her body. Her fingernails would continue to curve imperceptibly, and had she still retained her hair, that too would have continued to curl round her head. But in the moon-filled room, the putrefying bacteria were also at work.

Dagmar lay stiffly in bed, her blue eyes staring at the ceiling above, and she twitched at the series of raps which rattled across it like the distant report of a machine-gun.

30

The rain kept falling. Those who ventured into the open wrapped up well and felt in their bones the change of season was upon them. The funereal weather soaked into the clothes and buildings, but people got used to it. It was in their nature to expect a certain amount of hardship. They thanked their lucky stars that the window breakage had not occurred during a spell of bad weather.

Whatever the elements were playing at outside, the Coffins lay in the perpetual gloom of closed curtains. Sister Ursula had sealed the room, and at regular intervals she came to check on their progress.

'My you are ill,' she declared, and so took to wearing some faded pink rubber gloves in their presence. She searched her memory for the types of affliction which were sent to teach the wicked a lesson, or those which were created by the devil to torment the innocent and good. She spent long hours just staring at the two bodies, weighing up whether God or the devil were responsible. Her mind whirled in confusion. Although they remained silent, Sister Ursula sometimes had the uncomfortable feeling that in some quite mysterious way they were chatting to themselves. She pinched her arms with the rubber gloves, but she couldn't stop watching their eyes, and although they didn't seem to move much, she could swear that when they did, all four would be co-ordinated.

'I know, I know,' she once cried into the silent room, 'talking, talking, behind a person's back,' and that night she brought no food, for however they were affected, food, which had been the centre of their daughter's life, now became the same for them. Beneath the sheets their bodies were filling out, the wrinkled skin was becoming tighter and layers of fat were beginning to build up.

And as her parents' desire for food increased, so Ethel's

diminished. Deep down inside herself she could feel something stirring, and her loss of appetite made the sensation all the more powerful as her stomach, bereft of food, seemed to grow ever more sensitive to itself. Despite the few morsels she allowed down her throat, her huge body still remained undiminished. She spent her days staring into space, listening to the rumbling whispers of her stomach. Occasionally her eyes would focus on the bustling body of her aunt, who had briskly taken over and begun to change the house. The ambience of a convent was being slowly created, a home from home, one in which any man would have felt immediately ill at ease. Carpets were rolled up to expose the light-coloured stone flags. At first, Sister Ursula had sought to provide some explanation for her actions. Carpets, she declared, could carry many germs, and the stone floor was easier to keep clean. But soon other items of furniture and decoration began to disappear, washed away in the tide of the nun's enthusiasm.

The night was lit by candles, the smell of hot wax spreading through the bare house. The interior was mystically transformed into a shaded façade of a church. There was a sense of expectancy in the cool rooms; it was not the house into which Ethel had been born.

Since the schism which had occurred in the kitchen, Ethel had not set foot inside the domain of food. Festooned around the kitchen were the paraphernalia of an altar; pristine white cloths with delicate embroidery were draped over household utensils, and using the candlesticks she had brought with her as well as some she found in the house, Sister Ursula had arranged them in front of the statue of the Virgin Mary which had been brought down from her bedroom.

Here it was she prayed and did the cooking. Genuflecting every time she passed the statue made the preparation of food quite an exhausting matter. Carrying pans of vegetables, she bobbed, shifting the pan so she could make the sign of the cross.

Although Sister Ursula wanted the house to breathe the peace and calm of the convent, a melancholy mood disturbed the days. Despite her most fervent prayers, no cure was

297

forthcoming, and however hard she tried to shake the notion from her thoughts, it looked as though God had forsaken her. She fought against the temptation of questioning her faith; the fastings and prayers were doubled. The waiting continued, and scarcely a word passed between Ethel and her aunt. The wireless which had interrupted the contemplative atmosphere had been disconnected. Her eyes often strayed to the frayed wires that dangled from the machine. Sometimes she thought the wireless was still sending messages to her. The nun covered her ears and prayed fervently, as Ethel watched with round eyes.

As Ursula went cleaning round the house, the rising dust reminded her of the writings of Richalmus, Abbot of Schonthal, who had said the surrounding demons were as plentiful as dust in sunlight. She put down the duster. What could be more likely than the devil's minions trying to divert her from the path of sanctity? It was well known they plagued and tempted the pious. The rims of the nun's nostrils quivered. Emanating from two bodies was an unhealthy smell. She backed away from the odour, shielding her nose with the trailing wimple.

She felt stifled, and fled from the room and the devilish stink, just as Saint Christina soared from her coffin away from the smell of humans.

Leaning against the door, Sister Ursula concluded that she too could detect the dreadful smell of sinful human bodies. The nun wondered if Ethel also smelt, and with her nose leading the way, she went in search, sniffing the air occasionally.

She found Ethel, sitting, as she usually did, staring into space. It had been a disquieting morning and Sister Ursula was in no mood for Ethel's fixed gaze. Taking a deep breath, she sucked in the air. No strange odour assaulted her, and for a moment the suspicions about her niece evaporated.

'Ethel,' she snapped, as though calling for the girl to return from wherever she was wandering.

'What's trepanning?' demanded Ethel, and Sister Ursula jumped at the sound of the voice.

'Whatever next,' said Sister Ursula mildly. 'It isn't healthy to brood so much Ethel, not for someone of your disposition, far too morbid. Are you listening to me child?' The faint shadow of a smile brushed the nun's lips, but the eyes remained steady and cold.

'But what is it?' persisted Ethel unwisely.

'Heavens girl,' exclaimed Sister Ursula, 'as if there isn't enough to be getting on with in God's world without an endless stream of questions. Now then,' said the nun, 'I just have a little letter to write, and then we shall be going into town.'

As Sister Ursula locked the front door, she paused as though she could hear something behind it.

'Did you hear that?' she hissed to Ethel, who stood by with an umbrella in hand.

'I am summoning assistance,' she declared to the impassive door, and marched off to the post-box.

As the letter left her fingers, it was as if a burden had lifted itself from her shoulders.

'Winter is coming early this year,' remarked Sister Ursula breezily, 'look at those holly berries. That means we are in for a lot of snow.' Ethel glanced at the bright red fruit poking through the top few branches of the tree. 'Now tell me,' said the nun, 'do you know how the berries got that colour?' Ethel shook her head dumbly.

'It's a lovely tale,' said Sister Ursula. 'It was holly which was supposed to have been the thorn crown of our Lord, and as the poor man bled, his holy blood turned the green berries red.' She smiled down at Ethel. 'And the robin, he tried to pull the cruel crown away from our Lord's head, and its breast was splashed with the precious blood. From that day forth, its breast is a reminder of the suffering.' She smiled down at Ethel. 'Do try and keep the umbrella straight,' she said gaily, unaware that Ethel's smile was filled with images of trickling blood.

She stood heavily as Sister Ursula wound her way through the clustered stalls, comparing prices until she found the most reasonable, and even then she would check each vegetable before she handed over the money. Every penny saved, she told Ethel, could go towards buying a blessed candle, or a mass. She smiled triumphantly if she found any bruised apples, or a potato going to seed, holding it aloft for all to see.

'Fancy trying to cheat a bride of Christ,' she murmured to Ethel. 'Protestants the lot of them,' she declared, regretting that her coppers fell into such hands. Sister Ursula poked about the flower stall.

'Look Ethel,' she said, in a voice which she knew the proprietress would hear, 'forget-me-nots. They used to be white until Our Lady's robe brushed over them.' She smiled at the unsmiling woman. 'Such a lovely tale,' she said, and then wondered whether or not perhaps it had been speedwell. Still, the principle was the same. 'Do hold the umbrella still,' she said a little sharply to Ethel, aware for a moment of the softly falling rain.

'Is it the forget-me-nots you'll be wanting then?' interrupted the unsmiling woman, who was getting rather tired of the nun lifting her flowers about like that. 'Those anemones are delicate,' she commented as Sister Ursula caused some petals to fall off.

'I don't think they're as fresh as they might be,' said the nun sweetly.

'All freshly cut this morning,' declared the woman loudly.

'Really,' said Sister Ursula, sounding quite sceptical, and thinking that she knew full well the unsold flowers would be kept in pails of water overnight. 'How lucky you are,' she said, 'to be able to surround yourself with such beauty.' The woman grunted, and went over to serve another customer, glancing occasionally at the nun. The clock on the town hall struck twelve.

'I'll be closing in a minute,' said the woman, but Sister Ursula knew she was not the sort of person to turn away custom so she ignored the comment and continued studying the flowers, thinking how marvellous were the works of God. Although beauty had its dangers, it could take your mind from the spiritual life. Beauty was a superficial thing.

'Made your mind up then?' persisted the woman. 'Those roses are quite nice, they'd brighten up a hospital ward no end.'

'The flowers are not for a hospital,' said the nun without

300

looking up. 'They are for a religious purpose.' She wondered vaguely whether this would cause the woman just to give her the flowers. At the convent they either used those in the grounds or people would give them flowers for the altar. She had never heard of anyone buying any.

'Perhaps they wouldn't be right for a cemetery,' concluded the woman.

'They are for Our Holy Mother,' cried Sister Ursula.

Suddenly she became aware of the rain again. She turned round to remonstrate with Ethel and what she saw left her quite rooted to the spot. Sister Ursula stared straight ahead, and the flower-seller glanced sidelong at what the nun was looking at. She saw a fat girl with an umbrella standing and talking to a blonde woman; the umbrella was the one which had been held over the nun, now it was held over this other person.

'Seems like you lost your umbrella,' she remarked with a laugh.

'She is up to no good,' hissed Sister Ursula.

'Will it be a dozen roses then?' asked the flower-seller, anxious lest after all the sale should be lost. 'They'd look a picture on any altar,' she added.

'There are forces at work,' declared the nun darkly.

'All red will that be?' enquired the woman, who was carefully pulling the roses out.

'The devil's work,' spat Sister Ursula.

'White then?' suggested the woman. 'With a bit of forget-me-not thrown in.' She gazed uncertainly at the nun's back, and wondered whether she should tug her habit to bring her attention to the flowers that her hands were arranging.

'Will that be all?' she asked.

'She has a demon in residence in her bowels,' said Sister Ursula. With authority, and before the flower-seller had time to wonder whether she had heard correctly, the nun strode off towards the two figures.

For a moment the flower-seller was too amazed to utter a word and stood there with the flowers hanging limply in her hand.

'Hold your horses,' she cried out. 'What about these flowers?' She waved them in the air and a few pale petals detached themselves. Indignant, she thrust the roses back into the pail.

'Did you have any paeonies?' asked another customer.

'I'm closed,' snapped the flower-seller, thinking how these religious people thought they could get away with anything.

'You'll not get any more flowers here,' she shouted.

'Pardon,' asked the confused customer.

'I'll not turn the other cheek,' declared the flower-woman, 'coming to my stall and poking and prodding all my wares, and,' she declared, 'all freshly cut this morning. Look at these anemones,' she said, thrusting them towards the bewildered customer. 'That's right,' persisted the flower-woman, 'just walk away. Don't think I won't warn people about your carrying on. She used the word, bowel,' cried the incensed seller. She moved so she stood in front of the carefully laid out flowers.

'What's up Lizzie?' asked the vegetable man, emerging from behind a pile of cauliflowers. 'Have you been short-changed?'

'I wouldn't have believed my own ears,' declared Lizzie the flower-seller. 'Coming out with words that are best kept to the surgery, and her all got up as a religious.'

'You don't say,' exclaimed the vegetable man, scratching his head slowly. 'She's not all there if you ask me. Just look at her now.' All three stared through the falling rain to Sister Ursula.

'Having a little trouble?' asked Dagmar demurely. She had watched the approach of Sister Ursula with a little smile playing on her lips. Sister Ursula did not return the geniality.

'I think you know where the trouble lies,' she replied tersely, and tugged the umbrella towards herself.

'This is the second time I have soaked myself to the skin on your behest my girl,' she said to Ethel. 'Oh yes, I'm sure Miss Ehrenhardt thinks your old aunty is being a little hard on you, but then Miss Ehrenhardt doesn't know you quite as well as I do.' She looked Dagmar in the eye. 'I take a very dim view of all this,' she declared. 'I shall have to report your interference

302

to your employer,' she said slowly in her coldest voice. Dagmar laughed. 'I assure you, this is no laughing matter,' retorted the nun, 'you are encouraging this child in her bad habits. Don't think I can't see through your stratagems.'

'I assure you,' said Dagmar firmly, 'that I did not encourage your niece. In fact, I have no interest in her whatsoever.'

'It's not true,' screamed Ethel. 'You said you were going to show me Germany, teach me lots of things.' The tears welled up in her podgy eyes.

'So,' cried Sister Ursula, 'you were going to abduct my niece to Germany.'

'This is preposterous,' said Dagmar, her voice rising to combat that of the nun.

'If I had my way,' declared the nun, 'you would be clapped in jail.'

'Do I have to remind you,' hissed Dagmar, 'this is a public place. I will not be made part of a spectacle.'

'Youooo lied,' moaned Ethel. 'I'm special.' She swayed slightly as though unsure of what to do.

'Stop fidgeting,' ordered Sister Ursula, becoming all too aware of the eyes which were now on them.

'I suggest that you tell your niece not to pester me any more,' said Dagmar, 'rushing up and asking lots of questions. I have no time to chat to subnormal children.'

'How dare you,' shouted Sister Ursula, pulling Ethel towards her. 'Look how you have upset this poor child, and her parents lying sick in bed. You are not fit to be a nurse, you are a heartless creature. I shall see Mrs Booth about this!' Dagmar laughed again, it was a chilling sound. 'You won't be laughing then,' said Sister Ursula.

'She is dead,' said Dagmar, and Sister Ursula suddenly noticed the black clothes of what she took to be mourning. 'The poor thing gave up the ghost,' stated Dagmar, 'that is what you say?'

'I had no idea,' said the nun. 'I shall pray for her poor soul.'

'What about me?' wailed Ethel, tugging herself away from her aunt's protective arm.

'She needs treatment,' stated Dagmar, glancing at the small audience which had grown. 'There are special hospitals,' she said knowingly.

'I'll forgive you,' said Ethel pleadingly, making a big effort to please Dagmar.

'Stop it,' ordered Sister Ursula. Although she made no effort to take hold of Ethel, she had felt a strange fear when the girl had broken away, as though Ethel were capable of great violence.

'In the future such children will not be allowed to be born.' Sister Ursula gasped.

'You can judge by skull size,' instructed Dagmar.

'Blasphemy, blasphemy,' Sister Ursula crossed herself. 'Setting yourself up like God. Only he can decide whether a child is born. It is not for us to question his wisdom.'

'Nonsense.'

'I will not have this child subjected to such heresy. Oh yes! you set yourself up just like Satan who was hurled down from heaven.'

'Where are your thunderbolts?' asked Dagmar. 'The Führer is the herald of a new revelation, yours is a strange faith imported into Germany; National Socialism is the doing of God's will. The national church will have the loyalty of the people. On the altars will be one book and a sword. The cross will be removed for the only unconquerable symbol, the swastika.' She recited the words of Alfred Rosenberg with her pale blue eyes gleaming triumphantly. She only wished she had a copy of *Mein Kampf* to flourish under the nose of this Christian.

'I . . . will . . . pray for you,' gasped Sister Ursula.

'Keep your prayers,' announced Dagmar, 'you cannot be both a Christian and a German. Nor will it be possible to be English and a Christian. Save your prayers for yourself, you will be needing them.'

'I am a soldier of Christ,' declared Sister Ursula, at that moment ready to die for her faith.

'You have no guns or bullets, you will submit as a dog would to its master.'

'I shall try to forgive you!'

Dagmar laughed once more.

'You will not laugh at God on Judgment Day.' She clasped hold of Ethel's hand, 'Prayers will be useless then.'

'I shall pray for you,' said Ethel judicially.

'In bedlam,' grimaced Dagmar, as though an unpleasant odour had just assaulted her nose.

'I am leaving,' stated Sister Ursula. 'I had thought that once we had reached a little understanding, and I am sorry I did not realise sooner, foolish pride was in the way. That is a sin, but there are worse sins, and I shall pray for you, my dear,' she murmured, 'pray for forgiveness.' She lowered her eyes with humility.

Lizzie, the flower-woman, nudged the vegetable man. Her beady eyes had widened from press-studs to buttons watching the confrontation.

'Beyond the pale,' said the customer who was still standing there, moved to speak out at the whole nasty business.

'No call for language like that,' said Lizzie, her eyes moving to follow the departing nun and the overweight girl who trailed her, carrying the umbrella.

'Quite beyond the pale,' repeated the customer, not making it clear whether she was indignant at both the parties or merely one.

'Where's that other woman from?' asked the vegetable man, thinking that she had a fine figure. A body like that, he decided, could drive a man crazy. Then he blushed.

'She told me about trepanning,' said Ethel, trying to keep up with her aunt whose stride scythed through the damp air. She stared awkwardly at the nun who was as silent as a holy picture. 'I don't want blonde hair now.' She had secretly purchased a bottle of peroxide. 'Are you going to convert her?' she asked.

No voice came back to answer her, and try as she might, Ethel could not keep the umbrella over Sister Ursula, who now seemed oblivious to the weather. Walking through the familiar streets, she took to looking through the windows, her mind wandering as her feet scraped her along. Some people had net curtains up, so all you could see were shadows. Vases and little ornaments were piled haphazardly on display on the window-ledges. The most cherished possessions often took pride of place in the window; a sad-looking pot donkey with part of a leg missing stuck in Ethel's mind.

'There was a donkey in that window,' she whispered. 'They

have a cross on their backs in remembrance of the day they carried the Saviour.'

For some reason the donkey made her feel at peace with the world, even though one of her socks hung down and her feet squelched in the water from the puddles.

31

Nature had made it clear that winter was approaching. A cold wind blew over the land and while Persephone dwelt underground for the pomegranate seed she ate, scarves and thicker clothes were worn by the mortals. The calendar had reached one of the ancient turning-points of the year in pagan Europe, but few were aware of the fact. They knew about Hallowe'en, but now the fires were lit to commemorate the burning of a traitor five nights later than when the souls of the dead sought warmth. Although the town of Slackhall had been hounded by bad luck, a sense of relief could be detected and doors which had remained shut were now left ajar and the suspicion which had rested heavily was lifted. The fires burnt brightly in the grates and the town allowed itself to relax along with the rest of the country, closing its ears to dark rumours, and the warnings of politicians. Sometimes men would give a nervous laugh in the bar, and in ordering another round wonder why their hands shook as though they were frightened. The old soldiers who sat in the corner exchanged knowing looks, and sucked harder on their pipes. People talked, smiled, made love and died in this imaginary world.

As tanks which were supposed to be made of cardboard and always breaking down rolled over the tilled fields of the Sudetenland under the autumn sky, English ministers smiled at the vulgar German, who even had a portrait of his dead chauffeur in his private rooms. Such eccentricity might be allowable for the aristocracy, but not a painter of tiny, precise water-colours, inhabited by few figures, only grand façades.

As the Austrian painter stirred the European psyche with old prejudices, his talk of the elders of Zion turned the public mind towards the chosen people, but on Hallowe'en, witches and demons could feast with impunity. It was far more dangerous to light the seven-branched candlestick, and the wails would sound in nine days' time, amid the shattering glass and rifle butts.

The ninth of November was also the date on which the latest film at the Majestic would be changed, but on the thirty-first of October an orderly if excited queue waited on the pavement, occasionally stamping its feet, not from impatience, but cold.

'Next,' said the ticket lady mechanically.

'One for the circle,' said the filmgoer.

'Front or back?'

'Front.'

'That'll be one and six, then,' and she reached for the half-crown which had been pushed towards her. As she counted out the change and reached for the ticket, she looked for the first time at the figure outside the booth. 'Why,' she declared, 'I haven't seen you for some time. Isn't your friend with you?' she asked. 'A right little gentleman he was, always paid if I remember rightly.'

'You've got the wrong person,' said the figure, glancing at the long crowd behind her, and reaching out for the ticket and change.

'Suit yourself,' said the ticket woman sourly. 'That's one shilling change. I'm sure my eyesight isn't that bad that I've given you the wrong change,' she added as she watched the little woman count out a shilling in her palm.

'You've seen too many pictures,' stated the customer and walked into the foyer.

'Next,' said the ticket lady, thinking that in her profession you met all sorts.

As the cinema slowly filled and the bodies were packed next to each other, the chattering died along with the dimming lights. For a moment they were engulfed in darkness, and with a smile Mrs Wagtail settled herself back into the seat. Popping a mint in her mouth, she awaited the start of *Snow White and the Seven Dwarfs*.

Sister Ursula trilled, 'I'll get it,' as the knocking continued on the door.

Ethel raised her head in the bedroom as she heard the voice, but as she had no intention of opening the door, she

308

sank it once more until it rested on her layered chins. She knew who it was, but she had decided that tonight was the night when she would show them.

'Come in, come in,' said Sister Ursula, 'let me take your coat,' and before the man could object, the nun was tugging at the coat so that both of them became breathless and flustered.

'Ah, ah, thank you, Sister,' said Father Farnaby in a soft brogue.

The masculine voice seemed to hum and buzz in the bare hallway. He watched his coat being draped over the banister, and as his eyes took in the bare floorboards he caught sight of the print of St Lucy. The plate with the eyes made him shudder slightly.

'It's aah, a terrible cold night,' he said, rubbing his hands together noisily. Sister Ursula blushed at the sound.

'Come through and warm yourself, Father,' she said, leading him into the shadowy sitting-room.

As he stood in front of the fire, the nun took her first good look at him. She was surprised to see such a young man. He stood with his legs slightly parted, and Sister Ursula watched the red glow of the flickering flames dance over his dark suit. He was a handsome man. She trembled as she gazed at his swept-back hair. It was black, terribly black.

'You are not from these parts then,' she said, stepping back slightly as he turned to face her.

'Aah,' he laughed, 'and here was me thinking my accent was, aah gone. Not quite the missionary work I had in mind, but ours is not to reason why.'

'No, no, that's very true,' she said humbly. 'We all have our little cross to bear.'

Upstairs, Ethel was sitting cross-legged on the floor like some buddha. She was listening, not to the vague noises downstairs, but to her gurgling stomach. Since swallowing the pomegranate seed, she had slowly become convinced that the strange fruit was growing and ripening within her. The feeling inside made her hot and cold, but she couldn't explain this to anybody. She thought she knew what it meant, and now she had the solution. In front of her lay her father's toolchest.

'Is it one sugar or two?' asked Sister Ursula, failing to notice the frown on the face of Father Farnaby as he took in the religious effigies and artefacts which littered the place. The picture of Christ rose up before him, displaying the five wounds of Calvary.

'Only aah, one.' He continued studying the crucifixion; in the subterranean glow the blood had seemed to flow, welling up thickly.

'It's wonderful how Our Lord makes one feel at home,' she said, coming in with a little tray.

'Aa yes, yes. I could tell at once this is a religious household.' He reached for his cup.

'Indeed it is,' said Sister Ursula, leaping on to his words, 'and in a place like this, it is not easy, not easy at all.' She took a trembling sip of tea. 'I shall be frank with you, Father.' She fixed him with an uncanny stare. He tried not to look at her pinched white face and settled on the nailed feet of Christ above the nun's head. 'This community is a long way from salvation, and I have been besieged and beset for wishing to live a Christian life.' She clasped her hands together tightly. 'Abused in the streets, Father. Oh their souls are heading for purgatory. There are crimes here, great blasphemy goes on. They have hounded me for my love of our Lord. They have persecuted this household.' She wrung her hands, and Father Farnaby shifted uncomfortably in the chair. 'My niece has been led from the path of righteousness, poisoned by evil tongues to even deny our Lord.'

She clasped her hands to her cheeks, pulling the skin between thumb and finger, pinching her flesh until the priest could see a red mark appear. His cup of tea was suspended in mid-air as with a horrified fascination he watched the nun mortify her cheeks.

'I heard her,' she gasped, 'blasphemy spilling from the lips of my own niece. She must have penance, Father, as we all must. I am a weak vessel, not fit to anoint our Lord.'

'Aah, now Sister, surely . . .'

'Prayers and penance,' she pleaded. 'God must be brought back to this place, and we must all seek absolution.'

'You are, aah, distressed.' His shaking hand lowered the cup. 'Come, come, Sister, this will not do at all.'

'Salvation,' she cried. 'We must reject earthly delights, that is the true path to God. Humiliation is our allotted role in this

310

life. Our only desire should be to share the suffering of our dear Lord.'

Father Farnaby sat rigidly in his chair.

'I have suffered,' said Sister Ursula bravely. 'We are under siege; windows breaking, policemen and strangers entering, assaulted in the street, accused of unmentionable crimes, and hearing things, hearing things no modest person could repeat.'

'This is aah . . . terrible.' He felt at a loss.

'Yes, yes,' she clamoured. 'Oh, to be able to share my thoughts, to see light in all this darkness. My suffering has been terrible. But I would endure it all again, and . . . more.' She paused suddenly, and stiffened. 'Did you hear that?' she whispered, the whites of her eyes rolling towards the ceiling.

'I . . . ah.'

'Sssh,' she commanded, 'there again.' She clasped her hands together. 'We must pray, we must pray . . . *O Deus ego amo te, Nec amo te ut salvas me.*' She paused, and opening one eye, stared at the gently sweating face of the priest. 'You must pray. This is a pagan place.'

And as she closed her eye, she strained to hear his heavier voice, for his eyes had been very black, terribly black. But even the devil could not pray, the words would burn his profane lips. Soon she would know.

Ethel had managed to drag the heavy toolchest over to the bed. She paused for a moment, and listened. She didn't want her aunt to come poking her nose in. Stealthily her hand reached out and opened the lid. She froze as the rusting hinges creaked, and then, the box was laid bare. It was filled with strange implements. Some gleamed in the dull light, but others lay flat and uninteresting, their surfaces mottled with patches of rust, like dried blood. Her fingers cautiously slid into the box, and with a strange tenderness she laid her palm on the roughened surface of the rusty saw. She kept her podgy fingers away from the serrated edge, and as gently as she could, she lifted it from its place.

Mrs Wagtail popped another mint into her mouth, sucking enthusiastically as the cartoon figures paraded on the screen. She had a splendid view since the protruding head in front of

311

her had rushed out of the auditorium with terrible earache. The little shuffling boy who sat next to her had also fallen silent.

'Heigh Ho, Heigh Ho,' sang the seven dwarfs as they went off to work, their little picks sharp and gleaming, ready for the mining.

'What a strange question,' Dagmar had said, frowning down into the flushed face of Ethel Coffin. 'Whatever put that into your mind?'

'Please tell, please tell,' pleaded Ethel, glancing anxiously back towards her aunt. Dagmar gave a pale, flickering smile.

'It's a very ancient technique.' She paused slightly, relishing the desperation in Ethel's face. 'Lots of skulls have been found by archaeologists which have been trepanned. Merovingian kings were ritually incised . . .' She stopped. It was quite uncanny how this child had somehow picked a subject of which she knew a great deal. Her hand raised itself subconsciously and felt the rim of the indentation hidden by the blonde hair on her temple. 'Well, perhaps I won't bore you with the history, except it was thought that people were trepanned so their spirit could leave the body, so they could gain enlightenment.'

'But what is it, what is it?'

'Trepanation,' declared Dagmar, 'is making a small hole in the head, through the bone, so your brain is exposed to the elements, not a huge gaping hole, but very, very small.'

'But why?' gasped Ethel.

'Some people thought that it relieved madness, but they were mad themselves. In trepanning, a person raises his consciousness. Everything is heightened, thinking is clearer. It is wonderful.' She gave Ethel a rapt smile. 'But it carries its dangers. Some perforate the brain, or even have slivers of skull entering the brain cells, and the resulting abscess may kill. But some think the risk is worth it.' Her eyes gleamed down.

'Worth it, worth it,' thought Ethel as she sat in front of the toolchest. She felt that God was speaking to her. Wasn't our Lord a carpenter? She allowed her hands to be guided. She

312

lifted out a bevel, and then plunged her hand once more into the box of mysteries and pulled out a gimlet.

'Forgive me, Father,' said Ursula, 'for doubting.'

'We all have doubts, aah, even the most devout sometimes doubt their faith.'

'Oh no, no, you misunderstand me. I do not doubt my faith, I was doubting you.'

'Me?'

'Things are not always as they seem, Father. I had to be sure . . . you could have been his emissary,' she leaned forward, 'come to tempt me.'

'Really, Sister, I, aah, think that it's best that I . . .'

'There is no peace in this house. I am not at peace, Father.'

'At peace?'

'This place reeks of heresy.' Her nose quivered in the air. 'You heard them, they have been tormenting me, mocking me. You must hear my confessions, you must give absolution,' she sobbed. 'Forgive me, Father, for I have sinned.'

'I, aah don't think . . .' started the priest.

'I have consorted with demons,' she gasped, 'spoken to Satan's emissary.'

'Sister Ursula,' he commanded, 'stop this at once, I say stop.'

'In my pride I let them enter, I must be broken. I have betrayed our Lord, and I love him so.'

'I don't think,' began the priest.

'Forgive me, forgive me, they are mocking us, ruining us in body and soul.'

'Please, Sister, this is unseemly. You must use self-control.'

'The sons of Belial are here, afflicting us. He will not leave us in peace. They have made this house unclean, but I resist them, their tricks shall not overcome me.'

'Demons?' he repeated, with morbid fascination.

'We must make them howl and tremble and leave the bowels of those they possess. You must exorcise the devils in this place. They could not bear to listen to a voice which has tasted the host. They will try to make you hoarse; they have done this to me, and tormented me with doubts. They will try anything, even flatulence to mock our Lord.'

313

'This is nineteen thirty-eight, not the Middle Ages. Satan ruled fears then, but not now.'

'You are so sure,' she laughed. The sound was so brittle it tinkled around him like broken glass. 'There is good, so there is evil. To deny the existence of Satan denies the existence of God and the Church. The existence has been settled for Catholics,' she stared resolutely. 'I tell you demoniac action has been at work in this place, and only God knows how many others. If it is proof that you want, you shall have it.'

She leapt from her seat, and turning round, placed her trembling lips on the carved wooden feet of Christ. With wild eyes she faced Father Farnaby. The priest was pale, the seminary had not prepared him to deal with the hysteria of a nun. He wondered coldly what had happened to the other members of the household.

The lights came on in the Majestic and the audience blinked as the final credits rolled. The images of the screen were still in their minds and they talked of this scene and that, marvelling at the skill of the cartoonist who had plunged them into the magical tale.

'It's Hallowe'en tonight,' cackled Mrs Wagtail, 'you'd better lock the house so the wicked queen don't get in and bite you.' She poked the little boy beside her, who turned worried eyes to his mother.

'There's nothing they like better than popping a little boy in some dough and baking him on a fire.' She laughed and prodded him with a pointy finger.

'Mummy,' he began to wail, as he pushed himself towards her skirt. Mrs Wagtail darted out her tongue and wagged it at him, back and forth, like a magnet between iron lips. She made little smacking sounds.

'Heavens above,' said his mother who had not heard the conversation, 'just stop that noise at once, or you'll not have any supper.'

'She said she was going to eat me,' he sobbed.

'Don't be such a baby, they were only cartoon characters,' she sighed, and looked around for that scruffy little woman. She didn't want lice on top of everything else. Just the thought

314

of it made her feel itchy. She yanked her son's arm and let him snuffle quietly. She couldn't see the old woman anywhere.

Ethel heard the footsteps coming up the stairs and, instinctively, she tried to hide the toolchest. Her huge body was swathed in white. She had struggled to fit herself into the clothes of her first communion; a white veil hid her sweating face, topped by a wreath of white flowers made from cotton. They had been bent out of shape in the drawer, no longer looking fresh and pure. She waited until she heard the footsteps pass her door before letting out a long trembling breath. The veil did not hide the fixed look of ecstasy which filled her eyes. She lifted the veil with the delicacy of an illusionist about to astound the audience. She had chosen white because it was the colour of the operating theatre.

Sister Ursula stood in front of the closed door, her hand trembled on the handle. 'They have been grievously harassed by the demons,' she whispered. 'You must prepare yourself, the evil ones must already sense your presence.'

She pushed open the door and swiftly entered. Father Farnaby felt curiously reluctant to follow her. His throat was dry and, as the door opened, his nose was assaulted by an unwholesome smell. As he followed Sister Ursula, he could almost feel the darkness and his lips moved in silent prayer. Her anxieties fuelled his thoughts and he felt like vomiting. He could make out nothing in the gloom.

'A light, Sister,' he gasped into the humid air.

Upon illumination he blinked and took in the two beds. Slowly he approached them, forgetting Sister Ursula, who stood with her hand still resting on the light switch. With sickening certainty he knew that the smell came from the beds. He wanted to pull out a handkerchief to hold to his nose and wondered whether this was the smell of death or evil.

'They lie so still,' he murmured.

'They are possessed,' intoned the nun.

He reached out, and tentatively laid his hand on the sheeted form of Fanny Coffin.

'You must give them absolution,' whispered Sister Ursula.

315

'The Stations of the Cross for penance. Let them drag the cross, share the suffering.'

He had found her hand, and he could not prevent himself twitching with revulsion. His instinct was to drop it and run. He even wondered whether the demons were already at work on him, feeding off his fears.

'*Rosa Mystica*,' responded Sister Ursula, wondering whether Father Farnaby was too young to handle an exorcism. The priest's fingers had slipped over the cold flesh and he cried out as he felt the steady pulse.

'Oh sweet Jesus, save us, save us,' she gabbled, 'the hosts of Satan are upon us. Lord Jesus come, wash away our sins.'

Her jerking hand once more plunged the room into darkness. She gave a little shriek, as though not even aware that she herself had touched the switch. She pressed herself against the wall, any moment expecting to feel the claws of a demon. As the priest groped his way towards the sound of the whimpering nun, he wiped his hand back and forth over his trousers. He felt he had entered a madhouse. He had stepped from the street and was now enmeshed in a nightmare. His hand felt along the wall until it found the switch.

'They are . . . a . . . a . . . alive,' he said grimly.

'You see what I face. Oh the stench of sin,' she gasped. 'They try to drag us down to hell.' She fished for her rosary. 'Holy Mary, Mother of God! Holy Mary, Mother of God,' she began.

'They are alive,' he repeated. Sister Ursula stopped her rosary.

'They are possessed, Father.'

'No, no.' He shook his head with frightening rapidity, so that Sister Ursula took a step back, and tightened her grip on the rosary.

'Have you had a doctor now, Sister?' he said.

'Doctor,' she exclaimed. 'What use would that be, Father? Science has no place in this house; religion will heal, not probing fingers. Would you have me allow a Protestant doctor into this place? We are good Roman Catholics here.' Her eyes became as hard as nails.

'They are ill, Sister. They are lying in their own filth. Did you not know this?'

'How . . . how dare you. You know nothing. I have prayed for them, I have suffered for them, I have had signs.' She held up her hand from which dangled the rosary.

'They have a disease, Sister. They are not getting proper care. Perhaps the strain has been too much for you. Mother Barbara has written to me . . .'

'Mother Barbara,' she gasped, and reeled back as though she had been struck across the face. 'It is a mistake, there is no need for concern. The powers of heaven will heal them. I must write to Mother Barbara and assure her all is well. She has a bad heart; she must not worry. I have been away too long.' She looked at the priest. 'Not bad news, was it? There is a pilgrimage to our Holy Father, perhaps I am needed for that. We shall go round all the shrines, visit all the churches.' Her mind became filled with the glorious journey. She would pray to the head of St Catherine in Siena, to the tongue of St Anthony in Padua.

'A doctor,' he repeated, 'it's a doctor we're needing.'

'What is all this talk of doctors? Haven't I told you, this is work for God.'

'They are in a terrible condition, Sister, the sheets have not been changed. Shall I be taking you downstairs and then calling for the good doctor?'

'They have to be mortified. What use would a doctor be, taking X-rays? They would not show up the demons. All the hocus pocus of science would not help their poor souls.'

'But the sheets, Sister?'

'Didn't St Radegunde sleep on cinders, and St Oportune refuse to use water. They can clean their sheets with tears, good tears of contrition.'

'You are too harsh, Sister, they need help. There is nothing wrong with a doctor. You must think of them. Have they not suffered enough? They must be diagnosed.'

'The power of God will cure them. They are possessed. I could sense it . . . and their daughter, she is abomination.'

'I must, aah, insist now, Sister. This is no way to carry on. You are overtired.'

She frowned at him, thinking of her earlier suspicions, his black hair, and black eyes. Was the devil not supposed to take the form of a dark man?

317

'I have taken measures,' she gasped. 'They are heading for purgatory, like St Rita's sons.' She smiled. 'But I have prayed, like the blessed Rita, that they should die and be taken from further wickedness.'

Father Farnaby sighed.

Mrs Wagtail looked up at the sparkling sky. The dotted stars winked down like the diamonds in the mine of the seven dwarfs. A fire crackled in front of her, sending shadows dancing round the clustered trees and a huge wardrobe which stood with one door open. The interior was as black as the sky. She had a little wreath on her head made from the ivy in the churchyard.

'Let him who has keep hold,' she murmured, and spat into the fire. It hissed. 'Heigh ho, heigh ho, it's off to work we go,' she sang, nodding her head from side to side and thinking of the shiny little picks, as sharp as could be . . . 'With shovel and pick . . .' She couldn't get the tune out of her head.

Ethel wondered briefly whether it would hurt, but she knew she would have to give the plant light. It had curled its tendrils into her head, she could feel them. She wondered if she had swallowed an orange pip, or an apple, and whether they, too, would be growing inside her. The strange heavy fruit would need the sun to ripen, she knew that. She remembered from school, plants need light. 'Chlorophyll,' she murmured; she took wilful pleasure at the sound of the word, and her white veil rustled as she sank down to the floor next to the toolchest. She wondered whether Jesus had ever used a gimlet in old Nazareth; it lay so lightly in her palm. She raised her eyes from the implement when she heard a stifled cry. She rubbed it lovingly between her fingers, feeling how sharp its end was, like a . . . pick. She jumped at the thought, she could almost hear the branches of the strange fruit creaking inside her head, like tall trees under a star-filled sky.

'Let him who has keep hold,' she said.

Her hands moved over the gimlet, deft and loving. Like the Holy Ghost a huge pomegranate floated above her, splitting itself slowly. The bloody juice welled up, but did not drip on to her communion-white clothes. She saw it as her goal, a sign

318

of her specialness. She wished on it. Like a magic carpet she would be able to go anywhere she liked, even to Germany if she wanted. Her mind drifted for a moment; she felt a slight twinge in her foot as though she had pricked it, or stood on something sharp. She paused, would it feel like that in her head?

'We work, work, work . . . the whole day through,' sang somebody in the distance. And she suddenly felt afraid, and closed her eyes. She did not want to see. The branches spread inside her skull, she wanted to climb that big tree into the sky; she stretched up her hand and plunged the gimlet in.

She made the hole through her skin into the snapping bone as thin as the eucharist. The gimlet mined deep and a red veil washed over her podgy face. Her hand slipped away, her eyes fluttered and she let in the light. Its brightness blinded her, her mouth opened in wonder, a huge round 'O' and from deep within a scream, a thin tearing sound like membrane. The light shone through, and she could hear the angels singing in the white, their heavenly voices echoed as though in a cavern. Her corporeal form collapsed, the white, white clothes soaked up the bloodied map of her revelation, the continents of blood spread their borders.

And the angels sang to her:

'Heigh ho, heigh ho, it's off to war we go.'

IN THE YEAR OF OUR LORD
NINETEEN HUNDRED AND FORTY

PART TWO

'Savagery is necessary every four or five hundred years in order to bring the world back to life. Otherwise the world would die of civilization.'
                    Jules and Edmond de Goncourt

32

William woke with a jolt, and found that the train had stopped at another station. He straightened his neck, which ached slightly, and ran his tongue over his dry lips. He didn't feel refreshed from the sleep. He tried to close his eyes, but knew that he was unlikely to drift away again. The other occupant of the compartment was still there, still sitting in the opposite corner to William. She had spent the first half-hour of the journey reading a letter over and over again as though she were trying to memorise it for a recitation. William took to staring out of the window. He had had enough of seeing her eyes glazing over with a filmy band of water, as they shone with emotion and suppressed tears, and watching the landscape go by he fell asleep. He opened his eyes lazily as he heard someone struggling with the carriage door. The figure of an obese matron pushed a bulging suitcase into the carriage. He couldn't make out the wording on the name tag, and before it even occurred to him, the young woman had jumped up to lend a hand, tugging the heavy suitcase to one side and steadying the older woman as she puffed and panted into the small space.

'Thank you, thank you,' she wheezed. 'Can't get a porter for love nor money these days.'

She leaned over and pulled the door closed, and at once William was aware of the woman's cloying perfume which wafted about at her slightest movement. She smiled at the younger woman, but not at William. All at once it seemed the airy compartment had contracted. As though going through a prescribed ritual, the new passenger reached up and feeling around her hat, pulled out a sharp hatpin, and then lifted the hat with a little sigh of satisfaction. Her fleshy hands placed the prim hat on her broad knees, which seemed to strain through the tight skirt. With fascination, William watched as she suddenly plunged the pin into the side of the hat, as though oblivious as to whether it would penetrate right through. She patted down her greying hair which had been moulded into tight little waves, and looked as though it would be unable to become mussed even if the whole carriage were ripped apart in some frightful accident.

'That's better,' she said in a self-satisfied way. Her voice seemed to be pitched so anyone else in the carriage would be forced to listen to it.

Her eyes met those of the young woman again, and she smiled.

'Going far?' she said conversationally, and with a sinking feeling, William knew that the rest of the journey to Slackhall would be filled with voices. He swiftly closed his eyes lest he should be dragged into the conversation. As they introduced themselves, he heard that the young woman was called Sylvia Dewett, and the older, Mrs Joan Withington, the secretary of a girls' school. She had been visiting her sister who had cancer of the lungs.

He pressed his head against the padded backrest as though he were trying to force it out of the carriage. With one ear he could hear the muffled rumbling of the train, and with the other, the voices of the women saying how you wouldn't believe it would be June soon, and the weather looked as though it could do anything. Miss Dewett asked sympathetically about the sister with cancer.

'A bit of a tricky business,' the new headmaster had said to William, avoiding looking him in the eyes. 'Once the cat is out of the bag, it could be most awkward for you, Booth. I don't know just how long I can keep the lid on this sort of thing.'

He turned his back and seemed to be studying an old school photograph. William remained standing there, and in the distance he heard the bell to signal the change of class: he should be in history now.

'You see the position I'm in, Booth,' the headmaster said, and William looked to see what was in the old photograph that the head was staring at. Perhaps it was one with his uncle in it. 'They want to speak to you about it. I told the inspector that it would be better if you went up to see them, wouldn't do

to have them at the school, only start the tongues wagging.'
He turned to face William. 'How old are you now, Booth?'
William told him; the head nodded in an abstract manner as
though listening to some translation or conjugation. William
thought for a second that the headmaster was going to
apologise for all this embarrassment, instead he once more
turned his back on William, this time to stare unnervingly out
of the window.

'Lots of mayflies about,' he said absently. 'Peculiar insects,
once they emerge from the water they only live a few hours or
a day. The adult mayfly never feeds, but has vestigial mouth
parts. All they do is mate and die, seems a bit pointless,
really.' He turned from the window. 'Except from the fishes'
point of view.' He gave the ghost of a smile. 'Are you a
fisherman, Booth?' he asked, and then as though he couldn't
wait to hear from William, 'All boys must have done some
fishing.' He sighed. 'Something always gets through the net,
slips through.' The headmaster's hand strayed to the top of
his cluttered desk, his fingers made out they were looking for
something.

'Have you thought about the future, Booth? What occupa-
tion had you in mind, well, before all of this?' He shrugged his
shoulders slightly. Again he didn't wait for a reply. 'Difficult
times ahead boy, difficult times.' He spoke as though in pain.

'They have a cotton mill your family? Always be a need for
that, but if you have a different calling, just say the word, I'm
sure I can provide you with the ah, necessary . . .' His voice
faded out. 'We all have our duty, Booth, king and country
boy, king and country. Still, perhaps it will all be over before
you get your papers. I know you won't let the school down.'
He opened a drawer and pulled out a small metal box, and
fumbled with the key.

'Bit of a loner, aren't you, Booth? Mr Watkins told me you
have no particular friends, perhaps that's for the best, make it
easier all round, eh? I don't take to bullying, but when this
sort of thing comes out, bound to have a hard time of it,
bound to.' He opened the little box; it contained money.

'Now, don't worry about your things, matron will sort all
that out, just get what you need for the journey. I'm sure this
is all for the best,' he said, once more unable to look in

William's eye. 'I hope you understand, it's nothing personal Booth. Don't think that it's any reflection on you. Time heals all wounds.'

He held out his hand, and William thought he meant to shake it, but as he grasped it, he felt the money rustling against his palm. The headmaster's hand fell away without shaking that of William, and the note fluttered to the thick carpet. The headmaster turned away his eyes so he wouldn't have to watch William pick the money up. He sighed, at least it was all over now. He just hoped it wouldn't mean parents would not send their children to a school where there were connections with people accused of acts prejudicial to the state.

'For the train journey, Booth,' he explained, 'and perhaps there will be enough for a meal eh?' He carefully closed the little box, and put it neatly in the drawer. 'Well,' he said trying to sound more positive, 'I hope your conduct will be a credit to the school.'

He always said that to those who left. Somehow it sounded hollow in the study whereas at assembly the words had resonance. He didn't finish the speech, but turned once more to look out of the window at the mayflies dancing over the pond. William stared a moment at his back, and after quietly placing the money on the shiny surface of the desk he fled the room.

'Worse than the blackout,' complained Mrs Withington. William opened his eyes in the dark as the train rattled away in a tunnel, and there was a distant smell of smoke. He wondered vaguely whether that would also be the smell of a battlefield. 'Have you tried to get any torch batteries?' she asked Miss Dewett. 'You just can't get them for love nor money. I said to my sister, I said, I'll do myself an injury in these blackouts, and then where will you be? I should think it would be difficult to get compensation,' she added. 'I have a bit of knowledge in that department, I was secretary with some solicitors. We dealt with that kind of thing a lot; people slip and slide all over the place,' she gave a little laugh. 'It's a wonder we don't all get knocked down. It's all right for the men, they can let their shirt-tails hang out.' She snickered in the dark. 'That's better,' she said as they emerged from the glimmering shadow, 'can't stand to be cooped in like that.'

She glanced towards William, who swiftly closed his eyes, but not quickly enough. Mrs Withington had spotted he was awake. He must be listening in to their conversation, she thought. She eyed him suspiciously, his shoes were none too clean either. She wondered whether he was a deserter; somebody had told her there were quite a few about. She turned back to Sylvia Dewett who had lowered her head and was staring at the letter Mrs Withington had noticed earlier in her lap.

'Is that from one of our brave boys?' she asked.

'My fiancé.' She bit on her bottom lip. 'He's somewhere in France.'

'Now don't get despondent.'

'It must be terrible for them, fighting for those foreigners. He doesn't understand a word of French. I don't know what would happen if he got lost.'

'Now that's not very likely. The army don't go around losing their soldiers. My husband was there in the Great War and he didn't know a word of French either.'

'They don't tell you anything, though,' she said.

'Walls have ears,' replied Mrs Withington, and couldn't help glancing at William.

'I suppose you are right. I just hope he's all right, he only has two pairs of socks.'

'Now don't get despondent. Are you going to be a land-girl?' she asked. 'I would jump at the chance if I were a bit younger.'

'Well, no, I get hay fever,' admitted Miss Dewett, looking more despondent. 'I think I shall go into a factory, for planes or something like that.'

'That's very worth while; I gave all my saucepans away,' she said proudly. 'It's that new campaign, saucepans for spitfires, makes you wonder what bit they'll end up as. I hope mine go for bullets to kill them Nazis.' She smiled with satisfaction, and looked out of the window on to the peaceful, rolling countryside. 'Mind you, can't say it's helped my cooking.' They both laughed at the little joke.

'Did you say you were going all the way to Slackhall?' she asked Miss Dewett. The younger woman nodded.

327

'It's not far now,' confided Mrs Withington. 'I've got today off,' she explained, 'on account of my sister, but I can tell you, there's been some goings-on in Slackhall.' She exchanged a conspiratorial look with Miss Dewett and eased herself slightly forward in her seat. 'It started last week, right out of the blue the police came calling at the school.' She looked sideways, and leant further forward. 'It wasn't the first time, either. They came a couple of years ago, but this time they carted her off.'

Miss Dewett looked slightly confused.

'Carted who off?' she whispered, falling into the conspiratorial mood.

'The headmistress.' William felt himself stiffen slightly. He tried to empty his mind.

'I had my suspicions, of course. I heard that policeman. Acts prejudicial to the security of the state! And belonging to organisations which have association with the . . . enemy.' She took a deep breath and sat up straight, pursing her lips. 'You could have knocked me down with a feather. There I'd been working for somebody who was associating with the enemy, giving my pots and pans for planes, and she's probably sending hers to Adolf.'

'What's going to happen to her?'

'Whatever it is, it'll be too good for the likes of her. I had to help the police gather together all her files. Goodness knows what secrets she'd tucked away in those, makes my blood run cold just to think of it.'

'How frightening.' She paused. 'Do you think they'll shoot her?'

'It's better than she deserves.' She remembered all the times she'd had to make the tea for Cecilia Royce. All that carry-on about China and India. She smiled. She'd be lucky to get anything where she was heading.

'There was a den of spies in Slackhall,' she said. 'We harboured them unknowingly, but they've all been exposed now, but one is on the run, a German by all accounts.'

'A German!' gasped Miss Dewett.

'Oh yes, it all goes on in Slackhall.' She lifted her hand to pat her static hair. 'Never a dull moment,' she laughed.

*

'On the run,' thought William, forcing himself to be still despite a terrible prickling at the back of his head. He listened to the two women for a few moments; it had become difficult not to.

'Nothing to offer but blood and toil and tears and sweat,' declared Mrs Withington 'that's what he said, and he should know if anyone does.'

William couldn't get the image of large, snuffling dogs out of his mind, following the scent. He was glad. Or was he? The rattling train seemed to dislodge all his thoughts. He was finding it difficult to pick them all up behind his closed eyes. Why should he care what happens to her? He didn't even know her properly, and yet as the train swayed on, the knowledge of her seemed to loom ever larger, inside, behind his closed eyes. He had the image of the traitor the two women had just been talking of, and perhaps he also had the terrible knowledge that he could betray her. After all, didn't he have some of her blood flowing through his body? He had absorbed part of her, and she part of him.

Since the death of his grandmother he had often thought of that day, when he first met Dagmar. Running with fright she had found him, and they had talked and talked, Dagmar telling him of the traitor Hagen, and smiling as they became blood brothers. How he had wished to change the pattern of things. Over and over he had thought of that moment, trying to sort his feelings like some arduous task in a fairy tale in separating the grains of sand from seed to be sown, truth from fantasy.

And now he was the heir, and there was nobody left to love him. He should have listened to the words of Nanny Bradshaw. He knew what she would expect of him. She would never have paused to think about it, she would have had her revenge. Dagmar rose before him, her traitor's neck wound round with the gleaming pearls of his grandmother, and on her finger her ring, and at his will the smile began to change, it flowed and shifted. Her eyes began to widen with terror, her mouth pleaded with him, begging forgiveness for the hurt. He stripped her of the pearls, and pulsing in her neck was the vein, and in the vein her life's blood; take out the blood and you put out her life.

Until this happened, it was difficult to remember that they were at war. The firing was so far away you couldn't even hear the echo of a shot. It was the twilight war, sitting around and waiting for something to happen, scanning the blue skies for the planes and the bombs. He had received a shock upon hearing of the arrest of his uncle, but no greater than the news of the marriage with Dagmar, and now he was behind bars, an enemy of the people. Perhaps he was an enemy of the people as well. Mrs Withington would have seen him as such if she knew the German was his aunt.

In the swaying carriage everything seemed frighteningly solid. It was as though his closed eyes had opened upon a different world, that since the journey began changes had taken place. He felt as though he had been kissed by the Snow Queen and would forget the people he had loved and even his home. When first he had seen Dagmar he had thought of the fairy tale, there had been no rest or repose in the German's cold glittering eyes, and in the reflection from the window he saw them resting within his own familiar face. His thoughts were as broken as a frozen lake, and just like Kay he had busied with them, joining the sharp icy fragments this way and that, and it was only in his eyes that they were of the utmost importance. He shut his eyes, and saw words forming, phrases from his past, responses from the future, planning what to say but there was one word he never formed – it was eternity. In the fairy tale the Snow Queen had said, 'When you can put that together, you shall be your own master and I will give you the whole world, and a new pair of skates besides,' and William knew, like Kay, he could never do it.

'Wakey, wakey,' cried Mrs Withington, who had never noticed that William had observed her putting her hat into place.

He opened his eyes to the sound of the wheels, and the face of Mrs Withington staring down at him, and hazily in the background was Miss Dewett. They both had fixed grins on their faces. He didn't give any answer to the summons, just stared at them. Mrs Withington didn't like the look in his eyes; there was no need for a look like that, she thought to herself, and there was just no getting on with some people.

330

He was a queer customer; she was glad she hadn't been in the compartment alone with him.

'Slaaack-haal, Slaaack-haal,' came the voice of the guard, and the train lurched to a standstill. William watched Mrs Withington ease herself on to her pear-shaped legs.

'The end of the road,' she said to Miss Dewett.

She had decided she would not say, young man would you mind lifting my case. She would not be beholden to him, even though she had noted he seemed to have no luggage at all, as though he were indeed deserting. She smiled at Miss Dewett, who, with a sudden panic-stricken expression, began to rifle through her handbag. Her fingers made contact with the letter.

'Now, now, don't get despondent,' said Mrs Withington.

William pulled in his legs as she struggled past him, and even so the case rubbed against them. Tottering in the doorway, she stepped down heavily, leaving an overwhelming scent in the exhausted air of the carriage. Miss Dewett hurried after, almost as though she were jerking behind on a string. William heard her calling out, 'I'll carry that for you.'

'Why, you are a blessing in disguise,' said Mrs Withington, and in the distance he heard her voice complaining, 'You just can't get a porter for love nor money!'

Waiting in the empty carriage, William had the reckless impulse not to get off the train. But as a warning whistle blew, he stepped on to the platform. The whistle blew again, the flag was waved, and in a cloud of acrid smoke, the engine slowly began to move. He watched as the steam slowly cleared until the platform stood silent once more. He was home.

He looked up a while at the storm clouds and then as he started to walk down the platform, his attention was caught by a poster. He stood in front of it. Under a warm, pleasant summer blue sky, was a gleaming tank, resting on the rich brown, red earth, and emerging from the hatch was the smiling, suntanned soldier. Everything looked calm and comforting, there were no distant flashes of shells, no untidy bodies, just a fresh summer day and a happy soldier. 'Join the Royal Tank Regiment' it said. He lingered over the peaceful scene, part of him wishing to be under the blue sky, breathing the fresh air. A figure on the platform studied William's thoughtful and intense face.

'William, it is William, isn't it?' came a familiar voice. He swung round, and confronted the Reverend Roe. His eyes were now slightly higher, and it was the vicar of Slackhall who had to look up at him. Seeing him standing a discreet distance away, William fought back the impulse to deny his name. He knew he had changed, but not that much.

'Reverend Roe,' he said, and hearing his own voice say the name, brought back the old world he thought he had left.

'Good to see you, my boy, good to see you.'

He extended his hand and William shook it; he didn't know how many people would wish to shake his hand again. He wondered whether Roe knew. There was an awkward silence. And then at the same moment they both spoke, neither hearing what the other said.

'You first, you first,' said Roe.

'I, I, was just saying I hoped you were well.'

'Oh, as well as can be expected; it is Mrs Roe who is the victim, I'm afraid.' He shook his head. 'I'm off to see her today. She has to rest, you see, it's all been too much for her, and on top of everything the war. She was never a strong woman at the best of times.' He gave a sour smile. 'And you, William, how are you faring after all this time?' He looked probingly and sighed.

'Oh, I'm fine,' he said, knowing there was no conviction in his voice.

'Perhaps you will find the little town changed. You seem to have grown William.' He looked past him at the head of the soldier emerging from the tank, and the corner of his eye twitched. 'Or perhaps you will not find it changed at all.' Roe looked up and down the platform quickly, and then swiftly clasped William's hand. 'Nobody should blame you, my boy, nobody should blame you.' Then he let go of the hand, and with a strained smile, said in a louder voice than was necessary, 'It looks like we might be in for rain.'

William looked down the platform just as Roe had. He couldn't see anybody who could be watching them.

'Rain,' he said.

'Oh I should think so, it seems to have got very close,' replied Roe. 'Well, I'm afraid I shall have to leave you, William, my train is on the other platform. Still, I hope we can have a longer chat some time, that's if you intend to be in Slackhall long.' He gave William a dejected look as though somehow in meeting him he had fallen victim of bad luck.

'Goodbye,' said William.

'Don't change the world before I get back,' said Roe, trying hard to smile, and then with an anxious glance across the railway tracks, he made for the little bridge.

William watched the vicar, and then he, too, left the platform, walking past the bright poster. He handed over his ticket and stepped through the barrier and then he was at a loss, he wasn't sure where he should go. He felt the eyes of the ticket-collector on him, so he moved out of the station, looking at his watch as though checking on the time for an appointment.

'Mr Booth, Mr William Booth,' said the policeman. 'I'm sorry, sir, didn't mean to startle you.'

'Are you arresting me?' he stammered, looking at the uniform.

'Not that I know. My orders were to meet you, and ask if you'd mind coming to the station. Seems the inspector thinks you might be able to help.' He smiled like the soldier in the poster. 'I thought you'd be expecting me, we sent a letter to your school.' He stepped back to let a woman enter the station. 'I'll lead the way then, shall I, sir?'

He turned briskly and with a swagger of authority started off into the street. William followed, already feeling like a prisoner and when they passed anyone, he felt himself blush. The route took him past more posters, and with every step he began to feel how the school for all its training corps had been more distant from the war than this. Bags which had been filled with sand and soil were piled outside buildings and windows had been taped with multifarious designs, to prevent them from shattering as a result of bomb blast. He couldn't help wondering where the sand came from, perhaps some beach was being dug away, not for hour glasses, but shelters from bombs. He looked at his watch, it must have stopped

333

some time during the train journey. He decided not to ask the time. What did it matter? He even resolved not to look at the clock on the town hall.

'The weather's close,' said the policeman, 'wonder what the weather's like in France.'

'I don't know,' said William, feeling the lack of such knowledge was somehow a veiled reminder of the duplicity of his family.

'Can't wait to be out of this uniform.'

'It must be very hot,' he said feebly.

'I meant,' said PC Bowles, stopping to look at William, 'so I can get in another and get to some action. It's driving me mad traipsing around this place. You'd think half the time nothing was going on; cats still go missing, dogs bite people. I tell you, I reckon most of the folks round here reckon it's going to be over in time for Christmas.'

'You don't think so, then?' asked William.

'I should hope not, I'm just waiting for my papers to come through and then I'll be off from this place like a shot.' He spoke gruffly, and William felt more pathetic and unmanly than ever.

Yet PC Bowles was not just wishing to rush to the heroic struggle. He would be relieved to escape the closed community where his predicament could come to light in the gossip and where he might receive knowing looks. At first he had blamed his impotence on the shock of seeing the body of Mary Leech, and the worry about the pox, but she hadn't got it. So much relieved he thought everything was all right, but it wasn't. He had never missed the single hair which had been on his neat uniform, and which later, amid cackling laughter had three knots tied into it by dextrous fingers, and as others fell and broke limbs in the period of maleficium, so he lost his masculinity.

As they reached the police station, William felt ever more isolated. He was taken to the waiting-room, and then left for about half an hour, as though like expert chefs they were wishing him to marinate in his own anxiety, so he would be more tender for their ministrations.

'Ah Mr Booth, or may I call you William?' beamed a round face eventually. 'So sorry to have kept you waiting around like this, I just thought it might be useful if I could have a little chat with you.' He paused and extended his hand, 'I'm Inspector O'Connor.' His hand seemed very warm and slightly damp.

'What a morning, what a morning. I don't know, perhaps it's the mood or something, but there seem to be more con men and charlatans around. They feed off wild hopes. You wouldn't believe it, the cells are full of mediums and conjurors. They've got into people's houses to put them in touch, and then when the lights go out they help themselves to the valuables.' He laughed. 'The crystal balls I've got piled in the drawer of my desk couldn't have let on they'd be spending the night in custody.' He pulled out a large handkerchief, and mopped his fleshy brow which was beaded with sweat. 'You don't mind if I open the window?' he asked. 'I don't know what good it will do, there seems to be no air, it's far too humid.'

William watched as Inspector O'Connor struggled to unfasten the window. No breeze came between the metal bars, and the inspector had to mop his brow once more.

'How about a cup of tea?' he asked. And as though he couldn't stand to be idle, he went over to the door and called out for some tea and, looking round at William, smiled and added some biscuits.

'Your old Nanny was interested in that sort of thing, wasn't she?' he asked pleasantly, sitting down at the desk.

'What sort of thing?'

'Oh, you know, crystal balls, spirits and what not.'

'I don't think so,' said William firmly.

'Perhaps not, then,' he smiled. 'I hope you had a good journey.'

'Yes, thank you,' William said cautiously.

'Have you seen Mrs Bradshaw since she was dismissed?' he asked.

'Mrs Bradshaw,' repeated William, thinking how strange it sounded, 'she sent me a letter, but I never replied.'

'I don't suppose you have that letter, do you?' He noted William's shaking head. 'Of course not,' he said briskly. 'Why should you? I just thought that perhaps you knew where to get in touch with her, that's if you can't help us.'

The door opened and the tea was set down on the inspector's desk. He poured it out, handing William the biscuits. As they were passed back untouched, William thought the inspector looked disappointed, and he watched how delicately the policeman nibbled his own choice.

'I suppose you know why I want to speak to you,' he said, sipping his tea gently. 'At the moment we have no idea where your aunt might be hiding, and I'm afraid your uncle is either unable or unwilling to co-operate.'

'Is he in prison?' asked William.

'Well, for the time being. I'm afraid your uncle chose the wrong set to go round with. Still, I don't need to tell you that.' He reached for another biscuit. 'Perhaps it would be better to say interned, and don't think it's only a few; I've heard there are about three thousand or more German women to be taken to the Isle of Man.' The ginger nut crunched in his mouth. 'Mainly servants of course.'

'Is that . . .' began William, 'is that where Dagmar will be taken?'

'Oh I should imagine so, that's when we finally find her,' he smiled at William. 'Still, she's not quite the same as some of the other . . . er, enemy aliens, is she?'

'Well she did come over as a servant.'

'I don't think we can say that now, can we?' He leaned over a folder and wrote something down.

'No.'

'You see, William, I'm very anxious to find your aunt.'

'She's not my aunt.' He said it too quickly and saw the inspector's thin eyebrow rise. He nodded and wrote something else down.

'Well,' he said, 'perhaps that will make it easier. The trouble is, William, we know that she is a Nazi, and it's quite possible that she's been feeding information back to Germany. We shall hope to find that out, but the major thing is to find her. It also seems she might be armed.'

'Armed,' he gasped.

'Now, it might not be correct; we shall just have to be very careful.' He smiled. 'Perhaps they weren't joking in parliament after all, when they said that it was a fact that the female of any species is more deadly than the male,' he laughed. 'So do you think you can help us?' He leaned his heavy body over the desk. William could see the inspector's sweaty brow.

'I don't know.'

'Well, perhaps if I can tell you the sort of thing we are interested in, whether she mentioned any people she was friendly with, relatives, or contacts, that sort of thing, and whether you can remember the areas of the country she's been to, and which might be familiar to her.' He pulled out a clean sheet from the folder. 'If I left you in peace, perhaps it would be easier.' He handed it to William. 'You just jot down anything you can think of.' He closed the folder and slotted it under the arm of his ill-fitting suit. 'I'm sure you'll find it easier than an exam.' He smiled and left William alone once more.

Far in the distance there were the faint stirrings of thunder. William glanced up at the barred window; he could see the grey sky, and wondered whether the iron would attract lightning. He turned to the paper, and in the dimming light began to write all he could think of, hesitantly at first, and then with bolder strokes of the pen. He didn't know how long he'd been at it, nor was he aware of the inspector's eye which peered through the spy-hole, and the smile that spread across his face at the sight of William's head bent over the paper. When he finished he pushed the writing away from himself as though he never wished to touch it again and once more confronted the familiar cracks in the wall.

Inspector O'Connor entered, and without a word to William he went over and picked up the paper and read it. The face remained professionally impassive. He could just as easily have been reading the confession to a terrible murder, or a shopping list. Eventually he lowered it and looking at William he smiled.

'Good, good,' he said, and without another word, just left the room and William sitting there.

After a while another policeman pushed his head round the door. 'Would you like a cuppa?' he asked, and as William shook his head, the policeman slid from view without another sound.

337

Thunder rumbled again like a distant aeroplane. William felt how heavy the air had become, as though weighted down, it would soon have to split open.

'Well, William,' said Inspector O'Connor as he entered the room, 'you have been a great help.' He smiled warmly. 'I don't want to detain you much longer, but I wonder if you have any hunches, where you think she's gone.' He looked evenly at William. 'Of all those places you mentioned, what do you think's the best bet?'

The inspector saw the vague look enter William's eyes, and he held his breath, not wishing to disturb the workings of intuition. He saw William frown.

'What is it?' he pressed.

'Well, I don't think it's very likely,' said William, and he paused for a moment. 'I don't know what made me think of it, I didn't even mention it in the . . . in the writing.' He looked embarrassed.

'What isn't very likely?' asked the inspector.

'I'm sure you've alreaoy looked.'

'Looked where?' He gripped the folder tightly and tried to keep his voice even.

'In the grounds.'

'Ah yes,' he said, loosening his grip, 'we searched the grounds.'

'I thought you'd have checked the old wardrobe.'

'Wardrobe?' repeated the inspector, looking puzzled.

'The old one in the wood,' said William. 'I once showed it to her; she thought somebody was using it as a hideout.' He smiled. 'Not a very good idea I'm afraid.'

'Just hold on a moment,' said the inspector and he disappeared again. William looked blankly at the wall. He had never thought about where he would stay or anything. He wondered whether the inspector might know. The door opened again.

'Now tell me about this wardrobe again,' said the inspector, and he placed a map on the table.

Later, William stood against the wall as he listened to Inspector O'Connor explain the plan to the other policemen; the rough position had been marked on the map, near the bank of Gore Brook. He heard how he was to lead them

338

through the garden to the woods, and then return to the house. Nothing more was said about his role, but he listened to the commands given to the officers and the warning about a gun.

He thought as they walked through the sticky air that the policemen kept a distance from him. Inspector O'Connor had given him the keys for the house and grounds; he could feel them lying heavily in his pocket, an unnerving reminder of his perfidy. He wondered what had made him think of Great Granny Grime's wardrobe? It had been so hot that summer, and the river ran dry. He looked up at the sound of thunder; there would be no chance of its running dry now. He saw his home rise up before him like an unwelcome spectre, and in the fulminating light the windows were chasms, and the ivy looked dark and wild. It had been deserted and William lowered his Judas eyes, and making his way along the wall, pulled out the bunch of keys and opened the door into the tangled garden.

He never turned to watch the policemen follow him, nor did he look at the key to see whether it was stained with blood which would never wash away. His betraying eyes rested guiltily on the foliage ahead. He wondered whether he should make as much noise as possible to alert Dagmar, let her know somebody was coming, so she could flee her final refuge. He didn't know if the policemen were armed. Would they shoot her dead? All the while he was pondering the fate of Dagmar, he was winding his way through the massed saplings, his feet moving him closer and closer to the garden proper.

The grey sky hung over them, making the green look livid and sullen and in the tangled grasses the quickly moving bodies of hundreds of spiders could be seen. They danced through the stalks, confusing the eye and making the intruders stumble as they looked this way and that at the strange phenomenon. Yet not a word passed the grim lips of the five heads bowed beneath the high thunder-clouds. They slithered down the ha-ha and, never glancing behind, failed to see the green grass slowly straighten itself from their passage, as though wishing them never to return. The stone satyr still stood, staring uncaringly at the humans who dared to enter the wild realm. The dull water reflected the grey above, and no fountain played to break the mirror surface.

Sweat trickled down the faces, and further on they saw the tall trees, and their path seemed beset with thorns and briars like the road to righteousness. The light was foul and grim and seemed to keep changing, and as they struggled on they had the peculiar sensation that they were not getting any nearer. A waiting pair of eyes watched the five forms. The watcher gave them no chance to see her. As soon as she could make out their heavy breathing, she swiftly darted between the trunks of the trees. No twigs cracked under her feet, and soon she was at the bank of the stream. In the gloomy elf light, the solid smell of moss and earth hung in the air. The watcher looked down into the gently murmuring water, and then with a curious leap she was on the other bank, and off once more among the trees. They cast protective shadows around her tiny body. The woodland sprite flitted over the pine-needles and leaves, disturbing not ing in her passage. She melted into the shadow of a tall tree, tall enough to have been a rudimentary scaffold, and from the blackness she stared into a dull glade and in the glade stood a large wardrobe, and in the wardrobe a grimy figure with wild eyes, and in the figure a burning fire like hell.

The watcher saw the fevered figure slowly stretch out her pale limbs, until she emerged from the box of wood. Damp, stained strips of cloth had been wound round the legs where they were swollen, and after standing for a few seconds she collapsed towards the muddy ground. The gloomy and monotonous light produced a somnambulistic calm, and after slowly raising her head, Dagmar laboriously leaned over and reached within the wardrobe. Her slightly trembling hand groped about and from her lolling head came the sound halfway between a groan and a sob. The sensitive nose of the watcher wrinkled as Dagmar opened the second door of the wardrobe, and the stale smell hung in the open space of the glade, the unmistakable odour of human excrement, and as though in some attempt to hide it, the exhaled scent of eucalyptus sweets. The door creaked audibly as it swung open, exposing the interior, and as if on order, a shaft of filtered light broke through the heavy grey clouds. It swirled

340

with tiny seeds and spores and fell on the wardrobe like an unwelcome spotlight. Dagmar raised her trembling hand to shield her eyes, as though like a troglodyte she could no longer endure bright light. Within the wardrobe were a pile of soiled clothes and sheets, and where part of the rotten floor had collapsed were stacks of slowly rusting tins. The labels had begun to peel off in the damp atmosphere.

It was clear that she had been here for some time. Several tins had been opened and the contents had spilled out, dribbling and congealing where they fell. Flies buzzed around the rotting leakage, feasting on the condensed milk and heavy syrup of preserved fruit. Dagmar no longer made any attempt to brush them away. The very smell of food had become repulsive to her, and even if she wanted to, she would not have been able to keep any down, but in the burning emptiness of her stomach lurched the rocking pond of nausea, and any motion sent it lapping up towards her dry, burning throat. Under the heavy lids Dagmar looked up, as though the mere effort of opening the door had been too much for her. The fevered eyes had grown dim, and were now without expression in her torpid face. Saliva dribbled from the corner of her mouth as though mocking her dread of food. A large fly landed in the gelatinous string of spittle, crowding round to the corner of her mouth as another landed. She closed her eyes against the shaft of light and, lowering her hand, as though blind, felt along her other arm, and with a trembling sigh began to take her own pulse.

As though a switch had been broken, the membrane of sky which had split to let the light through coagulated. Dagmar began to rifle through the shadowy contents of the wardrobe. Jars and bottles of pills were knocked over by the numbed hand. Her collection of vitamins and medications rattled and with weary resignation she watched tablets spill from an overturned bottle. She let her hands rest on her knees; one trembled slightly, like the faint vibration of the wings of an insect. With a look of determination she reached once more into the depths of the wardrobe and the greying hair fell into her eyes, which now shone inwardly with a light so dull it would have been difficult to guess the source, like the faint embers of a giant pyre buried under cold, grey ash.

Fresh green ferns were starting to uncoil in the withered bracken, and in the clearing the delicate heads of bluebells seemed to nod as though there was some movement in the air, trembling delicately at the approaching footsteps, and yet the five figures had not yet reached the wood. With a grunt of triumph, Dagmar pulled out a bottle; sealed within it moved a dark liquid. It would have been difficult to say whether she smiled, so heavily shaded was her face. The bottle contained a label, '*Unvolkung*', and as she slowly lifted it to the safety of her knee, the colour could be discerned: it was red. Her torpid fingers caressed the glass gently, and she almost appeared to be crooning to the contents. She bent her body over it, and murmured in a low husky voice.

She looked up at the distant cawing of a crow, and for the last time reached into the gloom. Her arm stiffened as she closed her hand round a syringe. Beads of sweat ran down her face, like thick tears of lament, and she gave a smile, animating a visage which seemed neither living nor dead, and for a second, as lightning flashed in the heavy sky, a human expression flickered across her features, revealing a strange nobility. She remained absolutely motionless, like a strong tree before it topples, cut through by the forester's axe. With the fixed determination of one who had put everything she cared for behind her and with the knowledge that some infection had already set in, Dagmar held the syringe proudly towards her arm, and then plunged it into herself. Her skin had become so translucent, that the metal needle could be seen probing for a vein beneath the surface.

Within her sallow face her eyes shone like the fires of Beltane as she drew out her own blood, she stared ahead as though she were looking on some great landscape. The dark forests of Bavaria, the steep valleys and mountains of her homeland, and at cities which would last for three thousand years. Greater than Imperial Rome, stronger than the Ice Age, a new Garden of Eden. The trees became transformed to marble columns, row upon row, surmounted by eagles of silver and gold, and fluttering between, the flags, red as blood. Her eyes closed gently and opened on the gloomy glade; the finery had disappeared. Clumsily she pulled out the needle. Blood welled up and as she stretched out her stiff arm, it dribbled weakly along her white skin.

The bluebells were flattened under their heavy tread, pressed into the ground. Dagmar heard them, and she vainly struggled like the stricken flowers, but she could not raise her head, the syringe fell from her fingers and like a dart quivered in the earth. Twigs cracked like rifle-shots. Their voices were distant and harsh; her body twitched and she waited with open eyes for the gun barrel to be placed at the back of her neck. Her dry lips would not lament or make a plea for mercy. They saw her body slumped half in the wardrobe. One lit a cigarette, his foot nonchalantly kicked a tin can, his eyes took in the squalor, and her naked legs tied round with rags, like a present with ribbons. PC Bowles looked into her open eyes, her body moved slightly.

'She's alive,' he said, and then taking hold of her ankles, dragged her fully out of the wardrobe. Her limp form flopped on to the ground, and the labelled bottle was dislodged and tumbled with her, spilling and splashing its contents.

'Shit!' exclaimed a policeman. 'Just look at this mess.'

The others moved over, and as Dagmar's Germanic blood soaked into the earth, they took in the woman's body and the thin rags which covered her were turning red as though she had taken a bath in blood. One of her fingers pointed up at the sky, and her lips moved and although she thought she screamed at them, just a low quivering sigh emerged as her pure blood was lost.

'Better clean her up a bit,' said one, and taking hold of her legs they pulled her away from the bloodied earth, and in scraping her along, the thin, rotting material gave; she was completely naked.

Behind a tree, fingers were slowly unpicking three knots which had been tied in a single human hair. The last knot free, the hands let the hair float to the ground, as though after all the effort they had lost interest in it, and the figure slowly moved off among the trees.

'Who's to know?' said PC Bowles, his voice dry with excitement, and the heavy air seemed to tingle with static electricity. They exchanged nervous smiles. 'She won't know anything about it, we're doing her a favour,' he grinned, and prodded Dagmar's thigh with his hard boot.

'We just don't leave any marks, nobody the wiser. This fucking bitch might have betrayed some of our lads.' He felt strong, towering over her and. as they looked at each other, their burning eyes exchanged the understanding.

PC Bowles leant over and caressed her breast. They laughed vigorously at their daring and lit cigarettes nervously. The three of them stood, drawing on the cigarettes, listening to the gasping movements of PC Bowles. The sounds throbbed in the small glade and they coughed expectantly as their libidos responded.

'Turn her head away,' said one. The others laughed at his modesty.

William looked at the buds which were bursting open, the bright green leaves pushing through, slightly sticky to the touch. His eyes reflected the grey sky. He had run from the wood and as he stood panting in the shadow of the house, he could hear his blood pulsing through his body. His side ached as if somebody had kicked him in the ribs. The thunder rolled.

'Ah, ah, ah, ah, ah, ah aah, ah,' came the sound of a human voice. It rose and fell with the even rhythm of panting, groaning, screaming, crying, laughing, moaning, sobbing, choking, breathing, dying. The universal sound filled the glade. Echoing round, it told of collapsing buildings and buried bodies clawing the dust, the dull thud of bullets entering the fragile tissue, the blinding pain of explosions, the sting of piano wire, and much more besides. It told of sad partings, faces only to be remembered in fading photographs, brief visits and nights of passion. Children who would never see their fathers, the groans of starvation, the shocked faces, the trenches, the dugout pits, the naked bodies lining them, the rattle of guns, the banging and thumping of the showers. The silence of the dead. The crackling of the fire. The dripping of the blood, softly, softly from the back of the neck. The sounds the world had heard before, but not so loud, not so loud.

Standing in the still pond, Mrs Wagtail hitched up her skirt. She looked into the grey sky and then gently splashed her

344

hands about in the water. The lapping sound set up its own rhythm, back and forth, back and forth, and so it was joined by another sound: that of falling rain. A downpour began, splashing and dancing in the moving water, cascading and sliding over the vegetation, coating everything in a slippery mantle which flashed and shone in the lightning. Down came the rain and the grey sky released a torrent which bludgeoned the waiting earth. It was not a gentle sound. Like the faces of the drowned, people looked up into the sky and were blinded by the onslaught. Gasping and spluttering they made for cover, sodden clothes heavy and sticking to their frames. The flanks of the grey cloud quivered like a running wolf and the frenzied rain lashed stone, wood and flesh. It was relentless and unyielding. It was not the gentle rain of cool balm; it hissed through the air with the bitterness of unshed tears.

In the glade, the rain fell on the scene of the rape, on the victim and the conspirators, making no distinction in its idle force. The crimsoned earth glistened under the fulminating heavens. The rain fell on heads and limbs, the cruel evidence was drenched, purged by the striking, flawless water, wounding all alike. They opened their eyes to their deeds, and the senseless body lay before them, white and naked. With bowed heads they let the rain wash away their sin, as it washed away the bloody red, purifying the ancient spot.

The key was slippery in his wet hand, and the rain coursed down his plastered hair into his eyes. He fumbled to open the door, the thunder rattling over the scene. Shivering and dripping, he stepped in and closed the door on the portentous weather. As though he had been submerged in the river of forgetfulness he stood for long minutes just listening to the rain, staring into the gloomy interior as though unaware that he was back in the house he once left. Motionless save for the odd fit of shivering he listened to the roaring sky. The windows rattled.

The overcast sky spread and uncoiled over the undulating water of the channel and in France the heavens were filled with a different drone, but still the windows rattled. Along cratered roads, grimy, weary soldiers hurried from destruction. The British Expeditionary Force was surrounded and retreated towards the gently lapping sea. Gathering on the beaches they faced their homeland, lighting their cigarettes on matches from a box imprinted with the image of Captain Webb who swam across the great divide one August day in 1875. Crowding together they held the cigarettes inside their cupped hands, cherishing the warmth on the bleak sand.

As the troops gathered in their thousands by the coastal town of Dunkirk, they clambered over the rubble of the seaside resort, and then inexplicably as though waiting to get into a football ground, or cricket match, they began to form long orderly queues leading into the sea where they waded among floating bodies to reach the ships. The Luftwaffe were hard at work, bombing the small town and the evacuating soldiers; rifles did not deter the Stuka raids, and in clouds of dark smoke and flying sand, weary soldiers died while trucks and cars were driven into the water to make abstract piers out of the age's innovations. And as the Luftwaffe droned overhead, turning people's eyes to the sky, not only destruction fell, but also softly fluttering pieces of paper. Like snow they covered the blasted landscape, some soaking up the muddy earth, and others, the spilled blood. What floated down from the heavens was an ancient prediction made by a sixteenth-century doctor who dabbled in the occult. His name was Nostradamus.

Frau Goebbels read of the visions of Nostradamus, waking her husband from sleep, and he too read how in a simple bowl of water, the seer had visions of the future, a vision that he too shared. Providence must have been on their side, and in the new court the astrologer Krafft was appointed to plan the future, choose the right moment, and read the omens in the entrails which were spread about Europe. With the firmament within their arsenal, the ministry of propaganda printed the quatrains, predicting the victory of Hitler, changing a letter here and there.

> Bestes farouche de faim fleuves tranner,
> Plus part du champ encontre Hister sera.
> En caige de fer le grand fera treisner,
> Quand rien enfant de Germain observera.

346

And with wide peasant eyes they read, 'Beasts wild with hunger will cross the rivers, the greater part of the battlefield will be against Hitler. He will drag the leader in a cage of iron, when the child of Germany observes no law.' Amid ribald laughter, and as a sign of contempt, the British troops who could not read the French, put the paper to a more practical purpose, and soon the latrine trenches were full of prophecy and excrement.

As words of great doom fell from the sky in the climate of destruction, a minor prophecy began to unwind within William's mind; the phantasma of his betrayal pursued him like the furies, and he began to wander the rooms and passages of the house, as though trying to find comfort. His damp clothes clung to him. The relentless embrace followed his every move, giving him no peace of mind. Distracted, he passed the cold, empty grate of the kitchen, and as he flung open the doors, as though he wished to make enough sound to fill the house with the sad illusion of life, he beheld the interiors swathed in huge dust-sheets.

In the ghostly realm of white sheets it was easy to become confused. Like grounded sails they draped furniture and ornaments as familiar aspects were changed and like fields under snow, it was difficult to judge direction. All familiar landmarks had disappeared. It was as if the whole interior had been measured for a shroud, and William wandered round and round. Spectres of his memories were conjured in the dead rooms, and in desperation or perhaps nostalgia, he violently pulled away at the sheets, exposing fragments of the concealed furniture. Part of a table, indiscriminate chairs, heavy urns once more became victims to dust. He shivered, and leaving the semi-draped room, he cautiously climbed the stairs. He felt like an unwelcome intruder.

Along the empty corridor he made for his room, opened the door, and then gasped as though he had stumbled across a corpse. He backed out of the room, looked intently at the door, and then entered again, and stood in amazement as though perhaps he were hallucinating. The room was completely bare, not one white sheet was to be seen. Whatever had once filled his room had been removed, as though an attempt had been made to eradicate all traces of his occupancy.

All that remained was a single, rusting drawing-pin, and a corner of the 'Keatings' poster which once hung on the wall. With his sense of unreality growing he left the hollow chamber. Every step he took made his old life more remote, and he shivered. He stopped. He could hear the rain drumming on the roof, a sound which might be comforting when curled in a warm bed now seemed ominous, and it carried within it the distant memory of a nightmare. He shivered again, and in the deserted corridor he slowly peeled off his wet clothes until he stood naked and defenceless. With a new freedom he ran along the cold passage, rubbing his hands together as though about to light a fire. He came upon an old linen box, and pulling off the white sheet, wrapped himself in it, and rubbed his flesh roughly. He glanced up and down as though afraid he was not alone. He could still hear the rain and, draped like a stage ghost, he flitted along until he paused at the stairwell leading to his grandmother's room. Then slowly, in his spectral apparel he climbed the steps until he reached the dressing-room. He half expected to be able to hear her stentorian breathing, but all he could discern was the rain.

He entered her bedroom, his fragile figure draped in white merged with the hidden furniture, and he knew this was where he belonged. Everything felt so good. He breathed in deeply and traces of the old familiar smell were there – a comforting reminder of his past. With the calm precision of an illusionist he began to remove the dust-sheets, each one revealing a remembrance and helping to build a shrine to her memory. He lay himself down on the bed in which she died, and knew that was where he would wish to die as well. He rose slowly, still wrapped in his makeshift shroud, and he looked out of the window. The rain ran down the pane of glass making visibility difficult, so he flung it open.

He saw the four policemen struggling along with Dagmar. She was draped in what looked like grey rags, and they pulled her like the spoils of war. She seemed to be limping in one leg, and the black figures of the four men supported her drooping form.

His eyes were riveted upon the slowly-moving bodies, and his look was both harsh and tender. He could see there had been suffering, whatever had been proud was lost. The policemen dragged her with casual indifference. She was too far away to see her expression clearly, but he imagined that her pale blue eyes were closed. She would be carried along in blackness.

In the room of memory he stared out at the present. Nearer and nearer they came, and then he could see her. He turned his eyes away, like a soldier at a firing squad unable to watch his handiwork. He had lost courage. And yet the half-draped room, with the heavy sheets, seemed like the sign of a death foretold, and so he looked out once more. They were nearly under the house. He could see her vacant stare, her eyes were open. Her eyes were more serene than his own; they seemed to reflect the quiet imminence of death. She collapsed to the floor and they slipped on the muddy ground trying to heave her up; their hands were not gentle. He heard her groan, but could not answer her. Fascinated he leaned out of the window, and she stared up at him. With an almost physical jolt their eyes met. He felt sick, and he saw his betrayal dawn within her eyes, and as his filled with pity, hers reflected a horrible truth. The policemen picked her up like a corpse and holding her under the shoulders and by the ankles, they steadied themselves. She raised an exhausted arm, and pointed up towards William. He was the only one who saw it, but it was the policemen who through their panting heard her voice croak out: *'Hagen, Hagen Hagen . . .'*

Stepping back, William felt himself tremble, and like butchers carrying a side of meat the policemen moved off, leaving William to brood in the empty house.

He sat down on the bed, wishing he had never seen what had happened. He felt as though he had just given the order for the bullets to fly. He could have forgotten, blamed the world if he hadn't seen her eyes. He had no answer, and the only thing he knew was that he wished to leave this place. He wondered whether he would sleep calmly again or would his nightmares be filled with what he had just witnessed. He tried to forget how alive and warm that body had once seemed to him, and he left the room and went in search of clothes.

In his uncle's room, he found some which he started to put on with cold hands. He had grown, and they fitted him well. It was only his frozen fingers which fumbled with the buttons which perhaps wished him not to wear them. He never looked in the mirror, taking things at random, and like a thief he stepped out, and finding his own shoes, he left the rest of his things like a swimmer who had the intention of drowning.

He stepped out of the house, closing the door with the key locked inside. The rain was more gentle now, and he turned up the collar of his jacket and walked towards Slackhall. Wrapped in his thoughts, he did not know he was being followed.

People had begun to emerge. There was a strange wild smell in the air, like the acrid odour of a circus, and like trapped animals people paced about as though they expected another deluge, and the wise had not yet stirred. His feet splashed through the oily puddles, and he thought that in Dagmar's face he had seen the expression of death, and rejected and lost, he walked in borrowed clothes.

'Don't I know you?' came an aggressive voice. 'Aren't you called Booth?' Startled, he swung round to see a man.

'I don't know what you're saying,' he stuttered. 'I only came this morning,' and denying his name, he walked quickly away from the muttering man. He bumped into a woman.

'Sorry,' he said.

'Wait a minute,' said Miss Boothroyd, 'I know you.' She frowned at his face.

'I don't think so,' he replied starting to walk away.

'Wait a minute,' she cried, causing a few other passers-by to stop. 'I do know you. I used to work for your uncle.' She turned to the other people. 'His uncle is that traitor.'

'You've got the wrong person,' he persisted, looking desperately at the staring faces.

'What's your name then?' she hissed. 'Getting decent folks to work hard, and then sending everything to them Nazis.' She pursed her lips and stood in front of him. He moved forward, she barred the way.

'Excuse me,' he said weakly. She didn't shift, and so he tried to push past.

'He's attacking me,' she screamed, and in fright he gave her a hefty shove and she fell backwards screaming.

His feet pounded down the street, he heard others following, but he didn't turn. He saw those ahead staring at him, and like the wail of a siren the thin scream continued, pursuing him like the feet. He dashed down a back alley, and no longer quite sure of where he was, clung to the wall, breathing heavily, and as he heard the pursuers he started running again. He thought that perhaps he was near the station. In the distance he could see an iron bridge. He threaded his way through dustbins and turned another corner, and before him lay another brick wall. He had found a dead end.

He look around wildly for a way out, and heard somebody knock over a dustbin. He felt his hands shaking, and with a desperate lunge tried to scale the wall. Like a hostage to gravity he fell back. A gate creaked; the wood was blotched from the rain, and screwed in place was an iron number, it was seven.

Scrambling to his knees, William made for the gate and reached it just as his stalkers rounded the corner. They seemed to howl as they took in the dead end.

'Please,' he begged, 'please,' and as though he had said abracadabra or some other magic word, the gate swung open, and standing before him was a small figure.

'Great Granny Grime,' he cried, and despite the danger gazed in amazement. A strange cruel smile played over the withered lips, and she glanced down the alley at the approaching figures.

'I'm not expecting company,' she hissed, and she stared into his eyes until he thought he was looking at a sheer wall, and felt all hope going.

'It's me,' he whispered, 'William, please,' he clutched at her, 'Mrs Grime.'

'You're pushing your luck,' she growled. 'Just take those hands off,' and obediently they fell away, almost senseless with fear. 'Trespassers will be prosecuted,' she whispered.

'We've been looking for you,' barked a voice. 'Did you think you'd missed us?'

Rigid, he looked into the impassive mask of Great Granny Grime. She smiled at him. He heard them laugh behind, but daren't look round. He didn't know how many there were.

'Tried to break in,' declared the old woman. 'Came here calling me grimy, like a wild thing. He escaped from somewhere then?'

351

'Granny Grime,' he sobbed.

'There he goes again,' she crowed. 'I'm Mrs Wagtail, Mrs Wagtail of number seven, and I don't know you.'

'We know him, though,' said another voice.

Like a rag doll they turned him round; he felt hands pull away his jacket.

'Walking around in a black shirt,' one exclaimed, and he was pushed into the wall.

'I know you,' said one called Dickinson, 'you bloody fascist. You're called Booth.'

'No, no, no.' He said it so faintly, they laughed, and on the third denial kicked him.

He staggered and fell down and one spat in his eye. They booted him and he rolled to protect himself. He could hear his groans, but they seemed to come from someone else. He felt the bones break as a foot was ground down on his hand. The blows fell on him, his head jerked and his nose snapped and he felt he was choking on the slippery blood. His position became determined from the force of the blows, like dark shadows the attackers stooped over him. His eyes rolled gently and he could suddenly see the sky. It seemed so vast from where he was lying and soon his eyes reflected the grey expanse, the sky of his youth.

'The devil will find work for idle hands,' said Mrs Wagtail. And the gate clicked shut.

> Men at some time are masters of their fates:
> The fault, dear Brutus, is not in our stars,
> But in ourselves, that we are underlings.
>
> Shakespeare, *Julius Caesar*